Published by Cici Edward
www.ciciedward.com

Cover Design & Interior Format by
The Killion Group, Inc.

POSSESSION OF THE HEART

THE POSSESSION SERIES

CICI EDWARD

THE POSSESSION SERIES

by Cici Edward

Possession of the Heart
Possession in Lace
The Last Gift
One Last Kiss
Possession in Moonlight
Possession for Innocence

CONNECT WITH THE AUTHOR

Website:
www.ciciedward.com

Sign up for my newsletter
for the most current updates.
www.ciciedward.com/contact-me

Facebook
www.facebook.com/cici.edward1

Instagram
@ciciedward

Twitter
@CiciEdward

This story is dedicated to my parents,
Edward and Portia,
who taught me my love of books.

CHAPTER 1

COLE BARLOW SQUINTED against the dying sun that sank behind the mansion he'd never called home. Penniberg stood before him like an ominous creature, a dragon he needed to slay. The last rays of light reached out over the silhouette of the building like clawing fingers.

He hated this place. Only when it was gone would he be free. He'd destroyed and rebuilt many real estate properties, but this one was different.

This one belonged to his father.

No, he had to remind himself that *he* owned the monstrosity now. Not his father. His father was dead.

Demolition should have started hours ago, days ago, a lifetime ago. It was long past time to shatter the last connection his controlling father had on him by tearing the mansion to the ground. When you needed something done, you had to rely on yourself.

The fact that the building still stood showed his father's control over this sleepy town. Hank Barlow had never given anybody a break, not his son, not his wife, no one. And if the workers could be believed, his father's spirit was tormenting them too.

There'd been too many problems trying to get this place destroyed, so he'd had to come here, the last place he wanted to be, and see what all the damned hoopla was about.

Now that Cole was forced back to Dalewood, he wanted to tear at the shutters, punch in the windows, shattering the glass, anything for it to be over. A gaping hole should have been smashed into the side of the Spanish Mediterranean style mansion. The mental image had a smile tugging at the corner of his mouth. A great big hole in his father's most prized possession, all of the antiques exposed in each room like a child's large doll-house.

He gazed at the perfectly, intact gray limestone. A shadowy figure shifted in one of the upstairs windows, and he narrowed his eyes. Then he realized it must have been the shifting sunlight that hit the glass, reflecting an orange glare.

The heavy oak door of the mansion banged open and Ted, the foreman, rushed through. Cole vaguely registered the older man's ratty overalls as he ran from the house. Eyes wide and face tight with fear, Ted's block-shaped chest lifted with each heavy breath. That same orange sunlight reflected off the brass buttons of Ted's overalls like a little warning light.

"I quit, Cole. I'm done." He lifted his arms and brought them down to slap against his sides. "Done."

Cole kept his face smooth and unfazed, even as a headache pulsed white-hot behind his eyes. "You can't quit, Ted," he ordered. This was the last thing he needed.

"I'm sorry. We're out of here. I can't stay another minute." The burly man pushed past with more strength than Cole expected.

"If you don't finish this job, you'll be in breach of contract."

"I should've listened to Jack. But no, I wouldn't believe it until I saw it for myself." Ted reached down to grab his wooden toolbox from the manicured lawn. He lifted the case and shuffled across the driveway to his battered pickup.

Launching the tools into the truck bed, he turned. "Jack told me it had ghosts. Hell, what place doesn't? I never thought he meant real ghosts. And I sure as hell didn't think he meant your bastard of a father. No offense."

"You don't believe in that nonsense, do you, Ted? Let's be realistic." Cole stalked toward him, feet crunching on the gravel drive. Ted backed closer to the truck.

"I don't believe it. I know it." Ted raised his hands palm out. "I've called it quits on this worksite. I can't risk any of my guys getting hurt. You understand, don't you?"

"What are you talking about?" Cole didn't want to hear any of this? "I'm paying you for a job that's not getting done."

Ted shuffled his feet and whispered, "I damn near fell down that flight of stairs." He seemed worried someone would overhear, which was ridiculous because the site was emptier than any ghost town.

Ted hitched a thumb back at the mansion. "Something pushed me. When I turned, nobody was behind me. I was shoved by nothing, I tell you." His face paled to stark white. "This worksite is shut down. It's dangerous."

"I need this mansion demolished."

"You could sell it."

"That won't be enough. I need it leveled."

"Your father's ghost isn't happy with the idea of knocking the place down. He's made that pretty damn clear." Ted shook his head slowly. "I can't help you."

"I don't care what my father wanted. He's dead." The words *he's dead* came out sharp and heated.

"You can do whatever you want, Cole. Maybe some other crew can help." Ted jumped into the truck's cab. "But that won't be easy with Hank's ghost spooking everybody." Ted slammed the door and leaned an elbow out the window. "I don't know what to tell you. Get an exorcist, or hell, call Angela Haven." Ted started the engine.

"Ghosts don't exist, Ted," Cole said through the truck's open window, but Ted had stopped listening. This town had always feared Hank Barlow, and with good reason. He'd been a bastard, that was true, full of anger and spite, especially when he was drunk. "If you don't finish this job, I'll spread the word that you don't complete your jobs."

"Do what you've got to do, Cole." The engine

revved.

Cole stepped back as the truck sped away, kicking up dust that choked at the back of his throat.

He could ruin Ted's business easily enough. He'd become a master doing it to his father. But what was the point? He had one reason to be here. He could not lose his focus. He'd find another contractor. He should just call the Greeleys and suck it up. He'd helped them when his father was trying to ruin Max and they would reciprocate now, but he couldn't do that. He wanted to close off any connection to Dalewood and calling them would create more ties to this place, re-open wounds he didn't want to face.

A crane cruised overhead. Its long neck speared through the shadowed sky. Black starlings jumped from limb to limb in the tall birch trees with light flashing off their wings as they flitted from branch to branch. Cool autumn wind brought the scent of the raging Steele River as it blew through the red and gold changing leaves.

Silence surrounded him with an eerie chill, no jackhammers, no grumbling diesel, only the pounding of his heart.

He'd finish this. He was so close. Penniberg had been his father's most prized possession, more important to him than his only child. Cole would relish the day when he destroyed his father's legacies and eliminated everything his father had built. Destroy his father in the way he had tried to destroy Cole and Max Greeley too.

Pulling in a deep breath, Cole walked toward the large oak front door. Solidly closed, he felt like the mansion blocked him, not wanting him to enter. To hell with that. He owned this place now. It was his and he'd be damned if anything would keep him out.

With a swift twist of the brass handle, Cole shoved at the door. For a moment, it stuck, barring him, but then the door gave with a small pop. With an unrelenting step, Cole walked over the threshold. The same old scents hit him in the guts, lavender and lemon. A sprawling staircase led to the second floor. A long hallway with parquet floors guided guests to the various rooms. The drawing room was to the right, the dining room off to the left, while the library was further down the hall. The kitchens were set deep in the house all the way at the back.

Cole headed for the drawing room and stopped in the doorway, reacquainting himself with the room he hadn't stepped foot in for the last ten years. He closed his eyes, pressing his fingers against the lids. He never understood why his father hated him so much. Maybe it was childish, but for a brief moment he wished, even now, that he could turn back time to make his father love him. What a ridiculous thought. He shook his head and pushed away from the door jamb, entering.

Mahogany and maroons dominated everything in the room. His father had spent hours with the decorator, selecting the perfect oriental carpet to match the camelback sofa and draperies. Appearance and connections had been everything. Cole had been jealous of all the time Hank had spent with the decorator. His father had been annoyed with him. Hank Barlow never could hide the angry man inside even though he'd tried, at least, until the guests left.

Cole sat on the sofa and pulled out his cell phone. Time to get to work.

Number after number, business after business, he tried all afternoon to get someone to take Ted's place, but gossip traveled fast in Dalewood. Damned small towns.

Cole opened the glass door of the liquor cabinet. It still held crystal decanters filled with Glendronach, Port Ellen, Ardbeg. Only the best for Hank Barlow.

As a boy, Cole had watched his dad take a few too many swigs straight from the decanter. It was never fun to watch. A drunken Hank was not a nice Hank, but then again, was Hank ever likeable? Nope, he was only mean or meaner with a tongue sharper than any saw and a fist like a hammer. He'd be glad once every remnant of his father was gone and so would everyone else in this town.

Cole removed the round stopper, leaned into the bottle and sniffed. The hot scent of scotch stung. He poured a generous amount into a cut-crystal rocks glass and took a healthy swallow. It burned through his throat and tore a path all the way to his belly.

He filled the glass again, almost to brimming. With glass in hand, Cole scanned the drawing room. The place felt as hollow as his insides.

The longer he stayed in the mansion the deeper

his depression would grow, but he refused to leave. He'd been run out of town once. He wouldn't let his father run him out again. Not until he finished what he'd come here to do. Dalewood needed it as much as he did. Cole took another long drink.

"You can't hurt me anymore, you bastard. You're dead, Hank Barlow." Cole saluted the air with the glass and took another drink. "You're finished, old man. I'm going to destroy everything about you, just like you tried to destroy everything about me and Max. I'll make sure everybody forgets you ever existed."

Cole wandered the room sipping at his scotch. He stopped in front of the wedding portrait on the wall. The couple seemed happy enough with glowing cheeks and big smiles surrounded by white flowers and gauzy fluff. Cole knew better. He pulled the heavy filigreed frame from the wall. He didn't recognize either of them. His mother had run off shortly after he'd been born. She'd lost control of the car and died that night. He hated her for that. How could she have left a new baby with the likes of a man like his father?

Would Cole's life have been different if his mother had lived? Would his father have been a loving man? Cole shrugged at the thought. Who knew? It really didn't matter.

Tossing the frame on the sofa, he turned his back on their false grins. His future awaited him and all he needed was the inheritance his father had taunted him with every birthday since he'd been five.

"You'll get what's yours, boy," Hank sneered those words time and again. "One day you'll get your inheritance when I'm good and ready to give it to you." That had been the closest thing he'd gotten as a present.

Cole moved to the mantle and rested a hand on the marble lion's head that adorned its center. It had been hand-carved in Italy and reminded him of the running credits in an old movie. The lion's head seemed to lift its upper lip in a snarl reminiscent of his father's.

"What are you looking at?" Cole slurred back at the offending animal. The alcohol made his head cloudy, and his surroundings brought out the worst in him. "You're about to get your head knocked off." He grabbed the poker from the fireplace and raised it like a baseball bat. As he started his swing, the poker shifted in his grasp as if someone had grabbed it from behind, then it clattered to the floor before the fireplace. Cole stared at the poker.

"What the hell? I must really be drunk." He touched his toe of his Ferragamo to the metal rod. All his fight was gone. He didn't give a shit anyway, so he abandoned it lying on the floor.

His head spun. Half-empty, he'd had too much to drink from the bottle of whiskey. Flopping on the couch, he stacked his feet on the coffee table, not caring that the heel scuffed the tabletop. His father would have gone into a rage. Cole liked that his dad couldn't do a damn thing about it.

Cole rested his head on the back of the couch, closed his eyes and listened to the eerie silence, but it was too quiet to sleep. The alcohol had dulled his migraine and sitting had stilled his mind.

When he opened his eyes, his gaze fell on the wedding photo hanging on the wall. Cole froze. He hadn't hung that picture back on the wall. Had he?

He must have. How else could it be back?

The place was driving him crazy. It really irked him that he'd spent years building a wall around himself, protecting himself from all the pain of the past, but getting right back into the mansion could easily open all his old wounds.

He refused to be that vulnerable boy again. Cole pulled out his cell phone and punched in the phone number for another demolition crew he'd found in the phone book.

"Hi, this is Cole Barlow…"

"Sorry, I can't help you," the female voice sounded high-pitched with fear. "Nobody around here will take that job. Alive, he was a jerk. I can't imagine what he would be like as a ghost." The phone clicked and there was silence.

"What in the hell? Does everybody around here believe in ghosts?" Cole tossed his phone onto the coffee table, hitting the newspaper. It skittered off the edge and fell to the carpet. The pages flipped as if caught in a wind so the paper opened over the toe of his shoe.

"Unbelievable." Cole read the advertisement, then scanned the room. His gaze rested on the wedding picture placed perfectly on the wall.

He reached for his phone and punched in

another number. "I can't believe I'm doing this."

When a sweet voice answered, he said, "Hi, uh… yeah, I guess I need a ghost hunter."

CHAPTER 2

COLE NEVER THOUGHT he'd resort to something so idiotic, but drastic times and all that crap.

This was the right place. Black letters on the glass pane spelled out, *Angela Haven, Follow Your Path Paranormal Investigations.*

There was no turning back. He grabbed the silver handle on the glass door. What other options did he have? Give up, tuck his tail between his legs and let his father beat him again? Absolutely not.

He took a step inside. The bright white walls reminded him of clouds in sunlight. Four beige cushioned chairs piped in white surrounded a round table near the bank of windows. A stack of magazines sat neatly in the center of the table. The entire place gave off an aura of welcome.

This was not what he'd expected. Where were the dark colors and blood-red velvet curtains? There wasn't a single skull in the entire place. Instead of smelling like candles and incense, the air was as fresh as the autumn breeze and he pulled in a deeper breath. Cole liked it, and that made him immediately suspicious.

Before he could explore the empty room any further, a door at the back of the reception area opened and a woman walked through.

She was attractive in an unassuming, kind of ordinary way. Her face held barely any makeup. Fair, smooth skin highlighted by blush tones enhanced her golden eyes. Her hair was pulled back in a waving honey ponytail while a fall of bangs brushed just above those unbelievable eyes.

She paused, startled, then squared her shoulders and walked confidently toward him. A fissure of energy shot between them and he wasn't sure how he felt about that. Usually, women reacted to him in two ways, with trepidation or with wanting a night with him. This woman didn't give off either reaction. Instead, she exuded strength and confidence.

"Cole Barlow?" She glanced at her watch. "You're early." Smiling, she lifted an eyebrow. Just as quickly, she dismissed him with a wave of her slim arm toward the windows. "Would you mind having a seat? I'll be right back. I'm almost finished with my current client." Her smile was sweet and hit him dead in the stomach.

"I've made a mistake in coming here." His life was shifting out of his control and he'd be damned if he'd sit and wait in the chair like one of her crazy clients.

"You can leave if that's really what you want to do."

Those damned eyes glimmered as if they saw too much. He crossed his arms and leaned his shoulders back.

Instead of cowering, her smile stayed firmly planted. She sure wasn't intimidated. A secret part of him was impressed but he wouldn't dwell on the thought.

"But you shouldn't run away." Her gaze challenged.

"How's that?" Embers flared deep in his belly and heated his insides.

"You've got a problem with your father and no one can help you but me. Isn't that right? You're too scared to face it."

Did she have a death wish? "I'm not here for therapy. Stay out of it."

"Too late."

Cole placed a cold, mocking smile on his lips. "Did the ghosts tell you to say that?" Why was he being an ass? Did he really care? He didn't believe she had special powers.

She closed her lips in a tight line. Her chest lifted with a breath as if she disapproved. He couldn't stop his eyes as they followed the rise of her breasts through the navy dress.

"I have a client waiting for me. You can have a seat and wait one minute. Thank you," she clipped the words as she pointed in the opposite direction. "Sit."

Cole watched as she angrily stormed toward the closed door. Her skirt swayed just above her knees and her heels ate up the carpet with each brisk stride.

He had nowhere else to go but back to his hated house, so he followed her order and took a seat.

The only way to get the people of Dalewood to forget about Hank Barlow's ghost was to hire the ghost hunter. That would make them believe she could exorcise the house and capture Hank's spirit in her ectoplasm box or whatever it was called. Then they'd believe she'd sent Hank to the hell he deserved. He could tear down the damned place. Problem solved. Goal accomplished. That would make himself and everyone else in Dalewood happy.

Cole reached for a magazine on the table and flipped through the pages.

She was everywhere. Golden brown eyes stared up from the glossy page. They haunted him. The article was written by none other than Angela Haven. *THE ROAD TO THE OTHER SIDE, stories about the dead and their journey into the afterlife.*

He skimmed the compilation of essays she'd written. When he got to the end of the article, he read her bio. A whistle slid between his teeth. Her credentials were stacked. That was good to know. He planned to pay enough for her fancy tricks. At least he'd be paying for a Masters degree in Psychology from the University of Chicago and many years work helping family members with the loss of their loved ones. Impressive.

A noise at the back of the room pulled him from the pages, so he tossed the magazine back onto the table and turned. Finally, the door swung open.

Anxious that he was about to see Angela again,

he felt disappointment when an older woman with a white puff of curls stepped out. It took only a moment before he recognized the woman. She wore a pink silk blouse and a pair of gray pants. Faint wrinkles, probably helped by Botox, lightly etched her face, but he couldn't deny the many years that had passed since he'd seen her last.

Fran Greeley.

He recalled her kind words, kind treats, kind hands. Focused on one goal in the passing years he hadn't allowed himself much time to regret what he'd left behind. Now that he was back, he'd get reacquainted with the Greeleys, the couple who had treated him like the son they'd always wanted, but never had. He owed Max everything, his success, his knowledge, his independence.

"Come any time to talk, Mrs. Greeley." Angela stepped out after Fran. "Pay attention to the signs. You don't need me to validate your experiences. You'll know if it's your husband's ghost that visits you. Trust in your own feelings."

Cole's stomach dropped.

"I know you're right. I'll do that." Fran sniffed and dabbed a tissue to her nose.

Shit, Max was dead. A piercing arrow of fire seemed to shoot through his heart. Cole closed his eyes to block the pain. It had been Max Greeley who'd taught him the importance of hard work and the ins and outs of running a contracting business. Max who had shown him how a father could, no should love a son.

And he'd walked away from Max like he would

be around forever. Cole swallowed at the guilt. Both of the most influential men in his life were dead. One deserved it. He took the pain of Max's death and stored it away in the lockbox of his cold heart. He was more like his father anyway. Max was the past, representing a time when Cole had tried to be a good guy. But he'd spent the last five years honing in his warrior's skills, hardening his heart to become the man he was today. The man who would destroy his father and all his father had built. He would not get distracted by the knowledge that Max had died.

"If you ever need to talk, just call." Angela's voice broke into his thoughts, like an alluring siren's song, soft and sweet.

"Thank you, dear. You're always a great help. I'll see you next week at the seminar." Mrs. Greeley flounced toward Cole. Her marshmallow hair fluttered to the jangle of her gold bracelets. Everything about her was just as he'd remembered, though she had aged, she still filled the room with her ready-to-take-on-the-world energy.

"Oh my goodness." Fran's hand flew over her heart. "I swear by my eyes that I'm seeing another ghost."

"Hello, Fran. It's been a long time." Cole forced the words through the tightness in his throat. Her eyes shimmered making Cole feel like a bigger heel for not coming back sooner. God-damn, he thought he had moved beyond these weak emotions. Sadness, guilt, shame had all been eliminated by his drive and determination for revenge. But in the matter of one day, one damned day his defenses had turned from a stone fortress into a chain-linked fence with an opened gate, for every emotion to flow right through like they were made of water.

"And you are all grown up. I don't know if I should slap the back of your hand or grab you in a big bear's hug, you brute."

"I, um…"

"You come here." Pink painted fingertips pulled him close. Her powdery perfume brought more memories that choked away his breath. He felt awkward but her hug was comforting and chipped at his cold heart. Rusty at emotional displays of affection, he wrapped his arms around her and patted her back. Strangely, he didn't want to let her go.

His eyes caught with Angela's, who was standing back with an open expression, curious and filled with wonder.

Cole stiffened and narrowed his gaze at the gawker. She blinked, her face brightening with embarrassment just before she turned around, giving her back.

Fran leaned away, but held him by the arms. "I hoped you'd be here for Max's funeral. I know why you weren't here for your father's funeral but I wish you could have been here for Max's farewell."

"I didn't know." He sounded foolish. They both knew he wouldn't have come even if he'd known. He swallowed back the nausea that roiled in his stomach. He refused to let himself feel sick over it.

"You're here now." She smiled and gave his arm another squeeze. Then she tilted her head to the side. "What are you doing here?" She looked around the bright room. "This is the last place I'd expect to find you. You were always so…" she tapped an electric finger nail against her lower lip. "…practical."

"It's a long, tedious story."

"The story is probably best shared over a glass of my famous lemonade." She laughed. "I remember that it was your favorite."

That and her apple pie and her pot roast dinners.

"I would die for a glass of your homemade lemonade." He'd said it without thinking. He'd forgotten how much he loved the stuff. Wow, had it been forever since he'd tasted it? And why did he care? He couldn't, wouldn't start caring now. He had to focus on his goal. If he let the past resurface, then he would get distracted from the plan. He'd worked too hard to get sidetracked now.

"Or better yet, I should throw you a welcome home party."

"No, don't do that for me." He really didn't want or deserve a warm welcome back to Dalewood.

She brought her hand to his face and patted his cheek in the way she'd done a thousand times when he was a kid. "I'm sure Liza would love to see you, too. You're even more handsome than I ever expected."

Liza. He'd played on the scrap woodpile behind her father's construction trailer and caught her watching him through the window. She'd worn cotton white dresses back then. He'd been embarrassed in his torn jeans and dirty t-shirts.

Fran brushed his cheek with the pad of her thumb. "A party will be just the thing." With one last pat against his face, she disappeared through the glass door.

"It's clear you know Fran." Angela said. "So, you're from Dalewood I take it?"

Cole dragged his eyes from the glass doors. "Yeah, but that was a long time ago. She knew me as a child." He wasn't the same boy who longed to be loved and looked for a home like a stray. "She doesn't know the man I've become."

Did she just scan him with a once over? Yeah, she sure did.

"Fran's a wonderful woman," Angela said as their gazes locked for a split moment before she turned away. "Shall we go into my office?" "I have all the paperwork in there. You'll need to sign those before I begin the investigation." She didn't wait for a response, clearly expecting him to follow. He gave her a once over of his own. She was small, but had nice curves. Her ponytail and butt both bounced nicely with each commanding step. Yeah, he'd follow.

The room was small, painted in a shade of pale blue.

She slipped around the desk and gestured to an empty chair. An old leather-bound book engulfed the desk. The tome crackled and creaked as she closed it with the touch of a lover's caress.

He didn't think her skinny arms could carry the weight of the book, but she swung it around and placed it inside an opened cabinet as if she'd done it many times before.

"That book looks like it belongs in a museum," he said.

"It's an old family heirloom." With a decisive twist of a skeleton key, she locked it away. The key dangled from a golden chain that she placed around her neck and then tucked inside the scoop of her dress nestled between her breasts. Cole would bet any money that she had no clue how damned sexy she was and damn it, why was he noticing?

"Shall we begin?" She reached into a file cabinet along the wall, displaying her curvy assets as she leaned over. He sat back and enjoyed the view. Had he thought she was ordinary? Distancing himself from others had become second nature, but as he watched, she made him think of cool water and he was suddenly very thirsty. Not good at all.

She pulled out a stack of papers and set them on her desk.

He looked past her. "I didn't realize you were famous." He nodded toward her smiling face plastered on the framed magazines lining the cerulean walls.

"Only in a few small circles. I believe in my work and people see that. Are you here to discuss your issues or my background?"

Touché, pussycat. He kept his face clear of any

reaction.

"Since you're so good, I'm sure you've heard the rumors about my father by now?"

She laced her fingers and placed her folded hands over the papers. Her steady gaze made him feel like she could read his thoughts. He didn't like it.

"Ghosts are my business and I've heard a few rumors, but why don't you tell me the story yourself?"

"Listen, I'm here to end all the crazy gossip of a haunted mansion." He leaned deeper into the chair and crossed his arms over his chest. Did she think she was his shrink answering questions with a question? She was pretty and all, but he didn't need a therapy session.

"Tell me what's been going on?"

"My father is dead. Supposedly his ghost has tried to push my workers down the stairs."

"Mr. Barlow, if there is poltergeist activity, then it's a lot more than crazy gossip. Harm attempted on your workers is serious." She picked up her pen and rolled it in her hands.

"I have a business to run. I need this nonsense finished quickly."

She carefully placed the pen back on the desk. "I help the dead move onto the next realm. This process can't be rushed or forced into a timeline. Some ghosts are ready to move on while others need to work out their problems."

"You really think you can see ghosts, huh?"

"Yes, Mr. Barlow, I really see ghosts. And yes, I really help them."

"You're a ghost shrink?" It was all too absurd. He tried to school his facial features but he was sure a little of his feelings showed. Ah well, he wasn't here because he believed her.

"You could call me that." She shrugged. "I was a grief counselor, still am, but the deceased would cut in during the sessions to connect with their loved ones. Now I focus my ability and training to work solely with ghosts. I have an easier time dealing with the ghosts anyway." She pierced him with a razor gaze that seemed to say that the dead were a lot less judgmental than the living, specifically him. Yep, she'd read his thoughts through his expression.

"I'm not worried about helping the dearly departed. Damn my father's soul for all I care. I'm hiring you to allay my workers' fears so they'll finish the job." A headache began to throb like a ball peen hammer in his skull. "Let's get this straight, Ms. Haven. I don't really care if you can see ghosts or not. Honestly, I don't believe you can, but the people in this town do and that's what counts. They think Penniberg is haunted. Save the explanations for somebody else. I'll pay you to perform your hocus-pocus." He waved his fingers like he was sprinkling confetti. "Then you can tell all of Dalewood you've hunted the ghosts. Simple, right?"

Her eyes dripped icicles. "I'm not a ghost hunter, Mr. Barlow. If that's what you're looking for, you should call the Ghost Busters or Zak Bagans. They're famous ghost hunters. I don't hunt ghosts. I help them." Two bright spots of color brightened her creamy cheeks.

Maybe she fought hard because she wanted more money. Fine. It would be worth it to get rid of his father.

"I'm willing to pay you more than your asking fee." He pulled his checkbook from the inside pocket of his jacket. "Double the amount?"

"You don't get it. What I do is more than a job. I can't say a few *magic* words and make it all better." Her lips tightened into a fine line.

"You don't think you can exorcise the demons from my house?" He closed his eyes. This was an insane conversation. Never had he planned for a situation like this. If his head wasn't pounding, he'd probably be laughing.

"Ghosts were once people. If they are still here, it's because they have unfinished business."

"I can't wait to see your tricks in action. Do you perform séances, play Ouija?" At her stricken expression, he knew he'd hit below the belt. He shoved the inkling of regret aside.

"I don't play children's games. This is not a parlor trick. It's not a game."

"The thing you and this shitty town need to figure out is that ghosts don't exist."

Angela slammed her palms on the desk and leaned over it so her face was inches from his. He held his ground and glared. It didn't seem to affect her, though. She was tough.

Nose to nose, her spicy cinnamon scent swirled around him. He resisted the need to move closer. She was stronger than he'd given her credit for and she was not easily cowed.

"Let me make one thing clear, Mr. Barlow." She snapped out each word, crisp and precise. "Whether you believe in ghosts or not, I'm good at my job. When you deal with me, ghosts come first."

Suddenly sure, he knew she'd make the town believe his father's ghost was gone.

"Fine, when do you start?"

CHAPTER 3

ANGELA PACED BACK and forth along the fluffy white carpet in her small living room. She clipped past the TV, then around the glass coffee table, and back again. Cole Barlow had upset her in the office that morning and she'd yet to get over the incident. The big beastly guy had been domineering and downright rude. Brutally handsome too, but that was beyond the point. Every time she thought of his arrogant presence in her office, taking up the space, bossing her around, the image of Fran touching his cheek popped in her mind to soften the image. How was that possible? He was a jerk. And why did she feel compelled to take on the job?

When she looped around the room another time, she shot a glance at Emma. Her younger sister sat on the couch with a legging-covered leg hanging over the armrest. She swung her dangling black suede moccasin up and down, up and down like a pendulum. She had brown curly hair, beautiful brown eyes and a smattering of freckles across her golden cheeks. She was still young with the fresh glow of innocence at twenty-three.

Angela didn't think she'd ever had that look and she surely didn't look like that at twenty-eight.

Emma flipped through her *In Touch* magazine, and clearly wasn't paying any attention to Angela's agitated pacing.

Angela paused and crossed her arms. Emma didn't even raise her head from the Brad and Angelina article.

"Did something strange happen today?" Emma asked in a monotone voice that seemed like she didn't care.

Angela angled her head. "Strange things happen to me on a daily basis."

"I know, but it must be worse than normal."

In some ways, Angela hated that she was different. The gift, her grandma had called it. When others referred to her differences, it made her feel like she had a chronic illness. Grandma had been the only person who had understood her. She'd known better than anyone what it was like to have their special gift. She'd had a version of it too. When Grandma Haven had died after her eighteenth birthday, Angela had decided to be as normal as possible, pursuing her psychiatric career. She'd worked really hard to put her weirdness to the side and she kind of had in college, ignoring it as best she could, until Paul. Then her strong hold on the ghosts had broken and they came barreling through stronger than ever. As if trying to block the ghosts had only made her connection to them stronger. Now, helping ghosts was her full-time job and she felt good about it.

Emma swung her feet around and sat upright on the couch. "You're upset. What's bothering you? You're making it really difficult to concentrate on my rag mag."

"Nothing much. I got a new case today." She shrugged, trying to act nonchalant.

"Was it from my advertisement?" Her eyes widened and she straightened with enthusiasm.

"Probably."

Emma clapped her hands. She'd recently graduated from DePaul in May with a degree in business marketing. When her first job fell through, she'd moved into Angela's apartment. Now Emma was the brains behind her Investigation's marketing department. It was also Emma's idea to branch the business into seminars.

"My new client mentioned something about the ad we placed in the paper."

"Wasn't such a silly idea, was it?" She nodded proudly.

It took everything Angela had to keep from rolling her eyes. Call it fate, coincidence or Emma's advertising strategies, it had worked like a charm and Cole was her new client. "I'm afraid I might regret it. He is paying a ton of money for my services, though."

"What's this new client like? Your strange response has made me highly curious."

"He's an absolute jerk. Emotionless, other than easy to anger and irritation." He'd seemed much larger in her small office than he had in the reception area. His broad, workman's shoulders and well-muscled chest had been overpowering in that suit jacket. Worse than his physical size was his hulking attitude. She would not be steam-rolled, especially when it involved her business.

"No wonder you're all worked up. How will you possibly work with such an idiot? I guess the pay will make up for it, but still." She rolled the magazine in her fist. "Do you think the money is actually worth it?"

"I'm afraid I signed a deal with the devil." A pair of mocking quicksilver eyes flashed in Angela's brain. "And he is Sinfully handsome and so smug about it."

"It's a good thing I'm here. I'm your sidekick." Emma smiled reassuringly.

"What? I'm Batman to your Robin?" A smile pulled at Angela's lips.

"Of course."

Her little sister had a way of cheering her up. They hadn't always been close. With a five-year age difference, she didn't blame Emma for being embarrassed when they were younger. Angela was the weird one who could see ghosts. It couldn't have been easy having a neighborhood freak as a sister.

Emma flopped back into the soft cushions and opened the glossy magazine. Without looking up, she said, "I'm here whenever you need me, Batman."

"He thinks I'm a fake, a simple table tipper." Angela started pacing again. "Do you use Ouija?" she mocked in a lower voice mimicking Cole's earlier tone. "He made me so angry."

"You?" The magazine fell to the floor. "My

unemotional sister who never gets fazed by anything?" She looked intrigued by the notion.

"I have emotions." Angela crossed her arms over her chest. No emotions? She had to be kidding. Even though she let most things slide off her back didn't mean she couldn't feel. Dealing with ghosts made most other life issues easy to handle.

"You've dealt with some pretty big jerks before. Remember Annie Rogers?"

"Annie was a typical school bully." Who had poisoned her best friend against her, but still. "I was just a kid back then. I've worked hard to build my reputation. I won't do anything to risk it. Cole Barlow questioned my integrity." She eyed Emma.

"Hmmm," Emma said, clearly unconvinced by this argument. "And he's sinfully handsome."

Her heart ticked in her chest and she could feel two hot flames burning her cheeks. "And he's too arrogant for his own good. An absolute ass." And too handsome with his smoky eyes and his slightly too long charcoal black hair that begged to be touched. God, she hated herself.

Could she be easily swayed by a handsome man? Was she that gullible?

It wasn't his handsome face that had gotten under her skin, she realized with a start. It was that pained look when he'd learned that Max had died. It had only been there for a fleeting second. There and then gone so fast that she could have made it up. She hadn't made it up. He'd covered it. She'd seen a vulnerability underneath all that brusque exterior. She'd seen it and she couldn't let it go.

"Lots of people question your abilities. It's not the first time."

"I know." Angela took a deep breath. Just the mere thought of that guy ruffled up her anger. "And it won't be the last time. He just made me mad."

"He can't be all bad or you wouldn't have agreed to work with him."

"That man was infuriating except when he was with Mrs. Greeley. He seemed sweet with her and sad when he heard of Max's death. After Fran left, he turned into a total bear."

"Interesting."

"Why do you say that?" Angela froze. She clearly was a lot more transparent than Mr. Icy Hot.

"You feel like you need to help this guy as much as you need to help your ghosts."

"He seems very capable of taking care of himself."

"You little liar."

"He's on his own." Angela flopped down on the large couch. "I'm not a therapist anymore."

"Hah. I don't believe you." She picked up the magazine and started thumbing through it, turning each page with a loud crinkling sound.

"The dead need my help."

"I know. I've heard this all before."

"Fine. You're right. I want to help both." Angela slumped into the corner of the couch and pulled a white throw pillow over her lap. "I really think

Cole is torturing himself. Ghosts tie themselves to this realm and I have no doubt that his father is haunting that mansion because of some connection to his son. Why shouldn't I want to help both of them?"

"It doesn't hurt that he's a looker too."

"So far, that's all he's got going for him." But she couldn't get that moment when he looked like a devastated, vulnerable boy out of her mind.

CHAPTER 4

ANGELA THRUMMED HER fingers on the steering wheel as she sped down the curving road toward the Penniberg mansion. The estate was located near the older historical district on the opposite side of town. She passed rows of Victorian and Queen Anne style mansions that lined the streets.

She traveled over the stone bridge that crossed the Steele River and followed the narrow road that led to the private property. Late evening sunlight filtered through the archway of trees, casting dappled shadows along the pavement. The beginnings of autumn were her favorite time.

The road narrowed down to one lane until finally, the driveway forked off toward the mansion. When it came into view, it was as if the building grew larger and more ominous as she approached. The driveway led up to the stone and marble portico. The columns stood like sentinels protecting the door's entrance to the limestone behemoth.

Parked along the rocky side of the drive, not quite under the portico was a silver Camaro

2SS Coupe. The car was sleek and manly, with smooth edges. She wasn't surprised Cole would drive a sports car. Perfect face, perfect body and perfect car.

Practical was the only way to describe her Toyota 4Runner. She parked the car and slid from the driver's seat.

Cole must have heard her pull up, because he leaned casually against the doorjamb watching her with his devil's stare. He wore a black button-down shirt and a pair of dark jeans that showed off muscular legs. Sinfully black hair ruffled in the autumn breeze. Damn him and his perfection.

"You're late," he chided as he pushed away from the jamb.

"Barely." She glanced at her watch. It was only a few minutes after the hour. "Not all of us go to appointments extra early." She glanced at him from the side of her eye then turned all her focus on the estate. "The ride up is lovely." She circled to view the rolling green lawns flanked by ancient birch and oak trees

"Nineteen twenties original."

"I would haunt it too. It's beautiful."

"It is, but don't get too attached. This place will soon be a condominium complex."

"What are you talking about?" She whirled to look at him, but a movement in an upper level window distracted her. A curtain fluttered, then fell into place. A shiver traveled through Angela. Maybe a certain ghost didn't like the talk of condo complexes.

"That's why I hired you. I need to get rid of the place so I can rebuild over everything my father owned."

She stepped closer to the entrance, ready to begin, but Cole blocked her way. Did he have trepidations about letting her begin? She wouldn't be intimidated by his scowl. She'd been intimidated by scarier than him, that was for sure.

"Is there a problem?" She tilted her head back to make eye-to-eye contact. He towered over her by a foot and was taller than she remembered. But then, she had been on her own turf back at the office. "Must I investigate from outside, or have you found someone else to take care of your ghosts?"

Cole leaned against the door, arms crossed over his chest. He seemed like he wanted to resist, but then he shifted. "After you, Madame Investigator."

She pushed past him to get into the hallway. Tiffany sconces gave everything in the hall an iridescent sheen. Her footsteps tapped on the herringbone wood floors. The hall led to a wide-open alcove with a large set of stairs that led to the second level.

"Do you need a tour? The first room on your right is the drawing room."

She turned and caught him staring at her. "I don't need a tour. Can I just wander a bit?"

"Sure. Look around all you want."

She trailed her fingers along the wall as she walked down the corridor. A rush of energy tingled through their tips.

"This place has high energy." She could feel the rush of it through to her elbows.

She brushed the wooden doorway, feeling for the brass knob. The door swung open on well-oiled hinges.

"I've pretty much been living in there. This place is too damned big for one guy."

She entered the drawing room. The oriental carpet and its red riot of colors dominated the room. A settee and two matching wingback chairs sat in the center of the room in front of a glossy coffee table. Bookshelves lined one wall and a fireplace ran along the other. Rich, velvet curtains flanked windows that looked out into the gardens.

"I'm not surprised this place is haunted. So many beautiful things would make it hard to let go." The room was charged. Energy flowed in waves. Angela took in a deep breath and tried to pinpoint the origin. It was fresh and raging that she couldn't decipher the center. She'd start her investigation in here. Pulling the video camera from her bag, she set it on the far table near the entrance doorway and pressed the record button.

Angela wandered around the room, brushing her fingers along the back of the couch. The roughened weave of fabric scratched against her fingers. It was like playing a game of hot and cold since the ghost had decided to hide from her. She brushed her thumb against her fingertips to rub away the charged tingles of electricity.

"Have you had any strange experiences since you've been staying here?" She glanced at Cole.

"Nope, nada." He flicked a glance toward the wedding photo on the wall.

She felt like he was leaving something out. Hadn't felt any ghosts? Either he blocked the feeling or he refused to acknowledge them. The guy had so much self-control.

"Were they your parents?" She nodded toward the portrait.

"I guess." His tone was flat.

That was a strange answer. Angela had always been close to her family even though she'd been different. She already knew he had problems with his father, but his pain ran deeper than she'd thought.

To push away the returning wave of compassion, she picked up the glass on the coffee table and sniffed. She scrunched her nose against the offending scent of scotch, then set the tumbler back on the table and pushed it away from the edge. Reaching down, she picked up the newspaper from the floor.

"Emma, my sister, was glad to hear that the advertisement worked."

His large presence was distracting. She'd work better if he wasn't here.

She wandered around the room hoping the ghost would show itself. She continued to touch her way around the room. Fragments of energy filtered through her hand as she slipped her fingers along the wooden part of the winged back chair. Getting a ghostly connection, even small, she reached in her bag, took her camera out and snapped a few shots.

Hopefully, she'd capture a few bits of physical evidence and then hotshot would have to admit he believed in a ghost or two. She tucked the camera away and continued toward the fireplace.

"Interesting piece. A lion's head in full roar."

"It was commissioned in Italy, especially for the mansion."

"It looks like it belongs in the space. I've never seen anything like it." Jagged marble teeth slid beneath her hand.

Sharp unexpected shivers ripped through her arm. Angela bit at her lip to stop the cry that almost tore from her throat. To catch her balance, she gripped the lion's face tighter, hooking her fingers around the sharp teeth.

The tingles were unexpected. Her mind was pulled, pulled to the past where old emotions drugged her senses. They were very old. She could tell from the vibrations that flowed through her. They were calmer and didn't fully dull her senses like the full onslaught of a spirit. The air wavered, shimmery and foggy like a dream sequence in a movie, and a couple took form before her. Angela intercepted their conversation in mid-sentences. Were they actual ghosts or just apparitions replaying a scene from the past? The energy felt old.

Angela watched and listened, hoping to learn something that could help her connect with the ghosts that haunted this mansion.

The girl was young and very pretty. Her black hair framed her face in a short bob that barely reached to her chin. Her thick bangs cut a straight line over her forehead. Bright red lipstick exaggerated the sweetheart shape of her full lips.

Angela watched those lips move in a hazy shifting. She spoke words Angela couldn't hear at first. But the words became louder and louder until their voices became clear, high-pitched and ringing like they rattled through a hollow metal tube.

"Harold Barnes, my dear Harry, don't you look all together smashing?" The girl faced a boy. He seemed a few years older than the girl. She reached with delicate fingers and adjusted the bowtie to his tuxedo. His hair was almost as dark as hers with a blue tinge in its blackness. Neatly combed, it was parted down the side and slicked with a shine.

"Daddy is going to move you up in the company for certain."

"Do you actually think so, Brooke, m'dear?"

Angela watched as Harry wrapped his arms around Brooke and pulled her close to him. The movements were as fluid as flowing water. She knew she was seeing an old image, something from a past long ago.

"Once Daddy makes the decision, he will make you manager, then we can be married and all will be made right." He lifted her chin so she looked up at him. "I love you Brooke Dalloway."

Angela watched the images play out before her until they wavered foggily and faded just as Harry leaned down and pressed his lips to Brooke's in a passionate embrace while their touches became more intimate. Angela was glad that the image drifted away. If she had seen more she would be uncomfortable.

The ghostly play completely disappeared and she was back in the sitting room.

Before she could catch her balance from the scene, white stars flashed behind her eyelids and a piercing hot bolt of electricity shot through her temple. She pressed her palm to the side of her head, trying to stop the pain when she noticed the glittering stars weren't in her mind. They shifted and swirled before her.

The temperature of the room chilled to iceberg level. She tried to blink her vision clear. A large shadow stepped away from the wall and the out-line of a figure took shape.

The shadow was menacing, but she refused to cower. She could make out his head and shoulders, but she couldn't see a face. There was darkness where his features should have been.

The shadow blew its angry chill toward her and tried to penetrate it into her body deep to her bones. Angela would not let this creature scare her. She reached deep down into her core and touched the white energy that swirled just below her belly. She needed it to gather her strength. Angry energy radiated from the dark entity in a searing wave of hatred. She wanted to take a step back, but she held her ground.

"I'm here to help you," she rasped. Her throat burned with the effort to say the words.

The spirit pushed through her every cell like icy fog. She dragged in a deep breath and steeled herself. He was furious and wanted to scare her from the mansion. But she was tougher than that. She pulled at every ounce of her power and held herself against the ghost, pushing him from her body. A roaring sound whooshed through her ears and rattled through her brain. The invader was gone. Relief and fatigue weighed on her.

She turned toward the couch to sit for a moment, but became startled. Cole's large, solid body stood before her like a wall of strength. He was mere inches from her, and she'd never heard him take a step. Now all she wanted to do was lean on him for support.

"Are you alright?" Cole asked. He'd watched as she glided along the floor, touching everything like a blind person memorizing every detail.

Mesmerized by her movements, he'd been unable to drag his gaze away from her delicate touches over his couch, his table, his fireplace mantle. She, at once, seemed strong and independent while somehow vulnerable.

When her body froze, his protective mode kicked in. He'd walked up to her, but she did not see him. He didn't want to startle her, so he waved a hand in front of her face.

Nothing. Not a flinch. Not even a flutter of her eyelids.

Then his suspicions flared. Had she performed a trick to convince him she was doing her job? He was about to say *boo* in her face when he noticed her pale skin. The color in her cheeks had gone from raspberry bright to the pallor of cool putty. While her eyes swirled like molten gold, they'd stared off into nothingness.

He rested his hand gently on her and the spreading heat surrounded him, jumping between their bodies.

When her distant eyes focused, the swirls seemed to still and she was back to herself.

"You were staring off into space. Are you okay?" The normalcy of his voice surprised him, especially when his emotions were in turmoil and had kicked into overdrive.

Surprise splashed over her face just before she stumbled into him. With a quick movement, he wrapped an arm around her waist and pulled her close. Her cinnamon scent enveloped him.

"I'm feeling a little off kilter. I just need a minute." Her laugh came out like a weak, miserable sound that grated his insides.

"You're as pale as a ghost or more like you've seen a ghost." He chuckled, wanting to lighten the mood.

When her eyes narrowed, the laughter caught in his throat. "Oh, come on. You aren't about to tell me you saw a ghost while I stood here the entire time."

"Didn't you see anything?"

He gave her an incredulous look and a grunt escaped from his belly in a disbelieving laugh. He'd seen her with a faraway gaze, but there'd been nothing else that he'd been aware of.

Pink rushed into her cheeks and her small hands pressed into his chest. She shoved without warning, throwing him off balance. He stumbled to right himself, then realized how much he missed the warmth of her hands against him. He must really be hard up if he noticed her perfume and the softness of her skin. He'd been focused on his revenge for so long and now was not the time to let a pretty face distract him.

"Are you feeling better?" he asked annoyed with himself, annoyed with her.

Her mouth opened, then closed, then opened again. "Much better now." Her clipped tones made it clear she was referring to the release from his arms. The implication stung more than probably reasonable.

"I'm sorry that you find me intolerable." The words came out with a coolness he wanted her to feel.

"You're the one who has a problem with me. You continuously insult me."

"I insult you? What are you talking about?" Anger bubbled in him.

"You hired me because I see ghosts." She seemed to deflate like a balloon with a slow pin-prick. Confusion fogged over her features. "But still, you can't believe it. You can't even believe something that is right in front of your face."

He had the urge to reach for her, stroke his fingertips along her cheek that now flared with bright color to bring back that confidence he'd seen a short while ago. But he couldn't let himself care too much. Better that she hated him. If she was angry with him, it would be easier to keep her at a distance.

"What happened to you that makes you so untrusting?"

"How can you expect me to believe in something that's not real?"

"It's real."

"Oh yeah? Then maybe you should talk to my father instead of me."

"Oh, don't worry, I will. That's why I'm here." She snapped her fists to her waist. She was gaining back her color. Good.

"Then why don't you start?" He shook his head at his own absurdity. He couldn't believe what he was saying. "I want to be rid of this place. All of it. Get rid of the past." He thrust a hand through his dark hair. "This whole town has gone crazy and it's taking me with it," he said under his breath, though he knew it was loud enough for her to hear.

"People care about the past. It's their history. What else do we have?"

"I want to forget my history." He stalked toward her and growled as his anger erupted.

The glass on the table popped up in the air, then fell to the floor with a thud. They both watched the dark stain spread on the carpet.

Cole's immediate response was to fall to the ground and clean up the mess before his father noticed. He closed his eyes and stopped himself. Even now, so many years later, he still reacted like his father was breathing down his neck. The response ran deep in his bones. Now that he was in the house again, the old ways trickled back.

Angela rushed to the glass and held it up in front of him with a large grin. "They never do anything like this unless it has meaning."

He opened his mouth, then stopped. He'd been caught in his horrible thoughts, he'd barely registered that the glass had moved on its own. He

narrowed his eyes. She must have faked it somehow. He was convinced of it and he was pissed.

"You're the ghost hunter. You tell me what
this means." Without waiting for a response, he
grabbed the glass from her fingers and strode out
of the room. He had to get away from her and
the things she made him remember.

Cole took the steps two at a time and headed
down the hall to his childhood bedroom, a sanctuary and a prison combined. He slammed the
door like the child he'd been reminded of just
minutes before, relishing the sound.

Rainbows flashed through the etched crystal
as he inspected the glass. How had she done it?
He rubbed his thumb along the bottom, but the
indentation was smooth, without any sticky res-
idue. There had to be a contraption to get it to
bounce like that. Some sort of trick. He should
have watched her more closely, but he'd let his
defenses slip a little. He couldn't figure out how
she'd gotten the glass to move on its own.

She had a reputation for being the best for a
reason, and she was probably rolling with laughter downstairs because she'd tricked him.

He gripped the glass between his hands. There
were no signs of tampering, but then again, she
was good. So good, he could almost believe his
father still tormented him from beyond the grave.

Almost.

No one would manipulate him again, trick him
into believing something that wasn't true. Not his
father who was supposed to love him, but never
did. Not this woman who said she saw ghosts but

didn't.

With a jagged laugh, he tightened his hold on the glass and hurled it at the far wall between the landscape and the window. Crystal shattered and fell to pieces in tinkling shards on the carpet next to the end table.

Cole's breaths came fast and ragged. Now that he was back in Dalewood, back in the mansion he couldn't control the emotions or the memories from battering through him. He scrubbed his hands over his face, unable to stop the flood of memories as they broke free from the barrier he'd kept tight for so long.

The echo of breaking glass rattled in his ears while his cheek stung from the tears after his father's tirade.

"What's wrong with you boy? Don't you know what I had to do to afford that?" His father grabbed at Cole's collar. "You're wasteful, useless." He pushed a much younger Cole to the floor. "You think I work for all this money so you can just break everything?"

Cole stumbled like the klutz he'd been accused of being. Pain seared through Cole's hands as he fell into the broken shards. Blood beaded, then trickled from the sliced flesh. He wiped his hand on his jeans, not wanting his father to see the injuries since his dad already thought he was a wimp.

He gripped the large piece of glass tighter and tighter, willing his father to leave before he did something bad. He dragged heavy breaths in and out.

"You're such a waste. An unwanted burden. Clean up your mess." His father's heavy boots thumped from the room.

Cole's pulse pounded in his ears. Blood pooled into his palm, covering the glass with slick red. He'd vowed, that day long ago, his dad would never berate him again. Cole was no longer a cowering baby. He was an adult and could take care of himself. He didn't need a father pointing out all his flaws and telling him how worthless he was.

He hadn't realized he'd been reenacting his memory until he saw that he was kneeling on the floor near the pile of broken glass. He held his right hand cradled in his left. The puckered scar crossed his palm right over his life line. The old scars were a constant reminder of the terror his father had inflicted. The scars inside had hurt more. They slashed deep through his heart.

Angela stared into the hallway, debating whether or not she should follow Cole. She must have touched a sore spot in him, hit a nerve. Somehow, she had really upset him and now she didn't know if she should apologize or continue with her job. She shrugged. She had nothing to be sorry about anyway.

Floorboards creaked in the hallway behind her just as she was about to take one last loop around the drawing room. She stilled, listening for more sounds. Another creak resonated. The hair on her arms stood up with charged energy.

"I'm here to help," she called.

Another creak sounded in the hallway as if leading her. She followed the sounds.

The moment she stepped out of the drawing room, she could feel the buzz of ghostly energy along the skin of her arms.

"Hank Barlow, are you here? Did you move that glass?" The experience with the dark shadow had caught her off guard, but at least she had some contact. "Hank, I'm here to help you."

Footsteps clomped on the stairs, step by heavy step. She knew the ghost wanted her to follow, so she obliged and followed to the second floor. Sparks tingled through the soles of her feet with each step in the ghostly footprints.

"Why won't you speak to me?"

The footfalls continued down the darkened hallway. An oriental carpet runner covered the wooden floor. A Tiffany style lamp sat on a side table flanked on both sides by two leather chairs. Leather bound books lined up like waiting soldiers in a bookshelf on the other side of the wall. A tall grandfather clock stood in the corner, its golden pendulum swinging back and forth in time with her heartbeats.

Another creak sounded down the hall in front of her. Slowly, the brass doorknob on the second door at the end of the hall turned.

"We don't need to play, Hank. I'm here to help you."

A click of the releasing door was the only reply. Then the door popped slightly open, casting a silver spray of light on the floor.

Angela reached for the knob and a rushing river of hot ice shot through her. She pushed at the door and entered, peaking into the room.

Decorated in masculine dark tones of green, the bedroom had a large, neatly made bed. Clearly, no one had slept in it.

Light from the newly risen moon filtered through the window causing something on the floor to sparkle. Broken glass. A dark shadow huddled on the other side of the bed shifted. She realized it was Cole, crouched, staring at the shards. She moved to help him.

She must have made a sound because Cole turned. His haunted face took her breath. His eyes were hollow, the irises dilated, almost completely gone. She remained rooted to her spot. His pain ran deeper than anything she could have done. This might have started because he was mad at her, but this wasn't about her. This was something older, deeper, more painful. She felt that pain as if it was tearing her insides, shredding her stomach into bits.

"Let me help you." She knelt next to him, reaching for glass pieces.

"What do you want?" he snapped. "Haven't you tormented me enough?"

She blinked at the harshness of his words even though she knew they were about something else and not about her. "You asked me to come here."

"Not in here." He thrust his hand out, pointing toward the door she had just entered.

"What happened?" She grabbed for another piece of glass. It sliced through her thumb like it was warm butter. "Ouch," she said before she could stop herself. The chunk of glass fell to the floor.

The hand that had been angrily pointing to the door snatched up her injured hand. He turned it into the moonlight.

He gripped his large hand around hers.

"Let me see it," he cajoled. Even angry she could tell he did not mean to hurt her and she relaxed a little releasing her thumb to his view.

Cole's fingers were hot against her cool touch. Calluses roughened the mounds and a thick scar ran across his palm. It was puckered, but old and long healed. He had such strong, masculine hands. His wealth had not come easy. He'd worn a fancy suit when he came to her office, and his shoes were expensive. But those were the hands of a working man, not someone who had made his millions from behind a desk.

"It's not that bad." She reached for a tissue from the box on the nightstand next to the bed. "I'm sure it's nothing to worry about."

"Let me be the judge."

She tried to pull her hand away, but he held her fast. He slid the tissue from her fingers and dabbed at the wound. The heat from his hand instantly warmed her, energizing her, making her fingers feel alive. She shouldn't like it that much, but she also didn't want to break the contact.

His lips skewered with concentration as he checked the cut for glass. He no longer looked lost or broken. He looked determined. His cheeks filled with color and his eyes, trained on her hand, were back to being the silvery color of the moonlight. A thick lock of black hair fell over his forehead. She wanted to brush it back and the thought shocked her. For all his bluster he couldn't completely hide his kindness when it escaped through little crevices. Was that the real person he was? She wanted to find out.

"You've caused enough trouble, already." He gently squeezed her hand. "A little anti-bacterial cream and a bandage will do the trick. It's just a small cut."

Before letting go of her hand, his thumb brushed along the sensitive flesh of her wrist sending a tingling sensation through her. She realized how big his strong, capable hand was next to her small delicate bones. She swallowed. He could have easily hurt her if he'd wanted to, but his touch had been kind and gentle.

She lifted her gaze to look at him. The intensity in his silver eyes startled her. She swallowed, but didn't look away.

"Why did you try to trick me with the glass?" he whispered. The corners of his eyes crinkled, accusing, but also disappointed.

"Trick you? I didn't try to trick you." She pulled free from his grasp.

"Tell me how you did it." He clenched his hands at his sides.

"What are you talking about?"

"Your job is to get the town to believe the ghosts have been vanquished, or whatever it is you do." His shoulders sagged and the rest of his anger faded. "You don't have to play your games with me. I don't need convincing."

He bent and tossed the larger pieces of glass into the wastebasket with loud clinks.

"I told you already," she defended herself. "I don't play games. When it comes to the dead, I do whatever I can to help them."

"Then why'd you pull that fast one with the glass?" He looked over his shoulder at her.

"I didn't make that glass fly off the table."

"You are never to do anything like that again."

"I don't take orders from you."

"When you work for me, you do."

Angela clenched her teeth as rage pooled in her belly. He was not going to tell her how to handle the gifts she'd honed over the years. "Strange things happen around me. You'd better steer clear if you can't handle it."

His hands stilled and he slowly twisted at the waist to look up at her. His eyes burned like mercury. "There's nothing I can't handle."

A shiver ran down her spine. Yeah, there probably wasn't much he couldn't handle.

The bedroom door banged against the wall. She jumped, breaking their silent stare.

"What in the hell?" He shot her an accusing stare.

A breeze fluttered through the room as more bangs and thumps rattled down the hall.

Angela shrugged her shoulders and raised a brow. She didn't dare laugh at his outraged expression.

Thankfully, he pulled his heavy gaze from hers and moved into the hallway. She followed him.

The neatly stored books lay in a scattered heap on the floor.

"What are you doing to me?"

"You think I did that?"

Without responding, Cole strode to the pile and kicked the top layer of books, sending some skittering across the carpet. He leaned down and picked up the book closest to his foot. "When I was a boy, my father caught me looking at these," he said in a distant voice. "He told me I'd never amount to anything since I was too lazy." He flipped a page and read. "He said I wasted all my time reading instead of working with my hands." He clenched and unclenched his free hand. "Don't bother reading, boy. You're not smart enough."

His back stiff, his head lowered, she felt wave after wave of pain emanating from him. Angela stepped closer and placed a comforting hand on his wrist. He didn't seem to notice her touch. Firm muscles flexed under his shirt with each movement of his hand. His pulse throbbed with a strong and vibrant rhythm.

"Cole, I…" She always knew what to say to a ghost in need, but she was at a loss when it came to him.

"I don't know how you did this." He raised the book. "You're good. Clearly the best."

"You think I faked this?" Angela pulled her hand from him as if she'd been burned. "I was with you the entire time." She felt defensive at his slap of words. "These poltergeist activities were happening long before I got here."

"I never experienced any of this until you walked inside."

"I doubt that. You refuse to pay attention." She threw her hands in the air. "Typical. You only see what you want to believe."

"Are you saying that I'm as crazy as you?"

"You're the one who hired me." She propped her fists on her hips.

"Maybe I am the damned, crazy one."

"You can stay here and wallow by yourself. Maybe you'll have a chance to think it over and you won't be such an arrogant know-it-all when I return tomorrow. I'm done for the day."

She took the book from his hand and read the title.

"Hamlet. Your father beckons you," she mocked as she handed back the book.

Their eyes caught.

"Pay attention to the signs, because this ghost is clearly trying to connect with you."

His face filled with disbelief. When he took the book from her, she turned and walked down the stairs and out of the house, leaving him with an open book, a pile of glass shards and years of unwanted memories.

CHAPTER 5

COLE PICKED UP another book and placed it on the shelf. He needed to think about this logically. Angela couldn't know any of the problems he'd had with his father. No one but Max knew any of the specifics.

Maybe her tricks weren't special to his past experiences. They could fit into a typical scheme for poltergeists pulled from any good ghost movie.

First an object moved. A glass was as easy as the next thing. Then books fell off the shelves. That wasn't very interesting or very ingenious. Books flying off shelves were practically a scary movie cliché.

Next, his kitchen chairs would stack themselves. Good thing he didn't have a parakeet. He'd never owned a single pet to bury in a backyard cemetery. Check those things off the possibilities list.

Ted said it wasn't enough that Angela had come into the mansion. He wouldn't start work until she gave the all clear. Only after she said the ghosts were gone would he feel safe enough to reenter.

Cole would give her a couple more days and

that was it. Instead of getting rid of his father's ghost, or at least faking that his ghost was gone, she was creating more problems, making it seem like his dad was back loud and strong.

That didn't make sense. Why would she do it that way? He was the only person to see her magic.

If others found out about those things, he would know instantly that Angela was trying to drum up business for herself.

Cole looked down at the old scar in his hand. Dull throbs pulsed through it. He'd been lost in his memories, and hadn't noticed Angela come in until she'd been right up on him. Then she'd cut herself. Her hand had been small, but strong. He hadn't wanted to let her go. How ridiculous.

Those big golden eyes, so confident, had looked at him with concern.

When was the last time someone had worried about him? Not since he was a young boy helping on Greeley's worksite. He'd injured his foot when a stack of two-by-fours fell off a pallet. Fran Greeley had wrapped his ankle when it swelled.

Angela had looked at him with that same mix of concern and care. But if Angela cared enough to help him, why had she played those tricks?

She didn't need to try so hard, not with him. He wasn't the one who needed convincing. He didn't care if ghosts existed. He'd be better off getting rid of the demons in his head. They resurfaced ever since his return. He had to get out of here soon.

If that meant suffering through some "poltergeist activities" created by the pretty trickster, then so be it.

When the last book was on the shelf, he noticed how still everything was. Not a single weird thing had happened since Angela had left. Just a little more evidence that she was behind it. He was more convinced than ever that she had something to do with the activities.

Alone in such a huge mansion. More like a mausoleum, Cole couldn't understand why his father had stayed here for so long. It was too big with too many rooms.

The creaks and pops of the old house along with the torture of his thoughts was driving him out of his mind. He'd taken residence in only a few rooms. Sleeping on the couch in the drawing room had turned old after the first night. His old bedroom had remained as it was when he'd left. Not too many changes.

But there wasn't much to change anyway. It had never been a boy's room. He'd never had posters on the walls or trophies on shelves. He'd never been allowed to hang a single model airplane, not one poster.

No, the room was that of a man and it still was. He slept in that room anyway. He hadn't gone anywhere near his father's room, yet.

"I hope it was all worth it, Dad," Cole said aloud. "Maybe you are haunting this place." He didn't believe it, but he continued anyway. "I hope you are, so you can rot in your own hell. Show yourself. Or are you scared to face me now that I'm grown?" Cole's voice had raised up to a near shout.

A floorboard creaked behind him. A chill ran up his neck, raising the little hairs there. Cole swung around, gaze darting to every corner, every shadow. A shaft of light from the window reflected off the wooden floor. The doorway was empty. Had he expected to see his father filling it?

"Creaky, damned house."

Cole could hear his father in his head laughing at him. *Stupid boy. What, now you believe in ghosts? Pretty soon you'll believe in fairies and leprechauns bringing pots of gold. The world don't work that way, boy. Better for you to learn that from your Pa than from the world.*

Unable to relax, he decided to wander the halls, room by room. When he was at the top of the staircase, he looked down at the entryway. It was a grand place. Shiny floors, hand carved banisters, plaster walls with crown molding and hand sculpted plaster work. Cole hated everything about it.

Had anyone ever been happy here? Cole hoped that the original owners had some happiness here, because his father hadn't known the definition and neither had he.

A sound like rustling fabric crinkled behind Cole, or that's what he thought it seemed like. He turned to see where the sound came from. Were there mice in here?

That would be funny. The that his father loved so much, infested by rodents. But Cole hadn't seen any evidence of mice. There weren't any chewed holes in the walls. He hadn't seen any little nests of paper bits. Cole knew the signs of mice. He'd lived in a few rat holes in the past.

When times were tight, he'd lived in any place he could afford. No, he didn't think any rats had taken up a home in the pristine Penniberg mansion.

What had made that sound? It had to be his active imagination after he'd met a certain ghost hunter. Cole traveled down the hallway to continue his tour of the mansion. *His* mansion. To do with as he pleased. He could spray paint the wall, cut down the curtains slash by slash. He'd start with his father's bedroom by getting rid of all his special possessions. Getting rid of his father one piece at a time would have to do for now.

Cole walked down the hallway to the bedroom at the far end of the hallway near the back of the house. From what he remembered, it had a view of the gardens and the ruins of what used to be an aviary. The original owners loved rare and exotic birds. Why did Cole remember that? He must have heard that somewhere.

His foot faltered and he froze in his spot. His father's bedroom door stood open. Every door on the second and third floors should be closed. Why was this door open? Maybe the latch slipped. He closed the door, then gave it a push. It stayed firmly closed. He jiggled the handle, but it was secure. Everything worked fine, so there was no reason why this door should have been opened. There had to be a reason. Maybe Ted had been up here when he'd been pushed? That was the only plausible explanation.

Gripping the handle, he unlatched the door. Pulling in a deep breath, he walked into the room for the first time since he'd been a child.

The room hadn't changed much. There wasn't much to be afraid of or have trepidation about seeing. His father was dead and gone. The pressure in his chest dissipated.

The master bedroom had a sitting room and its own bathroom with a large closet that should actually be called a dressing room. The room connected to another bedroom that also had a set of attached rooms. The honeymoon suite. Cole almost laughed. It all sounded romantic. He moved through his father's room and looked out the window.

The Steele River peeked through the trees beyond the gardens like a secret place in a fairy tale. He dropped the curtain from his hand. It would be easier to simply toss out some of his things.

He opened the closet and a wave of Brut and lemon balm overwhelmed him as if his father was standing right there. He pulled his shoulders back and raised his hands, ready for an assault, but it was just his residual scent. His shoulders deflated and he chuckled at his automatic response. *Just a closet, you wimp* he chided himself.

Cole scanned the rows of suits, filling the closet in colors ranging from gray to black to navy. His shoes were arranged on the floor, toes pointed out, lined up as if they had been straightened with a ruler, not a single one out of order.

Suddenly very tired, he realized he couldn't deal with this. He had to get out of here, away from his father. He moved toward the door, ready to leave, when he saw a small wooden trunk with brass hinges at the foot of the bed.

Where had that come from? He didn't remember seeing it when he'd entered. Had it always been there and he simply hadn't noticed it like so many things, a clock on a wall, a lamp? Like an object passed over many times unseen?

The patinaed hinges groaned when Cole lifted the lid and peered inside.

Cole pulled out the top item, a brush with a black and brown swirled handle that was too heavy to be made of plastic. Could it be real tortoise shell? The bristles were thick. They must have been old boar bristles. Surely an antique. It was something he would have played with in the attic. Why in the world would his hardened father place an item like this in a chest like a treasure?

Cole set the brush on the dressing table near the window. Moving back to the trunk, he looked at the other items. There was a baby blanket yellowed with age, hand embroidered with blue silk thread in the shape of the letter B. Was the B for Barlow? But the blanket looked like it came from and earlier era. Sitting on top of the blanket was a black velvet bag with the strings tied in a bow.

A glint in the corner of the box distracted him before he could check out the other items. How had that gotten in the box with all the old items? He had watched his father throw it in the trash.

Grasping the medallion by the chain, Cole

raised and held it out in front of him. It twisted, dangling from the chain, swirling round and round like a hypnotist's trick. He couldn't stop looking at it. The round chunk of metal he'd given to his father long ago was in the bottom of the trunk of things his father clearly thought were special or important.

God, that just pissed him off. Rage boiled in him. It had hurt very badly to see his father toss the piece into the trash like yesterday's junk and now to find it all these years later mixed in a box with these obscure items. How cold his father was to hurt him like that to his face but then save the piece. Why had he saved it and put it in this box for all these years?

Cole placed the medallion around his neck as a renewed reminder of his revenge. The rejected gift of a small child. It felt hot, throbbing against his chest. But maybe that was the anger from his own beating heart. He turned to the other items from the box. What other treasures did his father have hidden away?

Cole reached for the square of cotton. It looked like a man's handkerchief. Faded yellow, at one time it would have been pristine white, and the black embroidered H and B were now a muddy brown. Cole traced his finger over each letter. He felt a strange attachment to the handkerchief even though it was unfamiliar since he'd never seen it before. It could have been his father's though it seemed too old.

A hand-blown atomizer bottle held a brown layer of dried perfume. It smelled of the cloying scent of honeysuckle.

He placed these items next to the velvet pouch and then picked up the pouch. Cole slid the ribbons apart. At first, he thought it was empty, but then his fingers brushed against something silky. He gripped it between his two fingers and slid it from the bag. He held thin strands of fine brown hair tied with a faded blue ribbon. The hair was too silky to belong to an adult. A baby's first haircut? He placed the strands back in the pouch and cinched the closure.

For some reason he could not explain, he wanted to keep the items. He arranged them in the box, then set the pouch so it sat on top of the blanket and closed the lid. He gripped the medallion that hung heavily around his neck with one hand and tucked the trunk under his other arm to carry it back to his room.

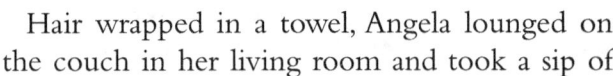

Hair wrapped in a towel, Angela lounged on the couch in her living room and took a sip of her merlot.

Emma had gone out with some friends, so she sat alone in the living room enjoying her solitude. The melody of "Ordinary Love" by Sade wafted through the air.

Taking another drink of her wine, she closed her eyes and snuggled more deeply into the cushions. The music surrounded her.

Just as she was drifting off, a pair of silver eyes flitted through her brain. He'd felt so strong and reassuring when his arms held her after the attack by the dark spirit. And his hands, those large hands, roughened with scars and calluses had tenderly cared for her and taken away her pain from the cut. Before he realized she had cut herself she'd felt his pain running through him, tightening his shoulders and vibrating from his body. She'd experienced it in almost the same way that she felt a ghost. When he'd looked at her with angry mercury-filled eyes, she knew it was misplaced. He needed to put his energy on his father, but he'd placed it on her instead.

She jumped when her cell phone buzzed, shattering the mental images. She reached toward the end table and grabbed the phone, stopping the jarring ringtone. Who would be bothering her now?

"Hello?" she said, not trying to hide the annoyance in her tone.

"Hi, Angela. It's Cole."

Her stomach jumped into her throat. Had she made him materialize by simply thinking of him? She felt her cheeks flare with heat and pressed cool fingertips against them. What a relief that he was on the phone and not at the door.

Imagining his handsome face and hearing his voice over the phone were two completely different things.

"Yes, Mr. Barlow. How can I help you?" Yes, coolness in her voice would surely travel through to his side of the phone.

"First, how's your thumb?"

"It's fine. It was just a shallow cut."

"Good, just keep an eye on it. Second, I need

to apologize."

"Oh." She practically slipped to the floor. A little care about her injury and then an apology, from him, was the last thing she'd ever expected.

"I was angry about the glass. Let's just say it shocked me a little."

"I'm sure. Something of that nature would surprise anyone. Ghostly activity is sure to surprise someone who isn't used to it."

"Yeah, well, that trick set me off"—he cleared his throat— "and it rekindled some old memories that I thought I'd forgotten."

"Hmm." Should she comment that she hadn't been tricking him or should she focus on the fact that he actually told her it had caused some bad memory to resurface? Maybe she could get him to tell her more since he hadn't said very much about it last night.

He didn't trust people easily. But why? Yes, his father had been a bad guy, that was true, but she wanted to know more. If she understood what had happened between Cole and his father, maybe it would be easier to help the ghost move on to the other side. Could she ask him outright? Should she? She words popped right out of her mouth. "What was it about the glass flying from the table that upset you so much? What was the memor…"

"I don't want to be tricked, Angela." His words were stiff and curt.

"I was doing my job, Mr. Barlow. Is that why you called me? To scold me for doing what you hired me to do?" Nope. He didn't like being asked outright one bit. She'd pull the info from him somehow.

There was a pause on the other side of the phone and then he cleared his throat.

"Everyone in this town feared my father and that's why I'm sitting in this mausoleum as we speak instead of working on a leveled construction site. Ted is the only guy who will do the job, but he won't come back without your approval."

"I take pride in my work. Let me do my job."

"This town trusts you, so I have no choice but to trust you too." He continued as if he hadn't heard her, words rushing out as if he was afraid she'd back out, abandoning the project.

"Thanks. That's so reassuring." He sure knew what to say to a girl. "Your confidence in my abilities comes through loud and clear." She said it in such a way that she knew he could not miss her sarcasm.

"You can't expect me to believe so easily."

"With guys like you, I thought seeing was believing."

"Yeah, well…" he trailed off.

"And still you don't believe. I do not perform parlor tricks and I don't play games. I have no need. What you experienced was real. It was a message to you, not me. How do I know? I can tell by how much you were affected by it. It resonated with you. I tell all my clients to pay attention to the signs."

He was silent on the other end, so she went on with her tirade. "Mr. Barlow. I signed a contract, but more than that, I made a promise. I take my job very seriously. Spirits don't have a voice anymore. There is no one who can help them like I can. This is why ghosts come first with me. That's my priority."

"I need you. It's long past time to help my father move on."

She wasn't fooled for a minute. "You need Ted and I'm the only route."

"It's practically the same thing. Isn't it?"

She rolled her eyes. Was he trying to be a jerk? Or did it just come naturally? "I'll be there tomorrow."

"Angela," his warm tone would have sent shivers up a weaker woman's arms, "I'll see you tomorrow."

"You're impossible." She couldn't completely blame him. They were similar. Two people who didn't trust easily.

She ended the call and tossed the phone on the table. He didn't believe in ghosts. Spirits and hauntings were her life. She couldn't drop her guard with him even if he was handsome. Especially because he was so handsome. He'd be watching her every move to prove her out to be a fake.

She went to the stereo, hit the replay button and raised the volume. The sounds of Sade flowed like ribbons around her. She laid back on the couch and let the music block out all her thoughts. She'd deal with the jerk tomorrow.

CHAPTER 6

"WHAT IS THIS?" Angela asked as little vibrations of energy tingled through her fingers where she touched a brush. She'd lifted it from out of the trunk she'd been rummaging through. Being back in Cole's bedroom after the glass incident had her a little on edge.

She shot a quick glance over her shoulder knowing Cole would be there since he'd been following her around all day, waiting to prove her as a charlatan, no doubt.

"That's called a brush." He uncrossed his arms and pushed away from the doorjamb. Wearing a gray T-shirt that stretched over the muscles of his arms and chest, he looked sexier than anyone should. He reached for the brush and their hands touched. Ripples ran through her fingers. Each time he touched her it did things to her that she wanted to ignore. He was too distracting.

Disheveled after exploring, she tugged at the hem of her navy button-down top, pulling it lower over her hips. How could he look so good while she felt frumpy?

He flipped the brush over in his hands. Angela

turned back to the chest to give herself something else to do other than watch his hands. She sifted through the items, lifting a pink dress with ruffles along the bottom edge to create a wall-like barrier between them. "The brush looks pretty old."

"Where do you think it came from?"

"This is your house. How should I know where it came from?" Angela dropped the dress back inside the box and stood to face him. "Hasn't it always been there?"

"I don't know where that old chest came from either." He slapped the tortoise shelled back against his palm. Tap, tap, tap.

Angela's eyes were drawn to the motion. His thick, solid fingers stroked the handle almost lovingly while he stared off, distracted by far away thoughts.

Where had that brush come from? It was too feminine to be his.

"Maybe it belonged to an old girlfriend?" She lifted an eyebrow and held back a smile.

"I haven't lived here since I was sixteen."

"Forgot all your girls already?" She grabbed the brush from him and pointed it toward his chest. "Too many to remember, huh?"

He crossed his arms again and leaned back to eye her with his silky stare. "Would that bother you?"

She felt a blush rise into her cheeks. She wanted to throw the brush at him to wipe that smile off his mouth. She turned away and tossed it on the bed instead. "No girl wants to be forgotten." Why was she curious to know about his past? She wanted to know if he'd had a lover in this room. It was his bedroom. It was driving her crazy being close to him and a bed. Which didn't make sense. Yes, he was hot, but still, he didn't trust her and insulted her work. Why was she feeling this way?

"You had too many women to remember whose stuff was left behind?" She grabbed the dress and waved it like a dancing girl. She didn't want him to think she was interested in his answer.

"I left this place long before I ever had a girl-friend. And what about your love life, Ms. Curious with the angel eyes?" He pulled the dress away.

Angel eyes? Her stomach fluttered. No one had ever given her a compliment like that and she kind of liked it, but she wouldn't let him know that.

"There is so much work to do." She crouched in front of the box and coughed to hide her ner-vousness. "I want to sort through each article to see if I get any residual energy." She dipped her fingers back into the box and yanked out the first thing she touched.

"Let me help you with that." Cole took a blan-ket, his large hands deftly folding the delicate crochet of blue and white wool before setting it on the bed. He ran a long stroke across the fabric.

"Was that your blanket?" Angela was surprised at the way her heart tugged.

"It must have been mine." He pulled his fin-gers away. "There were no other babies, just me, the only child in a loveless marriage." He pushed away from the bed. "It's getting late. How much more is there to go through?"

"I think this is okay for now." She closed the box, ignoring the vibrations that fizzed through her from the lid. She'd hoped she would have connected with the ghosts again by going through the stuff in the chest. But she'd felt nothing more than the energy coming from the brush and the tension crackling between her and Cole. "I can finish tomorrow."

"Do you really need me to be here?"

"I can work with my assistant." She smiled at him. "Okay, she's my sister. The best assistant anyone could ever have." She might be able to help him if he was around, but he was far too distracting. And did this mean he trusted her enough to leave her here alone?

"I think I'm too busy to be around tomorrow, anyway."

"I'll manage without you." She'd have to convince Emma to take the job. She loved working with her sister, but Emma was averse to anything that creeped her out.

She knew Cole was running away from his past, just like he ran away all those years ago at sixteen.

"Okay, that'll be goo..." The bang of the door broke off the rest of his sentence.

Cole stood, frozen in place.

Angela laughed at his bewildered look. "Ghostly things." She shrugged. "Happens all the time. Occupational hazard." It was about time. She'd been waiting for a ghostly connection since she started today.

"Who is here with us?" Angela asked into the

air.

"Just stop, Angela." Cole scanned the room. "I've had enough fun for one day." His face lost all its relaxed calmness, replaced with disapproval. He reached for the doorknob. "It's stuck." He jiggled the handle. Still nothing. "What the hell?"

"Is it locked? It can't be locked." A sliver of uncertainty slipped under her skin. "Who is here with us?" She asked again. Where was her recorder? Maybe she would catch a disembodied voice. She reached into her pocket. Empty. She'd left the recorder in the drawing room.

"It's jammed." Cole yanked again, but it held tight. He used muscle and leverage, but the door wouldn't budge.

"Are we trapped?" she asked Cole. "We can't be trapped. We need to get out. Whoever is here with us, why are you locking us in this room together?" Interesting that the ghost did that when she was already feeling uncomfortable with the bed and Cole in proximity. "Please, unlock this door." Angela called out into the air again.

"I'm trying. Let me figure this out."

"We're locked in this bedroom?" Alone, together? Angela sat on the edge of the bed and tapped her foot. She knew she was stating the obvious, but she couldn't stop herself. She hated being out of control, and being locked in a room with Cole was definitely not something in her control.

"Yes, Angela, we're stuck in this room." Cole glanced over his shoulder. She looked small, perched on the edge of the king-sized bed. She looked like she belonged there. All day he'd watched her, looking for something negative, but the longer he was around her, the harder it was to find things to dislike.

The sun poured stray rays through the window, creating a halo in her golden hair. Her creamy skin was very touchable and very pale. His fingers had a will of their own and itched to skim along the soft skin of her hand again. He turned back to the door and yanked harder.

"You've got to get us out of here." The pitch of her voice rose.

"Aren't you used to things like this happening?" He was surprised that she seemed nervous. Maybe she was scared to be trapped in the room with him? Cole used his strength on the handle. The knob shifted and bent slightly in his fist. If he tried that again he'd pull the brass knob right off the door. Shit. He needed to get away from her. "We won't be able to get out that way. It's jammed tight." He moved toward Angela. "I have another idea." His knee brushed hers as he leaned across the bed, getting into her space. He was purposely trying to make her uncomfortable but he couldn't stop himself.

She gasped and leaned away from him.

"I'm not that much of a beast," he said in her ear. Her closeness messed with his head. Ordinary Angela wasn't as plain as he'd first thought. "Don't worry. I'll get us out of here, even though I haven't thought about this in years." He opened the nightstand drawer. "They're still here, wow."

"What did you find? What is it?"

He leaned in a little closer to Angela than he needed to, reaching deeper into the drawer. A slight shift of his head would bring his lips just inches closer to hers. He could feel the heat of her body and smell her cinnamon sweetness. Maybe she should be damned scared of him. Hell, he was a little afraid of himself right now. He slammed the drawer and straightened. She seemed even more pale than a minute ago as she stiffened and sat up straighter on his bed.

"Were you fixing the doors so we could be trapped alone together?" He was baiting her.

"Why would I do that?" Her cheeks flared. Pink was better than a frightened gray hue. He must have hit a nerve. Maybe he did affect her like she was affecting him?

"These will do the trick."

"Why do you have a deck of cards?" She glared. "You want to play card games?"

"We are stuck in here." He gave her a mischievous smile that he knew the ladies loved. He'd rather have her annoyed so she wouldn't slip into a panic. "Are you scared to be caught in this room with me?"

"No. I just don't like to be trapped. Period."

"We won't be stuck for long."

"We're not going to get out of here by playing a game of gin rummy."

"Do you have something better in mind?"

"No. I can't believe you want to play games."

He flashed her a smile. "There was a special way to get this to work. I have to think about it for a minute." He climbed onto the bed and stretched out, arms bent under his head. "Let me concentrate." He liked these little games he'd started playing with her. Definitely hard to keep disliking her.

Angela stood at the foot of the bed, glaring down at him. "If I didn't know better, I'd think you were the one who planned all of this. Did you? You're always blaming this kind of stuff on me, but I wonder..." She tapped a finger against her pink bottom lip.

"And why would I do that?" Pure pleasure simmered low in his belly and tugged at the corner of his lips. Even she couldn't be immune to his charm, what he had left of it anyway. "You've been the trickster around here. Not me."

She huffed from the end of the bed. "You did this. Is this some kind of joke? A way to punish me for something you think I may have done? Which I didn't." She said the last part under her breath. She thrust her hands on her hips.

Cole stared up from his relaxed pose and enjoyed her tirade as she strode away. She moved to the door and jiggled the knob herself. It still wouldn't turn.

"You're trying to play some type of reverse psychology. I never caused all that mysterious stuff to happen. Believe what you want." She bent over and peeked through the keyhole. He admired the curve of her butt as he tried to remember the way to escape. He used it many times as a kid. They'd spent enough time in here together and he had tortured himself enough with her presence.

"Quit it over there." Angela called. Cole barely

heard her over the creaking floorboards as he moved toward the opposite side of the room. Exactly where was it?

"I'm trying to figure out this lock, Cole. And you're no help since you want to play games."

He glanced over his shoulder to see her peering through the keyhole. He knew she couldn't see much, only the white wall across the hall. How many times had he been locked in here trying to figure ways out? More times than he could count on his fingers.

"Where's the key? How is this door locked? What is that? What are you doing?"

Cole stood next to the armoire along the wall opposite the bed. "Remember, this was my room as a kid. Some things you don't forget." He flicked the king of spades from the deck. Hunching, he purposely blocked her view. "I had to use this old trick each time my dad locked me in here."

"He locked you in your room?"

He heard sympathy in her tone and it ruffled his hackles. He'd just said it out of nowhere, not thinking. Why had he revealed that? He'd gone that far and he couldn't stop as his tongue kept wagging. "It was one of the better punishments, but sometimes he'd forget I was locked in here if he passed out cold drunk."

Silence. Clearly, she had no response. That shut her up, got rid of her sympathy. It was true and what had made him who he was now.

With a twist of his wrist, the card wedged into the thin space in the paneling. With a distinct click, the wall slid open to reveal a secret passage.

Musty, dust encroached air seeped out, burning at the back of his throat. "How did we get locked in here in the first place when the lock is on the outside of the door?"

"We're trapped in here because a ghost wants us to be stuck together in this room for some reason."

"You're never trapped when you have a secret passageway that leads to the kitchens." He turned, catching her confused, amazement-filled look. A smile tugged at the corner of his mouth. She flashed him a silly little grin that pulled at his belly. How could she get past his defenses so easily? "Let's get out of here." He bowed and swept his arm, urging her toward the opening. "After you."

"You knew this passage was here the entire time?" Her tone was that of a scolding school teacher."

"I found it when I was a kid." He straightened, pausing for a few beats, then he turned and pushed into the darkness of the passage, not waiting for her, but knowing she'd follow. "This hall brings back bad memories. Grab that candle off the nightstand, will you?" he called over his shoulder.

"Secret passages are pretty exciting."

"Especially when you're trying to find a way out of your dad's punishment. Yeah, thrilling."

"Are there more passageways like this in the house?" He could swear he heard a slight tremor in her voice, as she stepped into the darkness.

"I know of two others." The passage was much

more narrow than he remembered, only slightly wider than his shoulders, now. He bumped his shoulder against the wall. "I'm a lot bigger now. As a boy, I could slip right through the passage without a backward glance." Gray shapes formed as Cole's eyes adjusted to the dim light. He traveled down the corridor and Angela followed behind.

"There's a lever somewhere over here that opens the door." He rummaged along the corner.

"What does the lever feel like?"

"It feels like a metal light switch. It's here somewhere."

"Let me try to find it." Angela slipped under his arm. "Take this candle." She darted her other hand forward and skimmed the wall.

He delighted in the cloud of her essence, her scent surrounding him again. Was it her closeness or the darkness that made him more aware of her? He could hear her breath and feel her body without even touching her.

Caught up in his reactions to her, he forgot to take care of the door behind them. It creaked then clicked closed, enveloping them into pitch-blackness.

"Not again." Fear laced her words. She grabbed onto his arm.

"Do you have that candle?"

"Right here. I've gotten caught in small places a few times before, so the candle is a great idea." She laughed but it didn't contain much humor. "It never gets easier."

Angela found his hand in the dark and passed

him the candle. Her hand rested on his forearm and stayed there. He liked that she found comfort in him. She'd never been scared of him even when he'd tried to intimidate her.

Cole lit a match and the candle flared to life. The tiny light battled against the darkness. It flickered orange and showed brief bits of shadows, then little flashes of light created more shadows than illumination. "We need to find that switch." Cole gripped the hand that covered his arm. He didn't dare rub his thumb over her soft skin, though her pulse fluttered as he lifted it and placed it down by her side. "I haven't needed to escape from that room for a long time. I guess I'm as rusty as the old door hinges."

He searched along the wall for the latch. He swore it had been in the corner. He tried the same spot again. The latch was not where he remembered it. "Damn."

"What does that mean?" Her voice filled with fear.

"It means we are really trapped."

"We have to get out of here." Her voice rose with a slight shrill.

"I'm doing my best. Just stay calm." The calmer he sounded the calmer she would be.

"How can you tell me to be calm?"

"Let me figure this out"

"Stay calm, he says."

"And stop talking."

"This is a small room with no way out."

"I'm going to find the way out." Where that latch? He'd used a hundred times as a kid.

"I thought you said it was a passage to the kitchen."

"It is. I can't find the latch that opens the passage." He ran another hand along the wall. Where was that switch? "I don't want to be stuck in here anymore than you do."

"Why are they doing this?" Her words came fast without any pause.

"Who's doing what?"

"The ghosts are playing tricks on us. I have to get out of here."

"Stop panicking."

"Get us out," Angela shouted. "Please let us out." Her voice lowered to a watery whisper. "Please." She sagged against him, hitting his arm.

Hot wax from the candle splashed, stinging his wrist.

"Careful. You'll set this place on fire, then we'll be in a bigger mess." He set the candle on the floor. "What happened to all your bravado?"

"I'm…sorry…" She sniffled. "You have your bad memories and I have mine too."

"I thought you were used to this kind of stuff. Occupational hazards and all."

"It's just that the space is small and it's getting…so… hot in here." Her voice hitched on the words.

"Don't like small spaces?"

"No, I don't." Her words hitched in a hysterical way that he didn't like and neither of them needed.

He pulled her toward him. "Look at me." When she kept her gaze low, he shook her gently to get her attention. He couldn't let her lose it now. "I said, look at me." She raised her golden eyes to him. They shimmered with unshed tears. "We can't panic. Do you hear me? The bad times are in the past."

A stray tear escaped. Shit, he didn't want her to cry. "I'm going to get us out of here. Hold it together. You are tough. You stand up to me like no one else."

She shifted her head and this time he saw resolve in her eyes as she blinked away the last of the moisture.

"Good. Wrap your arms around my waist and hold tight like you're riding on a motorcycle."

"Okay, but I've never been on a motorcycle." She slipped behind him and wrapped her arms around his waist, fingers hooking into his belt loops.

"Just hold on tight." His lips curved in the corners, but he wouldn't allow himself the smile. The weight of her head settled in the curve of his back. He liked the way her cheek felt pressed against his back. He liked pretending it wasn't just fear that had her pressing into him. Maybe she was starting to trust him a little. Maybe he was doing a little of the same in return.

Good, now that she was out of the way, he could concentrate on his task. Ha, that was a joke. All he wanted to think about was her tightening grip around his waist and the location of her hands. He tightened at the thought before shoving his thoughts deep.

"Please, get us out of here," her muffled voice

floated from behind him.

He ran another hand along the wall. After a few moments, he touched the clasp.

"Found you." Cole flicked the switch. Angela sighed against him, but she didn't release her grip.

With a groan of long disuse, the wall opened a small crack. "I knew I'd get us out of here."

He placed his hand over hers and pulled her around so she faced him. Candlelight flickered shadow and light off the delicate curves of her face. He slipped her chin between his forefinger and thumb. "Never panic when you're with me."

"But I…"

"I know. You got scared. But you're with me now. I'll never let anything bad happen to you."

"How can you make a statement like that?"

"It's a promise."

"It's a tall one," she added.

"You're questioning my abilities as a man willing to protect a lady, huh?" He raised an eyebrow. "Especially after I rescued you?" He pushed the doorway open further, rusty hinges groaning. He rubbed at the sweat that beaded the back of his neck. Boy, it had been getting hot in there. He hadn't even noticed the temperature until now. Bending down, he took the candle from the floor.

"I'm sorry I started to panic in there."

"Totally understandable. That was tight."

"I know, but I shouldn't have freaked out."

"It's okay. I remember it being a lot bigger, but I was a kid." He squeezed her hand. "Let's get you out of this tunnel." He guided her through the opening.

Relief washed over him as they entered the kitchen. He didn't want her to see him as an unreliable screw-up. "Come on, Angel girl. Let me show you around the kitchen." He shut the passage door behind them. "You hungry?"

"I'm okay."

"Do you want a snack?" He smiled at her, then turned to a cabinet. "I could use a snack."

"No. My heart rate is still banging a hectic beat."

"Have you always had a fear of tight spaces?"

"I got scared really badly once as a kid, but I can control it better now."

"That was controlling it?" He raised an eyebrow.

"The space was very small," she sounded defensive. "It was because of a ghost too. Long before I understood my abilities and how to work with ghosts. Imagine being locked in a closet with half their face bloody and broken." She shivered.

"Here, take one." He tossed a Twinkie through the air and nodded when she caught it. He had no response to what she was saying. It was one thing to think of it as a story, but believing it as reality was too much. "These things last forever. Supposedly even through a fall-out." He tore open the plastic and took a bite of the cream filled cake.

"Gee, thanks." She looked down at the Twinkie as her slender fingers peeled at the wrapper.

Guilt tore at him because he knew he hadn't said what she'd wanted to hear. Maybe he couldn't believe in her story but he could understand her fear. "I don't like being trapped either." He finished the Twinkie.

"You were pretty cool and collected." Her mouth drew his gaze as she took a bite of cake.

"Hey, I've experienced a lot of bad things too. When they happen often enough, you figure out how to ignore your emotions."

Her eyes grazed him while she chewed. A look that hit him in the gut. Did she care or was that pity shadowed behind her eyes? He sure as hell didn't need pity.

"Let's check the bedroom door to find out what caused the problem." He didn't wait to see if she would follow, though he knew she would.

"Okay. But I have a sneaking suspicion about that." Her footsteps rang behind him over the tile floor.

"I'm sure you do." Cole led the way to the bedroom. The hallway was dark since there weren't any windows in this hall. He flicked the wall switch and bathed everything in the iridescent light.

"You've got to be kidding me." He stared, stunned at the open door before him.

"Things like this happen all the time when you're around me."

"Ghosts lock you into small spaces?" He couldn't stop the sarcasm dripping from his tone.

"Only once in a while." Fear etched in the corners of her tightened lips.

"Are you saying that a ghost did this?"

"How else could this have happened?"

"It must have gotten stuck."

"I know you don't believe me, but I can feel the energy from the ghost running through the door."

"Whatever, at least we're safe now."

"Are we?"

"Yeah. We're no longer locked in the passage that scared the hell out of you. Look, the color is finally coming back into your cheeks." He pointed toward the mirror on the bedroom wall.

"Are you still going to question the fact that this place has a ghost that's trying to tell you something?"

"There's nothing I need to know." What could he possibly learn from his father that he didn't already know?

"It has something to say. You can keep kidding yourself or you can start paying attention to the signs." Her lips pursed into a disapproving nurse Ratchet pucker.

"Let's get out of this room. It's late and I'm finished."

"Good. I can get more accomplished tomorrow when you and your disbelief are far, far away."

Cole put his hand to his heart. "Ow, you wound me."

"It's impossible to hurt your cold, stone heart."

"Stone hearted, huh?" She was right. He'd tightened the wall around his heart long ago and wanted it to stay that way. "It's better than being gullible and believing in things that don't exist." He was cold-hearted, so why did her words sting? Hell, if his own father couldn't love him, how could he ever trust anyone else to do so?

No, he'd never allow himself to be vulnerable. No one would ever hurt him again.

CHAPTER 7

WATER FROM THE Steele River rushed past Cole in a blurry haze. He'd come down to the river to clear his mind after Angela left a few hours ago, and he was still mulling over her comment about his stone heart. It was one thing to think of himself in that way, but it stung hearing it come from her. If he had to be honest, he liked her too much and was spending too much time with her.

The cold from the stone bench seeped through him all the way to his already cold heart. That was funny, wasn't it? The stone bench was warmer than he knew how to be. It was probably better that way. Protect himself and protect her from himself. And why he was even thinking of her in that way was ridiculous. He was an asshole, wasn't he? Hell, yeah. He'd honed himself to come off that way to keep everyone out. He'd kept every girlfriend at a distance, kept friends at arm's length. It had worked all these years. Why was he disappointed that it could work on her too? Maybe because he wanted her to get past his defenses? No, that was bullshit. He was good by himself.

He sat just off the river's walkway, far enough from the edge so that he was nowhere near the water and it's claiming depths. The wind blustered, pulling leaves from the trees, dropping them to the river's surface so they floated for a second before churning under the water.

The chilled air wasn't enough to keep away couples as they braved the cold and swung their entwined hands as they strolled the river walk. A twinge of jealousy seethed through him. He'd never wanted that before, why now? Cole turned his gaze away from their laughing faces and tried to clear his thoughts as he watched the frothing water. What a joke.

At first, he'd followed Angela around the mansion because he didn't trust her. He'd wanted to catch her in the act of deceiving him. As he spent more time with her, he'd actually enjoyed some of her quips and smart remarks. She wasn't scared of him. The thought pulled a smile from him. Then he remembered how they'd gotten caught in his room.

Angela had been too scared in the secret passage to be faking. She'd had real tears in her eyes and the sweat that beaded on her forehead wasn't staged. He was shaken by his need to comfort and calm her. He'd wanted to wrap his arms around her and kiss the fear from her brow. Kiss the wrinkles from her nose and the tension from her lips. The feeling had been raw and intense and now, he couldn't get her stricken look out of his mind.

Damn.

He was a fool and a screw-up. Just like his father had always said. His stupid reactions proved it. He couldn't go back tomorrow. Not while she was in the house. The further he stayed from her, the better. As much as he craved it, he needed to shut her out. It was the best way to protect her and himself.

"Fancy meeting you here, stranger." The cooing female voice pulled Cole from the images swarming his brain. Surprised by the diversion, he swiveled around to see who it came from.

Mrs. Greeley walked down the path, arm in arm with a woman in her mid-twenties. Six-inch razor-sharp stilettos made the younger woman stand almost as tall as Cole. Model thin in her skin-tight jeans, her pink trench-style jacket enhanced the narrowness of her waist. White-blonde hair caught in the wind to brush against her angled cheeks. She was stunning and totally his type, cool, independent and a heart-breaking, love 'em and leave 'em type.

"You remember my daughter, Liza?" Fran pulled the other woman forward and smiled expectantly at Cole.

"You were a baby back then," Cole said, blinking a couple times, recalling the young girl he once knew. She wasn't a baby anymore. Crystal blue eyes licked over his body. She was everything Cole found irresistible in a woman. He could appreciate her beauty, but the spark wasn't there. Nothing, nada.

Maybe it was because he'd known her as a child and his instincts thought of her like a sister.

He pushed the image of Angela out of his mind before it even solidified.

"I'm glad we ran into you like this. It's Kismet." Mrs. Greeley's tone was syrup sweet. "The two of you should spend a few moments together. Reconnect." Fran pressed her hand into the small of Liza's back and hooked an arm around Cole. "Come along, children. Sit. Chat about old times. It's been way too long."

Fran looked up at Cole through her lashes, coquettishly. The old lady was trying to manipulate him into flirting with her daughter. He would do anything for Fran, but he wasn't into the idea. So much for a little peace and quiet, but he bit his tongue and decided to be polite. It was the least he could do.

"My husband would be pleased. You two talk. I have an errand to run. Liza needs to rest those feet of hers, heels and all." Fran backed away and disappeared down the river walk toward a set of shops. Not giving Cole or Liza the time to protest.

"My mother is anything but subtle." Liza's laugh was light and relaxed, as airy as the cool breeze.

"She's been nothing but wonderful to me."

"And my father too. Why couldn't you come to the wake?" The cool air turned into a frosty chill at her words. He was an absolute ass and deserved this.

Cole turned away and scanned the water. "I'm sorry for your loss. I didn't know." The words felt lame. He should have known. Over the years, he'd done everything he could monetarily to keep Max's businesses afloat, to protect him from Hank's destruction. But he should have done more. He should have... What? Called, emailed, sent private messages. Yeah. But he didn't. And now it was too late.

"You were like a son to him." Liza squeezed his arm. "It was difficult for all of us. My father would have understood why you weren't there, though."

Even though he hadn't known, his throat still burned from his guilt of not being here.

"But you're here now. That makes Mom very happy." She settled her hand on his forearm, gentle and comforting. He didn't deserve this kind treatment. He was his father's son after all. As much as he had wished it as a child, Max was not his blood.

Silence fell upon them. Neither broke it.

The river flowed over rocks and lapped against the banks. Cole had always loved the river even though it scared him to death. It had been his solace as a boy, a place to hide when everything was violent and painful. The river had always calmed him until Hank had ruined that too. Now, its angry rushing waves mocked him.

"What brings you back to Dalewood? Must be something very important." Liza's tone was light and he knew she wanted to break the tension between them.

"Yeah. I have some things to deal with now that my father is dead."

"Death seems final, doesn't it?"

When he didn't respond, she continued. "Like

the end of a story. One you never wanted to start and one you can't believe is over."

"If it was only that easy. My father is dead, but his memory is strong."

"My mother believes in ghosts. She believes she connects with my father's spirit."

"I ran into her the other day at Follow Your Path Paranormal Investigations with Angela Haven."

"You know the woman? She has my mother believing she can talk to my father's spirit. I guess I understand my mother's need to hold onto my father, but to deal with that woman."

"That woman?"

"Yes. She's strange. I don't know why my mother would want to deal with a weird girl like her. She pretends to be normal. Probably helps to make people believe in her. Claiming to speak with the dead? Please."

Cole's hackles rose. The urge to defend Angela hung on the edge of his tongue. His mind knew that didn't make any sense at all. He'd had the same reactions. But something had changed when they were trapped in that passage. She seemed ordinary on the surface. But so what? She wasn't a social outcast. He'd seen how others respected her and she had a great reputation.

The sound of jangling bracelets drifted through the air like wind chimes. Cole knew Fran was on her way back before he even saw her. Was that what Angela did? What was it like to know something before you saw it?

"I'm glad to see the two of you getting along so

famously." Fran practically vibrated with excitement. How was he going to break it to the older woman? He would never marry Liza. He was too damaged to marry anyone. He would figure out a way to make it up to her, to make it up to Max, too. He felt a renewed surge to destroy the mansion. Get rid of everything that Hank had touched.

"It is nice to get to know Cole again." Liza looked through her lashes and actually blinked at him a few times. Like mother, like daughter. Her gaze seemed wistful with longing. He needed to nip this notion right out of their minds. Marrying Liza was not the way to make amends.

"Don't get too attached. Things weren't great when I left all those years ago. I have a few things to complete and I'll be leaving immediately after everything is final."

"Leaving already?" Liza sounded stricken.

"Dear, you've barely come home. We must celebrate your return. I want to throw you a party." Fran clapped her hands once enthusiastically over her decision, her large diamond winking in the sun.

"That won't be necessary. I'm only here for a little while." This wasn't home. But if he was being honest, he didn't have a place he called home.

"You were like our son. Max would have wanted it too." She gripped Cole's hand, then reached for Liza's. She moved his fingers so they covered Liza's. "The two of you have many things to catch up on. A dinner party will be the perfect opportunity."

"The prodigal son has returned." Liza laughed. "It is the perfect excuse to throw a party."

"I do love a good party. For both of you. It will give you more time to spend together. You're practically part of the family, Cole. Hopefully it will be official soon."

He'd planned to end all this, but now it was spiraling out of his control. Cole's face must have darkened with his irritation, because when Fran finally looked at him her face froze with a blanched expression. "Oh dear. Don't worry, we'll keep it small and simple. Only the most important people of Dalewood. No more than fifteen or twenty. A nice little dinner party."

"That sounds like a big party. Don't go to all that trouble. I really don't deserve it." Hell, that was the last thing he wanted. A welcome home party. Welcome home to a place he hated. Each time he felt he could get away from this place, he was dragged even tighter into the fabric of Dalewood.

"Nonsense. Max would have had it no other way. He loved you. You loved him. We love you. You deserve it." Was that sympathy he saw in Fran's gaze? Shit. "It's no trouble at all. It will be great fun." Fran scooped an arm around Liza.

"I can't wait to plan this party for you." Liza fanned her eyelashes at Cole. They were too perfect, too long. She was beautiful by anyone's standards. Angela's eyes, her soft skin haunted him even though it would be impossible and he didn't deserve her.

"It will be lovely. Liza is a fabulous little party planner." With a flourish, Fran twisted Liza away. "We must be going now."

He would bet a boatload of bananas that Mrs. Greeley was getting out of there before he had a chance to argue and change her mind. He didn't want a party.

The women headed down the path through the archway of trees.

The only party he'd endure would be one for that little old lady. What choice did he have? He'd do anything to please her. He wanted to eliminate his guilt and make her happy. He wished Max would be there.

No one had ever thrown him a party before. The realization hit him like a ton of bricks.

He was the weird outcast, not Angela. He was the unlovable one. Hadn't his father proven that to him over and over again? He hadn't liked what Liza said about Angela and maybe it was because the comments hit too close to home.

Yes. He'd go to the party that Fran was planning. It made him feel, oh hell, he didn't know how it made him feel. Warmer, softer somehow, like butter left in the sun. The feeling was foreign to him.

It was just a welcome home, not an engagement party. The thought of being trapped in a relationship solely to appease Max made him want to lose his stomach. That had been the implication Fran was trying to make. It would please Max if they got to know each other again, get closer.

Liza would make a beautiful wife for some

man. But not him. He was no good to anybody. He was ruined, damaged. How could he pretend to be something he wasn't? He would have done anything for Max, but not this. He wasn't the man they believed him to be. He'd focused all his strength and energy on destroying his father. He didn't have anything left to give a woman. Nothing left for Liza. And he especially had nothing left for a sneaky ghost hunter with twenty-four carat eyes.

CHAPTER 8

———— ✦ ————

ANGELA FELT LIKE a wimp. She glanced at her baby sister out of the corner of her eye. Emma sat in the passenger seat of the SUV, humming with the music floating from the radio.

When had Angela become such a big baby who couldn't handle her own problems? She'd finally gotten to a place where she was confident in her abilities and accepted the fact that she was and would always be different. But where was that confident girl she pretended to be?

She could see ghosts. That would terrify most anyone. In fact, in the last few years, she'd followed her calling to help the dearly departed move to the other side. Now it was almost an obsession.

But here she was, in her SUV with her sister because she was scared. Not of the ghosts she would face, but because of one guy. She wasn't scared of him. She was afraid of how he made her feel.

"Thanks for coming with me." They drove along the narrow road that led to Penniberg.

"Oh, you owe me."

"Don't be scared. It will be so much fun. I'll protect you from anything."

"You've never needed anyone. You protect yourself. You're the tough one."

Angela flipped her sister a scowl. "Is that what you think? I'm strong and I don't need anyone?"

"You were always the strong one. You had to be."

"As a kid, I was always trying to avoid a confrontation. Now I can hold my own against any snide comments and arrogance. I'm glad we'll be on our own when we investigate."

"The lady protests too much."

"Stop doing that." Angela flushed at Emma's half smile.

"What?" Emma's bright gaze filled with feigned innocence.

"Stop mocking me with your mind-reading stares."

"I can't read minds. You're the one with the special gifts."

"Sometimes I wonder. You have an uncanny way of figuring out my thoughts and feelings."

"You're easy to read." Emma laughed. "I don't have any special talents."

"Now who protests too much?"

"Okay. Let's talk about something else. How about boys?" Emma twisted in her seat, the seat belt pulling at her neck.

Nervousness skittered through Angela. She hoped Emma wouldn't continue the third degree throughout the investigation.

"I don't want to talk about Cole." She took the

tight turn a little faster than she'd planned.

"That's great since I wanted to talk about Matt."

"Oh." Angela felt her cheeks fire.

"But since you brought him up, my spidey sense tells me you like him. I'm curious about what went on in that corridor with Mr. Hunky that's causing your brooding angst."

"Whoever said he was hunky?"

"Who are you kidding? It's obvious that you think he's hot. Plus, you've been awfully quiet on this ride."

"Mind reader," she grumbled under her breath and planted her gaze on the road.

"Stop trying to butter me up with compliments and spill."

"Fine. It was miserable. I couldn't concentrate on the walk-through in the house yesterday. He was always a few steps behind me. Everywhere I went, he was there." She snorted her disgust. "I barely felt much of anything. A few tingles here, a chill there." She recalled the sensations. "Until I touched the chest."

"Wait, you touched his chest?"

"No. It was a chest filled with things. There were many old items in it. Things much older than his father. There was something important in that box that Cole needs to know about. But I can't figure out how it can be related to his father. His dad has only been gone for less than a year. These items were old. Art deco, nineteen twenties old."

"You'll put all the pieces together."

"These are messages to Cole. I know they are."

"And then you were trapped in the room together?"

"Yes."

"Why would a ghost want to lock the two of you together like that?"

"To scare us. To get me to stop."

"I'm not sure about that. You think Cole is cute," she sing-songed.

Angela glanced over to see an enigmatic Mona Lisa smile curving over Emma's lips.

"You can't deny it," Emma continued. "Maybe this ghost sees how much you like him."

"That's ridiculous. I don't like guys who are arrogant and think only of themselves." But, he'd ignored his anger to check her cut finger. He hadn't acted selfish in the passageway. He'd calmed her first and guided her out before panic could fully take hold. He'd done that for her.

"Did you walk around the gardens?"

"No. Maybe we should come back another time to check out the grounds if Mr. *I don't believe in ghosts* allows that." Angela focused on the road as the scenery flashed by.

"We'll have the entire place to ourselves? Barlow isn't meeting us there?" Emma asked.

"No."

"Oh, he wants you too, all right."

"What could possibly make you think that?"

"I don't know. You have your gifts and I guess I have mine. But if he hurts you, he'll have to deal with me. He won't like me when I'm angry." She growled in her Bruce Banner imitation. They giggled and the mood lightened.

Angela drove, letting her thoughts drift. He couldn't possibly be interested in her. But the look he'd given her in the kitchens, while they snacked on Twinkies, was burned into her brain. It haunted her more than any ghost.

"Describe the mansion to me. I have driven this way before, but you can't see the house unless you follow the private drive. The hill and trees block everything."

"The mansion is big and beautiful. It has a drawing room, library, study, kitchen and full dining room on the main floor. The second level has six bedrooms. It's magnificent."

"Do you think I'll see a ghost?" Emma broke into Angela's revelry.

"It's always a possibility. Are you worried that something will happen while you're there?"

"I don't think so. Should I be?"

Angela almost laughed. "This place has had a lot of action. Even if Cole didn't believe. He had no explanation how the door locked with us inside. Then he blamed me for tricking him."

"He wasn't angry like Paul used to get, was he?"

"He was pretty upset that day when the glass and books flew, but he never acted like he would hurt me. He was pretty upset though."

"Paul always made you cry."

"He couldn't handle my ability to see the dead. He wanted to prove it was something else."

"And he wanted you to become something you weren't. You are special. I love you just the way you are."

"You're my sister, but thanks."

"You're not all that different. Though it is a little weird to think you can see and hear things that others can't."

"Yeah well, Paul thought I was a bit delusional." She didn't want to think about him. He was long gone and a part of the past that she'd like to keep there. She'd become his little research project. That was when she'd learned it was easier to face ghosts instead of the living.

Some people were willing to suspend a little bit of their disbeliefs. They wanted to feel connected with their deceased loved ones. She could give the suffering a little piece of the person they'd lost. There were some people, most people actually, like Paul who thought she was crazy. Others just thought she was a fake. That was Cole. She'd rather be considered a fake than treated like she was a lunatic.

Oh well. She couldn't let Cole get to her. She'd been treated a lot worse. She could handle almost anything.

She slid the car through the driveway and parked near the portico. Cole's car was gone. It seemed desolate. He'd clearly meant what he'd said yesterday. He'd leave her alone to finish her work.

Angela reached for the car door handle, but stopped when Emma placed a hand over her forearm. "I have something for you." Emma rustled in the pocket of her purse.

"A gift?"

"Before we go into the mansion, I wanted to give you this." Emma held out a bracelet. The blue beads glistened in the stray rays of sun.

"They're beautiful." Angela slid the silky cool strand through her fingers before fastening it around her wrist. "Are these made of quartz?"

"Blue quartz. They're supposed to bring protection and peace. I think you could use a little protection and peace while dealing with this mansion and its owner. He seems like he can be a toughie."

"I'm pretty tough myself. He doesn't know who he's about to deal with."

Angela parked the car under the portico. Emma strode beside her as they headed to the front door.

"What's that?" Emma asked.

Angela pulled the scrap of taped paper from the door. The note was scratched in a very manly scrawl.

"He's making up an excuse. He has business to handle in town."

Angela crumbled the note in her fist. "We already knew he wasn't going to be here."

"Maybe he's avoiding you?"

Angela was irritated by the possibility that he could be avoiding her. "We have the entire place all to ourselves."

"Except for the ghosts. I heard one of the ghosts tried to push Ted down the stairs. I've never known him to turn down a job before. Never." Emma's eyes tightened in the corners and her lips pinched.

"Don't be scared. I'm here, nothing will hurt you."

"I'm not." But Emma's face belied her words. "I

just don't know how you do this."

"Do what?" Angela asked distracted. Stepping out from the shadows of the porch, she scanned the windows. Her gaze stopped at one of the windows in the middle of the second floor. She didn't see anything out of place. It was a feeling. She made a mental note to check out that room.

"Step into a haunted, creepy house."

She glanced at her sister. "Creepy? I don't think it's creepy at all. This house is beautiful."

"I guess it's the ghosts that are creepy."

"Ghosts were once people. I can help them. You wouldn't let a person stay trapped in a burning building, would you?"

"No, but that is a little different."

"Not much."

"Why do they choose to stay trapped here?"

"It's not always that easy. Some things force them to stay. Unfinished business. Traumatic accidents. That type of thing." Angela almost laughed when Emma gave a sidelong look up at the hulking mansion. She seemed to be pretty scared. "There is nothing to be afraid of, Emma."

"Tell that to Ted."

"That's why I'm here, isn't it? I need to help these ghosts before I can help Ted."

"Do you think the ghost will try to attack us like it did Ted?"

"I've never had a ghost try to harm me. They know I can help them. There's nothing to be afraid of." She gave Emma a reassuring smile.

"I said I'd do anything for you. Let's get this over with."

Angela twisted the beads on her wrist. It was comforting to know that her sister would investigate with her.

CHAPTER 9

"LET'S MAKE A sweep of the house." Angela held the EMF detector in one hand. The lights on the end flashed as it detected strong electromagnetic fields. They moved down the hall and the needle settled back to zero until she pointed it toward the door to the drawing room and it spiked to six.

"There are a lot of rooms here." Emma sounded awestruck.

"It's a lot bigger than our tiny apartment." Angela could appreciate the feeling. "What a place." She pushed open the door, half-expecting to see an entity looming in the middle of the room. "It's less ominous on the inside." Angela moved into the room and the EMF rose to ten. "We should get started."

"Okay." Emma shivered as she entered the room too. "Is it cold in here?"

"What is the temperature reading on the EMF detector?" Angela took slow steps around the room. The activity was concentrated in here. She was picking up magnetic energy now. She felt it tickling her skin. The glass had also flown from the table in this room that day when Cole got angry.

"The investigation could take longer than I thought. It's big. Don't forget, I have plans later," Emma said. "How do you work this thing? Oh, here's the button. Sixty-two degrees. That's cold, but not too weird."

Her sister was rambling. It was one of her nervous habits. She'd only helped her investigate a couple of times before. And this place had a lot of energy. "I'm going to try to catch an EVP."

"Okay. I'll be quiet," Emma placed one finger over her lips. "I don't want to accidently step on any ghost responses."

Angela pulled the handheld recorder from her pocket and began recording. "Penniberg mansion. Investigators Angela Haven, Emma Haven. The drawing room," she spoke into the microphone. "Is there anyone here who would like to speak to us?" She paused a few beats to give a spirit the chance to leave a response on the tape. "I'm here to help you. What's your name?" She paused again.

Emma sat in one of the wingback chairs as Angela continued her questions. "Why do you haunt this place?" The EMF detector fell to zero and stayed there, unmoving.

They waited in silence. There weren't any auditory responses, though she hadn't expected any. They would review the recordings later tonight to see if they'd caught any voices.

"Maybe I should try to provoke the spirits."

"I don't know about that." Emma's hands folded

tightly in her lap.

"I hate doing it." Angela sighed. "But sometimes it's the fastest way to get a ghost to respond."

"What if you irritate them? I don't want to get pushed like Ted."

"That won't happen to you. Ghosts know I want to help, even if they aren't ready for that help. I need to make a connection."

"Fine, but I don't like it."

"Here we go." She held out the recorder and began. "Why are you here?" Angela spoke into the darkness. "Do you like scaring people?" She paused for a moment. "Do you like running the workers out of this house? Why do you want to terrify them?"

Angela walked to the other wingback chair and sat. "It's time for you to leave. Get out." Her stern words hung in the air. She hated doing this, but it might be the only way to help.

She took a deep breath and continued. "This is not your house anymore. You don't belong here."

Both sisters looked at each other through the dimness. Emma shrugged her shoulders and tilted an ear to the silence. "This usually works on TV."

Angela opened her mouth to give it one last try. "Is there anyone here with us?" A thud sounded.

Emma froze, mouth opened. Angela bit the inside of her cheek to stop her smile.

"What was that?" Emma's eyes grew wide enough to show all the white.

"It came from the room directly above us." Angela pushed out of the chair. "Let's check it out."

Emma came out of her chair more slowly. "I mean, do we really need to? It's probably the creaky house."

They inched their way up each step. When they got to the top of the staircase, they stopped and scanned the long hallway. Angela pointed. "The sound came from that room." They tiptoed down the hallway toward the bedroom.

Angela gripped the brass doorknob to the farthest room and twisted it with a flick of her wrist. The door creaked open.

"Is anyone here?" She flipped the light switch to illuminate the room. A tortoise-shelled hairbrush lay on the floor near the white dressing table.

"How did that get on the floor? I thought we left that in the box?" Angela looked back at Emma and paused.

Emma leaned around the edge of the doorjamb peeking into the room, face pale and eyes wide with fear. She'd let her sister stick to the promotions end of the business. This part was too scary for her.

"It must have just fallen off the table." She darted her gaze around, scanning the room. "Is it all clear? Is there anything I should be ready for?" she asked before entering.

Angela grasped the brush. Tingles shimmered through her fingertips up to her elbows. Cole was the last person she'd seen with this brush. His long, heavy hands had stroked the handle. Why was it on the floor up in this room?

"There was something here, but it's gone now."

Something was trying to get her attention. Angela clasped the brush close to her chest. "Who is it?" She turned to look around the room. "What keeps you here? We can work together."

Suddenly, the door slammed. Emma let out a shriek and jumped in her shoes.

"Oh no, not again." Electricity shot through her hand from the contact with the brush handle. Instantly she slipped from the present to the past. She was in the same room, though the furnishings were different, feminine and frilly and full of youth.

Angela watched the scene as a voyeur, eavesdropping through foggy glass.

The large bed, covered in a white lace duvet, dominated the room. A matching canopy hung over the four posts.

Along the far wall, a girl sat before a white dressing table with jars, cream pots and a jeweled atomizer cluttering the dresser. The large mirror reflected the image of the stunning girl looking at her reflection. It was Brooke, the woman in her early vision. She wasn't as young as Angela first thought. She had to be about eighteen.

"Harry Barnes," the silky, sweet voice whispered, low and husky. The sound came from a far distance. As distant as the far-off past Angela had entered. Brooke adjusted her jet-black curls, setting the finger waves. She stood and leaned into the mirror to apply a layer of red lipstick to her heart-shaped lips.

A late twenties-era beauty preparing for a night out. Brooke wore a knee-length, white dress. The low neckline created a V that caressed her small, round breasts with twinkling crystal beads. She was a ghostly beauty of the past. Secrets surrounded her and Angela wanted to figure them out to help this tormented spirit.

"Oh, Harry, when you catch a glimpse of me, old boy, you'll be unable to resist." Brooke smiled into the cheval glass and continued with a one-sided conversation.

"Brooke, don't you look smashing." She responded to her reflection in a low voice imitating a man. Angela was currently an eavesdropper. Not wanting to scare Brooke away, she remained very still. She was so close she would do anything to make the connection. Locking every muscle, she continued to watch.

"Why thank you, Harry, for the wonderful compliment. But I've had this dress for ages." She giggled. "Of course, I'll have this dance. The Lindy Hop is all the rage and you know it's my favorite. But first I have a secret to share, old boy." She pulled in a deep, shaky breath. Her skin paled, making her pink blush seem darker against her cheeks.

"Do you love me, Harry?" she asked with intensity, all fun set aside. Her face held a stoic longing that tore through Angela.

Brooke ran her hands down the length of her dress, then dragged them back up and pressed them against her flat belly. "Because I love you, Harry."

With a shake of her curls, Brooke seemed to push away all her worries. The color returned to her skin. With a few bounces, she kicked her feet in an old-time dance. The pleats of her dress lifted, then fell back into place. She danced a few more steps, swinging the palms of her hands in little half-circles. "No time for fear. All will work out, splendidly," she said to her smiling reflection. She shifted the glittering headband so the diamond brooch rested in the middle of her forehead.

The bold ostrich feather stood like a proud, white guardian ready to protect her from anything the night offered.

Angela admired the girl's verve and beauty, her confidence. In a quick movement, Brooke turned from the mirror and strode straight toward Angela.

Bracing herself against the frigid onslaught of the ghost, Angela clenched her teeth and clamped her eyes shut. Brooke ripped through Angela's body like a cold wind on a wet night. The ghost disappeared through the bedroom door.

Cold shimmering icicles speared her body and tingled through her veins. The room was modern again, no longer the bedroom of a teenage flapper girl. The foggy haze was gone, but the shivers remained.

Angela rushed toward the door and looked into the hallway. Nothing was there except the soft thumps of running footsteps. They sounded delicate, distinctly female and accompanied by another sound. "Emma, listen." She waved her sister to the doorway. "Can you hear that? Soft and low?"

"Is someone crying? It's faint, but I hear it."

"It was definitely Brooke, again." Angela smiled

with excitement.

"I never felt scared, not once," Emma said.

"Oh, right." Angela laughed. "You were shaking in your boots. You used me as a shield to hide behind most of the time."

"I was startled that's all." She pouted. "I never felt terrified or threatened by anything we encountered tonight." She placed her hands on her hips.

Angela couldn't stop the laugh that escaped. "It's okay to be scared. I was startled when she passed through me to rush out the door."

"Why would the ghost scare Ted and the workers when it runs from you?"

"I'm not sure." She gave another scan down the hallway in the direction the ghost had gone. "I didn't fully connect with the ghost. But this was Brooke's ghost. The dark spirit I encountered in the drawing room was different. It was dark and menacing. Brooke wanted me to see her special night, but she wasn't ready to tell me everything."

"She will in time. And on her own terms," Emma said.

"I hope so." She'd have to come back to the mansion again, and the next time she wouldn't hide behind her sister. Whatever was happening in the mansion was important and he needed to be a part of it.

CHAPTER 10

ANGELA AND EMMA loaded the last boxes into the back of the SUV. "I know we caught something." Angela slammed the hatch closing the trunk.

"The crying ghost was pretty freaky, and I can't come up with an explanation." Emma slid into the passenger side of the vehicle.

"Hopefully, there will be more. She might have spoken in the recordings or maybe we caught something in camera footage." Even though they hadn't had any other experiences aside from the running ghost, Angela felt a tiny diamond of hope in the pit of her belly. "Brooke is slowly revealing her secrets, but something was stopping her."

"No one but you will be able to figure it out."

"Let's get back home. I want to go through the tapes right away."

She started the car. The horseshoe drive led past the gardens.

"Tonight? You want to go through hours of audio and video tonight?" Emma didn't sound happy about the idea. "I can work for a little while, but then I'm getting ready for my date."

"Don't worry. I'll prep everything tonight so we can look through it tomorrow." Angela drove down the tree-covered path she was beginning to love, down the narrow road toward the stone bridge. "You've already done me a big favor by investigating tonight."

"Maybe a little rest will boost my energy reserves, so I'm not too tired for later." Emma leaned her head on the headrest and closed her eyes.

The Steele River meandered below the bridge. Flashing lights in the rearview mirror surprised Angela. "This road doesn't lead anywhere else."

With eyes still shut, Emma replied with half interest. "It's a direct road to the mansion. It leads from the mansion to Main Street."

"Anyone on it would be going to or coming from the mansion?" The small specks of light grew brighter as the car gained on them.

"Right. It dead-ends at the house." Emma popped one eye open and glanced dubiously at her sister. "Then where did that car come from?"

"It must be Cole, returning."

"It's behind us. Meaning that it came from the house."

Emma leaned closer toward the side mirror. "There is a car behind us and it's traveling fast."

Looking in the mirror, Angela said, "I thought we were the only people in the house." She gripped the steering wheel more tightly.

"Maybe there was a groundskeeper."

"Cole said the workers wouldn't show up. I assumed that meant all the workers."

"I think he would have told you if someone else was going to be there."

Angela flicked her gaze toward the rearview mirror. The round bright lights of the car behind them moved back and forth across the thin winding road.

The lights grew larger and larger in the mirror. "It's speeding." Angela reached for the rearview mirror and shifted it so she could watch the reflection more easily.

The yellow rounded fender was closer in color to gold. It looked old, vintage, but well taken care of. It was shiny and newly polished, like a remodeled car she'd seen at the auto show in Chicago a few years ago.

Closer, closer.

The car took over the road until it was right behind them. Inching until there were mere feet between them. The mascot of a woman on the hood seemed to fly through the air as the car moved. Arms outstretched behind her, the statue bent with the metallic cloth flowing to look like wings. Angela recognized the Rolls Royce circa 1920.

"It's almost on top of us. Does he want to smash into us?" Emma's voice held a shrill panic. "I can see the outline of the person driving. It looks like a woman."

The road narrowed as the bridge crossed over the river and did not allow for maneuverability.

"If this maniac wants to speed, then I'll let her. But she's not going to run us off the road." Angela gripped the wheel more tightly and shifted the car to the right side of the road. "Better to let her pass before we're stuck on that bridge." She slowed along the gravel shoulder and threw the gear into park. The banks of tall grass rolled toward the river's edge.

The Rolls Royce sped faster and faster, rushing in a blur of gold, coming up just behind them.

"She doesn't look like a groundskeeper." Emma turned in her seat as the car reached the bridge. In a flash, Angela saw the girl's face. It was Brooke.

"She's too young. What is she wearing?" Angela caught a glimpse of the girl's attire. She wore a pink cloche hat pulled low to cover the slashes of her raven eyebrows. Her short black hair peeked just below the edges of the hat. Her hands fisted the steering wheel as she trained her gaze straight ahead, while not seeing anything. The girl kept wiping at her cheeks. "She's crying."

This girl was in some sort of trouble. Angela swallowed at the pain in the back of her throat. She could feel the emotions as if the anger and sadness were her own.

The car swerved again as it passed them, barely missing their front end, and entered the small expanse of the bridge.

"What is your problem, lady?" Emma shouted, waving her arms. "She shouldn't take it out on us just because she's upset."

Angela reached for her sister's waving fist. "She's hurt and needs help."

The car swerved again. Then, with one last jerk, the driver lost control and the car slid in a semi-circle.

"No," Angela screamed. Her throat tightened and sweat broke out on the back of her neck. She threw a hand over her mouth, knowing that this was the girl's end. Shocked, she watched the old car heave into the wooden barrier with the shudder of splintering wood, and the screech of bending metal. The car flew past the rail and disappeared over the edge.

Angela and Emma watched in horror, unable to move or speak. Angela came out of her stupor first.

"We need to help her." She jumped from the car and ran to the edge of the bridge. Her shoes skidded over the gravel. Tears streamed down her own cheeks. How could she have watched an accident like that and been unable to do something, anything?

Sliding a hand into Emma's she held onto her sister. Glad her sister was with her, Angela peered over.

Mangled debris, twisted burning metal in the Steele, an injured body. That's what Angela expected to see.

Below was the beauty of the trickling river, the swaying brush and dying grasses. A lone bullfrog leaped from the bank and plopped into the water.

No smell of burning fuel, no debris, no hot fire, no woman.

"I saw a car go over the edge. Tell me I'm not crazy," Emma whispered, her voice rasped as dry as that frog's croak. She slipped her hand from Angela's as she sank to the ground.

Angela wiped at her face, then sat cross-legged

next to Emma. The gravel pinched her behind, but she ignored it.

"Where's the damned crash?" Emma covered her face with her hands. "My heart is beating two-forty."

"Look at the railing. There's no damage, not even a scratch." Angela jumped to her feet and ran a hand along the unscathed wood. Shivering energy tingled over her fingertips. "You and I both saw that car go through it."

Emma waved a disbelieving hand. "The car almost smashed into us. It almost ran us off the road too."

A sliver a fear ran through her. Was the ghost trying to hurt them? Or was it simply an accident with no real malice?

"What just happened here?" Emma stood in front of Angela, her breath hitching in large gasps.

Angela gripped Emma by her shoulders. "Calm down."

"Calm down? We were almost killed."

"No, we weren't." She looked into Emma's honey colored eyes. She was still holding onto fear, but her face seemed to relax a little. "I pulled to the side and that was the right thing to do. We're okay. But she is dead." Angela scooped at the air behind her.

"But there's nobody there. I'm going crazy. Am I crazy?"

"Nope."

"Then what is going on?"

"I think we just saw someone's death."

"That was a ghost?"

"Not just any ghost. I think we just watched Brooke's death."

"What?"

"I need to do some research on the history of this place, and I want to review those tapes and recordings. I'm sure we caught something."

"I don't think I can handle another unbelievable thing tonight. This is too much for my little heart."

"I wish we had those cameras running a few minutes ago." She rubbed her upper arms to eliminate the chill. "Cole won't believe this." How would Cole believe this if she almost didn't believe it herself?

But Emma had seen the ghost too.

Yep, Brooke wanted to reveal secrets. For some reason she wanted to reveal them like puzzle pieces. Angela would put them all together and soon she would see the entire picture. In her gut, she knew it revolved around Cole. This had all started with his return. She would piece it together and help the lot of them, Cole included.

A new set of headlights flashed through the trees as the car turned the corner, giving a glowing haze to the dusk. Night was starting to fall. Gravel crunched under the moving tires of a familiar silver Camaro.

"It's Cole. Move to the side, so there isn't a real accident." Angela pushed off the bridge toward her waiting SUV. She was curious about what happened to the dead when they moved through the doorway to the other side. But not curious enough that she wanted to get run over, especially by Cole Barlow.

As Cole drove over the bridge, Angela stepped away from the road, closer to the side of her SUV while Emma slid back inside the passenger seat and shut the door. Angela felt foolish standing there, not knowing what to do, she lifted her hand and waved. He pulled the car to a stop, sidling up next to her car and lowered the window. Hard lines shadowed his face. She was getting used to that look.

"What are you doing standing in a dark road like that? Do you want to get killed?" He jumped from the sports car and paced in front of her. A vein pulsed in his neck. "Enough tragedy has happened in this very spot. God, woman. Seriously, what are you doing out here?"

His words hit her like cold ice and she skewered a look at him that she hoped would display her irritation and disbelief. Could Cole know the background of Brooke's death?

Angela remained quiet. What could she say? Hey, we watched a lady ghost go over the edge? He didn't believe in ghosts.

"My mother was killed in a car accident on that very bridge. What were you thinking?" Dark, steely eyes pierced through her in the waning light.

"Your mother died here?" That wiped her face clear of any readable emotions. She was glad she hadn't said something about a lady ghost. That would have been too painful. What else had this guy been through? She felt a pang of sadness for the poor kid whose mother had died in a tragic accident and who got stuck with a brutal father. That ghost girl in the car had seemed from a different era, not from thirty years ago. That ghost was Brooke, not his mother. Why would she be connecting with a much older ghost? It didn't make sense. Research was next on the list. That was for sure.

"Yes. When my mother ran off to her lover, abandoning her newborn son."

"I'm sorry." Angela blinked against this new revelation. It was no wonder he pushed everyone away. The closest people had damaged him the most.

"I don't need your pity," he snapped. "What were you doing in the middle of the road like that? Do you have a death wish?"

"You wouldn't believe me even if I told you." His hot anger only accentuated his lips and the cut of his rugged jaw. She knew his angry response was a cover up for his fear that she could have been hurt. That thought slipped to her belly like warm honey.

"I think you're trying to make me crazy, woman."

"That's not true. You're driving me crazy with your bad attitude." Her words caused the tightness to slide from his features. She needed to focus her attention away from his good looks because she was driving herself crazy. She was vaguely aware that Emma watched them but she ignored that.

"Tell me you're finished with whatever it is you need to do, so I can get the workers back in that house."

"It's getting more complicated," she said. He took a step closer to her. She was instantly and completely aware of him. He was so close she could feel the hear rolling off of his body and smell his smoky scent.

"It was a pretty miserable place to grow up. Trust me. And I'm sick of being here. I thought I had gotten over all the things I'd gone through. But being here has it all rushing back. It's like I'm right back to when I was a kid."

His gaze bore into her more deeply than she would ever admit. She lifted her chin. "I need to learn more about what happened in your home, what's happened in the past."

"It's not my home. It never was a home. It never will be."

"Fine, but I need to know everything about the Penniberg mansion and its history." He was being difficult, but she couldn't expect more. He harbored too much anger for his past and she was the easiest person to take it out on. "There are many strange things going on here and I need to learn how they're connected."

His gaze licked over her, causing frissons of awareness to shoot through her. Instead of facing her reactions to him, she turned toward the car where Emma sat. "It's getting dark. I think we've had enough for one day. We still have work to do tonight and I need to get up early to do research at the library tomorrow."

She didn't need to look back to know that he watched her. She could feel the intensity of it hanging over her. She straightened her back and stepped with purpose. She wouldn't allow him to lower her confidence. And with that, she climbed into the car with her sister and drove off.

CHAPTER II

ANGELA BLEW HER bangs from her eyes. She'd been sneezing every few minutes since she started sifting through the pile of historical journals. The dust from the old books swirled in little clouds, floating up to the fluorescent lights. She'd always loved the sanctuary feel of a library. Each good book lined up for waiting souls to enter through the pearly gates with anticipation and excitement to find out what was inside.

When was the last time she'd sat in a library for this long? In college, when she'd hidden on the third floor all the way in the darkest back corner, when she'd been hiding from Paul, her overzealous boyfriend, now ex-boyfriend, who'd been more concerned about his research project than he'd ever cared about her. That was ancient history nobody was interested in anymore, including herself.

Eyes burning from looking at the computer screen for too long, Angela pulled her yellow notepad close and read over her scribbled notes so she could re-focus on this case and forget about a past she never wanted to relive. She dropped her pen when she realized she'd been scribbling Cole's name over and over.

She scooped the pen up again and scratched through the doodles. He was getting to her. But why was she starting to like him so much? He'd been nothing but ornery and arrogant, a downright asshole, really.

She thought about that look he'd given Mrs. Greeley. His tough veneer had slipped and she saw the love he held for her. He was hiding so much more under his brusque exterior. She had scratched the surface just a little and it only made her want to see more. His reaction on the road made her think she might be getting to him too.

Her research divulged a few interesting tidbits about Cole. He was the powerhouse his actions claimed him to be. His business was top in its league and he was rich, not quite Oprah rich, but he'd never have to worry about money, that was for sure.

His father hadn't done too badly either. He'd owned a successful contracting business that was involved in many of the subdivisions that made Dalewood one of the leading Chicago suburbs. At least until Cole went after his father's company piece by piece. And now Cole wanted to destroy the beautiful mansion that had been an original part of Dalewood's history. Was destroying the mansion the only way he could heal?

Hank Barlow had built additions onto the twenties Spanish-style mansion. Cole's mother had died at a very young age, right after Cole's birth. If anyone should be haunting that mansion, it should be Cole's mother, Malory. Cole hadn't been exaggerating when he'd talked about tragedy at the bridge over the Steele River. Malory had died instantly and never had the chance to know her own child. Angela bit at her lower lip. That alone would have been enough to make any woman haunt her home. And enough to make a little boy feel alone without a mother's love. Angela crushed a scrap sheet of paper and tossed it toward the pile of books. Where was his mother anyway? Why wasn't she the one haunting him?

But the ghost driving the car hadn't been a beautiful blonde. She had been a young girl with black hair framing her face in a roaring twenties style. Angela knew the ghost had been Brooke Dalloway. Young and vibrant, she'd glowed from every picture posted in the Dalewood Daily. The two hours had allowed her to gain some new insight into Brooke's family as well. The information had brought her near tears as the tragic story of the Dalloways unfolded through newspaper articles and reports.

Frank Dalloway began as a middleclass manager for the quarry. After working himself up through the ranks, he met his soon-to-be wife. The relationship with Marjorie had been a whirlwind romance that created quite a stir in the small town. Through hard work and determination, along with marrying the boss's daughter, he eventually became owner of the limestone quarry.

Once World War I broke out, the factory was converted to make supplies for the troops. Those years were prosperous for the family. The Penniberg estates were built at the height of his wealth.

Frank and Marjorie Dalloway had two boys, William and Thomas. They were the heirs to the Dalloway fortune.

Both sons went to war to fight for their country. Frank was proud of his boys who became the heroes of Dalewood. Marjorie was terrified. And rightly so. At the end of the war, both sons were dead.

Frank and Marjorie Dalloway had a fortune with no heir. Brooke was the result of their attempts to renew their family.

Though she was not the son they'd hoped for, Brooke was spoiled in every way during the great age of consumerism.

As a teenage girl in the roaring twenties, she rebelled and broke every social taboo. She was the quintessential flapper girl, so the news reports said.

In a terrible twist of fate, an automobile accident took her life. She was killed at the age of eighteen.

The newspapers also included articles about Brooke's death. A death that took place in the same way and at the same place as Cole's mother, Malory.

Angela felt sick when she'd read the information. She felt sick now as she reread her notes. How right Cole had been. That bridge didn't need another victim.

Angela rubbed at her upper arms to cast away her goose bumps from the chill that fell over her.

All those who'd died on the estate had the potential to haunt the mansion. Taking the time to understand a ghost's sadness was Angela's specialty. Everyone wanted someone to listen to their problems. Ghosts were no different. They still needed to be heard. She'd vowed to help them at all costs. Tomorrow she'd start again. Today, she'd watch the videos and listen to the EVPs.

Before logging off the computer, she couldn't resist another peek at Cole's website. Clicking on the company profile, his handsome face looked at her with his piercing gray eyes and devil-take-all smile. He was far away from the image of the sad boy she'd been thinking about all afternoon. She couldn't picture this grown man as a helpless child who craved strawberry candies and an old lady's lemonade. Good grief, she was acting like a maudlin dope. With gusto, she closed the page and pushed her chair back from the enclosed oak desk. But before she could stand, a conversation from a group of librarian-looking women caught her attention.

"I can't believe Cole Barlow is back after all these years." The first lady, who wore a calf-length beige skirt, chirped.

"Now that his father's dead, what's to keep him from staying?" The second lady, in her button-down cardigan, agreed. Her mousy brown bob brushed just below her chin with each nod, accentuating her words.

"He didn't go to his own father's funeral. Can you believe that?"

Angela's teeth clenched to hold back the retort

that sat on her tongue, ready to burst out. Why would he come back when his father had been horrible?

The third lady in heavy, black-rimmed glasses leaned in toward the others to whisper her secret, but her words were just as loud as the others. "I heard that his father beat him. The last time was the worst. He's become so arrogant that maybe his father knew what he was doing. Maybe he believed in spare the rod."

"Even arrogant, a child doesn't deserve that. Plus, he's drop dead gorgeous and he's made a success of himself. It wasn't his father's abuse that made him into what he is now. We all know it was the kindhearted ways of the Greeleys."

Angela relaxed her fisted hands. How dare that woman think a little boy ever deserved a beating. At least the woman with the glasses had some sense.

Cardigan shivered. "I wish he would just leave."

Beige skirt tilted her nose in the air. "You have nothing to worry about, Greta."

"How can you say that? Now that Cole's back, he's going to ruin everything," Greta said.

"You're worried about nothing. They love each other," The one wearing glasses chimed in. "I know everything has been moving along perfectly, but Cole's return could send them right back to the beginning." Tears filled Greta's eyes. "My son has his political career to think of and the Greeleys are very influential."

"They love each other too much." Cardigan placed a hand on Greta's shoulder.

"I hope their feelings are strong enough to endure his return. And if not, I'll think of a way to get him out of Dalewood."

"I've heard he wants to leave here as quickly as you want him gone."

"I don't believe it. Why else would he return after all these years if he doesn't want to reconnect with Liza?" Greta swiped away the tears before they fell. "I know he wants Liza and it's going to break my son's heart. I'll never let that happen to Erik."

"Cole can't be that hardhearted, could he?"

"And why not? His father was an evil man and Cole is bound to follow in those footsteps. He is the product of one rotten apple."

That was it. Angela jumped up from her seat ready to defend Cole. He may be hardened and a little arrogant, but he wasn't his father. He'd been caring and protective. That didn't match anything she'd ever heard about the hated Hank Barlow. She moved around the desk, ready to speak her mind to the insensitive women.

The group had vanished. Angela looked down the aisle of desks, but they were gone. As quickly as they had appeared to start their conversation, they had dispersed.

No one deserved a punishment because of the father. Even more convinced to help Cole after what she'd heard, she shuffled her papers and stacked the books so she could leave the library. She'd help Cole get rid of the ghosts that haunted him and his home. He seemed alone and only she could help him.

Maybe he really did want Liza? The voice of doubt had her second-guessing how well she actually knew Cole. Once he got rid of the ghosts, he'd want to start a new life. It made sense that he'd want to start it with his child-hood sweetheart, the daughter of the man he'd loved above anyone. How was she going to slog through hours and hours of video and audio now? Deflated, Angela flopped back in the chair.

CHAPTER 12

HEADPHONES ON, ANGELA sat next to Emma at a long faux wooden table in the conference room of Follow Your Path Paranormal Investigations early the next day. Laptops glowed in front of them as they silently listened to their headsets and carefully watched the computer screens. Every so often, they would laugh at their silly conversations caught on tape, breaking the monotony. EVP took a long time to analyze. Laughter wound down the time.

They had caught the slamming bedroom door, but the recorders didn't catch any footsteps or the sounds of crying. Still they trudged on.

Two hours of listening to audio and watching the same room, scene after scene was boring work. Angela was getting tired and she knew Emma had to be ready to quit too. She reached for her headphones then froze as a voice, low and grumbling, rumbled through her ears.

"I got a hit." Angela's exclamation must have penetrated through Emma's earbuds because she ripped them from her ears and dropped them on the table. Angela passed her headset to Emma.

"Listen and tell me what you hear." She rolled the recording.

Emma's eyes bugged, then she passed the headphones back as if they were covered in slime. "I don't know what it said, but I can't get that guttural growling out of my head." Her face went pale, clearly terrified.

"I'm going to loop that. I want to hear it over and over again." Angela placed on the headphones and listened five more times.

During the EVP session, Angela had finished each question with a pause, a few beats of time to give a ghost the chance to respond. Sure enough, one did.

"Why are you here? Why do you haunt this place?" Angela's voice asked through the recording.

The voice was broken, barely audible, a grinding against the still air.

"*Not mine.* I think that's what he is saying."

"Why would a ghost say that? Usually they tell you to *get out,* right?" Emma's tone didn't hold as much enthusiasm for the voice phenomena as Angela felt.

"What he said is important, but what is even bigger is that he responded at all." Angela's heart hammered at a rapid beat. "That means we are having an effect. This ghost will connect with me soon."

Puzzle pieces began to appear, but the image was still vague. Angela didn't know enough information to put this puzzle together yet. But she was a step closer. If this was Hank Barlow's ghost, it was just a matter of time until he made contact with her. She had to get back into the mansion soon, and this evidence gave her an excuse to call Cole to see if she could come back tonight.

She restarted the video to watch the unmoving scene of the room again. This time, she looked more closely in the corners to see if she'd missed anything that occurred during the EVP. Nothing budged.

Lifting her arms above her head, she stretched the tension from her neck and shoulders. With a few hours of recordings and video left to watch, she hunkered down in her chair. At least they'd caught one thing so far. Ghosts were usually drawn to her and she usually connected more easily. She was determined to find the key to connecting with Hank Barlow. If Cole had learned anything from his father, it was clearly stubbornness.

With all her scattered thoughts, she almost missed it when something shifted on the screen. She sat up straight and leaned closer, narrowing the space between her and the computer. Could they have actually gotten two pieces of evidence?

"What is it? Did you catch something else?" Emma angled toward the screen with renewed interest.

"Look at this." Angela hit the replay button. "We caught a shadow."

The image of the drawing room played on the screen. At first, nothing interesting occurred as the seconds clicked by. The room was shrouded in shadows with the velvet drapes shut. The barest beam of moonlight flowed through a break.

Bookshelves, loaded with leather-bound books lined the back wall. A couch and chairs sat near the fireplace and a large desk, heavily weighted with papers, dominated the dark room.

The wall separating two bookshelves held the heavy darkness of night until the shadow shifted and took shape. The head and shoulders of a tall, six-foot body slipped from the wall, separating from the other shadows. Darkness emanated from the man-shaped figure. Even through the recording, Angela could feel the ominous nature pour from the being. A chill ran over her spine. She remembered that moment when the shadow-man had ripped through her, trying to get her to leave the mansion. It was Cole's strength and heat that had made Angela feel normal again and brought her back to reality.

The creature leaned out over one of the shelves to cover a portion of the books, hiding the titles. Was this Cole's father? He was even darker than she'd thought. Death only brought out a person's nature. They didn't become better beyond the grave. Cole must have endured more than he'd ever admit if his father had turned into this.

She felt a stab of understanding. She'd learn what had happened that caused Cole to protect himself deeply. She planned on starting tonight. Helping Cole was the key to helping this ghost cross over to the other side.

Just as quickly as the figure leaned forward, it slipped back to become part of the shadowed space between the shelves. He was gone from the screen, but that ghost was still in the mansion and so was Cole.

How long would both of them suffer from the demons of the past? Cole had to face that past or he and his father would be stuck in a self-imposed hell for a long time.

"Wow," Emma's shout shocked Angela from her reverie.

"We have more than personal experiences now. We have physical evidence."

Emma cheered, raising her hand in a fist pump. "It's a lot less scary watching on the computer."

"Good idea to upgrade our technology, little sis."

Emma smiled, warming Angela's insides.

"This needs to be prepared for the client. Emma, could you clean the tapes and get this put on a CD? I want to show this evidence to Cole tonight."

"This will change his tune."

"Doubt it. His type isn't convinced so easily." She snapped the computer closed. "Way too stubborn."

"At least we caught some good stuff on tape. Seeing might be believing."

"But I still feel like I'm missing something."

"You think the ghost is holding back?"

"That's for sure. He appears in a room while we were in the opposite side of the house."

"Don't worry so much, Angela. They'll connect when they're ready. They always come to find you."

"I hope you're right." Angela worried at her lower lip.

"I have hunches while you've got the real thing, baby."

"Your hunches usually prove right."

She needed to connect with the ghost. They'd been able to identify two entities in the house.

She had evidence she wanted to show Cole. Maybe she could make him eat a little crow after the way he'd mocked her abilities. He wouldn't think her a phony performer after he saw the tapes.

CHAPTER 13

W HEN THE DOORBELL rang, Cole grabbed for the pizza and balanced the box on one hand. He was looking forward to seeing Angela. How had he let her slip through his damned defenses so easily? How could he not? She had a way that made him want to trust her and believe everything she said.

So caught in his goal of destroying his father, he hadn't given a thought to anything or anyone else for the last few years. He was driven that way he guessed. His father had hurt many people and someone had to try to stop him. Cole had tried to do that in the only way he knew how. When he had his eye on the prize, nothing else seemed to matter. He'd almost succeeded in taking away all his father's power. Destroying Penniberg would be the final piece to the puzzle letting everyone know that his father's power no longer could control anyone anymore.

Somehow, Angela, this little bit of a thing who claimed the most outrageous things—ghosts for God's sake—had put a chink in the battle armor he used to protect his inner self. He'd had it in place so long that he forgot it was even there. He was hard. Could he ever be soft enough for someone like her? Did he even want to soften? To hell with it all. She was here and he deserved a little goodness, didn't he?

Why not enjoy some pizza and a glass of Chianti, instead of worrying about it? They could at least enjoy the time even if she wanted him to view some strange footage of the mansion.

Cole filled his lungs with the scent of pizza. Oregano and cheese blended with the savory scent of tomato sauce and yeasty dough. She'd surely appreciate a little dinner. Chicago-style pizza was the best.

Pulling open the door with his free hand, he greeted Angela. "Pizza guy." He held up the box. "Maybe a little wine too?"

"Isn't it supposed to be the other way around? Shouldn't the pizza guy be on this side of the door?"

Her smile was soft and sweet. He liked it. It wasn't a lusting predatory gaze like he'd become used to seeing in so many others over the years. It held a genuine laughter that made him relax.

"I'm a guy with many facets." He stepped back so she could enter.

She wore tight blue jeans and a white V-neck T-shirt. He liked that she didn't feel the need to impress him with her clothes, but damn, he couldn't take his eyes off her narrow waist and those curves in her Levi's. As she brushed past him, he could smell her spicy scent.

"I bear gifts myself." She pointed to the bag on

her shoulder. "Evidence to change your mind." She gave him a self-assured confident smile that made him want to believe her.

"Come on in. Let's have a little dinner first before we start talking about that stuff."

She threw a look at him from over her shoulder and suddenly, he was very hungry. "Keep an open mind, would you?"

"I've got an empty stomach. Let's worry about that first."

"Are you scared of ghosts?"

He conjured up one of his darkest scowls. It didn't seem to have any effect on her, since she turned away and continued toward the drawing room, completely ignoring him.

"Where's that wine you mentioned?" she said, before she disappeared from the hallway.

"It's on the table. I already uncorked it. Pour me one too, would you? I could use a drink." He needed a distraction from her. Had she always been interesting?

Her hair gleamed like fresh honey in morning sunlight, while her eyes were like the golden gates beckoning him toward a paradise he didn't deserve. He had a black hole for a heart and never kidded himself into believing he'd end up in heaven.

After setting the pizza box on the coffee table, he reached for the glass of wine and slugged down half of it. She pulled a couple of paper plates from the stack and placed slices of pizza onto each.

When she passed the first plate of pizza to him, he stared at her for a few seconds before reaching out. She returned his gaze with a confident fearlessness that surprised him. As much as he tried, she was not easily intimidated. Maybe he'd ramp it up a little to see how pretty Miss Cool held up.

Purposely, he brushed his fingers along hers when he took the plate. If he hadn't been looking closely for her tiniest reaction, he may not have noticed the slight cloud of pink that formed under her cheeks.

This time she shifted her gaze and took her pizza to the opposite end of the couch.

Good. His touch had affected her. The only thing was that it had affected him too. He could still feel her smooth skin against his rough fingers. Each time they touched was like a fire that blazed through him fast and scorching. If he wasn't careful with his rash actions, he'd be the one getting burned. Better to let her sit at the far end while he stayed on his side of the couch. He tapped his fingers on the arm of the sofa to try to remove the memory of her skin.

She folded one leg under her and set her plate in her lap. He picked up a slice of piping hot pizza but froze partway while his eyes trailed over her lips as she pulled off a piece of cheese and popped it in her mouth, then licked her fingers. She was trying to drive him crazy even though she seemed innocent. He forced himself to take a bite of his pizza and swallowed, not tasting it one bit.

"Pizza never tasted so good." His voice sounded like it had been dragged over a pile of stones. "Romano's is the best pizza in the Chicagoland area." He was ridiculous, saying anything to distract himself. He cleared his throat and continued. "It's a family secret. No living person knows the entire recipe. Each brother keeps one piece of the pie, so to speak." He sounded lame with that last comment, but he had to break the silence and get his mind off that spicy mouth.

She angled toward him, resting against a striped maroon and gold pillow. "How can they run a business like that?"

"One makes the dough, the other makes the sauce. It must keep everybody honest, don't you think?"

"What if one of the Romano brothers died, taking the secret to the grave?"

Cole shrugged. "They could always hire you." He'd meant it to be funny, but the look she gave him let him know he'd missed the mark.

"Just because you don't believe in what I do doesn't mean you should mock me." She placed her unfinished pizza on the table.

"I wasn't mocking. I was just trying to lighten the mood. The air in this place weighs on me and it's nice to have someone else here for a change."

"It weighs on you because of the negative energy between you and your father." She leaned toward him and lifted a hand. "You need to listen to your feelings."

His inner voice was the last thing he should listen to. He wanted to cup her imploring face in his hand and drag a kiss out of her. He wanted her to lick him like she'd licked the sauce from her fingers. Instead of pulling her against him, he shifted on the couch so less distance separated them. She was close enough now that he could smell her fresh, heady scent. Why was he making himself insane? He needed to get her out of here soon, but he couldn't bring himself to stop the torture.

"Tell me how to center myself? How do I focus on my feelings?" He couldn't believe those words had come from him. Feelings? He didn't have any. Or maybe he did have some once, a long time ago.

She blinked like a stunned rabbit in sight of a lynx. "Are you mocking me and my business again?"

"Absolutely not. I saw the phrase about learning to center yourself on your website." This was not going well.

"It's part of my philosophy."

"A mission statement of sorts?"

"To truly connect with the dead, my clients must learn to trust in their inner voice. Their inner self. That's the best way to understand the signs our loved ones leave for us."

"Yeah, well, I don't have to worry about that. I didn't have loved ones. No messages for me."

She took a sip of her wine. "My clients really don't need me." A little laugh escaped. "Everyone can connect if they center themselves and trust their feelings. It's as simple as paying attention to the signs."

"Those aren't the words that should be coming out of a hardcore business woman."

"I'm not hardcore. I want to help people."

"They won't trust in what you can give them if you undermine your services. Never tell a client they don't need you. That's business one-o-one."

"My sister is the business woman. I was always the odd-ball."

He filled his wineglass and held out the bottle. "Want a topper?"

"Just a little."

"Chianti is great with some Italiano." He filled her glass. "You're not that strange. Stop putting yourself down all the time. You're one tough cookie." He shoved a square of pizza in his mouth.

"I guess all the taunting on the playground gave me a complex."

"Or a thick skin. You're not afraid of me."

"I've seen some terrifying things over the years. Trust me, as much as you want to act like a demon, the real ones are a lot scarier."

That made him pause. She was sincere, but he couldn't go that far in the conversation and start talking about the other worldly. He'd focus on something he could relate with.

"The other kids were mean to you when you grew up?" He knew what it was like to be mis-treated as a kid. "That sticks and stones shit is a fat lie. Words can dig deeper than any fist."

"And the scars are there forever," she agreed.

The sadness in her eyes infuriated him. He was mad at himself. Why had he started talking about the pain that people held from their childhood? He held onto enough of it and he didn't like sharing. But there was something about her that made him lower his guard. He wanted to protect her and take away her pain. That look was on her face because of him. He'd somehow gotten her to mention things that obviously hurt her too much to relive. He had to get rid of that look in her eyes. He needed to wipe it away.

He shifted toward her and brushed his thumb along her cheek, brushing away the tear that left an invisible trail over her soft skin. He wanted to touch the little freckle at the corner of her mouth. Damn, what he really wanted to do was lean in and kiss it. She closed her eyes. Instead of pulling away, like he feared, she leaned into his palm.

His boulder of a heart gave one shuddering beat before he leaned down and brushed his lips against hers. That's all he would take. He was about to pull away when she let out a sigh that fluttered against him, sending thrills down his spine and raging along his nerve endings.

She leaned into him and he took more, slipping his tongue into her mouth. She tasted of wine mixed with her essence and it was the most potent flavor any sommelier could crave. She kissed him back with just as much thirst.

Wrapping his arms around her waist, he pulled her closer, hoping she wouldn't change her mind. Taut breasts pressed into his chest and he could feel her pebbled nipples. He pressed more deeply. They drove him nuts. But what drove him even crazier was the fast thrumming of her heartbeat.

Cupping her face, he lifted her chin so he could deepen the kiss. Her tongue met his thrust for thrust. She sighed into his mouth. Her breath mingled with his as he explored her mouth, wanting to know every bit of her. She was like a life-giving elixir. The beating of his own heart raged in his ears, making his head spin with the overwhelming need for more.

She slid her hands up his back to encircle his neck just under the jagged layers of his hair. She brushed her fingers over the gold chain he wore. Attached to the chain was the medallion that reminded him of why he was here, why he'd returned to Dalewood. He broke the kiss.

Stomach tightening, he pressed his forehead into the crook of her neck. He didn't deserve her soft touch. He was used to rough hands dragging at him. The delicate, sweet trail of her fingers against his bare skin unnerved him. Her soft touch over the chain reminded him of his dark need for revenge, a man torn between her light and his need for revenge.

He jerked away from her.

"What's the matter?" she breathed on short, choppy breaths.

He couldn't let her know how much her kiss messed with his brains, how much her soft touch challenged all his plans. With a sneer he said, "Is that how you run a business? Always sleep with your clients?"

Her gasp ripped through him. But worse was the pain that shimmered in her angel's eyes. He was the lowest of the low and he'd just gotten done talking about the harshness of words. He had to be. He earned the title of asshole. Only one other did it better than he could. He'd learned from the best, but still he hated himself in that moment.

"How dare you?" Her cheeks flared with anger. His gaze fell to her kiss reddened lips.

Oh, he dared. He had to protect her from himself. If he got too close to her, he would fuck up everything. He'd taught himself that lesson long ago. Never let anyone close because everyone gets hurt. He was damaged goods. He'd come back to Dalewood so he could destroy all ties to the past. Messing with Angela would only get in the way of his plans. If he, kept this up he'd never be able to start fresh. Damn it all, because he wanted to kiss those lips again, hear those sighs and bring that flush back to her cheeks, but he couldn't. Kissing her was just another piece of proof that he was as base as his father.

The only thing he could offer Angela were some tough lessons in the business of hard knocks.

He did one thing well. He could run a hardcore company. He'd teach her a few ruthless tactics so she could take her silly little business to the next level. At least he could leave her with something.

"Listen, Angela, I admire your dedication to this business and I might be able to teach you a few things."

"Is that right?" She crossed her arms over her chest. Good, she was blocking him out. Her hands stayed locked in tight little fists. He took that as a positive. If she wanted to punch him, then she wasn't thinking about kissing him with that hot little tongue. He crossed his own arms in front of his chest and leaned back a little. Hoping he could send a message that he would not cross over that line again.

"Yeah, that's right." God, she was pretty when she was angry. Her eyes flashed hatred at him. That was good. He could deal with hate. That sealed the deal even more. How dare he touch her like that? She was too delicate for his roughness. He was a beast, goddamn it.

"It's your lucky day. I'm going to teach you a few tools to get you past your too nice attitude. That way you'll let your clients know what you're worth."

"I refuse to learn any of your heartless strategies."

"That kiss proved how sensitive and gullible you could be." He gave her that condescending smile he reserved for his toughest negotiators. "You need me to help you."

"Hey, big shot, last I checked, you needed me." She waggled her finger at him. "Remember that little problem you have?"

That little minx had the nerve to give him the once-over.

"I think you need me a little more than I need you," she continued, reaching over the arm of the sofa. She dragged out her laptop and set it on the table next to their discarded pizza plates. "If you don't mind, I'd like to finish this little business meeting of ours. Then I need to do a bit of investigating since it is dark outside and that is the best time to make *real connections*."

She eyed him when she said real connections, clearly insinuating that he couldn't make real connections with her or anyone else. Good. He had gotten through loud and clear.

Turning haughtily, she gave her full focus to the computer with clear dismissal. His nastiness didn't seem to stump her as she pulled up the footage with a full amount of professionalism. That made him feel like the biggest heel. She could clearly handle situations with calm decorum, while he always went into the dark side and came out covered in shit.

"Here's the evidence, though you're so thick headed, you'd probably need to be hit over the head by bat-wielding spirits."

He watched the recording in silence. For a while, nothing happened. Just as he was about to look away the shadow figure moved. He'd know that shape anywhere, the breadth of shoulders, the height. The sound of his father's voice sent a chill down his spine. He couldn't believe what he was seeing and hearing. How could he? His father was dead. He didn't believe in ghosts. He wanted to curse at Angela, accuse her of faking this footage, but he'd already said too many terrible things to her tonight. He was an ass all right and had created enough of a disgusting display for one night. What would he say anyway? That he refused to believe what was right in front of him?

"I'll have to mull this over." Cole retreated to the library, letting Angela continue her investigation on her own.

Ever since he'd come back to Dalewood, he'd started to unravel. He'd spent his entire life acting tough. In the short time he'd been back, all his defenses crumbled. He felt vulnerable and he hated that feeling. And he'd crossed the line with that kiss, but all he wanted to do was pull her against him and do it again.

Staring at the empty fireplace, he'd been berating his idiocy since he'd left Angela. He knew he had a lot of his dad inside him, but continuously tried to prove he was nothing like the man he hated. If only he could get rid of this place. Then he would no longer feel the need to prove anything anymore.

Could she be telling the truth or was she messing with him? He buried his head in his hands and scrubbed at his cheeks. The sound of far off tinkling laughter snapped him straight upright in his chair. Cocking an ear in the direction of the door, he listened to the silence, but everything was still.

Angela was *working* somewhere in this house. When he heard the sound again, he realized the faint bubbling of female giggles must be coming from her. The problem was that Angela never giggled. She yelled at him, she pursed her lips, she stared at him with those sexy golden eyes and she'd kissed him with those hot, sweet lips. But she'd never giggled, he thought with a smile.

A fluttering sound passed near the open doorway. He waited a few seconds for Angela to enter, but she never did.

"Angela?" he called as he pushed up from the desk and moved swiftly to the hallway to catch her. He glanced one way, then the other, but she wasn't there.

They were the only two people in the house. Did he hear it again? Soft tinkling laughter floated from the staircase. He followed the sound of shifting floorboards. Each step clicked, one stair at a time, like someone was slowly ascending the steps over his head.

"Angela. What do you need?" he called.

Silence.

He walked farther down the hall, then turned past the banister. Still, no one was on the steps.

Footfalls paced along the second-floor hallway out of view from the stairs.

He followed them.

What was Angela doing? Why was she sneaking around like that? She knew she had the full run of the place. He'd made it clear that he would stay out of her way.

The first bedroom door on the left stood wide open, allowing a shaft of light to spill on the carpet.

He moved closer, then paused in the doorway. She was there. Blonde curls spilled over Angela's shoulders, down her back. He wanted to touch its softness, but instead he stayed in the doorway and watched her. She sat at the dressing table, holding a handheld recorder close to her ear. Every few seconds she jotted a note in a journal.

Lost in concentration, she must not have heard him come in. If she'd been sitting up here, she hadn't been the one running around on the first floor. Who'd been laughing?

Old shifting floorboards, maybe? Old houses

made strange noises all the time.

She hit the rewind button and the tape squealed. Hitting the button again, her voice played back from the recording. "Hi I'm Angela. I'm here to help you." She took this business seriously and he admired her perseverance.

Metallic laughter rang from the recorder. It was identical to the sound he had followed up the stairs.

"I know you won't sit and talk to me, but maybe you will talk audio recorder?" she continued.

"Can't." The responding voice was a feminine, almost childlike voice. A low growling was replaced by recording static. Angela wrote a few more notes in her book.

"What are you writing?"

She flinched before swinging around in the chair. "How long were you there? I didn't hear you come in."

He strode toward the table and glanced at her scribbles. "Not that long."

"Are you here to give me more problems?"

"What were you doing?"

"I'm having trouble connecting with the ghosts. Something is preventing it. There's more than one entity here."

"Not just my father?" Was he actually starting to believe her?

"I'm not even sure your father's ghost is the ghost that others have seen. When he passed through me that first day, there was a distance, a separation. I don't understand why, but he won't connect with me. What about you?"

"I haven't seen him for years, living or dead."

"I haven't connected with him at all. I've seen the shadow man, a few residuals and heard footsteps. Usually the ghosts trust me more. They let me into their world and accept what I can offer." The corners of her eyes crinkled and the tilt of her soft smile faded. She looked tired.

"Can you really see ghosts?" He scanned her notes without finding anything interesting.

She stiffened. "I thought you were going to allow me to investigate without any more interference tonight."

"I'm not trying to insult you. I guess my curiosity is piqued." She hadn't known he was watching her work and she seemed sincere in her efforts that he suddenly needed to know more. "What is it like to see ghosts? Is it difficult?"

"Seeing ghosts? No, that part is pretty easy. They find me. As a kid, I had to learn how to hold their visits at bay. The hard part is how living people treated me. It isn't considered normal. Kids aren't always the nicest. It's hard to make friends since most people think you're weird or crazy."

"When I first saw you, I thought you looked pretty normal, ordinary, really." He shrugged. Had she been insulted by that? A look flickered across her face, but was gone before he could interpret it.

"In fact, the hardest part is dealing with jerks like you."

"I deserve that."

"I'm kind of busy here."

"Have you been up here the entire time?"

"Yeah, why?"

"Collecting recordings like that one you just listened to?"

"After you left me to my investigation, I walked to the second floor and came straight to the bedroom. This was where Emma and I heard some noises, so I thought it was a good place to continue." She set the recorder on the table and eyed him coolly. "Why? What brings you up here now?"

"I don't know. I thought I heard you wandering around downstairs and I followed the sounds into this room, my father's room. You were sitting at the dressing table with the recorder."

"Describe the sounds you heard."

"You were here the entire time? But I swear I heard you wandering past the library a few minutes ago."

"It wasn't me. Tell me what you experienced."

"I thought I heard laughter. Kind of like the recording you just played."

"Really?" Enthusiasm filled her tone. "I think you had a clear interaction with a ghost."

"That's ridiculous." The air crackled between them. A heavy weight surrounded him, weighing his body and filling him with a soul-weary anchor. It was hard to breathe. "I'm getting sick of being stuck in this place." Maybe it was her steady, expectant gaze or maybe it was the mansion. Being back in Dalewood, not being himself. He felt like he was suffocating. "I've got to get out of here. A path leads through the gardens into the woods toward the river. Want to get some air?"

Unwillingness flashed over her features. But he wouldn't allow her to verbally reject the idea.

"Come on. It's not far at all and the moon is bright tonight. It's wild and I haven't gone that way since I was a kid. This place is driving me batty. There's something I need to find in those woods and it would be better if you came too." He felt compelled to show her something he hadn't thought of in many years. He thought she'd hold her ground and flat out refuse.

Finally, she nodded. The unease seemed to uncoil from her shoulders.

"Good."

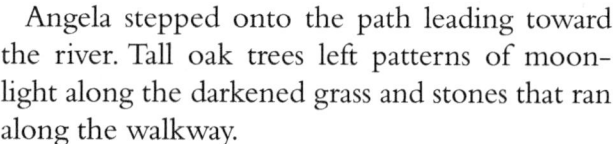

Angela stepped onto the path leading toward the river. Tall oak trees left patterns of moonlight along the darkened grass and stones that ran along the walkway.

"Watch your step in the dark, there are a few large stones scattered in the path." Cole walked a few steps ahead of her, hands jammed in his pockets, as he kicked at a rock to get it off the path. His broad shoulders strained against his jacket, shoulders that held all the weight and worries of the past.

The funny thing was that she had no fear of Cole. What she was afraid of was her reaction to him. If he tried to kiss her again, she wouldn't try to stop him.

The scent of water from the Steele River hung in the cool breeze. It blew her hair against her neck and tickled her cheek. She brushed it away and looked up at the bright yellow moon.

The soft touch reminded her of Cole's soft touches. Memories of their kiss burned against her brain and she let the hot feelings flow over her, through her, like a traitorous caress.

She could still feel his hands on her skin and she wanted to slide her hands over the taut smooth skin of his back, then up to tangle through his dark, wild mane that brushed along his collar. Her fingers itched to touch the silkiness.

He was a man of contradictions, softness with hard edges. Gentle kisses combined with biting words. She still smarted over his words, but her body betrayed her. Her brain betrayed her, because even as he was saying those mean things, she knew he didn't mean them. He was used to pushing people away. Knowing that made her want to invade his space even more. She wanted to force him out of his self-imposed barriers. She wanted to be the one to break his shell and help him learn to love again. Help him learn that he was worthy of love.

She stumbled over a stone. Love. Whoa that was moving too fast.

Enigma. Contradiction. Sometimes Cole made perfect sense and sometimes he made no sense at all.

The damage from his father ran so deeply, she feared it would be impossible to help this man. The old biddies in the library were right. Cole could be as bad as his father was. It rankled. She needed to help the ghosts in this place, but she knew, deep down, she couldn't help them without helping Cole first.

How could she undo the type of damage his father had done?

Cole needed to move on. He wasn't a little boy anymore.

The kiss had been perfect. Everything a kiss should be, hot, fast and all consuming. Then he'd gone and ruined it with his brutal words.

She thought she'd handled the situation pretty well. Instead of wilting like she would have as a young, impressionable college student, she'd held her ground and actually pushed back.

That was the way to handle Cole, especially when he was acting brutish.

Plus, though she'd never admit it to him, but he'd been right. A professional did not mingle with her client no matter how sexy he was and no matter how hot he kissed. She couldn't get it out of her mind. Especially when his long legs pulled him closer to the river and his butt moved enticingly against his dark jeans.

Thank goodness she'd been staring at his broad back because, without stopping, he stepped from the path, practically disappearing between some very old trees. Their trunks thick with age. His footsteps crunched into the brown ferns.

Annoyance sizzled. He didn't look back to see if she followed. He hadn't spoken to her either, intent on finding a particular spot in the woods. He climbed over a fallen tree branch and scanned each tree.

On the opposite side of the path, Angela could see a slight hill that dipped toward the sparkling river. A stone bench perched at the top of the slope.

She wouldn't follow him. She wasn't a doting puppy that would jovially trot along hoping for a bit of acknowledgment.

Angela moved in the opposite direction from Cole and sat. She closed her eyes and leaned her head against the back of the stone bench. His crunching steps increased and became more forceful in their movements.

She took in a deep breath of the sweet air, fragrant with autumn. The gurgling water had a calming effect, until Cole's face popped in her head, too beautiful and all too knowing.

To get rid of his smug gaze, she popped open her eyes. She pushed up from her seat, grabbed a few rocks and tossed them one at a time into the river. Each landed with a loud *kerplunk*.

She wished she could pick up a large boulder and throw it into the river to get a larger splash.

Cole's movements through the leaves behind her sounded like a person rummaging in a scavenger hunt. Why had he wanted her to come with him? If he didn't speak to her soon, the silence would drive her nuts. Maybe she could jump into the river just to get his attention.

She couldn't stand it anymore. She would be the first one to break the silence between them. Angela stood and turned, ready to do just that. But before she could speak, she stilled and watched. What was he looking for with such fervor? She twisted the bracelet on her wrist.

Cole pushed at the leaves on the ground and

shoved at the prehistoric sized ferns. Then he reached up and felt along the tree trunk. He repeated these actions with the next section of dirt.

"What are you doing?"

"It's got to be around here somewhere." He stood and ran his hands along another tree trunk, then the next.

"What are you trying to find? Can I help?"

"Everything's changed since I've been gone. This path wasn't here when I was a kid and some of the familiar trees are gone. Time makes things change." He moved on to the next maple.

"I think your father was the one who donated most of the funds to create the river walk. Do you think this path leads to the community walk?"

"My dear fantastic father? The Donald Trump of Dalewood?" His laugh was harsh and full of resentment. "My father would never donate a cent to help anyone but himself."

"I don't know his motives, but the river walk was a great addition to downtown Dalewood."

"I used to hide in these woods when I was a kid." He looked off toward the river. "Leave it to my dad to ruin my favorite place." He looked at her with eyes as cold as slate.

She had no response.

"Will you go a little deeper into the woods with me? There is something I need to find, if it's still there."

"What are you trying to find?"

"I wonder if my father destroyed my treasures like he did my life."

"There comes a time when you can't blame the present on the past."

He gave her a hard glance, then turned and stalked through the trees.

She picked up her stride and carefully followed him into the thickness of the woods.

He stopped dead in his tracks and she almost bumped into his solid back. He slowly turned to her. Through gritted teeth he bit out, "Don't think I overexaggerate. You have no idea."

"And how would I know that? I tell you my secrets, but you keep yours locked tight. How will you ever move past your hate?"

He didn't reply. Instead, he pushed deeper from the path. The chill of his silence made her shiver, but she wouldn't back out now. She was determined to find the soft place within him and get to the heart of his pain.

As they moved farther away from the mansion, she couldn't keep track of the direction they traveled. Each turn made it seem like they walked through a maze of trees. Finally, he stopped in front of the largest oak tree she'd ever seen.

"This is it," he whispered as he ran his finger along the carvings that left brown scars in the bark. He traced the letters CB. "I thought my father cut it down, but it's still here." The tenseness in his shoulders relaxed.

"Did you come here with your high school sweetheart as a kid?" She couldn't stop the words. She wanted to know. She felt oddly jealous of no one in particular, just anyone who had known him as a kid, before he became jaded.

"No. I was too messed up to worry about girls in high school." He scanned the ground, then walked a few steps from the base. "Here we go." He knelt down on one knee and pulled up his jacket sleeves before grasping the small boulder. Dirt partially covered it and grass grew along its rough edges. He gripped the rock, but it wouldn't budge. Grabbing with both hands, he pushed and pulled until it shifted barely an inch. He drew in a deep breath, making his back expand into a herculean size. He pushed, then pulled again with more force than before. A grunt ripped from him and the rock rolled forward. The momentum almost took him down. He caught his balance at the last minute by gripping at the oak. A satisfied sigh of approval rippled through the air. The hole left by the rock seemed deeper than it should be. Angela leaned over Cole's shoulder and peered inside.

"There's nothing but dirt down there. Was this what you wanted to show me?"

"Hold on." He reached into the hole and scooped some of the dirt away. "Well, lookie here." He scooped out another heap of dirt, then rubbed at something she couldn't see.

With great care, he pulled something from the ground. She leaned closer. "One of those treasures you mentioned? It looks like a big clump of dirt."

"Not a pile of dirt." He brushed at the thick black chunks that clung to the object. Clumps of mud and weeds fell to the ground in heavy plops.

She realized it was a painted blue clay object as

large as his fist. "What is it?" She reached for it, but he pulled it away.

"That's exactly what my father said when I gave it to him. Right before he laughed and tossed it in the trash."

"Let me see that. I can't tell what it is if you won't show it to me." She took another look. "Is it a..." She bit her lip while she struggled for something to say that wouldn't insult him.

His laugh sounded bitter. "It was supposed to be an ashtray. But I guess the old man was right. It was just a fucking piece of trash from his fuck up of a son." The harsh edge was in his tone again, his breathing ragged. He fisted the clay ashtray in a white-knuckled grip, forearm muscles twitching under the force. Each of his words pelted her like hale. He stared off into space even as he appeared to look at the old tree. Then he hurled it toward the tree, startling Angela with his swift movements. The ashtray rapped against the trunk and split into two pieces that thudded to the dirt before Angela's feet.

"Why did I need to find that piece of shit so badly?" Cole strode off into the dark woods.

She could see his silhouette in the bright moonlight. Angela stood a moment watching him, then she looked at the rejected gift. The pieces seemed oddly serene as they rested in the lonely dirt.

Nobody should endure such rejection from their own family. She'd had her share of problems as a kid, but she always felt loved. Leaning down, she rescued the two broken pieces that were once the ashtray from its dirt pile. She slipped both parts into her jacket pocket, then she chased after Cole, before he was completely out of sight.

"Wait for me," she called. "Do you plan on abandoning me in a dark forest?"

The words were meant to break through his anger and they must have worked because his steps faltered to a stop. Without turning back to her, he leaned against a white birch. The power seemed to deflate from his body. His hunched shoulders made him look vulnerable. She wanted to touch him, but she needed to protect her own heart otherwise he could break it like the ashtray. Was she willing to risk that?

She reached her hand toward him and paused. He'd been a beast only moments ago, full of pain and rage.

Then she rested her hand against his forearm. She needed to comfort him and that was the only thing she could think to do, other than to wrap her arms around his waist. He didn't pull away and she was relieved.

The tension in his muscles flowed from his body into hers and she felt him relaxing.

Angela placed more pressure on his arm and she could feel the hairs of his arm tickle along her palm. She willed him to turn and look at her. When he finally did, his gray gaze seemed hollow. She held back her gasp and returned his steady stare. She needed him to know she was here to help even if he didn't want or accept it.

His irises darkened and seemed to clear. She wasn't sure when it happened, but he finally looked at her, really saw her instead of the painful memories that tormented him.

He twisted his arm and gripped at her hand as if it were a lifeline. His grasp tightened, but she didn't pull away. He licked at his lips, then cleared his throat. "I'm sorry," he said the words as if he had to push them out.

Arm shaking, he pulled her into him and pressed her against his chest. His wood-smoke scent emanated from his hot skin. And she felt safe in his rugged arms even as he pushed her away with his words and his brusqueness. His lips pressed against hers, claiming and caressing with a gentleness he's never shown before. Cradled in his arms, she knew he would never harm her in anyway.

"I'm sorry I treated you that way." The words spilled from him faster than the Steele River rushed downstream. "When I said those terrible things to you, I knew I was no better than my father. I didn't mean them." He clung to her.

"I know," she murmured, and tightened her grip around his waist.

"I don't want to be like my father. I can't become him. But that's what I did. It was cruel. You don't deserve that. You're kind and sweet. I'm damaged and ruin everything I touch."

He slid his hand up and down her spine, gently, slowly. He needed this. He had to spill his guts of the bile that poisoned him.

"I needed to find that ashtray. I don't know why, but I needed to unearth it and show you. I needed you to see it. To let you know that I'm no better than my father."

"No," she murmured against his chest, snuggling deeper.

"I don't want to become him." The words tore from him.

"Then don't. I won't let him hurt you again." And she meant it. She'd do everything in her power so that Hank Barlow's ghost would never hurt him again. "He's dead. We get to choose who we want to be. The past is the past. You get to make your future."

"I wish I could believe you." He rested his chin against her hair and continued to hold her.

"You have to fight your own demons. I'll help you, but no one can do it for you." What more could she say? What she could do was help him face the past and maybe then he could work through it to create a new future.

CHAPTER 14

PURE SATISFACTION HIT Cole as he entered Angela's office building. It was clearly her space, calm and cool, with a subtle way of making him feel serene.

Last night he'd clung to her and spilled out his soul. She hadn't snubbed him and she hadn't made him feel inadequate. He'd never told anyone those feelings. Hell, he'd never even told himself.

In the blaring light of day, he should feel like a cockroach and scamper back to the shadows. Instead, he felt compelled to see Angela. He'd found himself driving down the street toward her investigation offices. Almost like an out of body experience, his feet moved of their own volition toward the entrance.

The front office was strangely quiet and empty. *Spooky.* The room was bright and airy with the faint scent of spice and dried fruit, like autumn and the forest. He pulled in a deep breath of the scent that was Angela. He loved her scent. He looked around. Where was everyone? Where was Angela?

It wasn't good form to leave the front end of the business unattended. Maybe he could suggest a secretary. Then he noticed the sign. It read *Seminar* and the arrow pointed in the direction of a room marked *Conference Center*.

Moving hastily in that direction, he pushed open the door. Was this what it felt like to want something, someone? It was foreign, but he couldn't wait to see her.

The conference center was really a large room with rows of chairs facing a small stage. Angela stood on the tiny stage, smoothly gliding back and forth, referencing a screen with the presentation in blue lettering.

Her name fit her. Light fell on her and radiated over her blonde hair, giving it a halo glow. Her sky-blue dress swirled around her, delicately brushing over her knees and displaying her very pretty calves. She exuded confidence in front of the large group and seemed to be in her element, at ease, effortless. The audience sat, writing furiously in white binders. At that moment, he knew why she was considered the best. She held the room with her enthusiasm and sincerity. She didn't need help from him on how to run a business. She was doing a good job all on her own. He leaned a shoulder against the back wall and admired her in action.

"Everyone has some level of psychic ability." Angela's voice echoed through the earpiece microphone that rested near her mouth.

The sweetness of Angela's voice rolled over him like warm water.

"Whether you call it the sixth sense or simply intuition, you must listen." The slide changed on the screen. "Honing your talents begins with trust. You must trust in your own instincts. This is the only way to build your psychic ability." Her gaze wandered over the audience as she turned around. Was that the slightest hitch in her step? Had she seen him standing in the back?

"And everyone has the ability."

She never made eye contact with him, but he was sure she knew he was there.

The attendees listened in rapt awe while their pens moved furiously along the paper. She had something he didn't. Maybe he could learn a few things from her instead of the other way around. She had the ability to connect with people in a way he had always avoided. She let people in with her kindness while he always pushed them away. That's why he had come here. He was ready for her help.

"I'm going to leave you with a task for our next session. A little homework." Her smile was warm and he wished it was for him alone.

"On the next section of your handouts is a page set aside for your own notes. Please write down each experience you have on a psychic level from now until next week. Include dreams, feelings, hunches or intuition. Remember, we can't hone the skill if we can't recognize our feelings. See you all next week."

The audience rang into applause. They got up from their seats to talk to one another. Others formed a line to speak to Angela individually.

When would she notice him? Look at him? Annoyance niggled, like jealousy, as he waited, though it was mixed with pride. She had many people at the seminar, but he still wished she would spare a glance in his direction. Maybe it was a bad idea to come here so soon after what he'd said last night. He'd been a mess and she was probably feeling awkward. He really was a screw-up. He should leave. It was stupid of him to come. He turned and started for the door.

But before he could leave, a hand, small and gentle, stopped him. He knew it was Angela. Air filled him and he could breathe again. When had he become a foolish infant? Yesterday after he'd spilled his feelings.

"Did you learn anything while you sneaked in a little bit of my lessons?" Angela's cheeks flushed and her eyes sparkled. "I won't tell Emma that you didn't pay your seminar fee to attend. She might send a bill if she finds out."

"Good to know one of you is cutthroat. I missed most of it, but your audience was very engaged." The words bumbled from his lips. She was pretty and fresh.

"I know." She laughed. "It wasn't always like that, but now we have a continuous following that attend each weekly session. It's amazing. Emma's marketing ideas saved the place."

"You also play an important part in the success of your business. Without you, there would be no trainings or people. It's your personality that brings them back."

She tilted her head and stared at him with gold

shimmers in her gaze. "Why, Mr. Barlow, is that a compliment?"

He had the strangest urge to shuffle against her stare. Instead, he crossed his arms and changed the topic. And why did he want to kiss her right here in front of everyone, claiming her when he didn't have the right?

"You are teaching everyone how to see dead people?"

"No. But I do believe everyone has some paranormal ability. It's nothing like the movies. It's a lot more complicated than that."

"More complicated? On television, it seems like the ghosts just walk right up and interact. Is that what it's like? They just appear before you?"

"Sometimes, it's a little like that. But most times it's trickier."

"Can you share those types of secrets?" He leaned toward her just to get a little closer.

"Oh, just stop, you aren't interested in what I can do." She put her hands on her hips.

He liked how she stood up to him and he almost smiled.

"Miss Haven, I'm sorry to interrupt." They both turned toward a woman who held her binder against her chest. "I have a question about one of the slides. Would you mind if I asked you for some advice?"

Angela turned back to Cole. "I hope you learned something by stopping by. If you'll excuse me…"

He'd learned something all right, but it was about himself. Cole turned to leave.

"Cole. Wait."

Cole stopped, to see Mrs. Greeley. She looked like she had just left the salon, with her hair pressed in perfect curls that framed her round face. She wore a pink silk blouse with a navy pants suit. Her bangle bracelets jingled as she waved at him.

"I knew I'd see you soon enough. I have something I want to give you."

He was surprised that she had a gift for him.

"I didn't want to wait for the dinner party, I've been carrying them with me since that day Liza and I saw you on the river walk." She rummaged in her large Chanel purse. "Where are they? I've been holding onto them for years and now I can't find them." She shifted into another pocket. "Ah, here we go." She handed him an envelope. "I thought you should have these. They're letters from—"

"Your husband? Max wanted me to have these?"

"From my husband?" Her face scrunched in a position that would leave wrinkles if she made it too often. He loved this old lady. "No. These letters are from your father. He gave them to Max."

Cole almost dropped the envelope as disgust seared his flesh. "Why would my father give them to his rival? I want nothing that came from my father and you know that, Fran." He pushed the letters back at her. "Take them."

"I think your father knew you would outright refuse them if they came directly from him. He wanted Max to give them to you, but..." She looked away for a moment, blinking. "They're yours and I won't take them back. You need these." Her features hardened and face was as stern as unmovable granite and it fueled his anger. He was sure his face held his meanest scowl and he didn't care. How dare she give him something from his father? She knew how horrible his father had been.

"You can no longer act like an obstinate child, Cole. Both men are gone. It's time to find a way to move on and make amends."

"How many injuries did you patch up for me, Fran? You knew more than anyone how bad I had it with my father and you give me these?" He crushed the papers in his fist.

"Do with them as you wish, but I hope they help you in your decisions. It's time you faced your father. You can't run from him forever."

"He never treated me as his son." Cole straightened the papers and then tore them in half and in half again. Fran flinched.

"Maybe those letters will help you understand more," she said.

"There is no reason good enough. I would never treat my son in the way he treated me." He never once had ever thought about having his own son before. His gaze slipped to Angela for a moment before returning to the letters.

"Max loved you like a son, so you could know what love was. You are not your father."

"I am my father's son." He wanted to get rid of the pieces. Wipe his father off his hands and from his life, but he feared he never could.

"No, you're not. Never say that."

"*You* think of me as if I were still the little child.

I'm a *man*. A successful one. All thanks to you and Max. Not *him*." He raised the letters.

"I remember when you were a boy. And I see that sweet little boy in you still. Why else would I trust you with my daughter? Be the man you were meant to be." She threw up her hands. "Fine, don't read those letters. But don't throw them away either."

He closed his eyes to stop looking at the ripped edges, their tattered roughness wore against his emotions. Anger roiled in his guts, deep and churning. He looked at Fran but couldn't bear the pity and worry in her eyes. "I live those days over and over in my mind since I've been back to Dalewood."

"Don't you remember a time when you were happy?"

"Don't do this, Fran. My father destroyed that boy. I'm what's left."

"My husband loved you like a son." She looked down and away. "He saw something in you. He knew you were strong."

Max Greeley taught him to hammer and nail. He taught him how to paint and repair the fence, how to build properties. He'd taught Cole everything about business. He'd do anything for the Greeleys, but he couldn't get distracted by his duty to them. He still had that same drive and focus as a kid, but that focus was now on one thing. Destruction. Revenge against the man who had turned him into the hateful creature he'd become. Revenge against the man who tried to destroy the family who cared for him and taught him. He would avenge Max. Nothing written in those letters would change that.

"You are much more than you think you are." She pressed her hand to his cheek. "Diamonds form under the worst conditions." She patted her other hand against his chest. "You have a diamond heart under all that rubble. The only one who doesn't believe it is you." Then she drifted away into the small crowd milling around Angela.

He looked down at the paper pieces still crushed in his fist. He walked to the trashcan in the corner, ready to throw them away. His hand hovered over the opening, but he couldn't bring himself to release the torn letters. He watched his frozen fist. It felt separate from his body. The fist that refused to bend to his emotional will. Lately, everyone refused to bend to his will. They were all starting to see through his bluster.

He pulled his hand back. The connection to his father was still there, buried somewhere deep. He tucked the pieces in his jacket pocket. The weight of the letters pulled at his shoulders and grabbed at his insides, but he couldn't throw them away.

Angela wrapped the extension cord around her arm in quick circles. All the attendees had trickled out and the conference room that seemed small a half an hour ago, now seemed to echo with its emptiness.

When she'd seen Cole standing in the back, watching, she'd almost lost her balance and her train of thought. How could he do that to her?

He could make her turn to jelly with only his presence. For the life of her, she couldn't figure out why he'd come. But she was glad he had come because it made her feel less awkward about what had happened yesterday. His mere presence had let her know there was something between them. And he was still willing to work with her professionally.

She placed the orange cord in the case with the screen projector.

"Another job well done." Emma's chirping voice shocked Angela from her thoughts.

Angela spun, knowing it was impossible for her sister to read her thoughts, but somehow, Emma always had an uncanny ability to get right into her heart and know what she was feeling. Recently, she'd been unable to get Cole out of her head and she wasn't ready to talk about it, not even to the person closest to her.

"I'll put the projector away." Emma took the box from her, then her gaze shot up to pierce straight through Angela's soul and she knew she couldn't hide. "What's the matter? You had the best success of this blooming business and you're brooding." Emma tilted her head to one side and blinked her brown, puppy dog eyes.

"I'm not brooding. I'm cleaning up." Angela placed the fattest cat smile on her lips hoping to sway the subject.

Emma turned with the box and Angela breathed a sigh. Emma took a few steps, then stopped and turned back.

"Why did Cole Barlow show his face here?

Last I saw him, he wasn't interested in the para-normal."

Angela swallowed, but said nothing.

"Did you turn him into a believer last night?"

"Something like that." Angela knew Emma was fishing for details about the other night. Angela had gotten home late, which wasn't odd considering her line of work. "I think he is coming to terms with the fact that he has to work through the problems he had with his father At least I hope he is."

With the seminar, Angela had avoided her sister's probing questions about the previous evening. She was telling her the truth without revealing everything.

What could she say anyway? That the arrogant jerk had a soul underneath all his brute exterior? That he kissed like no other man, with a sensitivity as passionate as his anger? Just the thoughts of his kiss made her feel vulnerable to Emma's intuition.

Her sister knew something more had happened last night, but Angela couldn't bring herself to share Cole's most intimate secrets. For some reason, it would feel like a betrayal.

She stood there like a mime, refusing to speak. Emma gave her one last knowing smile before leaving her alone.

The conference room felt large and over-whelming that she skittered from the space into the sanctity of her private office.

She shut the door behind her and sat at her desk. Out of breath, she rested her head in her hands. Even this room reminded her of him.

That first day he'd sat there arguing with her. He'd seemed large and looming, dominating the place that was her domain.

Last night in the woods, he'd had a darker quality. He'd seemed even larger in his despair with the moonlight accentuating his broad shoulders and corded muscles in an aura of pure vulnerability making him even more masculine.

Instead of being afraid, she'd been drawn to his need. He'd shared himself with her last night and she couldn't bring herself to talk about it. Not to anyone, not even Emma.

And then he'd been there today, standing in the doorway overwhelming the room, making it seem small because of his simple presence. For a split second, nothing existed but her and him looking at her. It had been a moment of tunnel vision. No sound, no feeling. Just him and his gaze roving over her body.

Or at least that's what it felt like.

He'd almost left without speaking to her and the thought made her feel bereft. She'd broken away from Ashley Clemer mid-sentence. The woman had been sharing a strange dream she couldn't interpret, but Angela needed to catch Cole, even for the briefest of moments.

Then she'd been pulled away again, just that fast, like the flutter of a butterfly brushing against her skin. Funny to compare that interaction with Cole like a butterfly. Soft and delicate and easily broken. Those ideas were nothing like the man he portrayed himself as. He was strong and unbreakable. Hard and brutal. He was much more than he showed the world and that was why she was drawn to him.

When she'd finally had another free moment, he was gone.

The pieces of the ashtray had burned against her side while they'd sat in her pocket last night. Now they lay nestled between her sticky notes and paperclips in her top drawer. She reached in and picked up one of the halves. Its heavy ceramic weight pressed against her palm. The paint was a mixture of blue and green swirls that reminded her of the inside of an old Victorian book cover. The fearless artistry of a little boy. It was painfully beautiful and tears stung behind her eyes knowing how he felt over the rejection. Pulling the tube of permanent glue out of the drawer, she repaired the broken treasure. It was a small gesture, but she needed to help Cole in some small way. Too bad it wasn't as easy to fix Cole's broken pieces.

She didn't understand why he would come to her today. And she didn't understand her own need to help him. But she did know something.

She was the butterfly attracted to his dark light. But she didn't think he would ever crush her into a splattered mess of wings and dust. He was too soft and sensitive on the inside. That's why he hurt so much.

Cole pulled out the scotch from the cabinet. Maybe it'd be better to get drunk than call himself every damned name in the book.

Every decision he made once he got back to Dalewood had turned into a mess. He couldn't get rid of this place so he'd called in Angela. Then he'd treated her to his asshole's best.

She must think him the craziest person. How could he break like that in front of her last night? And then, he'd gone over to her workplace like a stalker with no real reason to be there except to see her in the daylight after his ranting.

He wasn't a kid who needed his father's approval. He'd been on his own for a very long time. She was right. They were all right. He had to stop acting like a damned child.

When Fran had pushed those letters in his face, he'd seen red. To top it all off, she'd loaded him with the guilt trip of a lifetime. He loved Max and would always be grateful for the things he'd been taught. He tried to protect them and he'd failed. His father had still damaged the Greeleys. Over the years, Cole had to helped them and it seemed like Fran and Liza were doing well, now.

He pulled the stopper off the bottle and poured an inch. Before he could drink, his cell phone rang.

"You must come over immediately." Cole pulled the phone from his ear as Fran's voice rang shrill.

"What's the problem?"

"It's Liza."

His heart slammed against his ribs. "Is she hurt?"

"No, but she needs you. Please hurry." The phone went dead.

"What in the hell?" Cole's stomach tightened. Something was wrong. He'd have to hurry to get across town to the Greeleys' home. Scotch sloshed as he slammed the glass onto the table untouched, and ran out of the mansion to his car.

The road was slick with icy rain. The drops spattered on the windshield, obscuring his view faster than the wipers could clear them away. Their rhythm matched his blood as it raced through his veins.

What could have happened? What if she was hurt and Fran didn't want to tell him over the phone?

Could someone have hurt her? He may have been gone for a long time, but he was here now and he was the closest thing she had to a brother. He'd deal with anyone who would ever hurt Max Greeley's daughter.

Cole turned the corner. The back tires slid into a fishtail. Gripping the steering wheel with both fists, he gained control. He was driving too fast, but he didn't care.

Was there a single person who cared if he lived or died now that Max was gone? His father hadn't given a damn about the outcome of his darling little boy.

He swerved around another corner, into the downtown area of Dalewood. The small town he remembered had grown into a downtown district full of small shops and restaurants.

He passed a building with a long bank of windows. He recognized it as Angela's investigation offices. He wondered what she was doing right now.

He drove past Howard street and pressed the gas, speeding out of the district center. He had to get to Liza as quickly as he could. Mrs. Greeley had made it seem dire. He didn't know what he could do to help, but he owed it to this family.

Once past the downtown area, the neighborhood darkened. Without streetlights, everything seemed even blacker in the storm. He flicked on his brights so he could follow the narrowing road that led through the trees. An occasional home broke the monotony of woods. The Greeley mansion was easy to find. It was the last house at the dead end and sat on a small hill above the neighborhood. He pulled along the side drive past the row of cars and parked. He sat, waiting in the shadows as he looked at the golden glowing windows.

As a boy, the house had seemed much bigger and beautiful. Unlike Penniberg, it had white wooden siding and homey shutters painted in a cool green, though the paint was chipping to show the wood beneath. The home still held its glory even as it looked worse for wear. Large windows spread along the front veranda. A shining light beckoned him today in the same way it had when he was a child. He'd missed that warmth. It almost felt like coming home. He'd never felt accepted before he'd met the Greeleys. And he'd never felt that way again since leaving. How could he let himself lose touch? He had to. Once his father had gone after Max's businesses. He'd known what he had to do. He had to distance himself so his father would stop his attacks against the people Cole loved. He'd been trying to protect this family.

Maybe that was what he wanted. A little warmth. He was ready. He had learned to be a loner and he was fine with that. He had to take care of himself. But what would it hurt to let them back into his life? They needed him as much as he needed them.

Cole pulled his collar up to his ears to block the spitting rain and climbed the creaking stairs two at a time. The top step was loose. He pressed his foot into the sagging wood. The house was in disrepair. Maybe the monetary help he had given to Greeley hadn't been enough? Max was gone and couldn't fix it himself, but Cole could still remedy the damage. He'd be back to make some of the repairs. A loose step was easy enough to fix. It would be such a small token of thanks, but it was a place to start.

Once he reached the covered porch, he shook the water from his hair. Before he could knock on the door, it swung open with surprising force.

"Thank you so much for coming." Fran stepped back so Cole could enter the house. It smelled of apple pie and chamomile tea and a warm welcome, like a nice big hug after a hard day. The hard times the Greeleys had been put through couldn't take that kindness away.

"I didn't tell Liza you were coming." She led him through the hall toward the parlor. The carpet was worn, but still maintained. Nothing had changed since he'd been there years ago. It comforted him at the same time he felt annoyed. They had been unable to make updates because of his father.

"What's going on, Mrs. Greeley? I want to help, but I don't want to cause a bigger problem."

"Don't be silly. You have to cheer her up."

How was he going to cheer anybody up? He was the most miserable person right now, making it impossible to be a source of joy for Liza.

"She's sitting by the window. Only you can make my daughter happy right now," Fran said enthusiastically. Her face became overly bright which made his suspicions rear their ugly faces.

He turned the corner into the parlor and saw Liza's pale hair cascading down her back. She sat at the window seat watching the storm. The aged, faint yellow curtains still seemed homey. The interior of the house was not disheveled, just well-loved.

A flash of lightning played along Liza's profile and he could see she'd been crying. The big tears crystallized along the rim of her lower lid before slipping free to trail along her cheek. Her throat worked with each swallow.

Feet planted to the ground, all he could do was stand and watch her ethereal beauty. He hated when women cried. It made him feel inadequate and unsteady. How would he handle this? His stomach tightened with uncertainty. Where to start to console her?

He must have made a sound or a movement, because she twisted from her view of the storm as it blasted the gardens.

Unshed tears amplified her crystal eyes, making them seem almost clear. Bringing up a wad of tissue, she blotted at the moisture on her cheeks. She was painfully beautiful in her sadness.

"Liza." He didn't know what to say. He didn't even know what was wrong. He took a step toward her.

"I'm sorry. Did my mother call you?" Her voice held the moisture of her tears. She held her hand out to him.

"She said you were upset and needed cheering up." He shrugged, trying for a comforting smile. He was sure he'd failed.

"Ever since I saw you again, I haven't been able to stop crying."

"I'm sorry. Maybe I shouldn't have come." He took a step back and her hand slipped into her lap.

"Don't misunderstand me." She stood from the couch, raising her hand again, to stop him. "Please." Then she reached for him.

"I don't want to hurt you and your family, Liza. Your father was too important to me. You and Fran are too important to me." Her hand gently gripped his arm, making him think of how Angela had held his arm in the woods. How could their touch feel different to him? Angela's had gone right through his skin to where he could feel it in his bones. Liza's touch was soft and imploring, but didn't affect him in the same way.

"I think that's why I can't get control of my emotions." Her smile trembled, but her tears seemed to have stopped.

"Your mother wanted me to cheer you up, but I'm obviously causing more pain."

"Sit with me, Cole?" Liza sat on the couch, then patted the cushion next to her.

Unable to refuse the pain in her eyes, he couldn't say no. He sat.

"When we saw you, it brought back so many old memories."

"I know."

"I've been thinking about my father a lot since your return."

"I hold my memories of your father dear to my heart."

"We struggled so much after you left, Cole. My parents tried to keep it from me, but how wouldn't I know. My father barely held onto the business he loved. And the house has suffered, but at least we're still here. It took many years, but my father was starting to turn the corner on our finances. I think it was the stress of it all that caused his early loss. I miss him."

"I miss him too." Cole touched her shoulder and she crumpled into him. He wrapped his arms around her and pulled her into his chest while she cried. He patted her back to comfort her. He held her for what seemed like eons and eternity, not knowing what to say or do. He tried to think what Angela would say. She was so good with people.

"Do you remember when I was a small girl?" She hiccupped into his chest and then pulled back to look up at him.

"That was a long time ago." Her skin was

smooth and unblemished by even a single freckle. Unlike Angela who had that one freckle at the corner of her mouth. Liza's dark lashes fringed her eyes, making the blue seem even sharper. Cole couldn't remember Angela's lashes because her eyes were like pools of gold solace that he floated inside every time he looked at them. Next time he saw Angela, he would be sure to look more closely at her lashes.

"I remember." Liza continued, drawing him back to the past they shared. "I fell off my bike and you scooped me up."

He remembered, but he wasn't sure where she was going with the memory. He'd been frightened. He thought he'd be blamed for her injury.

"I hurt my knee," she continued. "You held me tight while you carried me all the way home. You were strong even then."

"I had to help you."

"I knew you were afraid that your father would blame you, make it as if you hurt me."

"He didn't like me hanging around your family."

She leaned into his side. "My father knew your character. He knew the difficulties your father faced. How he became suspicious of everyone and decided to hurt others before they could hurt him. You got caught in that. My father tried to help you as much as he could. He dreamed that we would someday be together."

"Liza don't."

"It was his wish." She leaned deeper into him, tilting her face closer to him until her lips pressed against his. At first, they were soft, bare flutters and then they became more demanding.

Maybe this was how it should be. He should do what was right, what his mentor wished. He would do anything for Max. Could he love his daughter? He should try. He owed Max.

Cole shifted his hand to the small of Liza's back, and turned so he could deepen the kiss. Liza's hands delicately pressed into his shoulders. There was intimacy, but no passion. That rising need he'd felt with Angela would not appear with Liza. He could get used to the intimacy of the touch, but something wasn't right.

Golden, fiery eyes flashed behind his lids. He blinked their image away. He needed to do what was right for once in his life. He deepened the kiss. Liza gasped in his mouth and her fingers tightened their grip. Cole was determined to make this work. He pressed deeper, but no matter how he tried to block her from his mind, Angela was there, haunting him like every ghost she claimed to see.

Somehow, she had possessed his every thought. He had compared Liza to her at every turn. Instead of kissing Liza, he'd been thinking of Angela's cool touch. It was her hand sliding around his neck and tangling through his hair. It was her breath against his lips. It was Angela's body pressed against his, instead of the pretty woman he'd known since childhood.

Wrong, it was all wrong. It felt dirty to kiss Liza while he was thinking of someone else. He couldn't take advantage of her while she was vulnerable. He couldn't kiss one woman while his mind was imagining another. His stomach clenched. Why had he come back to Dalewood at all? He gripped Liza's shoulders and gently pushed her back.

Liza's chest rose and fell with her heavy breath. Those tears brimmed, ready to spill again. "Why?"

"This isn't right," he growled between breaths.

"It is right. This is what my father wanted."

"You aren't thinking straight."

"You're the one who isn't thinking clearly. My father wanted us to be together. It was his wish."

"Is it your wish?"

"It doesn't matter what I want." She looked away and swiped angrily at her cheek. Was she mad at him? He had a suspicion there was more she wouldn't say. More about what she really wanted. And his guts told him that she didn't want him. Her kiss had been stringent, clean. There hadn't been any passion on her side either.

Cole shook his head.

"You would deny my father his last wish?" Her breaths came in tiny gasps.

"But is it your wish?"

"Don't ask me that." She jumped from the couch and paced in front of him, hugging herself. "I am more damaged than your father ever knew."

"I thought you loved him." She hissed, grabbing his hands.

"I'm no good for anyone. Not now, not ever." He broke free of her hold and charged for the door.

"Cole wait."

He couldn't stop. He rushed from the parlor and past Fran, who had been eavesdropping at the doorway.

Without looking back, he got in the Camaro and skidded away from the house. Wheels spun on the gravel drive as he sprayed mud and debris in an arc. He couldn't get away fast enough. The weight of expectations crushed in on him. Expectations that were all wrong. He had come back to Dalewood to make things right, but not like this.

Blindly, he drove. Rain smattered on the windshield and bulleted the rooftop. He wished the sound would drown out his pounding heart and stop the anger that grew in his guts like a monster. That was his father's gift to him.

He didn't want Liza. She was beautiful, everything a normal man would dream of. He wasn't normal. He was no good for any woman. He had to stop the feelings he was developing for Angela He couldn't let himself dream. Haunted men weren't allowed to dream.

The road was slick and he didn't care. He wanted to outrace the awful experience he'd just faced. He sped, taking the corner without hitting the breaks. The force shifted him in the seat, but he wouldn't slow.

Instead, he hit the gas. He refused to let the past force him to make choices. It was wrong. He didn't love Liza and she didn't love him. How could she? No one would be able to love him and he'd never be able to make himself vulnerable enough to love another.

What Max wanted was unattainable. He was never going to marry. Not even for the sake of the man he loved more than his own father. At one time, he thought he'd do anything for Max Greeley, but he would never hurt his daughter. He could not be forced by guilt.

The speedometer inched higher as his foot pressed the pedal, shifting the gears faster down the meandering road toward Penniberg. The bridge appeared up ahead. The dark expanse of the river glistened.

Cole pressed the accelerator all the way to the floor. Faster. He needed to get away faster. Away from it all. The Camaro bumped over the edge of the bridge and hit a wet patch of loose stone. Cole gripped the steering wheel tighter. The car swerved. The momentum and the speed caused a tailspin. Cole pulled his foot off the pedal and tried to brake, sending the car into an uncontrollable spiral. Time seemed to slow as he watched the forest rotate in a smear of moon-whitened tree trunks with beige and green pines.

The metal barrier came closer, closer, growing larger and larger with each second of his beating heart.

Holy shit, he was going to die.

The thought was clear in his brain. Was this it? This was how his pathetic life was going to end? Just like the mother he never knew. The screeching of his tires ground through his body. Was this the last sound she'd ever heard? It would be the last sound he would hear.

The steel barrier was right in front of him now. And in the last seconds before he hit it, a set of smiling golden eyes filled his head and he realized he did not want to die. The thought of losing out on something tender and beautiful with Angela was worse than anything he had ever endured in his life. He wanted to try to be a better person for her.

With one last pull against the wheel, he used all the strength he possessed.

The front bumper shifted and metal tore at metal as the car skimmed the edge of the barrier. The Camaro slowed until it jolted to a complete stop. Cole was thrown back against the seat. He leaned his head against the headrest and dragged in a few ragged breaths.

Once his heart rate cooled a little, he stepped from the car. The rain fell in sheets, drenching him through to his skin. Streams ran down his face and along his neck. He brushed the water from his eyes as his T-shirt plastered against his chest.

That had been the closest he'd been to death. But this was all his own doing. He didn't want to die, not this way. The realization amazed him. He wanted to live and it had nothing to do with his anger or need for revenge. It had everything to do with Angela. She had saved him at the last minute. She was the person he'd thought of. His old life hadn't flashed before his eyes. She had been his last thought when he thought it was over.

He leaned over the railing, his weight causing the metal to creak. The river raged as the rainwater poured from the hill in fast waterfalls, streaming with dirt and clumps of grass.

He should be down there too. Twisted metal and torn flesh burned by flames flashed before him. The image was sudden but clear. He might have thought the debris was down at the bottom of the ravine. But it wasn't his mangled body that he saw. A woman, first with long blonde hair, then short dark hair. He rubbed his fingers against his eyes to get rid of the horrifying picture. But as his eyes closed all he could see was the dark bobbed hair of a beautiful young girl of about eighteen or so. Her face was creamy and beautifully pale in her death. His throat burned and he couldn't swallow.

Just as fast as it flashed, the image faded like pebbles dropped in a smooth pond. A chill rippled up Cole's spine. Who was that girl? The only other person he knew to have died here was his mother. That girl in his thoughts was not his mother.

He inched away from the edge and backed up to press against the solid form of the car. The back of his legs pressed into the supporting surface of the bumper. He took a deep stuttering breath, then turned his back on the river and the past.

The scrapes on his car were a blend of black and silver streaks reflected in the rain and moonlight. He traced the scratches with shaking fingers.

What the hell had he been thinking? He hadn't been thinking. He slid back into the car and continued down the path to Penniberg, now that the rain had stopped. He was drenched and too drained to think. His muscles were weak from tension and strain. All he wanted was sleep.

The mansion grew ahead of him, a large hulking maw of despair. A shroud of lingering rain clouds floated around the large moon as it hung in the air over the roof and treetops, illuminating everything in a gossamer carpet, casting a spell of white light.

It was fit for the legends of fairies and angels. If he watched long enough he thought he might actually see their cellophane wings in the light. He expected the ghostly film of a white clad woman to float along the grasses and through the hedges.

A shiver pricked at the back of his neck. He was starting to believe the grounds were haunted like Angela claimed.

It was eerie to be back here alone in the night. Ghosts or not, he hadn't had the best childhood here and it would be better to destroy it along with the bad memories it held.

He pulled the car into the drive and got out. He stood before the mansion and felt his anger rise in him like a flowing geyser, hot and explosive.

"Why did you hate me, Dad?" Cole clenched his fists at his sides. His jaw tightened in anger. "How could you hate your own son?" His voice rose to a shout over the blustering winds that dragged at his hair and made his jacket flap around him.

The wind bent the trees like claws grasping at

the mansion.

"You don't control me anymore!" The blustering storm swallowed his scream. The sky opened again and the rain poured, pelting his skin.

He spilled his soul into the storm, shouting and releasing all the anger he'd held trapped deep inside for all these years. When he was finished, he fell against the car, hollow and empty. It was better that way. He needed to finish what he'd started. It was time to complete what he'd come here for. Time to end one thing so he could start something new, something good.

CHAPTER 15

IF YOU CAN'T get something done right, then you did it yourself. Cole had tossed and turned all night trying to figure out what to do about this albatross of a mansion. Dear old dad hadn't raised a weakling. Once the earliest peek of dawn broke the sky, he was out of bed, ready to take action.

All the things Hank refused to teach him, he'd learned from Max, including how to maneuver the forklift, the gravel trucks and the bulldozer. He learned to wield a hammer and build a few steps too. He planned to go to Fran Greeley's later to fix her porch. But first, he had a mansion to destroy. Cole turned the key in the ignition. The diesel engine coughed and sputtered and the bulldozer reverberated to life. The machine vibrated powerfully beneath him. It was like riding a bike—you never forgot how to do it.

He worked the gears and jerked forward. Holding his destiny in his hands, the towering mansion didn't seem menacing. If he could begin the destruction, then the guys would get over their fear and take over the rest of the job.

A gusty laugh escaped. This was freedom. He should have done this from the beginning.

When he'd stormed into Ted's office earlier this morning, everyone had been stunned when Cole wanted to know the running rate to rent a bulldozer for a few days. "What do you want that for?" Ted had asked. What did Ted think he wanted it for? He was tired of waiting and all the talk of ghosts was driving him crazy. He was finished rehashing the memories of the past. He'd come back to Dalewood to get rid of this place. Cole had been very patient, but he couldn't wait a moment longer. "Say good-bye, Penniberg. You've seen better days." Cole revved the engine and jerked the large basket toward the bank of windows. He needed to hear the crack of the windows and the splinter of wood under the crushing force of the machine.

Before he could shatter even one pane of glass, a man leaped in front of the bushes, waving and flapping his arms like an erratic bird.

"Holy hell." Cole slammed the emergency button that immediately stalled the engine. "What the hell is wrong with you? Are you some kind of damned lunatic?" Cole was already swinging down from the cab. He jumped onto the grass and plowed toward the idiot. "I could have killed you."

"Mr. Barlow?" the man asked.

Besides his twittering mannerism, he also had bird-like features—a sharp nose, beady black eyes and a high-pitched nasally voice. His greased hair was combed back in a neat part, but one piece stuck out in a feather-like cowlick.

"You're Cole Barlow, right?"

"Does everyone have a death wish around here? Do you know how close I came to killing you?"

"I'm glad I stopped you. You almost broke the law, sir. Kind of, well, anyway."

"What are you talking about? You're trespassing on my property." Cole stared down at the scarecrow skinny man, who was barely as tall as Angela. He used his darkest glower since he had an immediate dislike for the guy. What type of moron threw himself in front of a moving bulldozer?

"Actually, I'm not trespassing."

"You have three seconds to explain what this is about. After that, I'm going to throw you off my property." Frustration rankled against his every nerve. Everyone in this town seemed to conspire against him. "I was a little busy before you popped in." He might have to resort to throwing rocks at the windows and letting vandals handle the rest to even have a chance at getting rid of the mansion.

"I heard you were in the hardware store today, buying materials to fix things, wood, hammer, nails. Imagine my shock as I see you about to cause damage. Fixing the place up is problem enough, but damaging it is preposterous. Mr. Barlow, you cannot tear down this building."

"And why not?" Squaring his shoulders, he stared menacingly. All he wanted to do was get a move-on and start things anew. The only way he could see that happening was with the destruction of Penniberg. Why was everything difficult? He wanted to sigh. Better yet, he could use a drink.

"Your father signed a contract with the historical society. You cannot make any drastic changes to the exterior of this building."

"What?" That was news to him. Nowhere in the wills and property papers was there any hint of historical site proceedings. "This is the first I'm hearing about any of this. Who are you?"

"I'm Pierce Foster, President of the Dalewood Historical Society, elected by the people of this town."

"I own this mansion, now. Anything my father planned is no longer valid. I have all the legal documents that show I own this place. Nowhere was there a mention of my father signing anything about turning Penniberg into a historical site."

"Actually, sir, that's not the case. Hank and the historical society were in the process of finalizing the paperwork prior to his death. The board was unable to approve the final requests until after your father departed. But we still plan to move forward. We are starting the process of turning the Penniberg mansion into a historical site, protected by the people of Dalewood."

"He started the process?" Cole closed his eyes, hoping he'd wake from this nightmare. When he opened them, Pierce was still there with his curlicue bobbing behind his head like a peacock feather.

Pierce thrust a paper in his face. "This explains

all, Mr. Barlow. You'll refrain from any further damage to this mansion, or repairs for that matter."

"The repairs weren't for this place, they were for the Greeleys," he said absently as he looked at the official historical society letter head.

"The Penniberg mansion is an important site to the people of Dalewood, as the original town founder's home."

Cole grabbed the paper from Pierce's hands and growled, "We'll see about this. Now get off my land before I call the police."

Pierce scuttled away.

What else could go wrong? Every single one of his plans has been thwarted and now this new revelation. Just great. He'd call his friend in Chicago who dealt with records, documentation and permits to check on the validity of the historical paperwork documentation. If his father had started the proceedings, but hadn't finished them, they had to be meaningless. But he wanted to check first.

Now he had a rented bulldozer that was going to sit idle. Oh well. He would just head over to the Greeleys to fix their step. The painters would be there in a few hours to repaint the outside siding and shutters. It wouldn't hurt to get the steps fixed right away.

CHAPTER 16

ANGELA'S SHOES CLICKED on the cement pathway that led through the Penniberg gardens toward the remains of the aviary. Its white arches and metal bands surrounded thick panes of glass. It had once held hundreds of birds. Marjorie Dalloway, Brooke's mother, would hold tea in the aviary, surrounded by her collection of exotic birds and rare plants. Angela had seen one of the garden party photos in an archived newspaper article.

She loved the curving structure and wished she could have walked through it in all its glory during the nineteen twenties.

Tingling set her nerve endings on edge the moment she touched the door. Pushing it open, she entered. Stale air hit her. Old cages in a variety of sizes lined the walls on all sides. It was strange that Cole's father hadn't fixed up this building. Angela would have to ask Cole about that later. She touched the cage closest to the door, and ran her hand over the smooth enameled wire.

The atmosphere became heavy and the thick warmth swirled around her. The air seemed to sprinkle over her skin like little shards of glass.

"Harry, please."

The voice sounded in Angela's ear. She spun around to see who had spoken. No one was there. She was alone, but the cages weren't empty anymore. Everything was clean and freshly painted white. The humid air filled her with the musky scent of mulch and bird feed. Squawking birdcalls pierced the room. The thick air shimmered before her and two ghostly bodies appeared.

"Papa wants to send me to New York." The female voice rose with a shrillness matching the increasing crescendo of bird cries.

It was Brooke. Her form appeared. She wore a pink jacket cinched tightly at the waist with a matching thick belt and a large black buckle. Black hair framed her face in a disheveled mess of curls. Her cheeks flushed to a deep color of agitation, while the rest of her skin was deathly pale. The girl ghost wanted her to see the past, to understand something.

"What can I do to make you stay, my love?" A second voice, lower, masculine, but still tinny came from further away, making it difficult to hear. Angela sensed the words more than actually heard them at first.

"Tell my father how much you love me. Tell him how you plan to marry me." Brooke fell on her knees, imploring, grasping for his hands, her black shoes kicked out behind her almost prostrate.

Fuzzy and unclear, the ghostly image of the couple had the appearance of being projected on a gossamer cloth, waving and fading in and out of view, though the words were clearer, easier to hear. Angela could see the birds hopping from their perches through the couple.

"I already tried that and he refused." His jaw tightened and his face became hard. "He reneged on the promotion." Brooke's head fell lower, pressing against the backs of her hands as she grasped him.

Closing her eyes for a moment, Angela let the sounds and emotions surround her, fill her. She needed to feel Brooke, wanted to connect with her. She had to know what Brooke was thinking and why she was trapped here, haunting the mansion.

She stepped closer to the ghost couple and reached out. Surprise filled her as her hand came into contact with the cool shoulder. Tingling sensations traveled from the ghost arm into Angela's fingers and spread through her hand. The slight touch was enough.

Tears flowed down Angela's cheek as she felt Brooke's sadness. Rubbery legs barely held her up while her arms hung heavily at her sides as if she'd done a hundred push-ups. She didn't have the drive or energy to move them, so she sunk deeper into the emotions Brooke sent her.

Angela looked down and her jeans were gone, replaced by a pink silken coat. When she looked up, she stared into eyes that swirled like melted steel, dark and tormented.

Instead of looking at the ghosts, her perspective had shifted, no longer watching the scene, she had become part of the scene. Her hands gripped Harry's icy fingers. Her body sprawled on the cold white tile, stinging her knees.

Close to Brooke, she should know her every thought and feeling. But still she kept some secrets hidden, blocking Angela from understanding her reasons, her motivations.

Irritation rippled through Angela even as she reminded herself that this was the closest Brooke had ever gotten, finally letting her in, possessing her so she could see and feel the past. The ghost was letting Angela see another piece of the puzzle, but not the entire picture.

Without warning, a sense of overwhelming terror, mingled with sadness gripped Angela's insides and made her feel as if nothing would be right ever again. The emotions settled into a place below her heart as if Brooke could contain her panic in a secret little box. Resolve burned and bottled in her throat to block the pain.

Lifting her chin a little higher, Brooke's words came again, rattling through her instead of coming from her.

"Maybe it is better this way. I'd grow bored of you anyway. Maybe Father knew that." Angela spoke, but they were Brooke's words and actions. Pain flickered over Harry's face, crinkling the corners of his eyes in a bare, fleeting moment, before his face hardened, emotionless.

"You told me you loved me." Harry's face loomed before her, floating like an angry gray storm cloud. His grip fisted painfully around her fingers.

"Just leave." Brooke tore her hands away and turned from Harry, facing the caged birds as they squalled and screeched the inner torment she refused to release.

She raised her hands toward the thin metal bars. With the caress that she'd saved for the one man she loved, she slipped her fingers over the latch. Moving swiftly, she unlocked the cage and opened the door wide. The African Grey parrot bobbed to the back edge of the cage, shocked to silence. Black eyes reflected its fear and uncertainty.

She knew what she had to do and reached in, releasing the bird from its captivity. Wings flapping, the Grey thrust toward the ceiling and landed on the edge of the open window. Nodding its head in a few quick movements, it took one look back at its former prison, then gave a decisive flick of its red tail before jumping through the window into the air of freedom.

Brooke stood still and watched the empty window for a moment as if she too wanted to escape. Then she moved to the next cage and followed the same steps, gripping the white painted bars in a fist before releasing the Blue and Gold macaw. She watched as it flew up to the opening like a flash of rising sun against an azure sky, then disappeared out the window following the Grey.

Methodically, she opened cage after cage, freeing each animal. The surprised birds cried out as they flew around the glass domed building. Feathers fluttered to the floor before her feet. Raising her gaze, she looked at Harry. The words stuck in her throat for a moment before she pushed them out.

"You're free, Harry. You should go and never return. It's over." Tears stung her eyes, burned at her throat, but she refused their release. "We're over."

"Don't do this to us." With a swift, rough grab at her wrist, he pulled her to him.

Her chest pressed into his and she could feel the strength in his thin form. She wanted to melt into him, but knew she never could.

"Harry, I don't love you. I've never loved you." She willed her gaze to fill with anger. There was no hope if her father wouldn't allow it.

"I don't believe you." He shook his head. "You promised we'd always be together." Birds squalled and fluttered in a frenzy of wings around them as they flew to their escape. "Don't you remember saying those words as I held you naked in my arms?"

She gasped as his words hit harder than a slap. She needed to hurt him so he would leave. "We had a little fun, Harry, that's all."

"It wasn't that way for me." He raised a hand to her cheek.

"You little fool, how could you think otherwise?" The lies bit like a viperous snake at the back of her throat. She pressed a hand to her churning belly, willing it to still. "You could never give me all I desire, now that Daddy refused you."

Anger flashed mercurially in his dark gray eyes. "It can't be too late."

"It's already too late. I'm leaving for New

York. Daddy mentioned his plans this morning." The lies flowed easily now. She could keep her secret. No one would know, especially not Harry. "Leave, Harry. It'll be easier for you. Make it easy on both of us."

"Was I really nothing to you? I don't believe it."

"Did you think you could use me for father's fortune?" She couldn't control the words that spilled from her mouth. Hurting him now was the only way to spare him further pain.

His face crumpled in anguish, all pretense vanished. He brushed his fingertips against her cheek in one last gesture. "I love you and you know it has nothing to do with money. You damage me greatly with this talk."

"We're too young to know what love is, Harry," she said his name with disdain.

"Is that what your father told you to say?" He spread his arms out palms raised. "Give all this up and come with me. We'll make our own way."

"Aren't you excited for me, Harry? You should be. New York will be an adventure. I will have a grand spree there that only my father could manage. You could never do that for us." Her voice cracked, but she tried to cover it with laughter. Her misery overwhelmed her because their plight could not be remedied. Pretty to think they could at only eighteen and twenty with no prospects ahead of them, without her father's help.

Harry took an imploring step closer. His fingers twitched but he didn't raise them. Her stomach fluttered with wonder as a small bean of hope sprouted from his sweet words. About to throw herself into his arms and beg his forgiveness, she froze. He must have believed her harsh words. His shoulders stiffened and his fists clenched at his sides.

"You'll be back, Brooke, and you'll be sorry because I might not be waiting here when you return." He gave her one last glance, swiped his hat from the floor then turned and pushed out of the aviary. A white feather fell from his hat in a slow, back and forth flutter to the floor. The glass door slammed in a clatter of finality.

She watched him stride down the path through the wavering glass, slipping farther and farther away and out of Brooke's life forever.

A sob tore through Angela, ripping from her throat like shards of glass. All of Brooke's devastation and fear and regret sliced through her, causing more agony than any sword.

Deep shudders wracked her body as her guts poured from her. She buried her head in her hands and wept. But still she held secrets.

The time to reveal the past had come and Angela's abilities gave the ghost a way to reveal the old tragedy. Only then could Brooke move on from her painful decisions, to the other side.

Angela barely felt the hand on her shoulder as she came back to the present.

"Angela, are you okay?" The voice was gruff and filled with uncertainty.

She spun to see Cole touching her, tall and strong. She thought she'd wanted to be alone until he was there, a solid rock for her to find balance.

Angela swiped the tears from her face. Her body tingled with ghostly remnants, her hands moved with lead.

"What's the matter? Who hurt you?" The words, a roar that came from deep in him.

"Her ghost is everywhere. She torments me."

"Tell me what's going on. What's happened? My father..." his words caught in his throat. His hands gripped her shoulders like she was spun glass, turning her to look at him. "...did he... hurt you?" He said the words in disbelief, though he was saying them.

"No, not your father. He avoids me. It's another. She has secrets. She lets me know her pain, but she won't tell me the deepest secret." From the raw emotions and then from her tears, she couldn't catch her breath. "I'm feeling light-headed."

"Please, sit down." He led her to a white chipped wrought iron bench and sat next to her, rubbing her shoulder, taking up most of the seat.

"She refuses to come right out and tell me her secret. Something holds her back." She pulled in a quick breath as reason dawned. "Maybe she can't tell me."

"You have to slow down. I'm not following this conversation. A different ghost? A woman?"

"She's connecting with me. Just leave me. I need to stay. I need to try again."

"I can't leave you here alone. Not like this." Cole's brow creased as he tried to understand what she said. "You need a break," he demanded.

"It's okay." The images of the day flashed through her mind. "I'm missing something. She was close, too close for me to leave now."

"You're in no condition to continue out here by yourself. If you could see what I see, you'd know it was time to quit. You're too pale. You have beads of sweat on your forehead and your hands are shaking." He took one hand and rubbed it between his, bringing back the warmth with friction. Then he warmed the other hand in the same way.

She yanked her arm from his grasp. "I'm staying."

"You look like a wild creature. Your eyes are bloodshot and your face is streaked with tears. And your hair…" He reached for her, smoothing the loose strands.

"You don't look so great yourself. You're dirty and sweaty." Angela needed to shake off the icicle shards from the ghosts. They still shimmered through her bloodstream. "She's trying to tell me something. When she feels comfortable, she'll share more."

"You look pale." His petting hand stilled at the back of her neck in a warm comforting touch. His face filled with something that she couldn't interpret. If she knew better, she would read it as wanting to say something that he was too afraid to ask. Cole was anything but afraid, it had to be something else.

"This happens to me when I connect strongly with a ghost."

A puzzled frown pulled his eyebrows closer. "This ghost, this woman ghost, was she…" He turned away just as she noticed his cheeks turning pink under his tanned skin.

"The ghost I have been connecting with is a young girl from the nineteen twenties. I am almost certain, in fact I'm certain, she's Brooke Dalloway, the daughter of the original owner of this mansion, the family who owned it before your father."

"I know the history." Disappointment poured from him as he turned back to her. "How are you certain that was her and not somebody else? Do you speak to the ghost and they simply tell you?" His tone held a slight harshness that seemed to come out of nowhere. She didn't understand.

"It's a little more complicated than that."

"Complicated, this whole business is complicated. You see ghosts, long dead ghosts. My father's ghost haunts me. Why? Do you see every ghost that exists? There've been others who have died here. I'm supposed to believe that these are the only people that seek you out? The two ghosts that have clear histories in this town. You did your research."

"You'll never understand." His words slapped her. Just when she thought he was moving forward, he built his defenses.

"Maybe I won't." He turned to face forward, completely shutting her out, resting his elbows against his knees and dropping his head.

She looked at him, so big and so guarded. Her throat worked at the words she couldn't speak. Could she handle disdain? She knew he didn't believe her and that he had no trust in her abilities. She'd worked hard to get to a place where she didn't care what anyone thought about her. Why did she care what he thought? She wanted him to believe in her and trust in her. For all his bluster and brooding, she saw a sensitive man under all his scars. He cared with great passion for those he loved, protected them with everything. She'd seen that love he had for Fran. He was a good person deep down and she wanted to see that person all the time. Wanted to be free from his anger and pain that his father had caused him. She was more determined than ever to resolve the issues he had with his father.

"It's not simply speaking to the ghost. What I experience can be described as possession," she said quietly. She felt compelled to explain herself, to get him to understand. Understanding was closer to believing in her, right?

"Like in *The Exorcist?*"

She pushed down her irritation at his disdain. "No. I possess the ghost. Sort of. I don't know. I can feel their emotions. I know their feelings."

"And they tell you their secrets?"

"Only when they are ready. That's how I help them move on."

"It seems a little farfetched."

"Really? Because a minute ago you thought it possible that your father hurt me." Her comment caused him to pause for just a beat, then he smoothed his features.

"You need to understand where I'm coming from. I can't just believe in ghosts because you say they exist."

She lifted her head and their eyes held. His cool

steel against her fire. "You need to understand where I'm coming from."

"I want to."

He slipped his hand to her arm and they were close to each other now. Her ice-cold skin warmed under his touch. She lifted her chin a little higher. Instead, the movement brought her lips toward his. Even now, with all his annoying words, she still wanted his kiss. Her body absorbed every bit of heat he had to offer, languishing in it.

"I want to believe you, Angela." His breath, a warm whisper against her skin. He leaned closer until the barest space separated their lips.

"Then just believe me. Trust me." She closed her eyes, waiting for his acceptance. Betraying her mind and heart, she leaned toward him, wanting to claim a part of him that she wasn't sure existed. She longed for more.

"I'm just unsure." He pressed his forehead against hers. "It's just too weird. How could I believe something so crazy?" His words poured over her, icier than any autumn rain. The words reminded her of everything she'd heard as a kid in the playground. She was too weird. No one could ever believe a crazy person. He was no different. Could never be any different. The rage she'd been holding down flowed through her like Brooke's emotions, more violent than the rushing Steele. With a quick and sudden movement, she shoved him squarely on his chest with all she had.

"What the—" The push set him off balance and he slipped against the metal arm rail of the bench.

She would have laughed at his shocked face if she wasn't so angry. "I'm sick of constantly needing to prove myself." She stood up to look down at him and placed her hands on her hips. "I'm done. Do you hear me? Done." She pointed a finger right at his chest. "I've dealt with this my entire life, and you"—she jabbed at him—" you will not make me feel ashamed all over again."

With that, she spun and ran down the path, scarcely paying attention to where she was going. He called after her, but her eyes filled with tears and she wouldn't look back.

The path meandered around the house and still she ran. With a quick glance, she looked at the bay of windows. A figure stood in the window, watching. Then it was gone just as fast. She was too upset to care and continued down stone steps before entering the woods surrounding the grounds.

A small clearing opened and she could see the river just beyond. Two marble benches, shaded by an ancient weeping willow, sat on the bank.

She slumped down on one of the benches and let the tears flow. Her breaths came in ragged gulps. She had to get a hold of herself. It had been too much. The emotional connection with Brooke and then the argument with Cole had topped it off.

CHAPTER 17

SHOULD HE STAY here or go after her? Cole was in his right mind to let her cool off, but she'd been so upset that he couldn't. He followed her down the walkway.

What had she expected? She spoke of ghosts as if everyone could see them. He only saw the real world, the things that were right in your face. Things you could feel and touch. He wanted to believe her, but then she spoke of an old ghost of some long dead girl. A girl from the famous Dalloway family was pretty convenient, especially since he knew she went to the library to do research. Anyone could find that information. Why wasn't she connecting with the one ghost he would be curious about, one that he'd want to talk to?

He froze dead in his tracks. He didn't want to connect with ghosts. The thought was absurd. But there it was, bared wide open for him to see the gaping hole. He could care less if he ever saw his father again. What smarted the most was how he'd been easily abandoned by his own mother. If Angela connected with his mother, maybe he could understand a little better, maybe then he could release his resentment. Maybe he could actually believe in Angela.

Why was he chasing after her then?

Stupid, he knew. How ridiculous that he was starting to think ghosts existed. He was a fool.

His instincts told him to follow the path that led to the river. When he came out near the clearing, he almost didn't see her in the shadows created by the aging willow. She sat looking down at the water with her profile angled toward him. She was even prettier in the fading light that dappled along her soft skin. A sad angel, she looked like one of her namesakes. Absently tearing at a leaf, she dropped the pieces at her feet.

He had the sudden urge to haul her up into his arms and kiss every sad thought from her mind, tell her what she wanted to hear.

Those painful angles were etched on her face because of him. He and everyone else who had given her a hard time over the years made her feel that way. But he wouldn't lie to her. He took a step toward her, snapping a twig under his foot.

She tossed the bare stem to the ground. It fell in the center of the leaf confetti that was anything but cheerful.

"Let's get everything cleared up," she said as she looked at him, then looked back to the river that raged. A shaft of sun filtered through the tree, highlighting her hair into a golden halo. He wanted to reach out and touch it. To let the gold pour into the darkest parts of him to eliminate all his lonely places.

The medallion burned hot against his chest, reminding him of every reason he'd hired her. She was here for one purpose. She needed to make everyone believe the house was safe enough to reenter so they would destroy it.

"You hired me for a reason. And that's what I'm here to do. You clearly don't believe in my abilities and that's fine. Not everyone sees what I see. You didn't sign a contract declaring your belief in my abilities and that's fine." The sound of the river gurgled in complaint.

She ripped another leaf with bits of red and orange, from a low hanging tree branch, then stood and started pacing. "I should be used to this. I am used to this." She took a step back, moving farther from him and closer to the water's edge. "This is not new to me, you know. It's par for the course." She took another step back and her shoulder flinched back a little as if something unseen had pushed her. Before he could get to her, she stumbled. Her arms windmilled as she grabbed for the trunk of the tree, and catching only air, with a squeak, she toppled backward, feet flying up.

"Angela!" Cole lunged for her, but his reach missed by bare inches. Her smooth skin slid past his fingers and she fell into the river with a cannonball splash.

She dipped below the swift current. The beat of his heart froze solid in his chest. She popped up, sputtering, arms flailing, water droplets flying in all directions. Her hair plastered dark gold against her forehead. She jutted her arms in the water as she tried to paddle her way through the strong current while she drifted a short way with the river. She called for help, then she slipped under the water again.

"Angela?" he called again, but she didn't reply. His heart hammered a painful rattle in his chest as he came back to life.

With a swift jerk, he pulled his black sweatshirt and t-shirt over his head and tossed them to the ground. Cool air bit at his exposed skin and he welcomed it. He jumped into the river. The icy water pulled the breath from him. The current dragged at his arms and legs. He swam to catch her.

Her head surfaced and she coughed, the most beautiful sight he'd ever seen. He blinked the water from his eyes, and gave thanks she was alive. She hadn't traveled very far. His only thought was to get to her. Water rushed all around him and the sound roared through his ears.

"Cole," Angela called before she slipped under again.

He thrust through the water, back toward the river's edge, trying to get to her. Then she resurfaced with flailing arms. She grasped the thin branches of a tag alder. The branch broke and she slipped again.

"Grab onto the thicker branches of that log," he called. He wasn't sure if she heard him over the current. She grimaced but grabbed hold of the log in a strong hug. The rushing water propelled him toward her. He reached out to Angela. "Take my hand."

"I'll try." She balanced herself along the length of the log and reached to him.

As Cole reached out toward her, a branch scratched his neck, then looped around the chain holding the medallion. The chain stretched taut then, with a snap, it slipped from Cole's neck to drift into the water.

Cole lunged for it without thinking. The log groaned and shifted. The chain slipped farther into the water's darkness.

Angela's scream pulled him back to the present. She held the log in a death grip to stop herself from slipping into the river. Cole, abandoned the chain, clasped his hand around her upper arm. He pulled her into his chest. Her scent mixed with the water, so sweet, so fresh. Alive. He pressed his face into the crook of her neck and breathed deeply, closing his eyes.

The medallion was gone and he didn't care. He held Angela close to him. She was safe in his arms. He squeezed her more tightly to him.

"Let's get out of this water." He pushed them toward the bank. "Can you pull yourself out?"

"I'll try." Her voice wavered as she shivered against the cold and her adrenaline.

She pulled herself up. Angela's behind shifted as she dug her toes into the soft earth and her butt wiggled as she pulled herself out of the water. She was sexy in her wet jeans. Somehow, through it all, she had become important to him.

"Let me help you." He placed one hand on her thigh just below her ass and gave her a quick shove.

She let out a small squeak but used the momentum to get up over the edge. She fell into the grass, gasping and dripping wet, her hair splayed out in wet curves, haloing her face. Cole pulled himself up and sprawled next to Angela, their bodies touching. Heat sparked between them. Anger forgotten, replaced with the joy that they were safe and the pulsing energy that they'd survived a near tragedy from the river that had taken important people from him. But not Angela. He'd been here to protect her. Pride swelled in him and he knew he needed her with him. Cole turned to her and propped his head on his hand.

"I was scared." Angela's voice huffed out in breathlessness.

"I was too." He laced a strand of wet hair through his fingers. "When you went under the water, I thought I was too late."

"You jumped in after me. When you called to me, it gave me confidence. I heard you tell me to grab the log and there it was. I grabbed it. I was too panicked to think of that on my own." She let out a little laugh.

"I've always hated this river even as I was drawn to it. My mother drowned when her car went over the bridge. I come to the river to think about it and about other things. Somehow the river gives me clarity even as I fear it."

"There has been so much tragedy related to this river. I'm sorry I haven't been more understanding about it." She turned on her side to face him. "When you asked me if I hadn't talked to a different girl ghost, you meant your mother, didn't you?" Tears brimmed.

He looked toward the water unable to see her pity, her understanding. "Yes." He nodded. "I was resentful that you hadn't connected with my mother. If you want the truth, I can't understand how a mother could abandon her son. And then here you are, speaking to ghosts and still she abandons me. My father haunts me at every turn, my mother does the opposite." His laugh was brutal, scouring the hole deep inside him. Though the emptiness didn't seem large. He knew that it was because of Angela. Somehow, she was helping him fill it.

"I don't pick who comes to me. They find me. If they are tortured or stuck here, they find me like a light in the darkness. I don't know the rules of how it works or why I see who I see. I'm sorry that I haven't seen your mother." Her cold hand pressed against his cheek. He covered her hand with his, reveling in the warmth flowing from her palm into his cool cheek.

"It's not your fault that my mother won't come for me."

"I will do everything in my power to try."

He believed her. "You're cold as ice."

"So are you." She smiled and he smiled back. "At first, I thought I would drown, but then you jumped in the water and I knew you would help me."

"I'd never let anything happen to you."

"Thank you for saving me. I wouldn't have had the strength to climb out without you."

"It was worth it." He brushed a wet strand of

hair behind her ear.

"You act like you're hard, but you're not." Her mouth lifted in a barely perceptible smile and her hands came up. Her fingers were long and soft, as they cupped his cheek.

He lifted his hands to cover hers. Warmth from his own body filtered through her fingers. Her skin warmed his fingers in return. "Let me put life back into them."

Her eyes looked especially big and her lashes long, he realized, long enough to brush against her lids. They were darker blonde than her hair. But it was her eyes that affected him so much. He was more afraid of drowning in them than the river. Her lips beaded with water. He wanted to taste them, needed to taste them more than anything he'd ever needed in his life. Then his lips touched hers and they kissed. He loved the sweetness of her mingled with the taste of the river.

Her lips trembled and he wasn't sure if it was from the cold or from his kiss, but she didn't pull from him. Instead, she gripped onto him like she was grasping for the tree branches, like her life depended on it.

He crushed her against his chest, wanting all of her inside of him, filling all those dark places, getting rid of any of the emptiness that still remained from his childhood traumas.

Beneath her drenched t-shirt, her nipples beaded against the bare skin of his chest and his blood boiled, warming his wet body from the inside out. His breaths came short and choppy

as if he gasped for his own life's breath. He deepened the kiss and she kissed him back with the
same ardor. There was no other place he'd rather
be.

He pressed her into the grass, never breaking
the kiss. His nose rubbed against her and he felt
how chilled she was. Damn, his nose had to be
just as cold. Her skin pebbled with gooseflesh.
He pulled back and her fingers reached for him,
skimming over the wetness of his skin, as she
tried to pull him back to her.

"Angel, you're cold to the bone. It's freezing
out here and you're drenched. He was drenched
too and starting to feel the chill in the air himself
now that the adrenaline was wearing off.

"But you warmed me up." She gazed at him,
those amazing eyes sparking through her matching lashes.

He stood and strode the few feet to his pile of
clothes near the willow tree. He reached for his
discarded sweatshirt and tugged on his tee.

"Here, put this on. I'll turn. Take off your top
and put this on." He thrust his sweatshirt at her
and turned his back to her as he watched the river
without seeing it. His mind raved with images of
her pale exposed skin as she slid off the wet shirt
and removed her bra, which he imagined that
pale blue and lacey, though probably tame if he
knew her.

"Okay, you can turn around now." She looked
at him shyly, her pinked cheeks cheering him,
knowing he'd made the right choice in stopping
the kiss and getting her out of some of her wet

clothes. Instead of getting all of her wet clothes off and on his bedroom floor. He groaned at the thought and pulled himself to his feet, grasping her hand and dragging her up too.

"Let's get you home before I forget that I'm becoming a nice guy."

She laughed and leaned into him. He pulled her cold body tight against his to warm them both up as they headed back to the mansion, where he would get her warm and dry in the most chaste way and then send her to the safety of her own home. Being the good guy was going to be torture.

CHAPTER 18

ANGELA COULDN'T MAKE herself face the day, so she pulled the blankets over her head and snuggled deeper under the cover. It had all happened so fast and her memories jumbled in a blur. She remembered slipping over the edge and crashing into the water. But had she really slipped? One second her feet were on solid ground, and then she was flying back with her feet in the air. The shock of the frigid water had made her lose track of everything. She vaguely thought she could have been pushed by unseen hands. She didn't want to tell Cole because he had suffered enough pain from his horrible father. And any mention of ghosts brought out the worst in Cole.

The next thing she remembered was Cole's strong arms giving her the strength she needed. With the adrenaline pumping and the awe of being alive, they'd kissed. It had been the most tender kiss she'd ever experienced in reality or in her imagination.

Once he'd dragged her back to the mansion, she couldn't stop shivering, and he forced her to change from her wet clothes. She kept his sweatshirt on while he dried the rest of her clothes in the drier. He'd changed his clothes while he got her dry ones too.

He'd given her his oversized clothes to change into after her river dunking. Then, after her clothes were toasty, he'd pushed her into her car, given her a sweet little kiss on the nose, which he pronounced nice and warm, and sent her on her way home.

She hadn't removed his sweatshirt when she'd gotten home. Cole's sweatshirt tangled around her waist and legs. Still trying to convince herself that it was because she had been too tired to take it off, instead of the real reason she didn't want to face. It held the scent of him and reminded her of his strong, protective arms around her and wanted to hold the memory for just a little longer. She crossed her arms around herself, hugging the memories and the shirt tighter to her chest.

She was still trying to make sense of the events that had occurred earlier.

She'd connected with Brooke, then Cole had upset her so much that she'd run to the river. She was even more convinced that she hadn't slipped. She had a strange inkling that one of the spirits was trying to push her and Cole together. When he'd rescued her, she'd practically fallen into his arms and she couldn't stop that kiss, didn't want to stop that kiss. He'd revealed his feelings about his mother and it made sense to her. Caught up in connecting with Brooke, she'd never considered that Cole would wish to connect with his mother. And he'd shared that with her. She held that thought close to her heart.

When Angela stepped into the aviary, she'd been taken off guard by the sudden rush of connecting with Brooke.

Little by little, Brooke had revealed some of her secrets, but she didn't tell her everything. Penniberg held many pieces of the puzzle and now Angela knew another part.

Brooke had loved Harry Barnes and he had loved her fiercely in return. But that love had been severed. Angela needed to find out the reason.

The fight didn't make sense. She'd been inside of Brooke, saw what she saw, felt what she felt. Brooke hadn't been ready to share everything yet. Those secrets had been hidden for too long. It was just a matter of time. Angela felt that in her bones.

It was frustrating that she didn't know more. Once she learned that secret, the ghost would be free to leave this world. She had to help Brooke. She couldn't give up the case easily, not now. And she couldn't let anything get in her way.

Cole distracted her every thought away from the case. She had been angry with him today. The ghosts weren't the only ones with long hidden secrets. He covered his sadness about his mother's abandonment with anger, but when it came down to it, his mother was who he wanted to see most of all.

Then he had kissed her. She'd wanted that kiss, been waiting for it, wishing for it. The pull of him was electric and undeniable. It was too much.

Even now, lying in bed, reliving the possession of Brooke Dalloway, thoughts of Cole were strong. When she should be thinking about Brooke, her mind could not stop thinking about Cole jumping into the river to save her.

The last thing she'd seen before slipping under the water's surface had been his broad shoulders and sculpted chest. If she'd had to go, that wasn't a terrible final image.

She could have died, the current was strong, but somehow, she'd never held much fear knowing he was close. He didn't let her down. He'd been right there, giving her his strength and confidence.

Once she was safe next to him, dripping like a wet cat, he'd spilled more of his secrets. Falling into the river had forced Cole to face another of his demons.

Cole was making it hard for her to hate him. How could she hate him after he'd shared his story of a tormented boy?

As much as he thought he was tough and mean, he always thought of her before himself. He'd saved her without a thought of the risk to himself.

That kiss trickled through her veins and seeped deep into her bones, weighing her down more than all the water in the river. When he touched her like that, nothing else mattered, not her need to help ghosts, not her fears.

When had she started to fall for him? The guy who was such a brute on the surface had somehow found his way past her defenses.

That thought terrified her more than anything else. She'd learned the hard way not to believe in men. Men had a hard time getting past her ability to help the spirits of the dead. Cole was no different. His kisses were hot and his protective nature ran deep. But he had made it very clear that he didn't—couldn't—believe. That wasn't true. He was unsure about what he'd been seeing and experiencing. But it wasn't enough. He didn't fully believe. She had to remind herself as much since her body refused to listen.

He was too much of a distraction. If she let herself get sidetracked with an ill-fated romance, she would never be able to help anyone, especially the ghosts who couldn't move on.

She needed to focus on Brooke Dalloway and Hank Barlow. They still suffered, but had finally started connecting. She would do a better job of helping them without any distractions.

Shoving the covers from her body, she slung her feet over the edge of her bed. Cole's sweatshirt hung loosely over her. After that kiss, she couldn't bring herself to take it off last night. It still held the clean smell that always surrounded him and now it lingered on her skin. Angela decided that she'd brooded enough for one morning. With a swift movement, she pulled the sweatshirt off and placed it next to her pillow. It was a new day. One without any sidetracking thoughts of sexy, unpredictable men.

After a shower, she headed through the hall to her galley kitchen where the deafening buzz of the blender greeted her.

Emma poured a pink frothy drink into two glasses. She took a sip, then held out the other glass.

"Strawberries, a little wheat germ and some yogurt. That will get you off to a good start."

"Thanks. I think I'm going to need this after last night's slip into to the river." She took a sip. Emma eyed her over the rim of her own glass without responding. She just stared with those big eyes that seemed like she could see right into her. She turned away to avoid that gaze and noticed the pile of mail on the counter.

"What's this?" Angela reached for the top envelope. The creamy paper was thick and had a slick richness. She peeled at the adhesive.

"That's all your mail from yesterday. Mostly junk, but that looks like an invitation. Any of your friends getting married?"

"Friends?" She pulled out the card. "It is an invite." The cardstock was elaborately painted in bright purple swirls and black calligraphy.

"What's it for?"

Emma grabbed for the card, but Angela pulled it out of her reach.

"You have to get your own." She laughed, then handed it to her sister. "You have absolutely no patience."

"Invited to where? By who? Do you need to find a date for the wedding?"

"That's not a wedding invitation." Dread filled her. There was no way she could refuse. But she didn't want to attend. If she didn't go, it would be considered a major snub to her hostess.

"Oh my goodness." Emma looked up from the invite with wide eyes. "A dinner party at Fran Greeley's."

"Uh huh."

"That is not the expected tone. You should be jumping up and down to get an invitation like this. It could change everything for you and your business."

"Did you read it more closely? Look who is the honored guest."

"That hunky dark-haired devil?"

"He isn't a devil." She defended Cole automatically. The memory of how he rescued her flashed through her mind and then just as quickly the feeling of his scxy body pressed against hers seared her brain, making her feel flushed. She knew it would be a mistake to go to the party and interact with him on a social level.

"He is a demon. You've said so yourself." Emma tapped the card against her cheek and stared at her with a psychic's eye that made her think Emma could read her mind.

Angela squirmed.

"Are you getting a soft spot for him?" Emma raised a perfectly waxed eyebrow.

"Oh, please." What a stupid comeback. She willed the heat from her cheeks. What else could she say? She was starting to like him and he was the best kisser she'd ever known. She knew it was a mistake, too big a distraction from what she was meant to do. Help spirits move on to the other side.

Emma gave her one last fortune teller's look,

then scanned the invite again. "You must go to this party. You'll be eating dinner with the most influential people of Dalewood. Mrs. Greeley only invites the best people to her parties."

"Then why did she invite me?"

Emma rolled her eyes. "It's obvious that she knows you're the best. You helped her heal after her husband's death. How could you even question why she would invite you?"

"I don't know if I should go."

"Of course you should go."

"You don't think she's inviting me as the entertainment?" Why couldn't she let go of the past? She'd earned her degrees and her credibility. Plus, she knew Fran trusted and believed in her abilities.

"You've been helping her connect with her husband. This is a wonderful opportunity and you are going to take it. Don't let your fear and self-doubt get in your way. And that's an order from your Vice President of Marketing."

"Self-promoted to vice president, huh?"

"Everyone deserves a raise and a promotion when they move the business to the next level." She rubbed her hands together like a thief ready to snatch the prime jewels. "You already admitted that your biggest and newest clients came because of my advertising strategies."

"True, sister-dear." Angela placed an arm around Emma's shoulder and squeezed. "I'm glad you're on my side."

"Thick and thin," Emma added. "If she makes you do even one reading, you're sending her a bill."

"Absolutely not. She is a wonderful client and I would never insult her like that."

"When is this shindig?"

"Saturday."

"That's just enough time to get you a new outfit. You've got a great figure to show off."

"I have lots of suits."

"Do you want to look like a therapist? Come on. You can do better than that."

"What about that pretty robin's eggshell? The one with the scalloped top?"

Emma's lips pinched. "It's too plain."

"I like it."

"I'm making myself your personal stylist. Leave it all up to me."

"I don't know…"

"Don't make that face. You'll get wrinkles." Emma waggled a purple-painted fingernail. "Don't ruin my excitement. Hmm, what are your best colors?"

"Nothing fancy."

"You leave this all up to me."

"I really don't want to stand out."

"Stop worrying. I'll pick out the perfect something. You'll see how good I am at this." Emma grabbed her smoothie and swept out of the kitchen toward her bedroom.

Angela took another sip of her drink, resigned to let her sister take over her wardrobe. If Emma went overboard and Angela didn't agree with the selection, she could always wear the light blue skirt suit.

The doorbell jangled Cole from his nap on the couch. The loud sound rang in his ears. He was nursing a headache. After Angela had left, he'd continued to drink the rest of the bottle of scotch in the cabinet. Cole folded the newspaper he hadn't been reading and removed his socked feet from the coffee table.

He hadn't expected anyone. He'd been holed up in the mansion, brooding and depressed since Angela had left yesterday. The kiss by the river had been fast and hot and unplanned, filled with passion and adrenaline. It had been sweet and full of relief.

When he'd brought her back to the house, they'd moved awkwardly. Hands bumping and skittering when he'd given her a pair of his way-too-large sweats. She'd looked cute in his clothes with her pink cheeks and wet hair. Water spiked her long lashes like glittering diamonds, making it impossible to miss their beauty.

Instead of staring at her like a rabid teenager, he'd thrust a towel over her head just to block her from his gaze.

She'd rubbed the towel over her hair, creating tousled curls, and thanked him all prim and proper before she'd slipped into the bathroom. Once she'd changed into his dry clothes, she disappeared as quickly as any ghost.

Another rapid succession of the chimes jangled him from his thoughts. He must not be moving quickly enough because whoever was at the door pounded like a monster was on the other side.

Cole peeled himself from the couch. He still wore his jeans and black button-down shirt he'd changed into last night. He was sure he looked ragged and rumpled. He ran a hand over the stubble on his chin and through his hair. He probably made it look worse than it already had. That's what happened when you got yourself drunk and slept on the couch trying to forget a kiss that blew your mind. Trying to forget the sweet angel whose kisses inflamed him. The fear of being burned was enough for him to get drunk.

"Coming," he shouted.

He pressed a finger to his temple to slow the throbbing. Whoever was at the door had better have a good reason for bothering him.

"What do you want?" He swung the large oak door open, thinking it was that bird-guy, what was his name? Pierce. "Mrs. Greeley," he sputtered. "This is unexpected. What brings you to my happy abode?" He knew his tone held mockery, but everyone knew how much he hated this place.

"Hi, Cole. I had to come." She wore a gray fur wrap over her black sweater and slacks. A sheepish smile curled across her face and he had a feeling he wasn't going to like what she had to say. She scanned him from head to toe. "You're a mess."

"To what do I owe the pleasure?" Shifting the door, he took a step back.

"Ever since we talked at Angela's seminar, I've been worried about you. You were angry. Can I come in?"

"Of course." He waved her in and she breezed past him, heading straight for the drawing room.

It would be rude not to offer her a drink. She'd always taken care of him and he should return the favor, though he didn't have much in the cupboards. "Would you like some water? Some wine?"

"No, I'm fine, thank you."

He let out a sigh of relief. All he had to offer was some water and scotch. He wasn't sure if he even had a clean glass. The cabinets held a few cans of soup and maybe a leftover ravioli. He hadn't had it in him to buy food to do any cooking here, even though he was a good cook. Shopping and cooking seemed like something a person did if he planned to stay a while. He felt like he'd been here too long already. "Let's sit."

She headed straight for the heavy curtains and pulled them open. "That's better. You need to get some light in here. What would Liza think if she saw you this way?"

"I had a long night." He smoothed his hair and then tried to rub out some of the wrinkles in his shirt.

"When I gave you the letters you were really upset, but I needed to make things right. I haven't slept well since that day and clearly neither have you."

"I'm trying not to think about them." He wasn't about to reveal the truth about why he was a wreck. And he'd practically forgotten about those letters. He'd stuck the pieces in the drawer next to his bed and hadn't looked at them since.

"Maybe you'll find some closure if you read your father's letters."

"Closure? There's nothing he could write that would ever make me forgive him." Cole closed his eyes against her expectant face. He felt like a feral animal raged in his guts, angry and snarling and wanting to stalk the memory of his father. It came on him so suddenly that he could barely maintain his irritation. "After all my father did to you and Max? He tried to ruin you."

"You helped us so much, but all our problems weren't caused by your father." She walked away from him and looked around the room, trying to change the subject. "There are so many things missing from this room. Your father sold a lot of things to the historical society. Mostly old things in the attic, but he obviously sold some other things, I assume because of the problems you caused him." She turned over her shoulder and gave him a pointed look.

"Is that where all my childhood stuff went? To a museum?"

"He was in the process of turning this house into a historical site."

"Why would he do that to the place he loved so much?" Cole asked, though he knew the answer.

"He wanted to stop you."

"He was trying to thwart me. He knew I was coming after his company and he was trying to protect this place, right?" Cole had been thwarted at every turn by his father and even now in his death he could still control Cole's plans.

"He didn't stop you as you bought and destroyed

each of his properties right out from under him."

"Why did he do this with Penniberg?"

"He wanted to protect the mansion."

"From his destructive son? Hank might have been mean, but he wasn't stupid."

"He wanted to protect you from yourself. He knew what you were doing and he knew you would eventually come for Penniberg. He made a deal with the historical society. He wanted to stop you."

"He's not going to stop me. He never signed the final papers and I still own Penniberg."

"Penniberg is the oldest home in all of Dalewood. It was built by Frank Dalloway."

"I know Dalewood history. When you've lived here as long as I have you hear about most things happening in this town. The quarry mines were the heart of Dalewood and the town was built around them. I own this place now and I can get rid of it without a single qualm."

"It should be a part of Dalewood history. The historical society was overjoyed at the idea of restoring Penniberg to its prime. Pierce wants to bring back the art deco flare and the feel of the roaring twenties."

"What exactly does it mean to turn the place into a historical site anyway?"

"You still own the property, only there are some requirements for restoration."

Cole wanted to growl at the thought. Restore Penniberg? That was not the plan he had for the place.

"Cole?" She brushed a hand over his sleeve.

"Your father didn't do this to hurt you."

Cole wanted to push her hand away from him. He wouldn't do that to her, even if he felt a twinge of betrayal. "You knew what my father was like. How can you say that?"

"Maybe your father tried to love you in his own way."

"It's easy to say those things now that he's gone. Why do people want to make the dead better than they were in life? My father didn't love me. He hated me and he taught me to hate. He taught me to mistrust. I'm not a little boy, but those lessons stuck."

"You're not the little child you once were. You've grown into a man. A very thoughtful man that did way too much to fix my house."

"Max taught me everything I know and I thank him for that. A few new boards on your porch and a coat of paint is nothing." He looked at the woman and felt the deep love for her that he'd had as a kid. "And I thank you." He forced the words through his tight throat.

"I know you do."

He didn't deserve her trusting smile.

"You need to face your father. You're stuck with him just like you're stuck with this place. He is a part of you and you need to face what you fear the most. If you face the problems you had in the past, you could start your future here. I can imagine your sons running around bringing new joy to this place."

"I'll never have children." He wouldn't allow the thought to sprout into life.

"Don't say that."

He couldn't stomach the pity that brimmed in her eyes.

"I could never put a child through the same things I went through."

"Your father was hard on you."

"He was, and I'm too damaged because of it."

"Not the boy I knew. Not the man I see in you. You're a strong, handsome, hardworking young man. You've done very well for yourself, but I still think you deserve more."

"And you think I should thank my father for that?"

"No, but you can't keep running from the past."

Her words hung in the air like ashes floating above a fire.

"Please, Fran, I'm already tormented enough."

"I can't sit back and watch you destroy everything. Your father is dead. Stop letting him hurt you."

"I was never good enough for him. You're right. Now that he's gone it doesn't matter. But it matters to me. I will do anything I can to get rid of this place. He was connected to this place. I won't be able to move on until Penniberg is gone. Then he won't exist anymore."

"He'll still exist."

"Not after I destroy the mansion."

"I know you don't want to admit it, but he is in you. You're his son."

"I wish that wasn't true."

Tears filled her eyes. "You deserve more. Don't waste away all alone. Everyone deserves more.

I'd hate to see you ruin your life now that your father is gone. Read the letters and you will understand."

"I know you care about me, Fran."

"It's more than that, dear. You are my son. Maybe even more than you were ever Hank's son."

Like an arrow, her words pierced straight into his heart. She was the only mother he'd ever known.

"You owe it to this old woman to face your demons. My life is in its sunset. You have so much more to give, to experience. Don't waste your chance." She stood and straightened her black pants and rearranged her fur cover-up.

He stood too, since he had no responses for her.

She patted his cheek. "Think of what I've said and don't forget about the party Saturday." He escorted her to the door and as quickly as she had come, she was gone.

He felt dazed and off balance. The room was empty and he could feel the hollowness right through his body, traveling through the hole in his heart straight to his soul.

CHAPTER 19

"EMMA, I JUST don't get any of this." Angela scanned through the list of things she knew about the mansion. "I'm positive there are two ghosts. I thought there were three, but now I realize that one ghost was showing me two sides. The dark shadow that tried to scare me was what he showed of himself at first. I think he wars with some major problem and that's why he still haunts the mansion."

"The shadow figure is the ghost everyone thinks is Cole's father?" Emma asked.

"Yes. And then there is the ghost I know is Brooke."

"Have you ever had to deal with two ghosts at one time?"

"Not like this. The only time Cole's father connected with me was that first time. He tried to shatter my emotions and scare me off."

"He's scared everyone else out of that place."

"I feel like he's scaring Brooke too. She only gives me snippets of information."

"Do you think she's too afraid to tell you everything?"

Angela nodded, trying to let the pieces fall into place. "What secret could be so terrible that multiple generations want it buried?"

"Let's rehash all you know so far." Emma pulled a yellow notepad from the end table. She tapped the pen on the paper. "You talk and I'll write."

"When I first went to the mansion, Cole thought I was tricking him. That glass flying off the table triggered something in him. That's the only way to explain why he was upset and stormed away. He had a painful past."

"When investigating, we heard Brooke's woeful cries and her footsteps. Before that, she showed us how happy she was with Harry. Then, I almost couldn't believe it when she showed us her death when she went over that bridge."

"Did you write both those things?" Angela checked over her sister's bullet points. "Add how Cole's mother also went over that bridge." She narrowed her eyes, confused.

"Brooke went off that bridge. She showed us how she died." Emma scribbled more words on the page.

"He was a brand-new baby when his mother died in a similar way to Brooke. Where was she rushing off to? How could she leave her child that way?" She knew she'd never be able to leave her child like that. Not for anything. "Would feelings for a lover be strong enough to ever make a mother leave her baby?" Her heart tore with sadness knowing that Cole felt abandoned.

"Everyone says how Hank Barlow was a bastard and maybe it was her only escape."

"Then I hate her for leaving her own baby in the hands of a monster." The angry words ripped from her before she even realized how mad she felt. Suddenly, her entire body was quaking with the rage she felt for Cole's mother, Malory. "She left an innocent child to fend for himself. No wonder Cole is the way he is. You'd practically have to become a beast to protect yourself from a monster like Hank." How was she supposed to help a ghost that she hated? He didn't deserve a peaceful rest. Not when Cole was tormented by the treatment from his father.

"Your research made it seem like she drove over the edge on purpose?"

Emma's words pulled her back to the puzzle pieces. She had to stay focused if she wanted to solve this. "She and Brooke died in the same way."

"It's odd that both their deaths happened in the same place."

"Brooke wanted me to see her death for some reason. I could feel her sorrow, remorse. It was intense. There's a bigger secret here. Something that spans time." And she knew it was related to Cole somehow. "How is a woman from the nineteen twenties related to a boy abandoned by his mother a little over thirty years ago?"

"Why don't the ghosts simply tell you their secrets and get on with it?"

"It's not always that easy. Brooke will tell me her secret. She has to learn that she can trust me. She's scared."

"She seemed to run from something and, unlike Cole's mother, she wasn't married to a brute." Emma added.

"I think you're hitting on something. That first shadow I encountered was a different ghost all together, the angry energy of Cole's father."

Emma cocked her head. "The energy of his father's ghost?"

"He's portraying only his worst feelings in the form of a dark entity. Maybe his ghost is blocking Brooke." She had to figure out this riddle. There were many lost pieces to the puzzle yet. "Something's missing though and I'm going to find out what it is."

"Tell me another ghost experience. Do you have any pleasant experiences?"

Angela held back her smile. Leave it to her sister to want to find a bright side. "Brooke showed me her happy relationship with Harry before she showed me the fight. I like the idea of star-crossed lovers. Her father was the rich company owner and Harry was the lowly employee. I felt her strong love for him. It was more than puppy love." As much as she really knew about true love. Angela only had her one experience with Paul. She'd thought she'd been in love, but he had proved her wrong. "Then Brooke showed me how she ended the relationship with Harry."

"What a romantic and tragic story." Emma eyed Angela.

"I know. Brooke was barely eighteen when she died."

"She was young, practically a baby herself."

"Reread the list you created." Angela propped a pillow behind her and relaxed on the couch.

"Okay, let's see. Bullet point one: Dark shadow attack by Cole's father. Bullet two: Brooke excited to see her love, Harry. Bullet three: Brooke running through the halls, crying. Bullet four: Brooke's death. Drove over the bridge running from something or someone. Bullet five: Star-crossed, true love and a breakup." Emma looked at Angela with questions in her eyes.

"She is showing me her experiences out of order. We saw her death before her breakup. It's like she's slipping me little notes whenever she has the chance. There are other things that happened too."

"Like what?" Pen poised, Emma was ready to write more.

"The books that fell off the shelf. Being trapped in the passageway, being pushed into the river. All those things must be messages to Cole."

"I'm too confused to follow all this." Emma dropped the pad on the coffee table.

"Brooke's secret must connect to Hank's secret. I will solve this. Once the past is revealed, they will no longer haunt that mansion. I'm sure of it."

"I need a break and you need to relax. Clear your head."

"I don't need any distractions."

"Yes, you do."

"I'm close to connecting the dots."

"Your eyes look ready to cross and I know the perfect way for you to unwind."

"Oh really?" She was skeptical. "And what do you suggest?"

"I have just the guy for you. It will be perfect.

He's not exactly your type, but you'll have fun with him. Spend some time with Steve and all your problems vanish, poof, like magic. At least for a little while." Emma gave her best Bugs Bunny smile that always made Angela nervous.

"I don't know."

"Don't argue, just live a little."

Cole's quicksilver eyes flashed in her mind. Maybe she was getting too intertwined with his haunting. He was starting to haunt her now. "Maybe I should go out and have some fun. Get my mind off a few things." One thing in particular. A guy too handsome for the cover of GQ and too damaged for Disney's Beast. Letting out a deep breath, she agreed. "All right, I'll go."

Emma clapped. "You won't regret it."

Her heart rate increased like the heavy thump of bass music. She squeezed the bridge of her nose to release some of the pressure. She was already regretting her decision.

"Angela, it's time for you to get a life," Emma said over her shoulder as she headed down the short hall to her bedroom. "Just enjoy it."

The doorbell rang again, surprising Cole. It was like déjà vu. Whoever was at the door better have a good reason for bugging him. What the hell? Everyone thought they could just stop by anytime they felt like it.

Cole held back a groan when he saw Pierce Foster wringing his long, bony talon-like hands as he stood in the doorway. Cole was reminded of a buzzard circling over prey ready to swoop down to his meal. What did this guy want now? The headache came rushing back like a freight train to crash behind his forehead with a throbbing pain. Who had he expected anyway? Angela? Not likely. He hadn't called her since that mind-blowing kiss. Why should he? What could he offer? Not much. He could barely stand to be with himself, let alone force himself on her.

He ran a hand through his already mussed hair and stared daggers at Pierce. Maybe he'd take the hint and turn tail.

"I have a proposition for you, Mr. Barlow."

"Not really interested in what you have to offer." Nope. He had no luck when it came to this town and this mansion.

"You might want to listen to what I have to say," Pierce said.

"Last time your news screwed up all of my plans. I haven't quite figured out what I'm going to do about your little bomb, yet."

"Can I come in? Maybe I can help with your decision?" Pierce wheezed as he looked up at Cole with beady black bird's eyes. They were unreadable and made Cole feel on guard. The little guy grated on Cole's nerves.

Cole widened the opening and let Pierce enter. "This better be good."

Pierce sat in one of the wingback chairs in the drawing room. He shifted from edge to edge on his seat, nervously trying to get comfortable.

Cole tried to ignore the little vulture as he sat back on the couch. Pinching the bridge of his nose to ease the headache, he propped his feet on the table. Was it too much to hope that Pierce would disappear?

When Cole looked up, Pierce's eyes had widened and his mouth pinched in a disapproving pucker. Cole wasn't sure if it was because of his manners or because of his feet on the antique table and, to be honest, he didn't care. He rested his aching head on the back of the couch and ignored Pierce.

"Mr. Barlow…" Pierce cleared his throat.

Cole stared through one slit eye as Pierce continued.

"The historical society has come to the decision that we would like to place an offer for the mansion. We believe there is enough history here to turn the mansion into a museum. We know how much you want to be rid of this place and we would like to take it off of your hands."

Cole sat up quickly at Pierce's announcement. A stab of pain throbbed in his head at the sudden movement. This was great. The perfect opportunity to be rid of the past. Why wasn't he jumping at the offer?

"You want to take the mansion off my hands out of the goodness of your heart?"

"Well…" Pierce sputtered. "We think people would enjoy the mansion. The people could take tours of the house and the grounds, for a small fee of course. I can see it now." Pierce dragged a hand through the air. "Can't you envision it? The mansion restored to the art deco styles of the roaring twenties? The tour guides dressed as flapper girls. We would set up the cellar like a secret speak easy and teach people about Prohibition. We would also teach the people about the Dalloway family and all of their efforts in the community, how they built our little town from a small mining community to the thriving town we have today. They would see how we've grown since. It would be wonderful. And of course we would include information about your father's contributions to modernize Dalewood."

Cole crossed his arms over his chest. The guy practically vibrated with enthusiasm. It grated against his raw nerves.

"Your father sold us many antiques from the mansion. We would like to return them and turn it into a beautiful museum that all of Dalewood could partake." Pierce nodded. His cheeks flushed.

Cole found him utterly annoying. A museum would not help him achieve his goal. Even if he no longer owned the mansion it would still exist. He wanted to get rid of his connection to his father, not glorify and honor him by forever protecting the building with a plaque in his honor.

"What do you think? It's a great idea, isn't it?"

"I have to think about it," he heard himself say.

"That's great. It's the perfect decision for everyone."

"I haven't said yes, yet."

"We have one other stipulation."

Cole narrowed his eyes. "And what's that?"

"We know you have been working with Angela Haven. We want you to stop that connection."

"You can't tell me who I can see and who I

can't."

"We aren't telling you who you can keep an association with. What we are asking is that she discontinue any work she is doing here in the mansion."

A thump behind the couch stopped Pierce's tirade.

"Don't worry about that. Old houses make lots of noise. The longer you're in the house, the more you'll grow accustomed to the bumps and creaks." Cole smiled and raised a brow at Pierce.

Pierce swallowed and his Adam's apple bobbled up and down. "As I was saying, she needs to stop any dealings in the mansion. We don't want her to clear it of any ghosts. If there really are ghosts." He laughed nervously and looked around. "We think the tales of ghosts and the possibility of ghost sightings will lure visitors to the museum. We might be able to increase tourism to Dalewood as well."

Pierce had slipped farther to the edge of his seat. If he shifted any more, he'd end up on the floor.

"If you could please call her off and tell her she is no longer needed, well, that would be just great for the historical society and its plans."

Two more thumps behind the couch interrupted them. Pierce jumped and looked in the direction of the sound.

The shifting of floorboards could be confused for a woman stomping her foot in irritation.

"We haven't made a deal here, Mr. Foster." Cole stood. "And like I said, I'll have to think about it." He looked around the room. Instead of the reminder of his father and the horrible times he'd had as a child, he actually thought about Angela. She always seemed confident and sure as she walked around the room. She seemed to fit into the house. For whatever reason, he didn't want to make her stop. "I have to consider your offer from the historical society. I think I might become fond of this place."

He escorted Pierce out the front door and shut it with a resounding bang. He had a great opportunity to get rid of the mansion, but it wasn't enough. He wanted to get rid of the past. That was a fact, wasn't it?

He couldn't simply sell it to the historical society and make a museum of the place. He'd worked too long and hard to simply give up now. Pierce and the historical society could take a hike.

He didn't want to hear any more of Greeley's stories either. He didn't want anyone else telling him to face his past.

Honestly, he felt… He didn't really know what he felt, but it wasn't good. He was feeling confined, trapped and cornered.

Cole was sick of it. Sick of sitting alone in the large mansion that he couldn't get rid of. It was like mildew. You had a plan of attack only to realize that it was attached deeper than at first thought. Now that he had an option for getting rid of the place, all he could see was Angela walking around in here. Her fingertips skimming along the walls and the furniture. She'd seemed at home. Somehow, she'd entrenched herself into his thoughts of the mansion. She'd shifted his memories of the house so that her image popped into his mind, trumping the memories of his father. How had she done that?

Cole pushed up from his chair. He needed a drink. He went into the kitchen and poured a splash of scotch into a glass. A deep swig burned the back of his throat, but he couldn't calm his raging heartbeat. Disgusted with his father's drink, he wanted something else, something different, a cool beer, maybe. Setting the glass on the table, he knew he had to get out of the house. It was too quiet and too big. The memories pressed in on him.

All Cole could do was think, and he didn't want to think. He wanted to block it all out. He didn't want to wallow. He wanted to get good and drunk. And why not? He'd done enough soul searching to last him a while. Coming back to Dalewood was a mistake. A lot of old memories had resurfaced. Things he'd pushed deep, he'd thought he had eliminated them.

But no, they were there as strong as ever. He had to get out of here. He grabbed the glass and dumped the contents down the sink drain.

Cole couldn't stay here anymore. He pulled his jacket off the hook near the door and thrust his arms into the sleeves. He stormed from the mansion without a backward glance.

CHAPTER 20

THE ROW OF glass windows were thrown wide open to let the cold November air into the throbbing heat spilling from the night club. Angela's feet skittered with trepidation, but Emma's hand on her wrist was relentless. A stream of yellow and pink fluorescent lights edged the doorway.

"Time to meet Steve. He's a real hunk. I think he's going to make the Bears football team."

"Gee, sounds great." She really didn't feel like spending time out at a club with some guy. "Am I going to feel like an old geezer?"

"You're one hot mama, especially wearing my white halter."

Angela tugged at the top, pulling it higher over her breasts.

"Stop fidgeting. You look great. Anyways, Steve is two or three years older than me. You won't even notice an age difference. It's not like you're in cougar territory."

"It will be dark in there anyway, right?" She tugged at the low-cut jeans, reducing the slight square of exposed midriff. "Describe this guy again."

"Steve is big and blond." Emma gestured with her hands to estimate the size of Steve.

"He sounds like a giant." And just what she needed. He wouldn't look anything like Cole. Maybe she could distract herself tonight.

"And he's buff. Oh yeah, a real muscle head. Totally not your type. It will be great. Just fun, to get your mind off some things or someone," Emma said the last under her breath. "Live a little."

Emma gave her a little shove toward the rough wooden door. The light sputtered low and gave off a low hiss in the cool night air.

"Ooh, can't wait." Angela couldn't hold back her sarcasm.

"Just dance, have a drink and share in some small talk. You're not marrying the guy. And you don't have to sleep with him if you don't want to." Emma laughed.

Angela grimaced. "I don't plan on sleeping with anyone any time soon."

"That's your loss, sister." Emma put an arm around Angela's shoulders. "Let's get tipsy, dance the night away and forget the rest. Are you ready to meet lover boy?"

"Why not? Let's get this over and done with." Angela pushed at the door and the stale smell of beer, cheap perfume and fake smoke hit her with the banging force of the music.

Steve leaned over the high round table. Angela

resisted the urge to lean away. His eyes were bright blue and his hair was dusted a sandy blond. His high cheekbones gave him a pretty boy look that some other woman would find extremely attractive. The loud music beat from the DJ box and the dark room flashed with strobe lights, highlighting pink in his hair. The too-loud music drowned out his words and he shifted his seat closer to her, shouting the words a second time.

"You like to dance?"

Her ear rang for a moment. She shouted back. "I walked to the river yesterday and I stubbed my toe on a rock."

"Huh?"

"Stubbed my toe."

"Oh."

"It's sore. Don't want to put too much pressure on it." She sipped her cranberry vodka and blinked up at him with what she hoped was an innocent gaze.

"Uh, okay, no biggie." He sat back.

Angela looked into the darkness. Occasionally bright pink and blue lights flashed, burning her eyes and blinding her at intervals.

Steve gave her a big doofus grin. Definitely not her type. A burly jock in a green tee and basketball shorts in autumn was not a love match.

Emma whirled up to the table. Her hair was a floating cloud around her cheeks and shoulders. Her face was flushed from dancing. She took a sip from her drink and leaned into Angela's ear. "How's it going? Steve is great or so I've heard." Emma's laughter rang out. "Just relax and have a good time." She swayed her hips to the music and gave Angela a conspiratorial grin before melting back into the darkness.

"You ah…wanna get out of here?"

Angela jumped when she felt his hot breath skim her ear. His husky tone made the skin crawl up her back.

She felt stupid. She didn't want to string the guy along and make him think she was interested in something more.

She knew nothing about him and one-night stands weren't her idea of fun, so she decided to feign innocence.

Leaning into him, she could smell the lime from the Corona he'd been sipping.

Making her smile bright, she pointed to her ear and shouted. "Sorry, I couldn't hear you." She grabbed her drink and sucked down her cock-tail, eyeing him above the rim. She used it like a barrier, blocking him from leaning in toward her.

A crowd of people stood along the bar waving cash, vying for the bartenders' attention. Others played darts along the wall. The dance floor bulged with the swaying rhythm of those on the dance floor. Angela's gaze went to the large black door at the entrance and she stared with long-ing. Freedom was on the other side. She fished for escape excuses. The door swung open and the bouncer blocked the way, checking IDs as girls in silver tops and tight black pants and the shortest skirts giggled.

She racked her brain for excuses to get out of the bar and away from Steve. His big goofy smile irritated her. So did his short hair spiked in a way that he must have thought was cool. Angela rolled her eyes and took another sip of her drink.

The door opened again. She watched, expecting to see a new group of club hoppers.

Her breath froze in the back of her throat.

Highlighted in the glow of the red exit sign stood Cole. She'd have recognized him anywhere. His shape, so unlike the bulky, over-muscled linebacker next to her, was strong and fit. Cole's broad, square shoulders narrowed down in a perfect triangle to his waist. He strode into the club with cocky confidence.

How dare he come here? Didn't he know she needed to get over him, stay away from him? She willed her heartbeat to slow.

She could ignore him. She would just ignore him. He couldn't know how much his kiss had affected her. How much she wanted to be in his arms.

Angela gripped Steve's meaty hand. "Come on, let's dance." Pushing back the stool, she tugged him away from the table and dragged the beefcake to the dance floor. His spiky blond hair and wide shoulders got more and more attractive by the moment. The crowd surrounding Emma shifted slightly, letting them into the small circle.

"Whoo hoo, I knew you needed to get out and have a little fun," Emma said as the couple entered the floor. Emma bumped Angela's rump with her hip and pushed Angela closer to Steve. Her hips bumped against Steve's pelvis as he ground to the music. Angela let out a groan, which she was sure

Steve would think was in pleasure. Now she was in a mess and all she could do was move her hips to the music. Hot embarrassment tore through her. What was she doing?

She refused to look at Steve, so she looked around one of his beefy arms. Her gaze fell on Cole, who was walking in their direction.

Suddenly she wanted to make Cole jealous, so she swayed her hips frantically to the beat of the pounding music. She turned and gripped her fists into Steve's shirt, pulling him closer. Sweat beaded along his neck and rolled into the cleft of his chest beneath his shirt. She didn't care. And she didn't want to care about Cole. She swayed again, shifting herself so she could keep an eye on the guy she kept telling herself she didn't care about. Cole was weaving through the crowd until he reached the edge of the dance floor.

She wanted him to know that the little ghost hunter could get any guy.

Oh no, he would not just walk by as if he hadn't noticed her. Angela danced more frantically to the music. Raising her arms over her head and swirling her hips, she moved out of the circle closer toward Cole so she knew she was in his line of vision.

"Hey, babe, you're a lot of fun." Steve's hand came down to the small of Angela's back and pulled her closer. Angela twisted from his arms and danced in front of Steve, just out of his reach. He grinned and awkwardly shifted from foot to foot in his linebacker's dance. Angela tried to hide a grimace, turning her back on him so he could view her backside and she could see if Cole had noticed.

Her stomach sank to her feet and she missed a beat. He was gone.

She scanned the crowd, looking for his dark frame until she saw Cole leaning against the bar resting on one elbow, a beer hanging from the other hand.

Had he been watching her?

Eat your heart out, Cole. "Do you want to take a break?" she asked Steve.

When he nodded, she danced back toward their table.

"Babe, you've got some moves." Eyebrows slightly darker than his hair waggled.

Laughter that was heartier than it needed to be bubbled from her. She slumped in the chair and wiped away the damp strands of hair from her face. Purposefully sitting in the stool that faced Cole, she placed her hand on Steve's shoulder and squeezed. She wanted to see Cole's face darken when he realized she was with someone else.

"Your moves weren't too bad yourself," she purred.

Steve must have thought that was an invitation since he leaned into her. A meat hook of a hand played with her earring, twirling the beads between his fingers.

About to swat his hand away like an irritating fly, she saw the crowd shift, giving her a clear view of Cole. He stood rigid. A scowl tightened the angles of his face, giving his lips a hard edge.

Score.

Angela smiled brightly up at Steve, but her eyes kept flitting back to what seemed like an angry Cole.

"You want to get outta here?" Steve asked huskily.

With only thoughts of Cole's scowl and the hopes of increasing it, she responded, "Sure, I am feeling a little tired."

Steve wrapped his hand around hers, which seemed unbelievably tiny, in his beefsteaks. He guided her toward the door. Steve had pulled her quickly, so she hadn't been able to take a last glance back to see if Cole would follow.

She looked down at the solid grip that Steve had on her. How was she going to get rid of him? Guilt trickled through her. This wasn't such a great idea. She shouldn't string Steve along with false beliefs. If she had to, she would feign illness.

She let him drag her through the crowd while she planned ways to make herself sick.

Suddenly, she didn't want to leave the bar with Steve. She knew it was a bad idea to exit the club while he expected more. Digging in the spikes of her high heels, she tugged at her arm but his fingers clasped around her wrist like a vise. She had to stop him, but he was so much stronger.

"Steve, Steve, stop. I think…um… I guess…" She tugged again, with more force this time. "I'm going to be sick." She gave a loud gag.

Steve jerked to a stop. With the momentum Angela had picked up from Steve's determined dragging pace, she didn't have the chance to stop and banged straight into his back with an *oof.*

Her breath whooshed from her lungs. As pain ran through her chest, she felt a wave of relief that he had actually stopped. He may look like a meatball, but Steve had a back like a solid brick wall.

Grumbling rumbled through Steve's solid mass. Angela practically vibrated from it.

"Hey, what's your problem, dude?" Steve said.

"I'm not your dude."

Angela peaked around Steve's bulk to see a dark and seething Cole Barlow. She couldn't help the sense of relief and excitement that bubbled through her. Mission accomplished.

"Outta my way, man. You're being a real buzz-kill." Steve shoved forward, leaving Angela in her spot. "And a cock blocker."

Angela's eyes widened at that comment. She had been trying to figure out a way to dump ice on Steve's evening, but Cole seemed to be doing that quite nicely.

"Take your hands off her, you rancid chunk."

"The lady likes my hands on her."

"From what I saw, she said 'no'."

The situation was quickly deteriorating. She'd never heard Cole speak like that before and she knew she needed to intervene before the argument got out of control. A crowd was starting to form. Everyone loved a bar fight. She took a deep breath. She'd started this, now she had to stop it.

Scooting around Steve's bulk, she placed herself in the middle of both men. She ignored how small she felt standing between two solid redwood trees. With hands up, one palm facing the chest of each man, she yelled, "Stop."

Two testosterone-laden males in a face-off and neither were willing to back down. Hulky Steve seemed a lot bigger than the very fit Cole. *Think fast, think fast.* She eyed both of them, waiting until their gazes shifted to her. Then she took her cue. "I think I'm going to be sick." Angela wilted, covered her mouth and let out a small retching sound.

"You gonna puke?" Steve croaked in horror as he jumped back.

Cole, on the other hand, reached for her. His strong hands gripped at her with reassuring strength.

"Come on, let me get you out of here. You need some fresh air." He wrapped his arm around her shoulder and pulled her against his strong frame. He was warm and smelled delicious. She could feel the muscles along his ribs and waist when she put her hand around him.

Feeling his strength, she reconsidered. He could easily have taken the dumb jock. Steve may have had the body of a linebacker, but Cole's strength ran through him deep into his core.

He led Angela toward the exit. With a glance back, she noticed Emma. Her sister separated from the crowd and stood on the edge of the dance floor. Did her sister just roll her eyes at her? Angela flashed Emma a swift smile, then buried deeper into Cole's embrace. Emma wasn't a fool. She'd seen Angela perform that same trick many times when they were kids. If she didn't want to go to school or if she was embarrassed to perform in the holiday performance, she would get the stomach flu.

Angela didn't feel one ounce of guilt at resurfacing her tried-and-true trick. Fight avoided and not one bruise on Cole. Although for some reason, she knew it was Steve who needed to worry about getting into a fight with Cole. He'd been trained in the school of hard knocks instead of learning from the playbooks of a football game.

CHAPTER 21

———～～———

"I THINK WE'VE HAD enough fun for one night. And to think I wanted to get out of the house to relax." Why didn't Dalewood have more bar options to offer? Note to self—open a sports bar. Cole led Angela out of the steamy club into the cool, wet air. A snowstorm threatened in the dark gray clouds in the sky. Cole's eyes were just as dark and cloudy.

"Were you really going to leave with that guy?" Cole crossed his arms over his chest. He looked down at Angela where she had perched on a cement parking block between the empty parking space next to his car. He had the sudden urge to punch the side of the car he had worked hard for. How could she let that guy paw all over her?

"Why not? I'm single." Her chin lifted defiantly.

She was pretty and too innocent for him to believe she would want to be with a guy she'd just met. So, then what had she been doing? Driving him crazy, that's for sure.

He ground his teeth at the thought of her

dancing with that creep. He couldn't stand and watch while she walked out the door with that idiot. "I thought you didn't want any distractions? I thought the ghosts needed all your time and attention right now?" He unlocked the car doors.

When he saw her on the dance floor with that guy's sweaty hands all over her, he almost went into a rage. Cole shook his head. He couldn't understand his feelings. He didn't trust her. In fact, he thought she was a liar, didn't he? She constantly wanted him to believe that she could see ghosts.

Could she really be willing to have a fling with some guy? He didn't want her having an affair with anyone else. The only person she should be thinking about sleeping with was him.

Now where had that thought come from? He was just mad that she was willing to jump from him to some other guy. He wasn't planning to build a life with her.

This situation had become impossible. She was working for him and she might actually be crazy. But right now, he was the one who felt crazy. When he saw the two of them as they walked to the door together, he'd just acted. For some reason he felt like she should be his and he wasn't willing to share her. He ran his hand through his hair. Yeah, he was the crazy one. He turned around to find that she had been watching him the entire time. Hiding his embarrassment at being caught pacing, he said, "Are you feeling any better?" The words came out more gruffly than they should. "You were about to be sick."

"Huh?" Her eyes crinkled, confused. "Oh yeah." Her smile brightened with a little wisp of mischief.

What was she up to now?

"I guess you were right. I simply needed some fresh air."

He wanted to smile back, but he couldn't. He'd never thought of himself as an animal, but he had become a snarling bear tonight. "Come on, where's your car?"

"I don't have it here."

"Why not?"

"Emma drove. It's okay. I'll just wait for her."

"Emma looked like she was having too much fun back there. I'll take you home." He reached for her arm, but she pulled away.

"That's okay. Emma will take me home. This place is closing soon."

"Come on. It's the least I can do for ruining your date." He'd said it so he could get a reaction from her. Angela snapped her head around to look at him. Good.

She narrowed her eyes faintly. He almost missed it. "I guess you do owe me," she said. "Steve was a nice guy and you were pretty nasty." She walked to the passenger side of his car and opened the door. Was that a guilt trip? Two could play at that game.

She slid onto the leather seat and clicked her seat belt on. Then she pulled out her phone and texted someone, probably Emma. He got in on the other side. He liked her sitting next to him in his car.

"What do you have against Steve?" She turned to eye him. He noticed the sparkle. She was toying with him. If she wasn't careful, she'd bring the panther out and he'd be pouncing with anger again, or something else, like kissing that smirk off her lips.

"I didn't like the way he was touching you."

"That's not your problem."

"I made it my problem. I didn't like seeing his hands on you." The image of Steve's hands on her skin raged through him. Softly he said, "Maybe I got jealous."

Her eyes widened and her lips parted slightly. Clearly, he'd shocked her. Damn, he'd shocked himself by saying it too. He couldn't take his gaze off those pink lips. He couldn't stop himself from leaning closer and closer until his lips pressed against hers and he claimed her in a kiss.

At first, she pushed her hands against his shoulders. It registered in his brain that she was rejecting him and his stomach tightened against the painful thought. Just as he started to pull away from her, she deepened the kiss. His heart soared. She gripped his shoulders, fingertips digging into his shirt and muscle. The smell of her was intoxicating, a blend of flowers and spice and heaven.

He thrust his hand in the silken hair at her temple and pulled her lips deeper to his. Her hands slid up his arms. Trails of heat burned over his skin. Her hands covered his. They were small and gentle. She could never hurt anyone. Her touch was like a salve to his damaged soul and he needed her touch. She slipped her fingers between his and gripped them tightly, as if she was afraid to let go.

He was the one who was afraid. She could have been with another man tonight and he didn't like it, but now she was gripping him as if he was her lifeline.

Their kiss warred between them, their tongues slashing against each other's becoming a battle. Her emotions melding with his. The bruising kiss ignited a fire in him. He knew in that moment that he would fight for her. But the war was with himself, not with the Idiot.

He broke away, out of breath, gasping. The moisture of her on his lips drove him beyond the breaking point. Her cheeks flushed and her breaths lifted with each heaving breath. He needed to get himself under control. If he couldn't get it together, he'd be lost.

A gold flash of anger and a cloud of disappointment floated into her eyes—eyes he had loved from the start. They had mesmerized him that first day in her office. The eyes that haunted him, even now. He needed to stop this before it went too far. He'd been able to protect himself for years, but being this close to her made him want to forget each messy memory of his past. That was dangerous and made him feel vulnerable. He didn't like the feeling.

"You can't make me your concern." Her lips were red and pouty from the kiss. It was as if his thumb moved of its own volition as it stroked her bottom lip. "I can't stop these feelings. God knows I want to, but I can't," he whispered.

"You think you know everything, but you don't." Her voice rose at each word. She took a deep breath. "Take me home."

"Okay." He rearranged himself in the driver seat. She gave him the directions and he drove her in silence. He watched as she got out of the car and walked up to the lighted door entrance. He needed to leave her alone. She didn't need to be tainted by him. She was too pure and he was too damaged.

CHAPTER 22

A NGELA TUGGED AT the dress with one hand and tried to stuff her boobs lower. She wanted to make a good impression at Fran Greeley's party for Cole, but she was already late.

"Here goes nothing and everything," she whispered. With a deep breath, Angela headed toward the steps of the Greeley's Victorian-style mansion but paused.

She wanted to hunch her shoulders, but that would not do. She had to be confident, so she straightened her back and ignored the fact that her cleavage showed more than she was used to.

Emma said the amount was sexily respectable. Angela wasn't sure.

A shadow shifted near the outer edge of the wraparound porch. Angela froze. She couldn't see anything past the dim halo from the porch light.

Her heart fluttered into her throat. Why hadn't she taken martial arts with Emma?

With a clenched grip on the strap of her butter-soft, newly purchased purse, she took a step back.

A man emerged from the darkness. A scream

rose from the bottom of her belly but caught at the back of her throat. He was large and menacing while strangely familiar. Angela backed up a few more steps, then the man's large body entered the shaft of light. She relaxed in relief, but her heart flipped into her stomach.

"Hey, Angel girl," Cole said as he slipped his phone into the pocket of his sports jacket. She couldn't tell if it was navy or black. What she knew was that it fit him in all the right places. He was calm and cool, like he hadn't just terrified her out of her skin.

"My name is Angela. Don't call me that." She bit out the words.

His sinful mouth lifted in a half smile. *Oh no you don't.* He could make her feelings shift so fast that it was absolutely unfair. She wished she could have the same effect on him.

"Why are you hiding in the bushes?"

He didn't react at all. Not a twitch. He was too good for that. Too controlled and protected to give a reaction freely.

"I was talking to a client."

"You scared me half to death."

His gaze scanned up and down her body, scorching her with each look. "You look very much alive to me."

Angela couldn't decide if she should slug him or tug at the neckline of her dress. She compromised and crossed her arms instead.

He gave her another once-over that had her blushing. "I almost didn't recognize you."

She wanted to hide in the bushes he'd just

stepped out from. His gaze was like a searing fire. Did he think she looked pretty? "Who did you think I was?"

"No one. You just look"—he shrugged— "different."

"Should I say thanks?" She let out a small laugh and bit her lower lip.

"I liked the way you looked the other day."

"What's wrong with how I look now?" She knew she shouldn't have worn this dress. He knew just the right things to say to set her off. He was an expert. Button pusher extraordinaire.

Cole knew what he was about to say would make himself look like a big jerk. That's what he wanted. Better if he insulted her and kept her at a distance. Especially when she was so beautiful and he wanted to haul her up against him and forget about his obligations.

"I liked you better in your white top and jeans. You looked so fresh," Cole told her. *And unbelievably real and totally sexy.* Tonight, she looked absolutely beautiful and it made something shift inside him. His heart panged uncomfortably and he decided he didn't like it. Her hair was swirled up and off her shoulders. Except for a few escaping tendrils, her neck was bare. The creamy skin glowed under the pale lamplight. The yellow dress fit her curves with a sweet caress. Could a man be jealous of a damned dress? He was being stupid.

"This is a dinner party. Jeans aren't actually acceptable. But you make your own rules." Did she look him up and down in retaliation? The woman was something else. Most women simpered over him or completely ran from his scowls. But no, she stood her ground and even had the audacity to look disapprovingly at his wardrobe. He wore Armani, but she made him wish they were sitting under the ancient oak slugging beers in their jeans.

"I didn't mean to scare you."

"Why were you really hiding in the shadows?"

"You wouldn't believe me if I told you the real reason."

"Try me."

"I was avoiding the inevitable."

"The inevitable?"

"Yeah." He nodded toward the front door.

"You don't want to go into the party?"

"Something like that. But you happened to pull up at precisely the right time." He placed his hand on her bare elbow.

Soft and cool under his touch, the feel of her skin spread life into him. He couldn't resist touching her and wanted to feel more. He trailed his fingers up the back of her arm, then dragged them back down to her elbow. Goose bumps prickled along her skin. She couldn't hide the effect his touch had on her, and he smiled into the darkness.

"Let's go in together. It will take the pressure off both of us." He led her toward the hornet's nest of a party. He thought Fran was trying to secure his marriage to Liza, so why had she invited Angela tonight? Was Fran playing some sort of game? He'd figure out her goal soon enough.

Angela hadn't expected to see Cole so soon. She didn't expect to see him lurking in the shadows. But here he was and now he was escorting her inside. How weird. And why was he nervous? What could he possibly be nervous about? He was the most independent guy she'd ever met. She thought he didn't care what other people thought, but he was avoiding this party.

The butterflies were back in full swing. She bit at her lip before she remembered that it made her look nervous and self-conscious, which was the opposite of her intentions for the night.

She dropped her lip from her teeth and noticed Cole was watching her. Electric bolts shot between them. Then his hand slid to the small of her back and she stepped forward, letting him lead her into the party. His hot touch seeped through the fabric of the yellow dress and sent sparks up and down her spine and lower. The man was too much for her and it was driving her crazy.

Loud chatter greeted them as they entered. Lights blazed in the ballroom where the guests lingered, sipping wine in between small talk. There were seven people. She and Cole made an even ten after Liza arrived. Everyone wore designer dresses or suits to fit the occasion. Once everyone realized they'd entered, the conversations ceased.

"Cole, you've made it." Fran clapped and rushed toward them. Angela awkwardly stumbled out of the way as Mrs. Greeley barreled toward Cole with arms outstretched, clearly more interested in his arrival than her own.

Fran wrapped her arms around Cole's waist and squeezed before leaning back with sparkling eyes. "I wasn't sure you would come." Mrs. Greeley released Cole and looked up at him. "I started to give up hope when you were late. You were upset at our last conversation that I thought it might have been too…" She paused when she glanced at Angela.

Realization dawned and she stopped her train of thought as if she didn't want Angela to know what upsetting situation she was referring. She squeezed Cole's hands before dropping them. "But you're here now and that's what matters."

Fran wrapped a welcoming arm around Angela's shoulder and subtly swung her away from Cole. "Thank you for coming to the dinner party too. There are a few people I'd like you to meet." Fran turned over her shoulder to look back at Cole. "Liza will be down in a few moments."

Angela set her teeth. Mrs. Greeley was trying to hook up Cole with her daughter. Angela didn't like it. But Fran was a client and a wonderful lady at that. She needed to network tonight and really, what could she say?

"Have you met Pierce?" Fran waved over a thin man with a beak-like nose and black beady eyes.

"Nice to meet you, Pierce."

"Hi. I'm Pierce Foster, elected President of the Dalewood Historical Society." He shot out a slick hand. He pumped, rattling her shoulder joint. She couldn't wait to let go of his hand, but she had to be polite. He was very influential and if she wanted a chance to get into some of the oldest buildings in Dalewood, she'd have to make friends.

"Yes. That's right. I sent a letter a while back while trying to visit the old Lundford cabin." She pulled her hand back. "I'm Angela Haven."

His eyes narrowed at her. "You're that ghost hunter, aren't you?"

"I'm a paranormal investigator." His look irritated her. When would she be able to get past the disbelief others felt? Probably never, but she couldn't let it ruin her night, so she smiled brightly at him. "Yes. Did you receive my letter requesting entry into the old homestead? I never got a reply."

"That's true, I never replied." He pulled at the collar of the black turtleneck he wore under his gray jacket. "Other, more pressing, issues arose." He glanced nervously around the room to fixate on something behind Angela's shoulder. Then he focused his gaze back onto hers before bending to whisper in her ear, "Hank Barlow died."

"How are the two issues related?"

"With Cole in the picture I had to deal with him and that situation first."

"And what situation was that?" Her curiosity piqued at the mention of Cole.

"I was working with Cole's father. He was considering the possibility of turning Penniberg into a historical location."

"Penniberg was built by the Dalloways and since the town grew around the Dalloway Quarry, it makes sense that you would want to turn it into a historical site."

His face skewered into a pinched scowl. "That was before Hank's son returned." He shot a scathing look across the room.

"Cole called me to come to the mansion. Everything is fine. I finally have the chance to investigate one of the oldest homes in Dalewood."

"It's not fine, Angela. I don't think you understand. It is not wise for you to eliminate the ghosts in that mansion."

"I don't eliminate ghosts, Pierce." She bit out his name in a slightly scathing tone. *Make friends*, she reminded herself. "I help the souls that are trapped."

His snort reverberated through his honker and Angela dug her feet in to stop from stepping back.

"Seriously?"

His tone dripped with condescension and she fisted her hands. "Yes, that's what I do."

"That is the last thing I want to hear."

She hadn't expected that and blinked a few times. "What do you mean?"

"Let me remind you that I work for the historical society. I see strange things more often than I want to admit."

She had expected him to show disbelief like so many others.

"You need to stop your work on the mansion."

"I can't. I won't stop until the ghosts can rest."

"You will ruin everything," he huffed.

Before she could reply or learn more, Mrs. Greeley broke into the din of the party conversations. "If everyone could please move into the dining room, dinner will be served. Seats have been prearranged. Enjoy and celebrate the prodigal son's return." She held out her hand and Cole took it. "My dearest Cole has returned."

Mrs. Greeley practically bobbed in her dark pink, knee-length skirt. She wore milky pearls near as large as Wilma Flintstone's. With her free arm, she guided the guests through the large walnut doors into the connecting dining room.

The room glittered with candlelight. Ten place settings covered the linen tablecloth. Each plate was decorated with a peach mum holding a card with a name printed in calligraphy. Daisies and chrysanthemums popped shades of yellows and reds throughout the beautifully arranged table.

Angela started toward her seat when a tap on her shoulder stopped her.

"Did you come here with Cole?" The tall willowy Liza stepped in front of Angela and blocked her way.

Angela smiled soothingly. "Of course not."

"Then why did you walk in at the same time?"

"How do you know that? You weren't even downstairs when I came in."

"I watched from the window."

"Then you would have seen that we did not come together."

"My bedroom window gives a view to a small area of the porch. I saw you talking in the shadows."

"Eavesdropping?" Angela raised an eyebrow. "There wasn't much to overhear."

"I couldn't hear anything, but I can see."

Angela closed her eyes for a moment. She

needed to bolster her strength. For years people had hated her because of her ability to see ghosts, but in a matter of minutes she'd had two people hate her because of Cole. She wasn't used to this.

"What are you trying to say, Liza?"

"Cole and I were supposed to be married."

Angela felt the words like a slap in the face. Heat rose into her cheeks. She'd suddenly lost her appetite along with her need to network. She wanted to leave.

Liza's hair was perfectly straightened. Her teeth were as white as her pale hair. Long legs seemed even longer and more perfect in her heels. They made her model tall and more feminine than any other woman in the room, especially Angela. How could she possibly compete with her?

"But you're not engaged." Angela was surprised at how cool her words sounded.

"I saw the way you looked at him," Liza hissed. "Remember that he's mine." Her tulip skirt swirled as she spun and stalked off, leaving Angela in her wake. Angela needed a break. She'd barely been at the party for ten minutes and she couldn't handle being accosted by another guest. If she didn't take a small break, she'd end up chickening out and leaving the party all together.

She checked left and right to be sure nobody would notice and slipped from the room. She welcomed the quiet of the hallway. A few moments in the privacy of the bathroom would do her wonders.

The buzz of the guests disappeared as Angela headed down the empty hallway. Where was the restroom? She wanted to sit and catch her breath, fast.

She turned down another hallway. It was dark. Clearly, she'd taken a wrong turn and was in a part of the house that was not set for guests. She really didn't care at the moment. She wanted to be alone.

Angela twisted the handle to the first door she saw. She stuttered to a stop when the person sitting on the bed whipped her head to turn glaring eyes at her.

"I'm sorry. I didn't mean to bother you." Angela stepped back and began to shut the door when the woman faded into a mist and crumbled into the bed.

"Wait," Angela called. How hadn't she known there was a ghost? Too many distractions and flustered thoughts.

She pushed into the room and the static tickled over her skin. It was like walking through a large spiderweb. "Please show yourself. I didn't mean to frighten you."

Angela placed a hand on the bed. Energy flowed from her hand into the ghost. "Use my energy to reappear."

Angela felt the soft brush of fingers on her hand and then the feeling was gone.

"I only want to talk to you."

"What should we say?" The voice was like the high pitch tinkle of bells.

"Anything you want."

"I have lots to say."

"Why are you scared?"

"Because you are the first person to realize that I am here."

"The first?"

"Yes. I have always been free to do as I please and then here you come to surprise me."

"Don't be scared. I can help you."

Laughter floated in the air. "I don't need help. And I'm not all that scared."

"You don't? And you're not?"

"Of course not. I'm perfectly content to exist in this manner."

Angela had never met a ghost so happy to stay in limbo like this. "You don't know what you're saying. You're confused."

The woman's face flashed inches from Angela's. They could press nose to nose if Angela even shifted a centimeter.

"At first I thought you were simply plain. But you are actually quite pretty. Those eyes you have are stunning. They are absolutely marvelous and wasted on you. You haven't the first clue on how to use them, do you?"

Angela blinked. Electricity shot though her, but it wasn't painful. It was energizing.

"I'm sending you my power."

Angela was usually the one who gave away her strength. She'd never received such energy before.

"I think it is you who needs my help and not the other way around."

"What do you mean?" Angela asked. She helped ghosts, they didn't help her.

"My name is Beatrice. I think you need a fairy godmother of sorts."

"There are no such things as fairy godmothers who swoop down to wave magic wands."

"You're a silly one, aren't you?"

Angela tilted her head at Beatrice. This was the oddest conversation she'd ever had.

Beatrice flipped her hands palms up. "No magic wands here, but I can still help you."

"And how could I use your help?"

"You have those eyes and you have no idea how to use them. Now that's a tragedy."

"My eyes work perfectly fine." Angela shifted them back and forth to look from one end of the room to the other. Then she blinked three times. "Yup, they can see things all right."

"Tsk, tsk, tsk." Beatrice tapped an invisible foot on the floor. "I can teach you to use them to catch that fish."

"I don't like fish."

"You know exactly who I'm talking about."

"He's already taken." Angela crossed her arms over her chest.

"Hmm. You give up too easily." The ghost tapped a see-through finger to her lips.

"Hey. I don't even know you."

"You know me better than you think. Or you will soon, because I've decided to help you. You need me."

"This is absurd." Angela slapped her hands to her sides.

"You're scared."

"I have a dinner party to get back to." Angela walked out of the room, snapping the door closed behind her. So much for relaxing for a few minutes. It was time to get back to the den of lions before she was missed. But then again, who would even notice she'd left?

She had no trouble finding the dining room on her way back. Standing at the doorway, she took a deep breath before entering.

"Everyone's already seated," Beatrice's voice flittered in her ear.

"So what?"

"Liza switched the place cards. She put you next to Richard Portly."

Angela peeked through the door and found the one open seat. To the left sat a man who fit his name well. The buttons on his blue striped shirt pulled and puckered against his swollen belly. His head was bald but for the few strands greased to stick to his glossy scalp. Angela's shoulders relaxed. "He's a heck of a lot better than sitting next to Pierce."

"Oh really? Scan the rest of the table and don't lie about how it makes you feel." What was one of the librarian ladies doing here? What was her name? Greta she vaguely remembered.

Angela's breath hitched when she saw Liza sitting next to Cole. Just then, Liza shifted her chair closer to Cole. Her left arm brushed his right arm. They'd be brushing each time they reached for food from their plates.

"I see nothing wrong," Angela said, haughtily.

"You lie, silly girl. You have a lot to learn."

A push between Angela's shoulder blades tripped her into the dining room, making her stumble forward. She caught her footing, but heat rushed into her face, making her burn hotter than any fire. All eyes shifted to stare at her not-so-graceful entrance.

Cole jerked in his seat as if he were going to try to catch her before she fell. Angela began to smile at him until she saw a thin hand grip his forearm and press him to sit back in his seat.

Bitch, Angela thought, then squared her shoulders and locked eyes with Liza's pale ice blue ones.

"That's it, girl." Beatrice's high-pitched voice rang in her mind. "Walk tall, like you own it. You need a pair of heels."

Angela took her seat next to Richard. He stood as she approached and held the chair for her. Farthest from Angela, Mrs. Greeley sat at the head of the table. Cole was to her right and Liza sat next to him. Cole was at the farthest end of the table, but he sat on the opposite side from Angela. She couldn't see Pierce, who sat on the same side of the table. *What a relief.*

Angela had not yet met the couple sitting across from her. Richard sat to her left. He was the town councilman and probably the most influential of this group of top-notch people at the party. Why had Angela been invited? Although she had built a respectable reputation, she was not the most influential person in town.

"Who cares? Stop thinking like that. Lift your head and be confident." Beatrice's voice sounded inside her ear. What? Now this ghost could read her mind?

Angela waved her hand near her ear like she

was shooing a bug. When she saw Richard looking at her, she brushed a stray hair behind her ear to try to cover her actions and gave him a dazzling smile.

"What a wonderful evening we're having." He pushed his glasses up the bridge of his round nose and gave her a broad toothy grin before reaching for his wineglass and taking a hefty drink.

"It has been great so far." She wondered if he noticed her sarcasm.

The soup course had been served while she'd been gone. Richard's bowl was already slurped clean. Angela dipped her spoon into the creamy concoction and tasted.

Yuck. Mushroom soup. She hated mushrooms, but she didn't want to insult her hostess, so she dipped her spoon in again and took a bigger scoop, swallowing it like medicine.

She glanced down the table and noticed Liza swiveled in her chair. With batting eyes, she was too busy trying to distract Cole and hadn't even touched her soup. Cole laughed happily at whatever joke Liza told. Had she ever seen him laugh like that?

Angela took big spoonfuls of soup, trying to ignore the display at the end of the table. Before she even realized it, the bowl was empty. The earthy flavor and Cole's interest in Liza left a bad taste in her mouth.

She folded her hands over the napkin in her lap, not wanting to look at Cole, not wanting to look at Liza. She did not want to see the two of them sitting so close, enjoying their dinner.

"How do you know Mrs. Greeley?" The man to her right asked in a low husky voice. The timbre held a hint of painful sadness. He was more handsome than he needed to be with his manicured eyebrows and tinted blond hair. He wore a designer suit with a silk blue and gray striped tie. A small diamond winked from the gold tie clip. Should a man be so pretty?

She knew it was simple small talk, but how should she answer his question? She helped Mrs. Greeley connect with her passed husband, Max. Was there an appropriate answer? Could he handle the truth?

"Confidence, girl." The words flitted through her ear accompanied by a sharp pinch to her elbow. Angela almost jerked from the pain. She rubbed at her skin like she had an itch.

Here goes. Give him the truth. How much truth could she give without telling too much? Mrs. Greeley deserved a little client confidentiality.

"I started a business and Mrs. Greeley has been working with me."

"Use your eyes," Beatrice whispered. "Bat some lashes."

Angela's cheeks flared fire. If he could only hear this internal conversation, he'd think she was a lunatic.

"He can't hear. Get on with it. Show him what you've got."

"You have your own business? I admire small business owners, especially in this risky economy."

The table was cleared in preparation for the salad course. Angela lifted her chin, looking at him.

"That's it girl, coquettish. Yes. This is good practice. Don't forget those lashes."

"What do you like about business owners?" Was she really asking this question in a sultry Marilyn Monroe drawl?

His green eyes held a hint of smoke as he gazed at her. "I find them very tenacious."

A giggle slipped from Angela. She'd never considered herself the giggling type.

"Perfect. Look down at the other end of the table," Beatrice ordered.

Angela's eyes flicked across the table to see Cole staring at her with a dark scowl. Was he annoyed?

"Oh yes. That is one sour puss on his face. The point goes to Angela. And you don't need my help? Hah."

By the time dinner was served Angela felt uplifted. All through the course, she chatted with Richard Portly and the man to her right, who she found out was his son, Erik. Erik was following in his father's footsteps with plans to gain some political footing now that he'd finished law school. His mother sat to Erik's right. Angela recognized her as one of the women from the library. What was her name? Gretchen? No, Greta.

Through dinner, she never completely forgot about Cole and Liza, but at least she was pleasantly distracted for a little while.

"Let's retire to the parlor," Mrs. Greeley announced after the plates were cleared. "We can enjoy our desserts with some sherry or some cognac."

"Shall we?" Erik offered his arm to Angela.

The glass of wine she'd sipped had gone to her head and she felt somewhat giddy. Gingerly, she slipped her hand through his arm. "We shall."

"I see that Liza is showing a bit too much attention to Barlow." Erik tilted his head in the adoring couple's direction. Seems like she wasn't the only one keeping track of Cole's behavior during dinner.

"What do you mean?"

"She's been fawning over the bastard all night."

"He's not a bastard," Angela snapped.

Erik froze. "He is in my book." His eyes shot shards of cold anger.

"Wait a minute." Her head was a little fuzzy and it took her a minute to get it. "You're interested in Liza? This isn't about Cole?"

"I'm such a fool. I can't stop myself following her around. It makes me feel like a damned puppy."

Angela looped her arm through his again and squeezed him closer. "This is wonderful."

"That I make a complete ass of myself around her?"

"No, silly. But I think we can help each other a little."

"Let's get a cordial. I need a drink."

They entered the parlor. Cole sat on the love seat with Liza perched next to him. Angela tightened her jaw, then relaxed when she realized she wasn't the only one upset. Erik's hand was fisted.

"I'm going to break his nose and rearrange it."

"Don't do that." She clutched at his taut

bicep to prevent him from stalking up to Cole and punching Cole's extremely handsome face. Though the more she thought about it, she was sure Cole could take care of himself and he could easily handle an angry Erik. "I have a better idea."

"You're right. Could you imagine the headlines?" He guided her away from Cole and Liza to the window seat on the opposite end of the room where the bay window looked out at the garden. "Let me hear this grand plan."

"I really don't have one."

"I'm so obvious, I even disgust myself. She's so beautiful."

That made Angela feel dowdy in her fancy dress and makeup that Emma had fixed. "I know I am nowhere near the standards of Liza, but maybe we could try to make her feel jealous?" And maybe Cole would also take some notice.

"That a girl. You are doing great, dear." Beatrice's voice broke through her mind. "I think I'll leave you on your own for a while." The energy that had been running through her was suddenly gone and for a moment she felt unsure and self-conscious.

"You can do this." The words fluttered through her mind and then she knew Beatrice was gone. Yeah, she could handle it, especially after she had another drink.

"Erik?"

He turned back to look at Angela. His vibrant eyes were miserable. Clearly, he'd been watching Liza. She wished Cole would look at her like that.

"Could you get us a drink?" she asked.

"Sure."

"But do not look her way. Ignore Liza proudly." She gave him a little push.

Erik walked to the side table that held the liquor and crystal. Her gaze shifted and caught Cole's deep silver eyes. They held for a moment and her stomach tightened and dropped low to her feet. Had he been watching her with Erik?

Then Liza giggled and Cole broke the connection. The moment was over that fast. Angela shrugged. What moment? The one she was imagining in her head? Forget it. She wouldn't be able to make Cole jealous because he had no interest in her whatsoever. She was wasting her time. He was interested in Liza.

That was fine. She'd wasted enough of the evening worrying about him. She'd have a drink and enjoy her conversation with Erik and call it a night.

Erik came back with a small crystal rocks glass filled with a caramel-colored liquid. She took a deep swallow, downing a third of it in one gulp. Its sweet flavor stuck in her throat, but she swallowed the cough.

"Slow down there, sweetie. Sherry has a high alcohol content," Erik warned.

Angela smiled up at him. "Bottoms up." She took another deep drink.

"Tell me about your business."

"You don't really want to know what I do."

"I'll find out what it is whether you tell me or someone else does."

"Oh right, you're the man with many connections."

"I have my fair share." He laughed and took a drink from his own glass.

"I run a very exclusive little business with my sister."

"It's nice that you and your sister do that together. I was a twin, but my brother died at a young age." His face clouded.

"Oh no." Angela placed a hand on his arm.

"He was hit by a car while coming home from baseball practice. He was in a coma for a long time. It was hard seeing him suffer that way."

"I'm sorry." Angela squeezed his arm trying to comfort him.

"I don't know why I told you that. I just felt like I could. Like you would understand."

"It is what I do. I help connect with spirits. Would you like me to try to connect with your brother? Usually ghosts come to me, but I could try."

Thank you. That would be nice." He covered her hand with his.

CHAPTER 23

COLE'S BLOOD WAS about to boil over. If Erik put his hand on Angela one more time, he might actually drag her out of here.

"You've been distracted all night." Liza's voice sounded too close to his ear and the warmth of her breath sent a cringe down his neck. It took his will not to pull away, but he was getting tired from having to do it all night. He had stayed by her side because he couldn't bring himself to insult Fran. He'd been sure before and now it was absolute that he and Liza would never be together.

"I have a lot of things on my mind." Yeah, like if Angela was going to toss back another glass. She was getting drunk, her face flushed and her laughter escalated as she practically fell all over Erik.

The guy was great. Cole didn't have a negative thing to say about him, not one. He just wasn't right for Angela.

They had been chatting all night. A cute couple, anyone would think that if they saw them. Cole didn't like it.

They had been in a serious conversation just moments ago, and now they joked and laughed.

Cole glanced at Liza. Her eyes were pure, clear, like water. Her long thin fingers wrapped around his forearm with the grace of a swirling ballerina. He covered her hand with his, then met her clear gaze. "Why are you doing this, Liza?"

"What do you mean?"

"All this—the cooing, the hanging on every word."

She huffed and tried to tug her hand free, but he held it fast.

"You have no interest in me. This is all a show."

"How can you say that?"

"Each time you touch my arm, you don't look for my reaction. Whenever you say those sweet loving words, you can't hold my gaze."

"That's not true."

She looked away and he knew she was lying. "You don't want me. You love someone else."

Her blush was telling, but he wouldn't push her anymore.

"My father knew we were a perfect match. It was what he wanted. I want to fulfill his final wish that we be together."

Cole shook his head. "He wouldn't want his only child to be unhappy."

"You could never make me unhappy, darling."

"I make everyone unhappy. I'm no good to any woman." He glanced across the room at Angela.

"That's not what my father thought."

"He only knew me as a child. He never saw the terrible man I've become."

"You are not terrible." She leaned in and ran a finger from her free hand over the back of the hand that captured her.

He released her. "You have no idea."

He pushed quickly from the love seat, shifting it back in his haste. He'd had enough of this farce with Liza and he couldn't stomach another moment of watching Angela throw back another drink, then laugh at one of Erik's jokes. Each time she touched Erik, he wanted to rip him to shreds. This night was becoming more miserable than he'd ever thought possible.

"What are you doing? Where are you going?" Liza called after him.

He didn't answer. His ears buzzed with a roaring anger. He was terrible and selfish. He was domineering and always got what he wanted. Right now, he wanted Erik away from Angela.

He took the four strides across the room and stopped in front of the laughing couple. Angela's swirling gaze met his and she crinkled into laughter, practically folding over. Erik caught her by the shoulders before she slipped off the window seat onto the floor.

"You're drunk," Cole accused. His tone sounded harsh even to his ears.

"Why yes, I think I am." She snickered and leaned into Erik, gripping the arm of his suit jacket. "I think I'd like another sherry."

"The last thing you need is another drink." Cole took the glass and scowled at Erik before he had a chance to fill it.

Cole ground his teeth to stop himself from

dragging her out of the party.

Dragging her to what? The safety of his castle? He definitely was not a knight in shining armor and he had no right to act like he had ownership over her. So what if they shared a few moments under a tree near the river. So what if their kiss had been like no other kiss he'd ever had.

"I am perfectly capable of making my own decisions, thank you." She thrust herself up from the cushions but lost her footing and stumbled in a pretzeled mess.

Cole caught her easily in his arm and pulled her close so she could catch her balance. She fit so perfectly in his arms. He breathed deeply of the spicy autumn scent he'd grown to know as her. He'd never appreciated the fall season so much before.

"I don't need your help." Her hands pressed into his chest. "Let me go," she hissed.

He tightened his hold for a bare moment before releasing her. She sneered at him. He had the strangest urge to smile, but he bit it back.

"I think it's time for you to go home."

She blinked those piercing eyes and her mouth opened, then shut before opening one more time. "How dare you?"

"I dare. You're drunk," he snarled back at her.

"You certainly are the biggest buzzkill."

The sudden urge to laugh rumbled through his chest. He swallowed it back because it was unexpected. She was something else. He wanted to kiss her right now, right in front of everyone. Claim her as his own so no one else felt like they could move in. Instead, he shook his head. "Come on, Angel girl, it's not the time or place. This party's over."

"And you know all about time and place?"

Two spots of pink brightened her cheeks and he knew she was thinking about their kiss by the river. All laughter completely wiped away.

He glanced at Erik for extra help, but Erik had absolutely no support for Cole's flailing. In fact, Erik's distant gaze wasn't focused on their conversation at all. His eyes trained on something over Cole's shoulder.

"What's going on here?" Liza asked with a false smile in her voice. "May I join you?"

Erik stood silent with a dumbfounded look like he had no idea of what to say.

"Perfect timing, Liza." Angela's words held the slightest of slurs.

"Of course." Liza glanced first at Cole, then to Erik. Was it even possible for her pale skin to lose any more of its color? He wouldn't believe it could be possible until he saw her blush fade to wan. "But why is that?"

Angela's brightening smile made Cole's stomach tighten in concern. She was drunk and that meant she'd be unpredictable.

"I saw you all night." She wiggled a pointed finger at Liza's chin since she was so much taller than Angela.

Cole had never realized how petite Angela was. Liza may have dwarfed Angela in height but not in her larger than life presence. Angela tried as much as she could to blend, but there was a particular glow that emanated no matter what she tried to do. No matter how many sweaters or plain white T-shirts she wore, she had a way of standing out.

Whenever she walked into a room, his eyes immediately drew to her. She was a beacon that he always followed. Even if they weren't close together, he still watched her.

"And what did you see me doing tonight?"

"Your slippery little claws, pawing all over the wrong man." Angela thrust the accusing finger at Liza, then wavered forward precariously. At the last moment she pulled herself back before she stumbled into Liza.

Erik's slight intake of breath was just loud enough for Cole to notice. His eyes narrowed on Erik. Was this guy jealous of Liza's overzealous display of attention during dinner?

Liza hooked an arm around Cole's elbow. "This man is strong." Her eyes shifted away from Angela's and held onto Erik's. "And tough. He would fight for the woman he loved. He would stand up for her in any circumstance. He would protect her from anything no matter what the cost." Her pointy chin lifted toward the ceiling and she held more tightly onto Cole's arm.

Erik stood stoic but for the tick in his cheek. With each new word Liza said, the twitch deepened. Trouble was brewing in this cauldron. Cole felt it as much as Angela claimed to feel ghosts.

Cole braced himself for the lightning storm that was about to strike.

Angela let out a snort and thrust a thumb in

Cole's direction. "That guy? Ha. Just because he saved me from a river and kissed me under a willow tree doesn't mean anything. He has no idea how to stand up for a girl. No idea at all."

"You kissed"—Liza's lips thinned— "her?" Tears welled up, causing the ice blue to melt into a deep puddle gray. "What does she have that I don't?" She pulled her hands away like they were burned by fire and one hand fisted over her mouth. "I can't believe this. How could you do this to my father? And you too?" She turned to Erik. Then with a cry, she turned and rushed from the room.

Cole watched her retreating back, stunned. Where had that come from? He'd made it perfectly clear that they could never be together no matter what her father may have wanted.

Distracted in his thoughts, he never saw the punch coming. The only indication that warned him was Angela's worried squeal before hot pain ripped through his mouth. He shook his head and touched his lip. The copper tinge of metal drifted over his tongue. He licked at the tear in his skin before piercing Erik with a firm stare.

"I'll let this go for today because we are in the house of the only man who ever treated me like a son." He dropped his hand to his side and formed it into a fist. "And I'm going to assume that you have feelings for Liza. Those things alone are why you still stand."

Cole reached out and gripped Angela's wrist. "It's time to leave." He didn't give her a chance to respond. He didn't think she would have said anything anyway since she didn't resist as he pulled her toward him.

"You're not taking her anywhere." Erik stepped between Cole and Angela. Cole tightened his grip on Angela. She didn't argue, so he was sure she was fine with his grasp.

"What are you going to do, Erik? Punch me again?" Cole eyed him coldly. He hoped Erik would take up the challenge. He'd been raring for a fight all night. He couldn't stomach his dinner while he'd watched Angela and Erik chat across the table. He was sick while observing the two of them whispering closely in front of the moonlight glow coming through the bay window. He hated that they'd chatted with a connection that seemed easy and effortless while he struggled with every move in their relationship.

Erik took a step back, though he still held his ground. Cole was a bit disappointed that Erik wouldn't take him up on the physical challenge.

"You are not taking Angela anywhere. I'll drive her home," Erik said.

"Why don't you go after Liza instead? She thinks she's upset over me, but she's confused."

"What are you talking about, Barlow?" Erik rubbed at his raw knuckles.

"Ever since I've been back, she hasn't been thinking clearly. In fact, the entire Greeley family is messed up with their grief at Max's death."

"But he's been gone for almost a year."

"My return has opened their wounds. Go to her. I'll take care of Angela. She'll be fine. Liza needs you."

Erik took a hesitating step, then glanced back to Angela.

"Go to her, Erik." Angela's voice was sweet as a cherub's.

Erik looked unsure for one last moment before he loped from the parlor. That's when Cole noticed the silence in the room. All the guests had been watching their gaudy interaction.

"I guess we should be going." Angela's lips lifted in a slight smile. Her gaze darted around the room pointedly.

Cole followed her gaze to fall first on Greta, who seemed to be smiling gleefully, then on Mrs. Greeley, who held her hand over her cheek, drumming her perfectly manicured pink fingertips, pearl bracelets slipping to the ruffled sleeve of her sweater. Her face was unreadable, but he knew she was disappointed in him. It was a driving spike into his gut.

Cole scrubbed a hand over his face. This had gone totally wrong. His entire life had gone totally wrong. How had he let it happen? He thought he'd gotten everything under control. Boy, was he an idiot. He had to get out of here, fast.

"I'm sorry, Fran. I never thought it would be like this." She didn't say anything and her silence was more painful than any lashing her words would have made. Cole squared his shoulders. "Enjoy the rest of the evening, everyone." Cole strode from the room. He made it through the doors to the outside porch. The cold, crisp air felt good on his charged nerves. He welcomed the late-night darkness after the blaring light and all the stares.

"Cole, wait up."

He hadn't realized he'd dropped Angela's hand until she came running after him.

Cole slowed his pace and shortened his gait for her.

"Would you stop? I think I might be sick."

He really wanted to get out of there. But he stopped and turned. "You look pale." This was not another of her fake outs.

"I really can't handle my liquor."

"You're going to have a pounder in the morning, Angel girl."

"So are you." Her small hand reached up to cup his face where Erik had punched him. Her thumb skimmed along the small cut on his lip. "Does it hurt much?"

"Not when you touch it." His voice became low and gravelly. Her touch made him forget about the throbbing pain. Most of it from the embarrassment to Fran. But her hand made all the pain disappear. He wanted her touch forever and that scared the hell out of him.

"Why did you let yourself get drunk?"

"I can't tell you that."

Before she could pull her hand away, he covered it with his. He swamped its tininess with his monster-sized grip. Her hands were tiny and delicate. She was tiny and delicate.

"Am I too rough for you?" He hated that the question came out ragged and torn. "I'm too much of a brute. I don't know how to be nice or gentle."

Her hand moved back and forth under his to caress his skin.

"I'm a big girl, Cole, and I'm not made of spun glass."

"You don't get it."

"No, I don't. How could I? You don't let anyone in."

"I'm tainted and no good for anyone."

"I understand, maybe more than anyone."

"How could you understand?" He dropped his hand and turned his back on her. He couldn't take her sweet innocence. His skin missed her touch and he closed his eyes at the loss. He couldn't live with himself if he hurt her and that was the only thing he knew how to do.

"I can understand more than you think. I know what it takes to block people from my heart."

"Not like this."

"Maybe you're right. I know what it feels like to be unwanted. It may be different from what you experienced, but I know what it's like to be a social outcast."

She could never know his deep pain. "You have no idea what it's like to want the love of your family, your father, your own blood. You had that love. I never did. I never will. You can't understand what it's like to be hated by the one person who should love you the most."

"I'm sorry."

"I don't want to talk about this. Not here. We need to go."

"Fine. Your car or mine?"

He turned back to see her looking like a gilded, fiery angel in the moonlight, her hands planted firmly on each hip. Her golden hair flew around her in the wind like moonlight. Her hair had been in an updo at the beginning of the party before the sparks had flown with the fight, but had somehow slipped free. Though her frame was tiny, it was filled with power.

In that moment, he knew she could handle anything he dished at her. His breath constricted in his lungs. Somehow, she had pierced through a weak point in his dragon's heart.

"I'll drive," she said.

"Oh no, you won't. How many glasses of wine did you guzzle tonight?"

"You made me so angry that I lost count."

"I made you angry?" He laced his fingers through hers and dragged her to his Camaro. She didn't resist. In fact, she actually kept pace with him, as eager to leave as he was.

"Whoa, my head is fuzzy." She giggled. "Smart idea to let you drive."

"You drank too much tonight. You're in for one big headache tomorrow." He smiled at her, although he really didn't want her to suffer. "You better take some aspirin the minute you get home."

Just as he tucked her into the passenger seat, a crackle of lightning shot across the sky, setting the hairs at the back of his neck on end. By the time he slipped into the other seat, storm clouds had rolled in.

Her eyes were already closing and her hair

streamed across her face. Reaching out, he gently swept the strand behind her ear. It was the softest hair he'd ever touched, so soft he had nothing to compare it to. He trailed another lock through his forefinger and thumb before he ran his palm entirely over the silk strands. She didn't move. She didn't pull away. She actually sighed at his touch. He watched her with wonderment. He was nothing but a devil and she was confident in his touch, so relaxed and trusting. She knew he would never hurt her. The weight of the knowledge filled the deepest, darkest part of him.

"Why aren't you afraid of me?" His breath formed into a tight ball at the back of his throat waiting for her response.

"Is this car spinning?" She groaned before dropping her head back against the headrest. Disappointment was a green ooze in his belly. She hadn't realized he was touching her. Just as he was releasing his fingers from her hair, she gripped him, pressing her palm against the back of his hand, stopping it in place.

"You're not all that scary. I hate to disappoint you, but you're a lot nicer than you think you are, Cole Barlow."

He jerked back to look at her. "Men fear me. Women hold their purses when I walk too close."

"Yah, yah. You devour small children too." She waved a hand at him like she was swatting at fleas, before it slipped limply to her lap. "An absolutely terrifying beast."

"You don't know the half of it." He shifted into gear and set his focus on the narrow gravel road lit by the circle of his car lights.

"That's true. I don't know anything about you."
Her voice was low and sleepy.

"You know more than most."

"How sad."

Cole didn't reply. What could he say? He knew
how pathetic he really was to have wasted his
life. But he was in too deep to turn back now.
Destroying his father had become his life and
he couldn't move on until this was finished. He
needed to completely separate from his father
and destroy every little piece. If it meant destroying himself in the process, then so be it.

He glanced at Angela, her face hidden in shadows. She was too sweet and delicate, and alluring.
Her lips parted lightly as she slept. Her soft,
rhythmic breath echoed in the silence. He was
the biggest of fools.

He'd been pissed when he saw her with Erik.
His gut had roiled to watch them together while
at the same time he knew she deserved someone
decent, someone who had a future to give to her,
someone like Erik.

The sky opened and raindrops plopped on
the windshield like little tears. Cole shifted the
switch and the wipers swiped them away. He
drove down the narrow road into the woods. The
only light came from his headlights. It was how
he liked it. The darkness made him feel alone
without the worry of pain or rejection. The only
music to remind him that he was not in solitude
was Angela's even breaths.

He hit his brights and the circle of light

expanded. Along the side of the road, two bright white eyes reflected. Cole took his foot off the accelerator to let the car slow down.

He tensed, hoping the deer would stay frozen, but the eyes shifted and the deer ran across the gravel. It had moved early enough and disappeared fast enough into the opposite row of trees. As quickly as it had appeared, it was gone.

Angela's breath lulled him and he relaxed back into the drive until he saw fog form suddenly up ahead. Like a cloud descending in the center of the road, a gray mist materialized. Cole blinked, then squinted as the fog grew and took shape. "What in the hell?"

He gripped the steering wheel and leaned closer to the windshield to get a better look. His eyes widened when he realized it wasn't a cloud. It was a man in the road.

He had been driving too fast. There wasn't enough time to stop.

The man grew bigger and bigger as Cole hit the brakes. Wet gravel caused the car to fishtail and it slid like it was on slick ice. The shape turned and Cole looked right into the face of the man he was about to run over.

His blood ran cold. It couldn't be. The man with dark hair and dark eyes looked directly into Cole.

There wasn't enough time to shift or even throw his arms up to protect his face from the impact.

The man didn't move either. He stood, hands on his hips, and snarled at Cole with all the anger

Cole knew too well.

All Cole could do was watch as his father's face came closer and closer. Cole could not tear his eyes away from his father's dark, angry eyes.

The car hit into the body, but there was no impact, no jolt, no shattering glass. There was only the distinct freezing chill that ran through Cole's body, turning his blood into icicles. The contents of his stomach retched into his throat. He pulled to the side and flung the car door open. Gasping, he needed to catch his breath. His stomach roiled. The cold, stormy wind slammed into his face, pulling the last remnants of oxygen from his lungs as if he was suffocating.

He jumped from the car, pulled in a deep intake of air and welcomed the slap of the last raindrops from the fading storm. He couldn't stop replaying the image of his father's face. Over and over, his car crashed into his father in his mind. He felt sick at the thoughts. Wasn't that what he wanted? To destroy everything about his father? But being faced with it like that was almost too much to handle.

"Did you get sick? I thought I'd be the one puking tonight," Angela's raspy voice sounded. "Are you alright?"

Her question pulled him back into reality. With a swipe of the back of his hand, he wiped at his eyes and brushed the raindrops from his face. "I'll be fine." He let out a deep breath. What the hell was going on? He was going crazy. He was imagining things.

"You're not okay." She placed a soft hand on his

shoulder. "What did I miss?"

He couldn't tell her that he was hallucinating images of his dead father. "I'm just tired."

"You know I'll believe just about anything." She gave him a confident nonjudgmental smile and he broke.

"I'm going crazy."

"Oh, Cole." Her hand slid to his cheek. "Tell me."

He leaned into her soft touch and closed his eyes against it, but it was too late. Her soft touch melted at the ice.

"I thought my father was standing in the road."

"What was he doing?"

"Standing, staring angrily. I have always been a disappointment to him."

"No." She shifted her thumb over his lips. "That's over now."

"It's not over. Not yet."

She ran her thumb softly along his bottom lip, sending licks of fire though to his core.

"You can't do this to yourself, Cole." She leaned toward him. "The past is the past."

Her lips touched his in a bare brush. He squeezed his eyes tighter to resist her alluring embrace, but he was tired. Too tired to resist. Too tired of being alone and unwanted.

The restraint around his heart shattered and he could no longer resist his hunger for her. He'd worry about the consequences later.

He gripped her upper arms but didn't pull her closer. He wanted her to come to him of her own volition. He couldn't take it if she pulled back now that he wanted her to move closer. Holding her in his arms, he raised his head. "I'm tainted, Angela. I don't know if I have what it takes to give you what you deserve."

"You're not tainted." She brushed another kiss on his lips. "I wish I could make you forget." She kissed his cheek. "I want to make it all go away." She kissed his other cheek. As if she tried to kiss away the hurt and pain of his past.

A groan escaped from his depths and he tightened his hold on her, pulling her into his chest so they pressed together from waist to shoulder. He slid his hand up her arm to the nape of her neck and gently slipped his fingers into her hair.

He pulled her lips back to his. They barely touched. "Help me forget," he whispered against her lips before leaning fully into them and deepening the kiss, tasting cinnamon sweetness, craving more of her.

She didn't pull back. Instead, she kissed him with the same level of passion, and it made him want more. He wanted more than he deserved, but he took from her like a drowning man gasping for breath.

He slid his hand from her hair to the curve of her back, wishing she wore her cotton tee instead of the pretty yellow dress. He wanted to feel her bare skin. Touch her and know this was real and not his imagination conjuring images like his father.

He froze and fisted the hand at the small of her back. He broke the kiss and pressed his forehead against hers. Even now his father forced his way into his thoughts, ruining everything. "I can't." His voice tore from him.

Angela didn't pull away as he'd expected. Instead she wrapped her arms around him and held him closer.

"I understand," she said.

He'd never hated his father more than in this moment. "Why the hell are you so goddamned understanding?" He gripped her wrists and pushed her away from him. "I don't deserve it and I don't want it."

"Stop pushing me away. You've spent your entire life pushing people away. You can't keep doing this."

"Why not? It's worked in the past."

"Has it?" she whispered. The words hung for a moment then, like brittle glass, fell between them.

He had nothing to say. They got back into the car and hew turned on the engine, pulling onto the gravel road. They sat in an uncomfortable silence as they drove from the gravel road onto the paved street leading to the downtown area of Dalewood.

"We left my car there." She broke the silence.

"I'll take you back tomorrow to get it"

"What a night." She rubbed her forehead. Had he given her the headache or was she feeling the effects of too much wine already?

"Typical for me," he gave her a sheepish glance. "Things have a way of going to hell when I'm involved."

"You're too hard on yourself."

He shrugged and kept his eyes on the road. It

wasn't as dark now since they had driven into the well-lit incorporated region. Buildings and shops lined the empty streets.

He felt awful. He couldn't leave her like this. They were strained and it was his fault. "I'm sorry I ruined your entire evening."

"Not the entire night."

"Only some of it?" He smiled.

"I did have a little fun at dinner," she said.

"You did? I was miserable."

"How is that possible?" She turned her entire body in the passenger seat to face him. "You seemed to be having a fabulous time."

"You have me confused with someone else."

"I saw you." She sounded like she was accusing him of stealing. "You and Liza had a great time."

"She's confused right now." He pulled the car in front of her apartment building and put it in park. He didn't want her to leave yet. "My being back has caused old memories to resurface."

"She looked like she was very interested in you all night. Was there an old flame rekindled?"

"An old flame? Liza is like a sister to me."

"That's not how it looked tonight."

"And how did it look?"

"Let's just say, the two of you seemed very intimate."

"How could you notice? You were too caught up in your own little conversations with Erik."

"All Erik talked about was his undying love for Liza while the two of you only had eyes for each other."

"You and Erik were very cozy and laughing all

night. He sure didn't look like he was crying in his wine."

"He was, but I cheered him up."

"I didn't like it."

She licked her lips and eyed him so intently he swore she could see right through his body and soul. Then she turned, breaking the connection, and he felt deflated.

"You really piss me off."

He held back a smile at her curse.

"You push me away and then you say that to me? I feel like a yo-yo." She crossed her arms over her chest. "It's too much."

She reached for the door and stepped out of the car. Before closing it, she leaned back inside, her face glimmering in the interior car light. "The only person I want is you and for the life of me I'm struggling to figure out why." She swiftly slammed the door while her words hung with him in the small space of his car. Her words had shaken him. The ball was in his court, but the only things he was good at were destroying things and fucking up. Pretty much just acting like his father.

He was tired of being that way. Could he change for her? Yeah, because he wanted her too.

CHAPTER 24

"MY SKULL HAS a lightning bolt striking the back of my brain." Angela groaned as she pressed the heels of her palms into her eyes to release some of the headache tension.

"You got drunk last night?" Emma called from her own bedroom.

"Don't sound so shocked."

"What got into you?"

"Could you get me some water?" She pried her sandpaper tongue from the roof of her mouth. "I guess I got upset. I also left my car there and need you to take me back to get it."

"Dish it. You never get drunk."

"Water first."

Angela fell back into her pillows and closed her eyes against the glaring morning sun that poured through the sheer curtains covering the windows. What had she done? Why had she said all those things to Cole?

She knew exactly why she was falling for him. He was tough and arrogant and not always nice. But he was also sweet and caring. She'd seen the way he protected others. He wanted to protect her at the bar, but wouldn't fight Steve. When Erik punched him in the face, he still acted with reason and had Liza's best interests at heart. He cared for Fran and she cared for him in return. Even if he didn't believe it, Cole had a sweet sensitive heart inside him. It was no wonder that she was falling for him. She hoped she hadn't messed the whole thing up by telling him that she had feelings for him. At least she hadn't said the L word. Was she actually falling in love with him? Last night had made her realize just how much she wanted him, but was it love?

"Here you go, drunken lady." Emma returned with a bottle of water, icy cold from the fridge. She smiled as she tossed the bottle of water. "Now spill."

Angela caught the bottle and pressed the cold surface to her temple with a sigh.

"I have a better remedy for a hangover. Water usually makes it worse."

"If it has cayenne and an egg"—she gulped back the bile that pushed up from her stomach— "I'll take a pass."

"It's better than that. Hold that thought." Emma disappeared. Glasses clinked and can tops popped from the vicinity of the kitchen.

"Eew, what is that?" Angela skewered her face into a disgusted scowl when Emma returned with the concoction in a glass. "It looks like urine. I can't drink that."

"You can drink it and it'll make you feel great. Trust me." She thrust the glass into Angela's hands.

"I won't do it. Mama said never to trust someone who says 'trust me,'" Angela protested.

"Just do it. You'll thank me for it later. You'll be rolling out the red carpet and sprinkling flowers under my feet."

"What's in it?" She took a sniff. It didn't smell all that bad, citrus and something else.

"Drink first and I'll share later."

Angela lifted the glass hesitantly and took a tentative sip. It wasn't half bad.

"You don't sip it, chug it." Emma waved her hands to get her to drink faster.

Angela lifted the glass and gulped down a third of the contents. She took a deep breath. "I guess it's all right. What is it?"

"It's orange juice and an energy drink."

"What? I hate that stuff."

"Oh, sister, you have no idea." Emma shook her head. "Finish your medicine and you'll feel much better. Trust me. Vitamin C and all that."

"Fine. But if I get gall stones, I'm blaming you." Angela drank a few more sips of the bright fluorescent liquid and leaned back into the bed.

"Tell me about last night."

"There's not much to say. I met Erik Portly."

"I've been hearing some buzz about him. He wants to follow in daddy's footsteps. Politicians."

"He's actually very nice. We hit it off like fast friends."

"Like I said, slippery politicians."

"You've never met him. He is actually very nice."

"So what? Did you do shots together with your new biffles?"

"Biffles?"

Emma waved a dismissive hand. "BFFs, best friends for life. Oh, forget it." She flopped onto the edge of the bed at Angela's feet. "It was supposed to be a joke."

"I swear you'll like him."

"Are you trying to hook me up with him?"

"No. He's actually very much in love. It was really romantic."

"Stop changing the subject. I want the scoop. You and Erik, continue."

"You're relentless and I need to rest my pounding head."

"Lay it on the pillow, sister, but keep talking."

"He's not in love with me. He wants Liza. They seemed perfect for each other."

"Wasn't she jealous that you and Erik got along so well?"

"Actually, it was Erik who was jealous." She closed her eyes and willed her stomach to relax. She wasn't too sure about Emma's home remedy.

"Jealous of his girl, Liza? Pretty miss perfect Liza Greeley?"

"You hit it on the head. Liza was fawning all over Cole." Her tone came out like a growl.

"And Erik was the only jealous one at this party?" Emma raised a neatly styled eyebrow at Angela.

"We are only discussing Erik right now."

"Uh huh." She bit at her thumbnail and bounced her foot back and forth over the edge of the bed.

Angela ignored her sister's sarcasm and continued. "Like I was saying, Liza was fawning all over Cole and Erik was beyond miffed. He was scalding. It all finally spilled over when I blurted out that Cole and I had kissed under the old willow near the river walk. You know that one."

"Whoa, whoa what?"

"Didn't I tell you about that?" Angela turned in her pillows, trying to hide her embarrassment and growing blush. Great, she'd just spilled the beans again. "Yes, I did."

"Okay, but you didn't."

"On with the story."

"Avoider."

"All during dinner," she continued, ignoring her sister's words. "Liza drooled over every word Cole had to say and her fingers trailed along his shoulder and down his arm, practically molesting him the entire night. It was disgusting."

"Relax, girl, you're going to tear that pillow apart." Emma chuckled.

Angela looked down to see the pillow twisted in her hands. When had she even picked it up? She tossed it to the other side of the bed near her feet and took a sip of the energy drink.

"Erik was very jealous?"

"After dinner everyone went into the parlor for drinks. I had a drink and then another."

"Hence the headache today?"

"Cole came up to Erik and me, dark eyed, angry and accusing."

"Why was he angry?"

"I think he was jealous too."

"Of course he was."

"He made Erik angry. My head is a little fuzzy about the entire thing."

"What were you drinking?"

"Sherry. It makes me nauseous to think about it." She groaned and cradled her roiling belly. "I thought I would be safe with it. I'll never touch the stuff again. I opened my big mouth about that kiss and everything got out of control. And Liza got so upset that she ran off."

"Why would that make her upset?"

"Ever since Cole came back, she's been talking about the last wishes of her father. He always thought Cole should be a part of the family and that they should marry."

"Liza wants to give her father his last wish and marry Cole?"

"Not if Erik has something to do about it."

"Oh really."

"He was so upset at Cole that he actually punched him in the face. Cole could easily take him, but wouldn't."

"Even after he was punched, Cole didn't fight back?"

"No. Punched right in the mouth. No, he wanted Liza to be happy and he sent Erik after her."

"And you weren't the least bit jealous last night?"

"I was surprised, to say the least."

"I'm sure. If Cole sent Erik to help Liza, what did you end up doing?"

"From what I remember, Cole dragged me out of there."

"He swooped you away? Rescued you from a fate worse than death?"

"I guess." Her face began to burn.

"Did you make out with him again?" Emma laughed and got up to leave the bedroom. "You can't hide in your bed all morning. You need to stop avoiding and face the day."

Angela threw her pillow at Emma's retreating back.

"Somebody's got a boyfriend," Emma's voice floated down the hallway at Angela in a sing-song.

CHAPTER 25

———— ∾ ————

"THANKS FOR A great seminar, everyone." Angela clapped with the audience. She hadn't known how much she would grow to love this newest segment of the business. Emma had suggested the idea to create another avenue of revenue, but now it was such a positive experience that Angela looked forward to it every week.

"I see a lot of regular faces, but there are also new faces in the crowd. You make these seminars what they are. I'll take individual questions on the side."

She pointed to the left wall. "If you wish to include your story in the next seminar, please fill out a card. They are located on the back table. Thanks, everyone."

Angela brushed her bangs from her eyes and stepped from the platform to join the crowd waiting for her. A small man with dark greasy hair blocked her way. Pierce Foster. What was he doing here? She tried to brush past him, but he wouldn't budge.

"The line for questions starts over there."

"Angela, may I have a word with you?" Pierce

wheezed through his large nose. "We spoke briefly the other night. My name is Pierce Foster, Elected President of the Dalewood Historical Society."

"I remember."

"I must speak to you about that urgent matter. You know. About Cole Barlow and the Penniberg Mansion."

"I'm a little busy right now." She glanced at the line that was quickly growing. "Can we discuss this another time?"

"It's imperative that we settle this immediately."

"It may seem immediate to you, Mr. Foster."

"Pierce. Please call me Pierce."

"Pierce. The attendees paid to participate in this conference and right now their issues are more pressing. I promise to discuss the mansion with you after I am finished here."

"I simply cannot wait. There is a major problem."

"What's wrong?" The mansion was haunted with a poltergeist. They could always shift into a dangerous realm. Had something happened? Was Cole okay? Her heart slammed against her ribs. Suddenly, she wanted to shake the little man. "Explain. What's the problem?"

He cleared his throat. "The problem is you."

Angela hadn't expected that and flinched.

"You must cease and desist your ghost hunt on the properties of the Penniberg mansion and surrounding estate."

He thrust a hand toward her and she automatically took a step back.

"What?" she asked confused. "By what authority? Cole Barlow hired me to help the ghosts that have been trapped in the mansion and I intend to do my job." Angela felt the stares of the seminar attendees burning holes through her back.

"Mr. Barlow has yet to speak to you about the proposal set forth by the historical society?"

"No, I have no idea what you're talking about."

"Read this." He waved the paper in his outstretched hand. "The historical society has drafted a contract to purchase the Penniberg mansion and said surrounding estates. We plan to create a museum for all of Dalewood to enjoy."

"Out of the mansion? And how does this affect the contract that I currently have with Cole? They don't seem related."

"Your contract will be null and void. Mine trumps yours. Hank Barlow started the proceedings of the sale, but he died before every detail was finalized. In this newest draft, you are to leave any said ghosts to their own volition to haunt the mansion as they please."

"Why would you want those souls to suffer like that?"

"It would increase the tourism to Dalewood's new museum."

"You plan to use the ghosts for your own gains. I won't allow it." She slammed her fists to her hips.

"Ms. Haven. It will no longer be your concern. It will be the concern of the city of Dalewood."

"You said the draft was never finalized."

"All we need is Cole Barlow's signature."

"He'll never sign that contract," she said with more confidence than she actually felt. It was the perfect excuse for Cole to get the mansion off his hands and then he'd finally be free.

"I have no doubts that he will sign over the mansion to the historical society. It's best if you cease now."

Angela was relieved when Pierce strode from the center. She tried to focus on all the questions from the attendees. Once she'd spoken to everyone, she looked for Emma.

She located her boxing up all the brochures and schedules.

"Emma, I have to deal with a pressing matter."

"I'll take care of everything on this end."

"Thanks. It should be slow now that the seminar is over. We might get one or two walk-ins. Just take the info."

"It's all under control."

She grabbed her purse and headed to Penniberg. Why hadn't Cole told her about the historical society the other night? Or any time she'd been investigating? She could have avoided the entire disgusting display with that odious, pointy-faced rodent. That's why she was going over there right now to ask him to his face. She'd known that the mansion was part of the historical society's consideration, but she hadn't known that Pierce had taken a stand. Cole had some nerve keeping her out of the loop.

When she got to the mansion, she barely shut off her SUV before running to the door, then pounding on it. He'd better be home.

And waited.

She pounded again. He didn't answer. She walked around the bushes to the front bank of windows, looking for one that was open.

"Cole Barlow, answer this door." She went back to the door and pounded on it with both fists this time. Where was he? Was he avoiding her? Was he planning to skip town before he even told her about this?

How could he just leave? Did she mean nothing? Did the trapped spirits mean nothing? How could he do this to her? To them?

She was falling for him. The night of the dinner, she could barely keep her hands off of him. He was always on her mind. And clearly, she meant nothing to him. She pounded again.

"Where are you, Cole Barlow? If you're gone, you'll be sorry."

"And who's going to do that?"

With a gasp, she spun around to see him leaning up against a tree all cozy and calm as could be. Her blood boiled. "I am." Without a thought she rushed to bare inches before him. Her breaths came in short quick puffs of anger. "Were you going to stand there and watch me pound against the door like a fool?" His face was blank and unreadable and it irritated her even more. Where was his reaction?

"I was down by the river. What's got you in such a tizzy?" He stepped closer and she could feel the heat pouring from him in waves. At the slight distance she could see a small muscle tick at the corner of his mouth. Maybe he was more affected by her anger than she thought. Good. He could be as upset as she was. She was ready for an argument. She put her hands on her hips. "I had a visit from a not so lovely person today. Care to explain?"

He narrowed his eyes. "Who visited you?"

"You're going to play stupid?"

The lip that had been ticking a moment ago, now twitched with the essence of a smile. "I don't know what you're talking about."

"Your new business partner."

He tilted his head. Confusion etched his features.

"Pierce Foster came to my office today. Sat down to partake in one of my seminars, for free, I might add. Then told me how I was no longer welcome at the mansion. My contract was null and void."

"That little vulture."

"Why didn't you tell me yourself, Cole?" Disappointment tore through her, hot like searing lava to her sensitive nerves. It hurt more than she wanted it to.

"There was nothing to tell you."

"You don't think it's important to tell me that you're leaving?" Her voice hitched and she hated herself for it.

She couldn't read his face. He took the last step, closing the little space between them. Without any warning, he lifted his hand and cupped her cheek. Her breath caught.

"I never said I was leaving. That weasel should have stayed in his little hole."

"But you're selling the mansion to the histor-ical society."

"There was nothing to say because I never made any decisions."

"You're considering leaving?"

"What reason do I have to stay?"

He rubbed his thumb along the ridge of her cheekbone with a velvety soft movement. He meant more to her than she wanted to admit. With an electric shock, she realized she'd fallen in love with him. Hard. This insufferable, arro-gant brute of a man who had many flaws and wouldn't let anyone get close.

Hot shivers coursed through her entire body. He made her feel like no one ever had. He scared her to death. She felt alive when she was with him. Wasn't that what Emma wanted? She'd told Angela she needed to live a little.

Angela had forgotten all about living until Cole walked into her life and spun everything on its axis. How could she simply let him go? The thought of him leaving was too painful.

She wanted to tell him to stay...for her.

Instead, she said, "You can't leave. The ghosts need our help." It just came out of her mouth. She knew it sounded stupid, but she couldn't tell him the truth.

"They don't need *our* help." His gaze left hers and she felt a cool chill replace their warmth. "I'm not sure if they need your help anymore either."

Should she tell him? She was afraid. Afraid he didn't believe in her. Afraid he would leave anyway, even if she told him how she felt, especially if she told him how she felt. She reached for his sleeve.

"And why is that?" The words came out as a whisper and she was terrified of his answer.

"I should leave Dalewood for good. It would be easy. Just pick up and walk out. It would be easy to walk away and never look back." He shoved his hands in his pockets. "I could get rid of the mansion and be done with my father forever. This place brings back too many bad memories I'm tired of reliving. There's no reason for me to stay here anyway." Finally, he looked at her with eyes blazing, piercing her with intensity that took away her breath. "What's keeping me here?"

"I don't want you to leave."

"I know." He pressed his forehead to hers and closed his eyes. Then he stepped away and left her under the colonnade.

Bile burned at her throat and she blinked back the tears that flooded her view of the closed door after he'd slipped inside. She'd practically told him how deeply she felt for him and he walked away.

CHAPTER 26

COLE LAY IN his bed staring at the ceiling. Gold flashing eyes floated in his mind each time he tried to sleep.

Staying would be the worst thing for her. But he was far from knowing everything. He acted like he was a know-it-all. He had to.

Alone in his room, he could finally admit, at least to himself, that he wanted her. He needed every inch of the beautiful woman who had somehow started haunting his every thought.

When she'd stormed at him with her flushed cheeks and her lips spewing anger about selling the mansion, he'd wanted to grab her to him and turn her angry words into lusty ones that made him tight just thinking about it. He knew then that he was playing with fire. He couldn't stay.

He would call Pierce in the morning and sign all the papers. A small piece of his heart ached. He lay in bed thinking about those beautiful golden eyes and the woman who came with them as his eyes drifted closed.

Filigreed golden gates of heaven blended and swirled before him until they formed into the most beautiful set of eyes he'd ever seen, Angela's eyes. Clouds rolled in, covering them over. Their gray streaks parted to reveal a towering limestone mansion. Flickering candlelight in the window on the second floor glowed bright. Cole stared at the window, drawn to the light like a moth, riveted.

"You belong here. You can't leave." A voice came into his mind, low and demanding. It was a sweet, familiar voice that rang in his head. His gaze remained locked on the window. A shadow stood there, like it had always been there watching him, waiting.

A hand, white and transparent, beckoned from the window. He felt a sense of wonder and belonging. Somehow, he knew Angela was inside the mansion. He was drawn to the window, to the mansion and to the secrets inside.

"What do I need to know?" he whispered. Water rushed loudly past him. The Steele raged. Rocks crunched under his footsteps and he realized the path to the mansion lay before his feet. He moved along the stones, closer and closer to the mansion, knowing he was moving toward his future.

Though he tried to get to the mansion, it seemed farther away. Panic flooded through him and still he pushed forward. He needed to find out the truth. One step turned into another and another until he was running. The path twisted and turned until he realized it was gone. Disoriented, he was no longer on the gravel path. He was surrounded by ferns and bushes, caught in the garden maze, lost.

He needed to find the truth but couldn't. Blocked, he spun around looking for the opening, but the bushes boxed him in on all sides.

The truth was here. He knew it. He could feel it.

Pain tore through his chest and he doubled over. With hands gripping his knees, he gasped like a dying fish, dragging air into his tight, rebellious lungs.

Darkness surrounded him. The only light came from the golden glow of the low hanging moon, full-faced and giving a mocking, sinister grin. Panic bubbled. Cole knew he could be more than his father thought. Angela believed in him more than he believed in himself.

The truth wasn't in the maze. It was inside him, but he'd blocked it for so long he was too afraid to face what his heart already knew.

The leaves fluttered on the low hanging branches of the bushes. He walked to the edge of the living wall that blocked him from the mansion, from his future. Lifting his hand, he touched the manicured greenery.

"What the…"

He pulled back when the rough surface rippled like water. With one finger, he touched it, and again it rippled like a liquid surface.

He pushed.

His hand went through the bush. He took a step, then lifted his foot into the bush. He entered the cool darkness. It reminded him of the feeling when he and Angela had been trapped in the secret passage together. An electrically charged heaviness hung over him as if a lightning storm brewed. Another step pushed him through the barrier. The tentacles of the dimension he'd just escaped dragged at him. He pushed farther through until the fingers of electricity released their hold and he was free on the other side.

He didn't know what it was—a sound, a feeling—but he turned and Angela was there. Wearing a white gauzy dress. The hem and sleeves flowed behind her. Wind dragged at her hair, lifting it from her shoulders and dropping it back in soft flowing waves.

She was a goddess. His goddess.

Angela lifted a hand. Her slim fingers fanned, calling him without words. She stood, a bright golden beacon in the moon's halo.

Under her spell, he stepped toward her as if all time had stopped. He took another step and stumbled forward as if he'd hit a barrier in the path. His guts twisted and he couldn't breathe again, though he watched her the entire time.

Her sweet face changed and the gold faded from her eyes, replaced with pain. She shook her head and turned from him.

"Angela, please. Don't leave me." He grasped for her fading gown, but she floated through the darkness.

The wall of branches opened to reveal a solid oak door he hadn't noticed before. The door opened for her and all he could see was the darkness flowing from the other side. Without turning back, she walked through, slamming the door shut with a resounding bang.

When he looked up, the door was no longer in the bushes, it was attached to the gray Penniberg mansion.

Like a seething beast, the mansion towered over him. Lights blazed in every window.

Letting out a war cry, he slammed his shoulder into the door. Beating it, pounding it, until his shoulder ached and his fists were swollen and throbbed. "Let me in. Angela, let me in."

"All you need to do is turn the key. The choice is yours. It always has been." Her voice flowed around him like ribbons. Where was she? Why was she doing this to him?

Covering his face in his hands, he fell to his knees. What she asked was too much. He couldn't do it.

"Why would you want to do that anyway? You're too weak."

Cole head snapped up at the low, guttural words.

"She deserves better than you. You're no good. You'll just abandon her." His father's angry voice replaced the sweet comfort of Angela's. "That's what you do."

"No, it isn't."

"You run away because you're weak."

"No, I don't."

"You've always taken the easy route. You're so much like your mother."

"I left because of you. I'm more like you than you want to admit, Father."

"You're nothing like me. You could never be

like me."

"You'd love that, wouldn't you?" Rage built in Cole as if he were a rabid animal.

"I wanted nothing more than a son I could teach and leave my legacy, but I got you instead." Hank's laugh was like a punch so painful it ripped into Cole's heart and made him want to die.

"You won't turn that key. You don't deserve it."

"Maybe you're right." The weight of Cole's life as a child hung heavy around him. "I abandoned you. You were no father to me."

"And you were never a son."

How could he give Angela what she asked? He couldn't love her. Love only brought risk and pain. That was all he knew how to give her. That was all he'd ever known. His stomach lurched. Facing his father clarified the need to stop what they had started.

Why did he feel as if he'd rather die than tell her that? He raised his head and looked at his father. "Why do you hate me so much?"

"You prevented me from my dreams and hopes."

Anger so deep broke through the barriers and spewed from Cole. "How could you do that to a child? To me? I was your son."

"That's just it. There are secrets too deep to tell. When your mother ran off, I was saddled with you and it was too much."

"I don't need you. I don't need anyone." But Cole needed her. He needed Angela. Suddenly, he realized he couldn't be without her. He raised his head to look at the door Angela had disappeared through. Why was he wasting his time fighting with a dead man who'd never cared for him? Angela cared for him and he loved her. He'd been too stupid and too screwed up to realize how he'd felt all along.

"I think I do want to turn the key." It was time to close the door on the past and open a new passage. He could have a future. And now that he realized it, he was desperate for it.

Cole reached for the door handle, but before he could turn the knob, his father's face appeared on the door. It contorted into the unrecognizable figure of a snarling monster, twisted in rage.

Anger hit Cole in the belly like waves, punching over and over with unseen hands, knocking him back. He fell to the ground on hands and knees. His father wanted him prostrate, but he wouldn't let himself fall flat.

As he caught himself, his fingers brushed something cool and solid. He gripped at its thin length and hid it between his fingers.

Pushing to his feet, he steeled himself against his father's wrath. "You don't control my decisions anymore." With that, he raised his hand and held the key, shiny and golden. He speared it through the air like a knife, pushing past the anger and thrust the key in the lock.

All hatred dissipated and he was filled with contentment. Finally, he was making choices for his future. His father no longer controlled him. With a steady hand, he held the key and turned it in the lock.

Cole woke in his bed, sweat soaked and heart

pounding. His belly ached almost as much as his heart. Why couldn't it have been as easy as the dream? Why couldn't he forget his past and just get over it? He thrust the covers from him and sat up on the edge of the bed. Could Angela really be his chance to move on and get over the past?

In the dream he'd said he'd loved her and he knew she loved him. It was only a dream. He cared for her and she made him feel things he'd never let himself feel before. She was funny and sweet and cared about everyone else more than herself. Hell, she wanted to help his bastard of a father. He didn't know anyone kinder than Angela.

Cole flicked on the lamp and pulled the taped letters from the end table. Though he'd put them back together like puzzle pieces, he'd been unable to bring himself to actually read them, so he'd stashed them in the drawer and tried to forget they existed. But they called to him.

Did his father deserve any of his understanding? Fran wanted him to have the letters for a reason. Maybe he needed to read them just so he could take that first step at moving on. He folded the letters and stuffed them in his pocket. The air in the bedroom felt hot and thick. He needed to take a breath and get out of the house.

He decided to take a walk through the grounds in the dark. He went outside and walked around the mansion. It didn't seem as terrifying as it had appeared in his dream. It was just the house he'd lived in and now it was the house that he remembered Angela walking through. She treated the place like an infant. She was always loving and gentle when she slid caresses along the walls and traced the edges of the furniture. It was like she was consoling a crying child, kissing away any small injury like she could make it all go away.

She touched him like that too. When he was with her it did *all go away*. He could forget the past when he looked in her eyes.

He walked toward the river. Now it made him think of her. Everywhere he walked, he was reminded of Angela. She somehow was taking over every bad memory he had. Instead of his first thought being about his father, his thoughts were about Angela. How she'd wanted to walk through the woods. Or how she scampered along the grass to spend time in the aviary.

He kept walking and the path changed from a cement walkway to gravel until he moved farther and the soft ground of the woods silenced his footsteps. The cool autumn breeze blew, rustling the letters he'd pulled out of his pocket. The scent of the trees surrounded him, pine and birch. He took a deep breath. He was coming to like autumn. He didn't realize how much he'd enjoyed the changing leaves, their crunch under his feet when they'd fallen to the ground.

Angela loved the fall season. She said it was her favorite time. A time between life and death. She felt that way too, caught between the world of the living and tormented by her need to help the dead. He realized how much he was in limbo too, caught between the torment of his past and the possibility to start a new future.

Cole found the willow tree where he'd rescued Angela and they'd sat shivering, clinging to each other after she'd fallen into the river. He'd held her and warmed her, but she was the one who was thawing the ice around his heart.

He leaned against the tree and slid down its trunk. All the memories had rushed back once she'd entered his life. Like she was sent to make him remember, make him forget. Could he forgive? How could he? That was asking too much. It was like asking him to abandon himself.

He remembered the letters he held. He pulled out the little flashlight hooked on his keychain and scanned the lines. The paper was faded and yellow and the black ink was worn in places.

Max,

My reasons may not be good enough for some and they aren't good enough for me either. I don't excuse my behavior, though it was a relief when Cole left. I won't voice my reasons in this letter. I will take those reasons to the grave. I've hurt enough over the years and I know I caused that child so much pain. No one can imagine the pain. I endured all those years holding on to the knowledge that haunted me and to learn that history repeats itself only helped me realize that there was no point in revealing all I know about the irreparable damage that has occurred in this home generation after generation. This is in no way an apology letter. I could never apologize for my part in all that I've done and all those who owe me an apology are long since gone from this earth. Just know there is much more to the story than I am capable or willing to say. Thank you for giving Cole the education and the care that I was unable to give.

Yours, Hank

Cole crumpled the letter. Was this an apology? Was this supposed to assuage his raw heart? It didn't. "How can I forgive you?"

Cole pushed up away from the tree and walked to the edge of the river. The rushing water barreled against the bank, dragging debris. Water lapped up near his shoes. His insides churned with turmoil like the churning water.

Gold light glimmered from under the water's surface. Stepping closer, Cole leaned over and stuck his hand through the frigid surface. The object was hooked onto a branch that had gotten wedged. He gripped the golden circle. It was attached to a chain. He pulled. It was his lost medallion, caught on a branch with the chain wrapped around the knobs in the stick.

Cole untangled the medallion and closed it in his fist. The rejected gift of a small boy that he'd forgotten. It was a symbol, a reminder to stay the course, continue his goal to destroy his father. Damage his father the way he had been damaged. The little boy that had been hurt and destroyed by rejection, humiliation and abuse. The boy who had grown into a man who had nothing but revenge to keep him warm and fill his emptiness.

"Did you feel empty, Hank? How did you fill your empty spots? Or did you pretend they didn't exist?" Cole had learned a lot from his father. Too much. Fran had said he was like his father.

Realization dawned. All these years, he hadn't been trying to eliminate his father. He'd been trying to get rid of the parts of himself that were like his father.

But instead of changing himself for the better, he'd been making himself into what he hated. He'd made himself into a lonely, bitter man who cared about nothing but his need for validation. His own need had become more important than anything else.

The medallion burned his palm. What was once his talisman now seemed like a heavy weight around his empty heart. Was it too late for him? He'd learned too late and now what did he have? Nothing but an empty self.

Standing, he held out his hand and let the chain dangle above the water.

He didn't want it anymore. He didn't want to look at himself. With an open fist, he let the medallion slip from his fingers.

This time the river carried the medallion away. The current dragged it away so quickly it never had the chance to hook onto anything. Cole watched as it flipped and turned and flowed farther and farther away. It flashed once in the late night, then it was too far to see anymore. The river washed it away. He pulled in a deep breath and let it out, relieved.

Cole was too agitated and unsettled to go back to the mansion since sleep was beyond him. He wandered past the woods to the small clearing.

White marble headstones glimmered in the moonlight. Most people avoided the cemetery at night, but Cole felt drawn to it.

He read over the names of the dead. Some of the engravings dated back to the twenties or earlier. Carey Higgins lived to the age of twenty-eight. Loving mother and wife. He moved through the sea of names. Phillip Stanton died, age thirty-one.

Cole stopped a moment. This guy died at his same age. Cole was thirty-one. He felt older. Ravaged in his own world of hate. Would it be better if he was the guy buried in the ground?

Cole had to be honest. As an adult, most of the torment and pain had been created by himself. He could blame his father if he wanted. It would be easy to do that. Blame his father for every ounce of hate he held bottled inside.

But there came a time when he had to make his own choice. He was turning himself into his father. A hateful person who cared only about one thing. What one thing? Hurting his son? Granted those things might be different but did that really matter? His father wanted to prove to the world that he'd been somebody. But all he had to do was look at his son to realize he already was everything, everything to a little boy who only wanted to be loved.

Cole moved through the graves until he came to a large carved block of stone that was two tiers high. The front block carved with scroll writing read *Hank W. Barlow*. It was a grand headstone. Why Cole was surprised he couldn't explain. Now that he was here in front of his father's final resting place, he couldn't look away. He felt frozen in place and stared at the gaudy stone.

Everything Hank had done was for the show of it. Even to his death. A large bouquet of beautiful, bright orange dahlias and mums sat in a vase. Someone stopped here often to tend the grave. His father had probably paid a groundskeeper to keep up the show.

Memories were a funny thing. They seemed to have sides to them, just like a story. Every story had three sides, right? His side, her side, and the truth. "Right, Dad? What was your truth? I finally read your letter," Cole said to the grave. After the first letter, he couldn't stop and read through the rest. "You thought you were doing right by me? Was that the best you could do?" He wanted to kick the flowers, but what good would that do? With a shaking hand, he brushed back his hair. "What am I doing here?" He reached into his pocket and pulled out one of the taped letters. "You wanted a tough son, a son worthy to handle what you've created. You did that, didn't you? I have become so strong that I thought I didn't need anyone. And maybe I don't need anyone. I've learned to be strong and deal with it on my own. Yeah, I don't need anyone. I've scoured out my insides and created a sterile place where no one would want to be. Yeah, I've cleared it out so well that I don't think I can even stand myself."

Cole plucked a flower from the basket and ripped off the leaves. "It makes for a lonely place. But you already know all about that." He stuck his nose into the bloom and breathed in the scent. Sweet and spicy with a hint of something that reminded him of autumn, of Angela. He took in another deep breath and closed his eyes to savor her scent. "You learned that was a lonely place, didn't you, Dad? Is that why you wrote those letters?"

He crushed the flower in his hand. The emptiness was no longer enough. The flower didn't compensate for what he wanted. He wished his father stood before him like he had in his dreams. If his father was still alive, he would confront him in person. Was that what he'd wanted all along? Was that why he'd been going after each of his father's properties?

Probably. He'd been saving the mansion for last so he could gather the courage to confront his father face-to-face. But that too had been taken from him. But now standing in front of the gravesite made Cole realize it no longer mattered, not since he'd met Angela.

"Do I have anything to give her?" Everything he thought was important no longer mattered. His quest for revenge seemed hollow, more hollow than anything he'd felt in years. He wanted more. Whether he was ready or not or had enough to offer, he wanted to try. He was willing. If he could learn one thing from his father it was that it could be too late. He'd run out of time with his father and if he waited too long, he could lose his chance with Angela.

Maybe his father had learned something and that's what those letters were about. What did it matter? Angela was still alive and he realized how much she meant to him.

He'd been hard on her. She knew there was

more to life than what could be seen or what people wanted to believe. Cole wanted to believe his father had been a completely evil man, one full of hate and disregard for his own son. And that was true to a point. It was Cole's truth. But he had to decide if that part of his past would ruin his entire future.

If he succeeded with his plan for revenge, then what? So what? He'd have nothing. His entire life's goal would be over. He'd be nothing but a glob of hate and that was no longer enough.

The crushed flower hung limply in his hand. It looked bruised and pale. Small and sad. It reminded him of the boy he had once been.

Was he small now? Was this what he'd become—a withered, crushed piece of himself? Yeah. That was what he'd done. He'd wallowed in shame and fear for too long. Acted like that injured child for way too long.

He was more than that. He'd come from there, but he no longer needed to live there. Angela had made him believe that somehow. She saw more in him than he ever saw in himself.

He wasn't his father. Forged and molded by him, true, but he had been strengthened by his own experiences, by his own hardship and life. He'd also been molded by good. Max had taught about hard work and helping someone become more than they were.

He was so much more and he was ready to give so much more. Maybe he wasn't as empty as he thought he was. Angela had filled him in spaces he didn't realize he had. She was right. He had to face himself. Look into the mirror at himself to see the truth.

"You faced your own truth, didn't you, Dad? That's what these letters were about."

A cloud moved over the moon, blocking its light. He shivered as a cold breeze flowed through him. The temperature dropped and he suddenly felt very alone. He no longer had his revenge to wrap over him and make him feel confident with purpose and warmed with hatred. He zipped up his jacket to ward off the chill. The chill was inside, in his heart, in his belly.

Fog had rolled into the cemetery and clouded the markers like smoke. It came in so suddenly, he hadn't noticed. Just like he hadn't noticed Angela slipping inside of his most shadowed places, lighting them up. She just flowed in like a secret. Like the fog, she was suddenly there, in his bones filling his hollow places with her gentleness.

He looked over the cemetery with its row after row of headstones. They stood like soldiers in their ranks, standing at attention, waiting for something.

Angela cared about these people. The dead. She always said the dead came first. Maybe she meant it.

Fear. That's what he felt. Not of the ghosts, but of her choice. Did she have a place for him—a battered, smashed child?

But he was like a lost soul too. Maybe her light was like a beacon to him. He could find the love and strength in her to pull him back from the edge of his own destruction. She'd made him realize there was more to life than revenge. He couldn't live in his half world of hatred any longer and he was willing to risk it with her.

He scanned over all of the dead in the cemetery. Their time was lost, but his wasn't. He still had a chance for more. He had been a member of the dead, somewhere between living and not. He had been stuck in a place where he didn't need to feel or think or want.

Now everything was different. She'd helped him to the other side. Now maybe he could help her. Maybe she would be willing to trust in him and move to the world of the living too. She'd helped ghosts for so long that she felt comfortable in that place. Maybe she could find her way back to this side. Both of them had lived in a sort of limbo too long. They could find life together. Cole gripped the flower tightly to his chest. He was willing to try. He hoped she was willing to risk it with him.

Cole picked up the phone, then dropped it again. Grabbing for it, he scrolled through his phonebook. He couldn't ignore the dream. His life had gone out of control. He needed to get back a sense of balance. But the dream had made it clear he needed Angela in his life. She was part of his present. Could she change his future?

He ran a hand through his hair. Great, now she had him analyzing his dreams. Hell, he was already starting to believe in ghosts. He didn't want to believe. His heart couldn't handle it. But he also couldn't handle being without her. Somehow, she had slipped into his hidden, empty crevices.

He pressed the button on the phone. There was a beat of silence before she answered. He was afraid she was going to hang up and he held his breath while he waited.

"Please, Cole. Just stop."

"Hear me out."

"You have exactly two minutes."

"Angela, I have come to the conclusion that I need you." There, he'd blurted it out. It was not the most romantic thing to say, but he'd said it.

She continued as if she didn't hear his words. "Are you calling to hire me for another business deal? Do you need my spiritual expertise?" Her voice dripped with sarcasm.

"What?" He didn't understand what she was saying. Here he was trying to tell her how important she was and all she wanted to talk about was their work relationship.

"I had a dream," he said.

There was another pause over the phone before she asked, "A dream about what? And why do you think I care?"

"The dream was about you."

"I was in your dream?"

"Yes. You, me, my father, keys. I don't know. It's all a jumbled mess in my brain." He ran a hand through his rumpled hair again. In his mind, he'd imagined this, but things weren't working out the way he'd envisioned.

"Tell me more."

He caught the interest rise in her tone.

"I don't know where to start. I can't explain everything."

"You could try." She sounded so interested that the dream spilled from him and he described what he remembered. "The pain was terrible, it made me afraid to find out."

"Find out what?"

"I don't know. All I know is that I need you. I need to open this part of me that's been closed for too long."

He heard her ragged intake of breath through the phone. "I need to go back to the mansion. But this will only work if you allow yourself to trust in me, believe in me."

The words from the dream rang in his head like a bullet. It was time to bare himself.

"Okay," he whispered.

CHAPTER 27

THE GRAY LIMESTONE loomed, part terrifying, part beckoning. The night was cold. Cole took a step toward the mansion, then grabbed Angela's hand out of impulse. His large, strong hands enveloped hers. He'd waited outside so he would know the minute Angela arrived.

"You don't have to worry. You probably won't see anything," Angela soothed.

"What do you think will happen?"

"Nothing if you won't believe or trust in me."

He squeezed her hand, then tugged her forward. "Come on, let's get this started."

They walked down the driveway toward the colonnade leading to the oak front door. It was time to push through the barricade and start the future.

Cole looked up toward the bedroom windows on the second floor and was reminded of the feminine shadow that had waved on his return. He saw her now in his mind, dark hair, transparent skin. She'd been filled with secrets and now was the time to learn about the past that kept everyone frozen.

"I love these old limestone mansions. The stones were quarried not too far from here. They tend to hold a lot of ghost energy." Angela let go of his hand and glided toward the mansion. Cool, sad air filled the pocket of his palm where her warm touch had been a moment ago.

He closed his hand into a fist and slipped it into the pocket of his jeans, pretending he didn't miss the feel of her fingers.

Flowing like a witch in the dark fog, she swirled her slender fingertips along the granite curve of a pillar.

Jealousy flashed like a stranger. Lucky pillar. He wanted those fingers on him. All he needed to give her was his full belief.

In one moment, her skin was fresh and pink, then all her color drained. With an agonizing cry, she gripped her belly and doubled over, falling to one knee.

His heart thudded in his ears. Within seconds he was at her side. He reached toward her but stopped before he touched her pale skin. She was caught up in whatever she could see. She didn't seem to know he was near her and he didn't want to startle her. She was definitely experiencing something, but what it was, he could not say.

She reached out for something, for nothing. Fingers touched air. A lone tear streamed a path down her cheek, leaving a glistening train. He watched frozen as her mouth worked on unspoken words, then a low cry erupted and the words spilled from her.

"Wait, Daddy." The cry wrenched from her

throat and she sobbed, tears in torrents.

Her agony ripped through him. He could not bear it so he grasped her by the shoulders and hauled her into his chest. She mewed like an abandoned kitten. All he could do was stroke her hair, soothe with nonsensical words. "Hush, Angel."

Finally, her body relaxed. Her eyes filled with sparkling moisture that made him think of diamonds.

"Are you okay?" Her chest rose and fell against his to the beat of her heart.

"Yes," she breathed. "I think I'm okay." She gave him a watery smile that did nothing to calm his racing heart.

"What the hell just happened?"

"It's hard to explain. I need a moment."

"Let's get inside so you can sit down. That was intense. Then you can explain." Instead of waiting to see if she was steady enough to walk, he scooped her into his arms. "You're pale."

"This always happens when the connection is intense."

He pulled her tighter against him, and he relaxed when she snuggled deeper into his chest.

He carried her into the sitting room and gently placed her onto the red brocade sofa in front of the lion head mantle.

"Rest and tell me what happened." He brushed a stray lock of hair behind her ear. What he knew was that she was distraught, physically shaken and very pale.

"Are you going to believe me when I tell you

what happened?"

"Just tell me." He wished he could easily just say the words he wanted to say. He believed everything about her.

She looked up at him with disbelief and it pierced him, but he knew he deserved it.

"I'll try. Are you hurt? You fell." He kneeled before her and ran his hands, first over one leg, then slowly up the other, looking for any bumps or bruises.

"I saw Brooke and her father. I know it was them because he called her name. And she called him Daddy." She looked up at Cole, solemn. "Brooke is one of the ghosts haunting the mansion."

"A girl? I thought the ghost was my father."

"That's who I saw. But she's keeping a secret."

"No. My father is haunting me. That's what my dream was about last night. What exactly did you see?" He didn't mention the beckoning woman in the window.

"I feel more than I see," she said.

"What do you mean?" He was confused. He didn't understand all this ghost stuff. "You could be wrong?"

"It's hard to describe. I feel their emotions. We share each other's emotions. That's how they can accept my help." She turned from him and began to stand. "Let me explain what I saw, what she told me. She was sad and she was angry."

"How does this relate to me? I understand that my father wants to haunt me. I wouldn't expect any less from him. But what is this about a girl?

What does she want with me?"

"She showed me a small piece of the puzzle. There is a secret that holds her here."

"And it's related to me?"

"It must be." She began pacing in front of the fireplace. He swore the lion's eyes followed her every move.

"She had just returned from somewhere, a big city. She'd come home from a place where no one knew who she was. Her father was upset that she'd returned and he threatened to send her away again. Only this time, she would be gone for good."

"What was he going to do to her?" Cole asked. "Did the dad kill her?"

"No, the fight was about marriage. He was going to marry her off. Frank Dalloway didn't want to kill his only living child. He loved her but he didn't want a scandal either."

"You got all this from the brief moment before you fell?"

"It's about emotions and what they tell or show me. Brooke showed me all of this."

"What did she say about a scandal?"

"I've done all the research and there's nothing in the family history about a scandal. That's how I know I'm on the right track to help Brooke move on. She needs to reveal this secret."

"Didn't she show it to you just now?"

"Some of the story, but not all of it. She had no hope. I felt her devastation. She was in love with Harry Barnes. She wanted her true love and she couldn't have him."

"What was wrong with the other guy?"

"She was in love with Harry." Her eyes met Cole's. "She was desperate when her father wouldn't listen to her. She felt like she had no choice." Angela's eyes tightened around the corners and her lips drew in. "She ran away to Harry. She was going to marry him secretly, willing to give up everything for him."

"The fight she had with her father happened right there under the portico?"

"Yes. I saw and felt the entire thing. It was the night of Brooke's death."

"How could you know that?" He had to admit that she was experiencing something, seeing something.

"I know. Because She was wearing the same pink coat I saw her wearing when she went over the edge in the car."

He brushed away the tear that slid down her cheek with his thumb. "It's okay. It's over now," he whispered.

She leaned her cheek into his open palm and closed her eyes. "It's not over, Cole." Her voice was firm. "They suffer still. I need to help them."

"You will help them." He wanted to ask her if she would help him too. Instead, he leaned down and kissed the wetness from her cheek. He trailed kisses along her cheekbone toward the corner of her lips.

On a breath, she opened her mouth slightly. The warmth of her lips trembled next to his. Her breath was his breath. He knew she was still upset from her feelings with Brooke, but he hoped that some of the trembling was from his touch. He moved his hands down to her arms and trailed them along the smooth skin to the pulsebeats of her wrists, then trailed his fingers back up toward her elbows, pulling her close so she pressed along his length.

Her eyes stayed closed, blocking him from the depths of their golden light. The creases around her eyes faded and her face relaxed.

He took her arms and drew her hands around his neck. Cool and delicate, her fingertips skimmed his neck, raising goosebumps. When her fingers twined through the hair at his nape, a groan escaped from deep inside him.

He loved her touch. Suddenly starving, he needed her touch all over his body. She leaned into him, giving him her full weight and he accepted it, reveled in it.

He trailed his fingers up and down her bare arms. He wanted her to have as many goose bumps as he had, wanted her to be affected by his touch as much as he reacted to hers. A thrill surged through him when he felt the telltale sign on her skin and heard the whisper of a sigh escape her lips. She felt what he felt.

She deepened the kiss and it surprised him. Their tongues danced as she pressed and swirled hers into his mouth. Delicate hands skimmed down his chest to rest on his hips. His body ached. His fingers burned to touch bare skin. When his sweet little angel slipped her hands under his shirt and touched the small of his back, he pulled in a breath. She glided her fingers down his spine to the edge of his jeans, then under the waistband of his briefs. Their cool sureness sent those goose bumps to the surface again. He'd never been so confident about anyone's touch before. This felt right and it scared the hell out of him.

He broke the kiss and pulled back to catch his breath. Her brows creased in the middle and her eyes fluttered open filled with questions.

Her angry lips parted and he grew even tighter. He liked knowing she wanted his touch, his kisses. He leaned down and nipped her earlobe. He took it into his mouth and swirled his tongue around it. She moaned and leaned deeper, pulling him closer. Her hands had slipped lower and gripped his ass. He hardened and pressed into her.

"You always surprise me, Angel girl," he breathed against her neck. "I want to feel your skin. My hands burn for you. I burn for you." He growled in her ear.

"I want your touch too."

The flood gates opened. He edged his hands up her shirt to feel her soft skin, skimmed over her belly, then slid his fingers to the edge of her bra. He wondered what color it was. Probably white and boring, like the average person she pretended to be. She had a vibrancy that spilled into every-thing.

He slipped his hands over her no frills cotton covered breasts and the tips beaded in his palms. He flicked his thumbs over the buds and they tightened even more. Like a salve, her moans soothed his injured soul.

She arched her neck back, leaving it bare for

his kisses. So exposed, so trusting, yet vulnerable. He scraped his teeth along it, then licked the trail to soothe it. He stopped, pulled away. "I'm being too rough. I don't want to hurt you." All she knew was gentleness and all he could give her was a harsh destroyer. He wanted to hold her and never let her go, but doubt slipped in and he tilted away before it was too late and he ruined things with her like he ruined everything else in his life.

She gripped him, pulling him closer. "No, you're not. Don't stop. I want this. I want to feel alive. I feel the pain of ghosts. I feel their emotions and it's always laced with sadness. When you touch me, I can't think of anything but you. I want this. I need to feel you—only you."

"I want this too." Nothing would stop him now.

She grabbed the edge of his shirt and pulled it up, skimming her hands along the muscles. They tightened and he couldn't stand another minute, so he grabbed at the shirt and pulled it off the rest of the way, tossing it to the carpet.

She ran her fingers along his chest and down to his belly. Her fair skin stood out against his darker tone. His abs jumped at her touch and she gave him a sly smile. He liked this side of her.

"Am I bringing out your dark side, Angel girl?" his voice rasped.

She responded with a laugh as she guided her fingers to the button of his jeans. He leaned back slightly. He wanted to watch as she turned into a vixen.

He rose more to her, waiting, but the wait

would be worth it. "I want you to fall in the abyss with me."

With a swift movement, she unclasped the button, then looked up. "Should I be scared?"

"Oh no."

Those eyes of hers reflected the golden gates of heaven and he wasn't sure he was worthy to enter. She gripped the zipper while her eyes still held his.

Slowly, she lowered the zipper. Each click rang through the quiet room. She edged her hands inside his pants and slipped them down his waist. He didn't stop her. He'd rather burn in hell for eternity than stop her. But he covered his hot hands over hers.

"There's no rush." He needed to savor every moment like it would be his only chance.

He reached for her shirt and pulled it over her head, tossing it to the floor with his own. Her bra was the palest blue, not white, not beige. He smiled when he saw her plain bra, no frills or lace, so typical of her. He wanted to get rid of it. He slipped his fingers under the edge and pushed it up, exposing her breasts.

"That's better." Hard beads lifted to him. He drank in the sight of her like a sinner finding water in the hot depths of hell. "Anything but ordinary." He dipped his head and kissed first one round breast, then the other, spending a few moments savoring her sweetness before he moved on. He trailed kisses lower, toward her belly, then swirled his tongue inside the indentation.

He trailed kisses even lower just above the button of her low-rise jeans. He could listen to her indrawn breaths for eternity. His fingers brushed the metal with hot fingers.

She stopped him before he unfastened the button. She pushed at him. "It's my turn again."

"I'm liking this game." He leaned back, hands on his waist. His pulse quickened a beat and his fingers shook as she pulled his jeans off. He stepped out of them and kicked them aside.

The obvious bulge jutted from his black briefs. Her eyes looked right at it and the blood rushed through him. He wanted to grab her to him, but he took a deep breath to get himself under control and kept his hands firmly planted on his hips.

She swallowed and he laughed. Before she could change her mind, he swiftly discarded his briefs. His erection stood proud.

"Maybe I should be afraid," she said, but her eyes sparkled with mischief instead of fear. With one finger, she caressed his length from base to tip. A smile spread along her lips as he throbbed at her touch. Longing for more ran through him like rushing lava.

The groan rumbled from deep in his throat. She touched him again and he burned for her.

"Okay," he said on a breath as he gripped her shoulders and pushed her back a step. "My turn." He couldn't take much more if she kept touching him like that. He had to take over or he'd be finished before they even started.

He rid her of her jeans. Though he thought he loved lacey thongs, her matching cotton panties were more alluring than anything he'd ever seen.

He needed to get her out of them quickly.

Take it slow, he reminded himself. With controlled determination, he gently traced the band before slipping his hands lower to cup the swells of her buttocks in his hands. "Very nice. Just how I imagined." He kissed her neck, raising those goose bumps he loved.

With a swift movement, he rid her of her panties and she stood before him naked.

"You're beautiful."

"I'm not." She blushed.

Instead of arguing with her, he pulled her into his arms and kissed her breathless until he knew her silly thoughts were gone from her brain. Then he slid his hands between them, down her soft, ready body and slipped his fingers into the curls at her apex. She was warm and wet for his touch and she groaned, leaning into his hand.

He flicked a finger over her slick wetness and a gasp escaped. Her fingers dug into his shoulders and a rumble of pleasure vibrated through him as he trailed his mouth to hers. He slipped a finger inside her. And matched the movements with his kiss. She didn't stop him, instead she pulled him closer and he knew she felt the same way. He wanted to be closer. He needed to be inside her. With another movement, he slid his finger deeper inside her. She writhed against his hand and he knew she was ready for her release, but it wasn't enough for him. He needed more from her.

"I'm done with games," he said gruffly. They melted to the floor together and he knelt above her, resting on his elbows. "Open your eyes," he commanded. "Open your eyes to me, my angel. I want to watch you, to feel like I'm deep into your soul."

Her lashes flitted and her eyes deepened to molten amber, clear and open to him. They held the freshness of golden fields that he wanted to live in forever.

He leaned so that only their lips touched. The kiss was a fire between them. He was about to explode into flames and burn to a cinder. He couldn't take any more of the self-inflicted torment.

She was like no one he had ever been with before and somehow, she had become everything. His road to heaven, his redemption, a promise.

She lifted to him and her breasts tipped against his chest. One of her legs raised to rub along his thigh. "No more games." He ripped the foil and quickly put it on.

Her eyes sparked with golden flames and he knew he was ready to enter heaven. She lifted her body up to him. The tip of him was scorched by her growing heat.

"Please. I need you." That undid him. Her words were the last thing he remembered before he was lost.

He could no longer be denied the promise of her sweetness and acceptance through her glorious gates. He thrust into her and knew he was where he belonged.

He wanted to possess every inch of her and he thrust deeply, making her groan. With each thrust and her matching response, he knew he was the one being possessed by her. She accepted him and he wanted all of her. This was the heaven he'd been searching for.

He'd be in hell without her. She welcomed his thrusts and found her rhythm with him. She thrust up against him and cried out gripping him closer as she shuddered with her climax, dragging him deeper. The climax came up on him quickly and it roared through him. In a shudder, he fell on top of her. He never wanted to let her go.

Now that he had found rapture, he never wanted to give it up. Slowly he fell back to earth. Her breathing was just as ragged as his. She stroked her hand along his spine with her gentle touch giving him thrills. He'd been rocked to his core and turned inside out. Everything he'd lived for had been for nothing. He knew that now. Everything had become clear.

His insides started to rattle and he could feel himself shaking with his need. He was too afraid to move and shatter the moment. He felt vulnerable and exposed now that she'd torn down all of his barriers.

He was still throbbing inside of her. He pulled her close and smelled her sweet scent of dried flowers and cool breezes. He tried to catch his breath as he rested half sprawled across her and half resting on the floor, lips brushing her ear. What if she rejected him? What if all the emotion had been one-sided and she didn't feel the same? The quaking in his belly spread until his entire body vibrated.

"What is that?" Her voice was low and husky from their lovemaking.

He was about to answer by telling her that it was his fear of rejection making him shake when a loud crash cut off his words before he could speak them.

The vibration he thought was coming from his body rumbled up through the floor, reverberating through the room. The crystal in the cabinets rattled. The oriental vase on the end table wobbled and crashed to the floor, breaking into pieces.

Cole jolted to his feet, pulling Angela with him.

"Is that an earthquake?" She clutched him close.

The house creaked like an old man awakening from slumber. Another crash resounded through the room. "What in the hell is that?"

Vibrations rumbled through the walls, the house shook, books shifted from their shelves, some fell to the floor. A whisper grumbled lowly under the crashing noises.

"It sounds like the noises are all around us."

Angela froze and strained to listen. It quaked, muffled through the din. Angela grabbed at Cole's arm. "Do you hear that?"

"How could I miss it?" He yanked on his jeans.

"No, not the crashing, the voice."

"Voice? I don't hear anything over the banging and clatter of the chandelier."

"Listen. There it is again." The voice was louder.

Another booming sounded through the house, causing vibrations to clatter through the room. The voice sounded under the rumble, "History won't repeat itself in my house."

"I don't hear anything but the rumbling. There must have been an explosion at the quarry."

"That wasn't an explosion, Cole." Angela needed to get her clothes on. She'd already wiggled into her jeans. Scooping up her shirt, she pulled it over her head. Once she was dressed, she stood in front of Cole. "I have to help them, Cole. For some reason, the ghosts are connecting and I think this is it."

She saw a shadow of something cross his face. "All of this." She waved a hand at the fallen object that had crashed on the floor. "This is their way of telling me that they need me and I have to do whatever I can."

"Ghosts come first right?" he asked in a low resigned tone that made Angela nervous. "No matter what, right? You will always choose ghosts over everything else?"

She felt like she was walking through a mine-field and if she said the wrong thing there would be collateral damage. What was he trying to say? Helping ghosts find peace on the other side was her entire purpose and reason for living. He knew that. "I need to work quickly while the ghosts are active."

"Is the answer yes?"

"You've known that from start."

"Even now?" he asked. His shoulders sank and he seemed to deflate somehow. His face contorted and it ripped at her.

They had just shared the most amazing experience that she couldn't even explain what it had done to her. For some reason their lovemaking had made the ghosts respond.

"This might be my only chance to help the ghosts move on. I need to go. We can talk about what happened between us once I've helped your father move on to the other side."

"That's right. My father's ghost is more important than what happened between us. Even now he influences my life."

"I've got to go. We'll discuss what's happening between us after I help the ghosts."

"You've made your choice. Now go. Go and choose him over me."

He turned. His back was rigid and his walls were impenetrable again.

"Cole." His words had slapped at her. She took a step toward him, and another explosion rippled through the mansion, followed by what sounded like mocking laughter. "I have to help the ghosts move onto the other side. This may be my only chance to connect with them fully." He stiffened but didn't turn and she knew he didn't want to hear it.

Finally, he'd allowed her inside and his father's ghost was preventing his happiness. She wouldn't allow it any longer. Even if it meant that Cole hated her, she would get rid of his father once and for all. She turned and ran from the room. He would no longer hurt Cole. Not when she could do something about it.

Cole knew the minute she'd left the room. He felt ice-cold and abandoned. Never had he bared himself to anyone like he'd done when he'd made love to Angela.

Finally, he thought he'd found that one person who could shatter his walls. She'd made him realize that life was risk and baring your soul. But now he stood alone. He felt shaken and vulnerable. He was alone and barer than a newborn baby. She'd made her choice.

Why did it sting so much? He'd known from the start that ghosts were more important to her than the living. He'd always be second to her need to help ghosts. He'd always been second best, not worth being loved.

He should have kept himself protected. How could he have allowed himself to be vulnerable to her? Thank heavens he'd realized it before he'd done something he would have regretted, said something he would have regretted.

He pulled on his shirt and searched for his shoe. It was under a pile of fallen books. His entire body still thrummed from her sinful touches even as his brain knew he could never allow himself to be that vulnerable again. It was time to sell the mansion to the historical society and leave Dalewood for good.

Is that what he really wanted? He sank into the couch and the lion's face mocked him with its open-mouthed snarling grin. Could he really go back to that way of life? He was just starting to feel alive. Just weeks ago, when he'd first come home, he'd been a shell of a man, hateful and empty.

No. He didn't want that anymore. It was worth

the fight. He had to make Angela understand what he was feeling. He jumped from the couch, determined to find her and convince her that he was worth something. That together they could teach each other about life.

Once in the hallway, he looked in both directions, but she was gone.

A shadow moved at the end of the hallway and turned into a corridor. "Angela, wait." He followed after the movement.

CHAPTER 28

"WHERE ARE YOU, Hank? Why are you hiding from me? What don't you want me to know?" Irritation bubbled. Angela turned at the corner of the hall to find a dead end. The wall was covered in striped green wallpaper. She hadn't noticed it earlier when she'd been exploring with Cole during her investigations.

There was only one way to go and that was back the way she'd come. She stepped closer to the wall of the dead end and realized there was a space along the edge of the wall. Sparks jumped through her arm when she traced the opening. It was another passageway like the one she'd gone through with Cole to escape from his room.

Startled, she yanked her hand away. She hadn't been expecting the anger that raced through her. Hank's ghost was filled with rage. That had been apparent with the explosive poltergeist display that had distracted her out of Cole's arms.

The squeak of old, unoiled hinges filled the passageway. The space in the wall popped open, revealing a secret door. Angela gripped the edge of the wall and pushed it farther.

Anger overwhelmed her and she almost doubled over from the onslaught of emotions. She tried not to fight the feelings, then relaxed into the emotions, letting them rush through her.

They were easier to handle if she accepted the emotions instead of fighting against them. With a tighter grip, she held onto the secret wooden door.

Once the space was wide enough, she slipped through into the dark passage. Heavy booted footsteps plodded down the hallway away from her. The light from the door behind her slowly became smaller and smaller until it disappeared when the door behind her snapped shut, encasing her in complete darkness.

The beginnings of panic began. It started like the slow ripple of a raindrop on the surface of a smooth lake, but the farther it traveled the more it built.

Why hadn't she waited for Cole instead of rushing off and leaving him? He'd been confident when they'd gotten locked in the passage before that he had to know all the different secrets here. How could she foolishly allow herself to get into a similar predicament again? She pulled in a deep breath and channeled Cole's calm confidence.

Then she heard the clomping sound of hard soled boots on the wooden floor. When her eyes adjusted to the darkness, she could see a faint light filtering through a small rectangle at the far end of the hallway. Angela focused on the sliver of light.

She thought of Cole and his strength. He was

never afraid of anything. He would have helped her get out of this small passage easily. All she had to do was stay calm. She pushed down her panic.

With careful steps, she moved into the dark through the old mustiness of misuse swirling around her. It smelled like the far corner of the university library where she used to sit alone. She trailed her fingers along the wall like a blind person. Tingling sensations fired through her hands.

Gingerly, she continued down the hallway. She knew it must be another secret doorway at the opposite end. She got to the door, but this one wouldn't open like the other one. She was officially trapped now.

The door behind her had closed and this one was closed too. She held back the panic that wanted to take over.

She pushed on the wall in front of her. Blood rushed through her veins and palms and she broke into a sweat. *Calm down.* This was a secret passage so there had to be a way out. *Look for the latch. Find a switch.*

She wiped her wet palms on her jeans before she trailed her fingers along the molding of the doorway. She searched for hinges, a doorknob, buttons, anything. There had to be some way to open this door. Her fingers skimmed over a metal piece that jutted out of the wall. With a click, the door popped open and rays of light poured into the hallway, blinding her for a moment. She blinked at their brightness, then stepped into the room. Hard leather footsteps shuffled and thumped along the floor like someone who didn't want to be seen. Angela moved into the room that was covered in pink and frilled with lace. The room shimmered with a strange iridescent glow that made it seem real and magical all at once.

Tingles of electricity fired through her fingers and up her arms until they ran through her entire body. All the hairs raised on her body as if she'd been shocked. This was a room of the past, a ghostly image. Angela held her breath and stepped completely into the room.

Sitting at the white dressing table was the outline of a body. The feminine shape materialized into a hazy image until the full-bodied apparition formed. She wore a white flowing gown that fell over her graceful back and over the square stool on which she perched. She looked into the oval mirror and raised a brush. With slow sweeps, she pulled the brush through her jet black hair.

Electrical waves surged through Angela. She gripped the edge of the bed and willed back her disoriented feelings.

Brooke was now a full embodiment of herself. She appeared real, flesh and blood, pink cheeks over pale skin, red lips and big gray eyes. Eyes so familiar. They were Cole's eyes, although they were more innocent and less cynical. How was that possible?

Suddenly, the brush clattered to the table and Brooke's eyes dripped tears onto the white wooden tabletop. Angela walked toward Brooke's ghost.

Her hunched shoulders rose and fell in wracking sobs that were painful to hear. The sadness flowed into Angela and she wished she could absorb all the pain from the past. The electricity pulsed inside her with each beat of Angela's heart.

"Brooke, I can help you. Please let me help you."

The ghost turned in surprise, then began to disappear. "Wait, don't leave," she called out to the fading image. "I only want to help you. I can help you. Isn't that why you made me follow?"

The ghostly girl froze and looked at Angela. "And how can you help me? I am meant to exist through my suffering."

"That is not how it has to be. I can help you understand so you don't need to suffer, but you must tell me your secrets first. It will be better than suffering alone. I can share your burden." No one, not even the dead deserved to suffer. No one should have to endure that pain for all eternity.

Angela was flooded with Brooke's emotions.

"Let's start. What is your name?" Angela asked the ghost.

Brooke let out a laugh that was like shards of breaking glass. "My name, I still have one after this long, Brooke Dalloway. But you knew that already."

"I know some things about you and your family but not all of the secrets."

"We still hold a lot of family secrets." Brooke turned away.

"It's those secrets that hold you here. By holding onto them you are causing your own suffering.

Share them with me and it will help."

She could feel more than see the indecision in Brooke, who wanted to tell but was too scared.

"What frightens you?" Angela asked. "Do you feel like the secret is all you have left? You'll gain so much more by letting it go."

Angela wanted to get her talking. Holding the secret kept Brooke trapped in this place. It was a hell of her own making. If she could let go of the past she could move on to the other side.

"I saw you on the day you died," Angela prompted. She wanted to force Brooke to remember the past so she could feel the tragedy, then let it go.

"My death." The laugh was brittle, tossed like old used newspaper. "I was young. And I was in love. But Daddy had bigger plans for me. I loved Harry too much, you know. Harry and I had plans of our own. I loved him, and he loved me. We were going to elope." She shrugged. "Daddy found out and he was furious. I'd never seen him like that before. He didn't understand. He didn't want to understand."

Angela listened quietly. This was it and Brooke would finally reveal the last pieces to the puzzle.

"When Daddy found out about the little secret of my own that I carried, he wanted it hidden so he sent me away, to my aunt in the city. Then, when everything was all taken care of and I returned, Daddy was going to marry me off in a quick ceremony so all his dreams would come true. No one cared about my dreams. When I came back I..." Brooke stopped and turned quickly.

Hot rage burned in her eyes, making them swirl like mercury and with a jolt, Angela was again reminded of Cole's quicksilver gaze. "You must leave. Go now. He is furious. I've said too much already. Leave us. Leave this place. Leave the past and all the secrets alone."

"I'm here for a reason. I can help," Angela implored.

"There is no help for me. I made my own problems and they are beyond forgivable." She swiped at the tears with the back of her hand.

"There is nothing that is unforgivable. If you talk to me, I can help."

"Talking of it won't make my burden go away."

"No, but I could share it. What secret haunts you?"

"He won't allow the secret to be told." Brooke gave a quick glance over her shoulder.

"You don't need to speak your secret to let me know. Then it will still be a secret."

"How can that happen? How can you know if I don't tell you?"

"Can I touch you? That way I can feel your secrets."

"He will still be very angry. He has been protecting his secret for far too long. But I cannot hold this secret for eternity. It is time that it is revealed, for all of us." Brooke wrung her hands and shifted from foot to foot, looking down at the floor. Then she nodded her head and looked up at Angela as Brooke reached out her hand. "Hurry, he comes."

Angela braced for a moment, then opened herself to Brooke. Her hands felt as if they'd turned into cold stone and the ice flowed through Angela's veins. As a child she had pushed away from this but now she accepted it. Her grandmother had taught her how to acknowledge her gifts and use them to help the ghosts. She understood the feelings of the ghost this way. She embraced the joy, love, sadness, grief, fear that pelted her like frozen raindrops.

She felt all of Brooke's emotions. She knew everything. Every sadness, every agonizing choice. Each moment of love, choice, then the fear of her father and his anger when he learned about her shame. She knew the secret of the hidden life that Brooke bore. The child that was rushed away from this place and hidden in another place. She knew how Brooke had decided to come back to Harry. Once she reunited with Harry, she planned to tell him about the baby so they could be a complete family. But the fight with her father caused Brooke to rush off. She had been distraught by their argument. Crying so much, she couldn't react quickly enough when the car skidded and she lost control and plunged to her death. Harry never knew his child existed.

With a heavy heart, Angela mourned Brooke and her tragic death. She also had sympathy for the man who never knew his baby existed. "I know your secrets now, Brooke. I can help if you'll let me."

"I cannot give you permission." Eyes wide and mouth tight, Brooke floated farther from Angela. Her transparent arm raised to point behind

Angela.

"Brooke, wait. Let me help."

The ghost shook her head. "I must go. If he finds me, he will steal my energy for his own. He comes." The last word was barely audible as the image of Brooke faded way.

"Is there anyone here?" Angela called into the still room. "Speak to me. Let me help you."

But there was only silence. Looking around the room, she realized that it was no longer frilly with lace. She was in Hank's room with its modern furniture and décor.

Brooke led her here to tell her about the secret baby. How was her secret related to Cole? Her eyes. They'd been similar. Could Cole be a descendent of the Dalloway's? How could that be?"

Oh no. Brooke had dragged her away from Cole and she hadn't thought of anything but helping the ghosts in the house. Where was he? Had he left? She wouldn't blame him if he had. Maybe he was waiting for her downstairs? She needed to go to him and explain.

Before she took a step, searing hot pain tore through her right side. Ghostly rage bubbled inside of her. Fiery fingers of fury grabbed at her arm and a low rumbling voice thrummed through her mind. This time he didn't appear as a shadow figure. Hank showed himself in his full form.

"How dare you invade my home? How dare you use the past for your own gains?"

Angela reeled from the hot flames that fought

with the cold marble ice that filled her. She knew she must accept the feelings, the emotions, but the pain and anger were unbearable. Her breath pushed from her and she could not fill her lungs.

She needed to protect herself from the wrath that enveloped her. Gathering her inner strength, she pulled from everything in her to stop Hank's energy from taking over. She thought of Cole. He'd been able to shield himself from Hank's wrath. Channeling Cole's strength, she found the power to push back some of his anger. It held Hank at bay, but it wasn't enough to stop him. Pain gripped her by both arms and he yanked at her. She felt her body lift, her toes barely touching the floor as she elevated in the air.

"I am here to help you," she gritted out past her tight throat.

"We don't need or want any help from you. Brooke's indiscretions have nothing to do with you. The past has nothing to do with you. Stay out of it."

"Why are you tormenting her?" She needed to get him to talk.

"How dare you? I cannot have my family name connected with scandal. Digging into Brooke's past will only bring out the truth of my own."

"How does Brooke's baby have anything to do with you? You cannot rest if you are holding onto a secret like this."

"History tends to repeat itself. I won't allow anyone to know how true that is. I will do whatever I must to protect my name, now and for always." Hank raised his hand and brought it down in a slash.

Hot fire seared Angela's cheek while ice shivered through her body. Flames warred against the chills, fire and ice, like heaven and hell. The blow was too much for her and her head fell back. The hot fire moved to her throat and she felt her feet completely lift from the floor. His grip tightened around her throat in a strangling hold. She gripped at the ghostly hands and struggled to drag breaths into her lungs. Lights sunburst behind her eyes just before she was surrounded in iridescent white light.

At once all the heat and cold left her body. She was falling, falling, falling into an abyss that had no beginning and no end.

CHAPTER 29

COLE FOLLOWED THE bangs and crashes down the hall. "Angela, is that you?" Why was she running from him?

He couldn't pinpoint the location of the sounds. They seemed to move and change places. It was as if they came from nowhere and everywhere all at once. At first the sounds were in front of him, then banged on the wall next to him.

He was starting to realize that the shadow he'd been chasing was something else. It wasn't Angela.

The bangs clattered louder and louder, echoing in his ears, reverberating through his body, and he followed them down a set of servant's steps. He knew where he was being led. This was the way to his father's room. Trepidation filled him and his steps slowed. The air felt thick and filled with energy like a stormy night just before the rain fell.

He came to another hallway where, like a beacon, light splayed from the open doorway of his father's room. Drawn to it, he moved forward stepping into the triangular glow. He knew she was in there.

When he peered into the room, his body froze. The banging stopped as quickly as it had started, creating a tomblike silence. The only sound was his own throbbing pulse, roaring through his ears. His feet rooted to the ground.

Inside the room, Angela stood in an unnatural position. Her head angled back as she lifted up on her tiptoes as if held by an unseen entity. There was no *as if*. She was being held by an entity. The only angry ghost he knew of was his father.

He tried to shout *Angela*, but no sound left his stiff lips. He could only watch her through the doorway. Hands fisting at his sides, they ached with his need to get to her, but he was rooted to the ground unable to act. Something had a hold over him. Inside he raged at his body to move, but he was frozen in place.

Locked by pure terror he watched Angela's face blanch. Inside he shattered into a thousand pieces. As his anger crumbled away, replaced by fear, the unseen grip released him and his feet separated from the ground. He rushed to her, but an unseen field blocked him from entering. He splayed his hands on the invisible barrier and watched from the outside.

"Damn it. Let me in. I need to get to her." He battered his fists against the invisible obstacle.

Frozen, he watched as she lifted completely from the ground until her feet raised off the floor, as if she were being pulled by a tether on the ceiling. If he hadn't seen it with his own eyes, he wouldn't believe it. He knew it was his father.

Her chin raised and her neck stretched. She

clawed at her throat. Pink dots ringed her neck, quickly turning to blue bruises. Cole banged harder against the barrier. It vibrated like waves on a lake's surface.

Enraged and frustrated, he willed the barrier away. With only one thought in his head, he pushed at the invisible wall, pounded it. He needed to get to her before it was too late.

"Let her go, you monster. Go back to the hell you came from. Let her go or I'll kill you all over again. If you take her from me, I'll find you in hell."

Panic raced through him and he pounded more furiously. Was this his father? Even after he was dead, would his father still do anything he could to ruin Cole's life? The thought was unbearable.

Angela gave one last cry, before her eyes rolled back and her head fell free against her shoulders, body limp. Losing her was more unbearable than anything his father had ever done to him or ever could. The invisible blockade would not give.

Terror radiated through him. And he remembered how he'd been released a moment ago. He had to let go of the anger and think of his feelings for Angela. All he wanted was to be with her, now and always. He didn't know what he would do without her. Who would he be without her?

As she slipped to the floor in a pale heap, Cole let out a guttural howl that came from some deep place inside of him that he never knew existed. With a last violent push, the solid glass liquefied like the hedges in his dream. Only this time, he didn't wait to see if it was real. He pushed through the barrier that shifted like water, falling forward, flowing through until he sprawled to the floor on the other side, breaths heaving with his terror.

Cole crawled to Angela's side. A painful knot blocked his throat. She had to be okay. He needed her to be alright.

He reached for her and pulled her to him, grasping her in his arms, pulling her close to his chest, hugging her, rocking her. "Angel, my angel."

Gently, he lowered her, placing her head on his knee. With an unsteady hand, he brushed her honey hair from her forehead. Her skin was pale but for her bright red cheeks and the blue marks that marred her neck.

"Wake up, Angela. Open your eyes." He rocked her in his arms. "Come back to me." A knot tightened around his heart. He'd known not to get close to her. She lay here, damaged, because of him. He didn't deserve her or happiness, but he wanted both.

Her chest rose on a shuddering breath. Relief flooded him. He skimmed his thumb over the bruises that formed a necklace around her delicate throat. How could he have been so close to her and unable to protect her from this? He knew the evilness of his father, and now that his father was dead, how would he ever be able to protect her?

"You're going to be okay." He stroked his fingers through her hair, across her forehead. "I finally see. I get it." He cupped her cheek in his hand. "I can't enter your world. But I believe you."

He brushed a kiss against her lips. "I couldn't help you. But you can't leave me." He leaned his forehead against hers and closed his eyes. "I love you." The knot in his throat moved to his heart and constricted, crushing the small bud that had started to blossom because of Angela. His father would never allow him an ounce of happiness. "I love you too much," he whispered.

Her eyelashes fluttered. Her shallow breath butterflied along his skin and her hand slowly stroked the hand that gripped her arm.

The corners of her lips curved as she threaded her other hand through his hair.

"It's about time," she croaked in her dry scratchy voice. She put pressure on his neck and guided his face to her lips. "I love you too."

Slow and lingering, the kiss filled with longing and sadness and promises he knew he couldn't keep.

CHAPTER 30

"HOLY HELL, WHAT happened to you?"
Emma's screech grated as Cole carried
Angela into her apartment. He knew he'd have to
explain her bruises. He'd hoped he'd at least have
a few moments with Angela first, though.

"How did this happen to her?" Emma rushed
forward and grasped Angela by the arms. Accusing eyes drilled into him.

"That's what beasts do, right? They abuse
women, attack damsels." Was he always destined
to be on the defensive?

"I can take care of myself," Angela croaked.

Emma looked at Angela and then narrowed
her eyes at Cole. Then she shook her head as if
deciding something. "No. This wasn't you, Cole.
As much as you put on the bravado, you would
never hurt her. You didn't do this."

"Let me sit and I'll explain all." Angela's voice
was full of gravel. Each of the stones seemed to
settle into Cole's stomach.

"Cole, put me down." He hadn't realized he'd
pulled her closer to him. He pressed his forehead
to hers and breathed in deeply of her autumn

scent. Then he placed her gently on the couch, propping a pillow behind her head and another under her feet. He tucked a stray lock behind her ear, wanting to keep touching her, holding her, loving her.

"Who did this to you?" Emma asked. "You look like you've been run over by a Mack truck."

Cole raised his palms. "You won't believe me when I say this. I barely believe it myself, but I saw what happened with my own eyes. She was attacked by something, by nothing. She was attacked by my father's ghost." He ran a hand through his dark hair, then paced back and forth in front of the couch where Angela rested.

He knelt before Angela with his back to Emma. Dark circles smudged the pale creaminess under her eyes. A faint bruise marred her cheekbone. God, she was beautiful. He ran his thumb along her jawbone. He couldn't stop touching her since he'd gotten her out of the mansion. He'd laced his fingers through hers in the drive that had seemed like an eternity. He carried her up the steps to her apartment, just as an excuse to hold her. Now his fingers itched to feel her soft skin.

"All I could do was watch you get brutalized." He brushed her earlobe. "I watched, helpless." Then his gaze fell to the ring of bruises around her neck.

"A ghost did this to you?" Emma's eyes popped wide.

"I'm okay." Angela's voice creaked.

Emma raised a fist and shook it. "I'm not training to be a black belt for nothing. Your cheek's not too bad, but those other marks will be there for a while. Those are some doozies on your neck."

"Emma, could you get the camera? I'd like some pictures of this for the files." She brushed her fingers along the welts on her neck.

"You're always business, Angela." She shook her head but went for the camera.

"Would you like something to drink? Water?" Cole felt helpless and needed something to do.

"Check the fridge. There are a few bottles in there." Her voice rasped.

Cole moved to the kitchen to grab the water from the fridge. He hated knowing she was in pain and he had been unable to do anything to stop it. His father had hurt him as a kid, but he was damned if he would let him ever hurt Angela again. Hank needed to be stopped, sent to the hell he belonged.

When he returned, he covered her hand as he gave her the bottle. "Take a drink, it will help soothe your throat." He had been terrified he was going to lose her. "You should rest."

He brushed the hair from her face. It was another excuse to touch her, brushing her cheek, her hand, her hair.

"Tell me what happened. Give me all the details." Emma raised the camera to take pictures of Angela's injuries.

Angela relayed the story to Emma.

He wished he was alone with Angela. He wanted to talk to her. Tell her what he was feeling. But what was he feeling? He didn't know.

Everything had become a mess. Typical since everything about him had become a mess. Maybe it was better that Emma was here. He wouldn't say something he didn't want to. He needed to pull himself back together. Rearrange the scattered pieces his life had become. He stroked his hand over her leg. He listened to her side of the story. She never once talked of her own pain. She cared only about the ghost she was trying to help. All she wanted was to help the ghosts. He was sitting here in agony worried that he would lose her. Knowing he could not allow anything to happen to her. She was worried about the ghosts and not once did she consider how worried he was for her. He had nearly seen her die because of him.

Angela told Emma the entire story, only leaving out how they'd made love in the drawing room. She dropped her head back onto the couch and bent her arm over her eyes. "I'm tired."

"Off to bed with you then." Cole scooped her up.

"Cole," she gasped but then grabbed him, pulling herself closer into his chest. She gripped his shoulders like she was afraid he'd let go and disappear like one of her ghosts.

"Which room is yours?"

She pointed to the door on the right at the end of the small hallway.

"I'll tuck you in nice and tight before I leave." He looked into Angela's eyes. Eyes he had become used to. He dreamed of those eyes.

"Don't leave me so soon."

He carried her into the room.

"Thanks for taking care of her," Emma said before he disappeared into the bedroom. The guilt bubbled up from his gut. He hadn't taken care of her at all. He could only watch while invisible hands strangled and tortured her. He shut the bedroom door behind them.

"Here you are." He put a smile on his face as he set Angela on the cool cotton sheets. Even her room was ordinary. A blue bedspread over white sheets. Striped, matching curtains over the window. She tried hard to hide how special she was. But he knew her too well. She had her gifts, and she used them to find a way past his walls.

He tucked the covers up to her chin, pushed them under her shoulders and sides, then under her feet like he'd wished either of his parents would have done for him when he was a kid.

Her face was almost as white as the pillow she rested on. He brushed her bangs from her forehead. The mark on her cheek glared at him as a reminder that he couldn't protect her.

"I should go so you can rest." He turned to leave her.

"Don't go." She rustled in the comforter. "Get these covers off me."

He turned to see her struggle with the blanket like it was an octopus in attack mode. He held back a laugh as she thrust it aside. She reached toward him, those sweet hands that only wanted to help. Hands that made him feel accepted like he had never been treated before. "Don't go."

"You need your rest. You'll never feel better if

I stay."

"I'll feel worse if you leave. I don't want to be alone."

His heart tore into pieces. Had she been scared? She had seemed strong. He didn't want her to need him. Not even a little. He had learned never to rely on others and he didn't want someone to rely on him. He walked to her, a moth to golden flames, a lost soul to the golden lights of heaven. His mind wanted him to leave, but his feet moved closer until his legs bumped into the side of the bed. He gripped the edge of the comforter.

"Lie back down." He covered her once again. "I'll stay. But you need to rest. Lie there and close your eyes."

"Okay." She patted the bed next to her. "But only if you sit here for a while."

Reluctantly, he lay on top of the covers next to her.

"Could you hold my hand?" She gripped his hand and threaded her fingers through his. "My grandma used to hold my hand when I'd get scared when I was little." She closed her eyes and her lashes brushed her cheeks. She looked vulnerable. He could not allow her to be hurt. Not because of him.

"I have to go back there, Cole," she said sleepily, her eyes still closed.

"No." His grip tightened, squeezing her fingers.

"I must. Your father will never rest if I don't help him."

"Does he even deserve it?"

"I don't know. I don't have any choice."

"How can you even think to go back there after how he hurt you?"

"It's important." She sat up.

"No. I'll bulldoze that place before you ever go back there."

"I must go back there. He'll just keep hurting people."

"No. It's too dangerous. Or have you forgotten what happened to you already? My father doesn't deserve saving."

"Maybe not, but you do." Tears shimmered in her eyes and ripped through him like any silver tipped arrow. "You deserve a future. I love you."

"Don't do this for me. I don't deserve any help."

She covered his hand with her other one. "I know I'm close. I feel it. And just shut up because you do deserve it."

"I swear I'll bulldoze that place."

"You can't stop me now. We are close."

He leaned toward her. Yeah, she was feisty. Maybe she didn't need to depend on him as much as he thought. She wanted to pretend she was ordinary. He knew better.

He pressed his lips to hers and kissed her. This time the kiss was hot and alive with pent up anger and emotions he couldn't claim. He wanted all thoughts of ghosts and mansions and attacks to vanish from both of their minds.

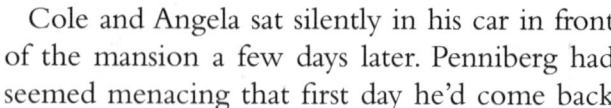

Cole and Angela sat silently in his car in front of the mansion a few days later. Penniberg had seemed menacing that first day he'd come back ready to tear it to pieces. The rays of late afternoon sunlight filtered through gray clouds. The mansion was dappled in spots of sunlight and shade from the trees that had almost lost all of their leaves for the coming winter, making the mansion appear less oppressive.

He should be less worried about her crazy plan to enter it on her own, but after what happened, he was even more terrified. The bruises still showed under her collar. But here they were, ready to go back into the place that had given her such pain.

"I'm not letting you go in there on your own." He set his jaw and looked straight out the window to watch the road. If he didn't look at her, see those eyes, he couldn't be swayed. He gripped the steering wheel and fought the irritation and fear.

"I need to go there. It's almost finished and I won't stop now." She sounded like she was going to be as stubborn as he was being, but she was obviously winning since he had driven her right to the very place where he said he would never let her go alone.

"It's almost done," she repeated.

"It better be," he snapped.

Cole got out of the car and went to the other side, pulling open Angela's door. She gripped his sleeve. "I need to do this alone."

"No." He shook his head. "After what happened last time? Absolutely not."

"I think Hank might connect better if he knows you are not there. Let me give it a try."

He grabbed her by the shoulders. "You think you don't need me? Is that what you're saying?"

"Cole, you're shouting."

"You can be alone, without me there. You don't need me, fine. Do it alone. Be alone." He had been alone for so long. Now that she didn't need him, he was being irrational.

"Go." He shifted away from her. "Go alone, since you handled things so well by yourself last time."

"All will work out. Trust in me."

"Sure."

She stepped onto the gravel path, ready to leave him. Something twisted inside.

"Angela," he called, stopping her.

She turned and smiled at him.

"Be careful." He said.

"I will."

He wrapped his arms around her pulling her tight against him so he could hold her for another moment. Then he kissed her with all the emotion and passion of the words he couldn't say.

Then she slid from his arms and headed toward the door.

He watched her as she moved farther and farther away from him. She wore a pair of jeans that covered her curves perfectly. Her white T-shirt was like a sexy uniform over her small shoulders and slim waist. He should be holding her in his arms, caressing her, kissing her, keeping her safe.

Instead he watched her disappear through the doorway heading into God knew what. She'd be okay. She could handle herself without him. He had to remind himself of that.

How could he protect her anyway? This was her world. He had grown to believe in her.

The one he didn't trust was his father, so he'd give her twenty minutes. That was enough.

CHAPTER 31

ANGELA REACHED FOR the doorknob with shaky fingers. *Confidence,* she reminded herself. This was bigger than her fears. Her future with Cole depended on it. He would never be able to move on with his life if his father continued to torment him.

She'd heard him tell her that he loved her, but maybe he'd only said that at the time because he thought she would die. Maybe he really didn't feel that way or maybe this relationship with his father was still holding him back from saying it again. He trusted in her, but Cole was too afraid of his vulnerability.

It was time to deal with Hank Barlow. There had been enough suffering in this mansion for many lifetimes. Enough was enough.

Readiness poured through Angela. It was time. Time to put an end to all of the suffering in Penniberg. Time to create a new start of calm happiness. If she didn't finish this, Cole could never start over and become the man she knew he was inside. They would never be able to continue the love blossoming between them.

The truth needed to be revealed. Her heart raced. This was it. Her heart knew it. Her body knew it. She knew something was about to happen. Change was on the air and she was ready for it.

With a strong resolve, she reached for the handle and firmly turned the knob and strode to the drawing room, not wasting her time on any other place. This was the room where she and Cole had made love. That had angered Hank so much that he rampaged through the house with his banging and rattling. It was time for all the secrets to be revealed.

"Hank Barlow," she called. "Stop being a coward and show yourself."

The door behind her slammed shut, making her jump. She tried the handle and it was locked. "Do you think that makes you powerful? I'm not scared of you."

"How dare you come back here?" The voice rattled through the walls. The chandelier clattered and books fell from the shelves, collapsing all around her, yet not touching her.

"I'm only here to help." She refused to cower to his wrath.

"I thought you would have had enough to leave and never return. How are you here to help me? You gave yourself freely in my own home, in this very room with that worthless man who carries my name. To be betrayed in this room twice? How dare you say that you want to help me?"

"Twice? How is that?"

The laughter shook the room like an earthquake. "Wouldn't it be easy to share that secret?"

"If you'll let me, I can help you. Tell me."

"Do you think you're in love?" Hank stood before her. He was solid with thick shoulders and broodingly, broad features. He was no longer a dark shadow hiding in a corner nor the misty image of a man. He stared at her with a timeless look, as a father whose child had shamed him. She felt seventeen again. Then he chuckled. "Youth is wasted on the young. You should not waste your life on what you think is love. Brooke thought she was in love. My wife thought she was in love. I might have thought that too, a long time ago. But I know better now." He shrugged his shoulders cynically.

"They let love kill them," he continued. "First, Brooke drove off that cliff. She rushed for love and lost control instead. Isn't it funny how my wife did the same thing? History repeats itself." He laughed again, only this time it held the sinister ring of deception.

"What did you do to your wife?" The chill that ran through Angela had nothing to do with the ghost that stood before her. Did Cole's father have something to do with his wife's death?

"You think you are so smart, Angela." He turned and began to fade. "Do you think that man I called a son can ever love you?"

"He loves me already. And he loves you too."

"If you believe any of that then you're a fool."

"Is that why you tried to kill me?"

"It has nothing to do with you."

"How could you do that to me? What did you

do to your wife?"

He turned solid again. "What I did to her was little compared to what she did to me. I had to live with her choices long after she was gone. You, dear, are the one who needs help. The apple doesn't fall far from the tree, or so they say. I hope my so-called son doesn't do to you what his mother did to me. Do not make the same mistakes as your elders. And yes, Brooke, though young forever, is still your elder. You seem to be following a similar path."

"The same mistakes as Brooke?" Her hand went to her belly. No, she wasn't in the same situation as Brooke. She and Cole had only made love that one time and it was too soon to know if there was a baby. "It's time that all your manipulation stops."

"If the truth is manipulation, then so be it. Brooke thought she knew what she wanted. Malory, my wife, thought she knew what she wanted. They both ruined it by letting thoughts of love cloud them, ruining the future for all of us. I didn't ruin Cole's life. His mother did that on her own."

"Why are you tormented? Tell me what holds you here? Let it go so you can rest. This secret causes you pain."

"I wish I could change the past. I wish my wife had loved me instead of another. I wish I could have been given the chance to love *our* son." His shoulders hunched and shook with pain.

"We cannot exist through our regrets. Malory made a mistake, forgive her. You made mistakes. I forgive you. Cole can forgive. You need to forgive yourself."

His grief changed suddenly into anger and he reared up, like an animal, becoming larger and oppressive.

He seemed to surround her in a tidal wave that took her breath.

"I can never forgive all that's happened to me. But who am I? I no longer want to carry this burden. It's not mine to bear anyway. If he wants to live with the knowledge that I've kept hidden, so be it."

"We all make choices, Hank. Good and bad choices. We don't need to live with them for all eternity. We create our own suffering. Forgive yourself and release the past secrets."

"Be careful what you wish for." Hank pointed a ghostly cold finger toward the roaring lion on the mantle. "Take the box. I'm tired. I can hold the secrets no longer."

The fang, jutting from the open-mouthed snarl of the lion, twisted. Rusted hinges creaked and old wood scraped against wood. The paint crackled and chipped as a secret panel opened in the fireplace.

"Take it, take it, take it."

The phrase rang in Angela's head even after Hank had vanished.

She reached into the dark opening. At first she only felt a dusty floor, then her fingers hit the hard edges of a wooden box. With shaky hands, she removed it. The box was lacquered all black with bright brass hinges and a brass key hole.

She tried to open it, but it was locked. There had to be a key. She shook the box. Whatever was inside shifted and slid. The box held the secrets to Cole's life and she needed to find the key.

Setting the box down on the coffee table, Angela put her hand back into the dark opening and gingerly felt around. In the far reaches of the square space, her fingers found the key. She pulled it out in triumph.

"What do you have there?"

She jumped at Cole's voice and whirled to see him resting against the doorjamb just like that first time she'd investigated in this room. He was handsome, and cool with confidence, but now she saw more. Under that exterior she could see his vulnerability. Love for him welled inside her until she thought she'd burst. She swallowed back the swell of emotions. He had to know what was in the box. It would be wrong for her to hope for too much when he had his father's secret to deal with first.

"Hank led me to this box. I think it is full of all your family's secrets."

"Aren't you going to open it?"

She inserted the key, then stopped. "I think you need to do this."

He shook his head. "I don't want anything to do with my father. You do the honors." With solid refusal, he crossed his arms over his chest.

She tried to turn the key, but it wouldn't budge. "There's too much corrosion."

"Fine, I'll do it." Cole brushed her hands away and twisted with only a slight grinding noise. The lid popped open a crack.

Angela raised the lid on creaking hinges. Old yellowed letters wrapped with a silken blue ribbon were piled inside, brown and brittle on the edges.

Cole pulled the top pile and untied the ribbon. He scanned the handwritten note, his eyes tightening in the corners. Then he read the next letter and the next.

Angela reached for a paper in the bottom of the box and carefully unfolded it. Her gaze shifted to Cole's, then back to the letter. Blood pounded through her ears. Her breath caught.

"These are adoption papers." She couldn't believe what she was reading. In black and white were family signatures. Male Baby X born to Brooke Dalloway.

Angela read the paper a second time before she handed it to Cole. "I think these things belong to you."

"No. I don't think they do." He shoved the letters back in the box. "None of this is mine." He waved a hand around the room. "Now I understand why he was selling this place to the historical society. It's not mine."

"How can you say that?"

"Those"—he pointed to the box— "are love letters to my mother and they weren't written by Hank Barlow."

"Then who wrote them?"

"My father."

The words hung between them for a moment like little fire crackers about to explode.

"I don't understand." She stared at him confused.

"I feel like my guts are being wrenched from my body." Cole sank into the couch and covered his head with his hands. "All this time, I wanted Hank to love me. I begged for his love. I never understood how he couldn't love his own son."

Angela sat beside him and put her arm around his shoulders. "Tell me what's going on."

"It's clear to me now. It all makes sense. He couldn't love me like his son because I wasn't his."

"What?"

"My father is the man who wrote all those letters."

The firecrackers exploded in her ears. It didn't make sense.

"All these years, Hank took me into his house and let everyone believe he was my father. He knew the entire time that my mother had cheated on him with another man. He knew that I was the son of another man. That's why he hated me all these years. How could he reveal the horrible secret without ruining his name?"

"You need to read these documents."

"What?" He took the paper. His face had already blanched from the knowledge of his mother's affair and became paler as he scanned the document. "What is this saying? What does this mean?"

"I think you're the descendent of the secret Dalloway baby. Brooke Dalloway's baby. Your father is a Dalloway descendent"

He looked up at her, eyes blank as they stared.

"You are a Dalloway."

"How can that be? These letters say that my biological father was named Patrick Allen."

"Harry Barnes was the father of Brooke's baby, the one given up for adoption. He was adopted into the Allen family."

"These letters are from Patrick Allen."

"I don't think it's a coincidence. I think Patrick is the son of Harry and Brooke's child. That makes you a Dalloway."

He stuffed the letter back into the box. "A lie, my whole existence has been a lie. My past has been a secret and a complete lie. That's my legacy." He raised the box. "This proves it. My great-grandmother was a sneaking floozy and got herself knocked up and gave away her baby. My mother was a lying cheat who abandoned her baby to a violent, abusive man. Boy, don't I come from great stock? This proves that I'm better off alone. I can't be trusted to love anyone. I will only ruin it. Everything this family touched has gone to hell. I'll do no better," he shouted.

"But that means your father wasn't your father. Your real father is Patrick Allen."

Her words made him feel like he didn't even know himself. The man who raised him, hurt him, never showed him love, was the man who had shaped him into who he had become. That had greater influence than any genetic connection. Who was he? Could he really be more than what he'd always thought? He wanted to be more for Angela, but maybe it was impossible.

"You need to go. I have to be alone." He fished

his car keys out of his pocket and tossed them on her lap. "Just go." Gripping the edges of the box until they bruised his palms, he turned his back on her.

She was shut out from his life that fast. She was abandoned by him and they still stood in the same room. She wanted to run to him, wrap her arms around his waist, tell him that he was worth love, that he deserved acceptance and love. But he was rigid, his shoulders tight and unwelcoming. She took one last look at him, then left him alone. He would come back to her if and when he was ready.

CHAPTER 32

COLE WAS NUMB. He'd always known his father hated him. He'd always been afraid that he was damaged and unable to show love to someone else. He'd tried to avoid falling in love at all costs. Now he realized it was too late.

Those letters proved what he'd always known. He came from a long line of screw-ups, generations of them. And the funny thing was, the person who had influenced him the most didn't share a single drop of blood. Max had been more his father than Hank ever had. And Hank wasn't his real father either.

His mother had an affair with another man, the descendant of Harry Barnes. Brooke Dalloway's baby was his grandfather. How could that be? All the time he'd wasted on a man who had no claims on him or ownership over him. Who was the man who produced him? Had his mother been like Brooke? Had she planned on coming back for him if she'd survived?

Cole closed his eyes, rubbed them with his fingertips, then scanned the room and registered every detail. Oriental carpet, red wall papered walls with oak trim, painted Italian tiles surrounding the fireplace and the snarling lion was where it all began and ended.

"This is not mine. It never was mine. But it is mine now and I don't want it. It's over. I'm finished with this place and the past."

He carefully folded each letter and placed them, one by one back into the box. With each letter his irritation flared and his anger rose. He slammed the lid with a smart snap. "I should burn this box. Burn all of this along with your burning soul. Burn it all for what you've done. You've given me a great legacy, a legacy to be ashamed of. You deserve it."

He gripped the box with whitening knuckles and strode to the fireplace. "I'm going to burn it all. What if I burned down this entire place?"

Cole shoved the lacquered box into the fireplace. Taking logs from the wrought iron rack, he arranged them around the box. He grabbed the long, wooden matches and fished one from the box. Before he could even strike the match, a log sparked into a small flame that quickly spread through the wood.

Cole jumped back in surprise, but he could only watched, stunned as the flames spread and grew in strength, flapping and crackling. The flames licked at the box, singeing the edges. Lacquer scorched, then melted and bubbled away exposing the old wood beneath.

Smoke clouded and hissed around the box. The smoke swirled and spiraled. Shapes danced in the gray cloud and shifted and reformed into new shapes.

Mesmerized, he let the box burn, let the past float away on the dark cloud of smoke. The edges of the box turned to char; the surface blistered in the waves of heat.

Angela gave him hope that there might be something more than the hell he had been living. His existence had been one of a person with no home, nowhere to turn to, no one to go to. When he'd seen those eyes, he'd felt kindness, acceptance. Even when it was clear he did not trust her, she still had that look in her eye. A look that said heaven existed for everyone. You just had to believe you deserved it. And sometimes you needed someone to believe in it more than you could.

She'd turned him into a believer. She had taught him that. He believed in her, but she had also taught him to believe in himself, believe that he had more to give.

He saw his future there in her eyes, in the smoke, in this house. If he let the mansion go up in flames, he would have nothing left.

He wanted more. The letters proved that he was so much more. He had a real father out there. His heart constricted and his guts roiled.

The box hissed and snapped as the flames roared. His entire body relaxed and it all became clear. He couldn't let the box burn. Cole fell to his knees and thrust a hand into the flames. They licked higher, burning at his skin. He pulled back. But he could not stop. He needed the letters in the box. They were his only connection to his real father.

The fire raged and flared. He thrust his hands deep into the heat. The acrid fumes of burned wood, the tang of melting paint made him pause for a moment. Pulling his hands back, he wasn't sure if he could get to the box, the fire was too strong.

His need to save it became a panic flooding his veins. Thrusting one last time, he found the box and pulled at it. The fire flew from the fireplace, wrapped around the box, licking it, refusing to let it go. He drew back quickly, letting go of the box. The flames seemed possessed with the need to destroy the box and the secrets within.

He needed to get that box out of the fire. The tongs. Where were the tongs? The fireplace tools had tipped over to the floor. He lunged for them and pushed them into the fire, grasping the box. It dropped to the tile floor with a clatter and a hiss, safe from the fire. The corners of the box smoked, some charred bits flaked onto the floor.

"It's over. I'm finally going to face it. Then I'm going to focus on creating a future."

The flames in the fireplace roared higher. Cole kicked the box away from the sputtering fire. Sparks flicked from the hearth. Embers flew from the pit to scatter across the carpet. They moved like crawling monsters, sputtering and spitting. The red sparks grew into fires that built until they turned into a wall of unnatural flame.

The fire licked and pulsed, drawing toward him like a live entity, forming a circle around him. The entire room glowed with red and orange light.

Cole planted his feet firmly on the ground and his hands fisted at his sides. He felt like it was Hank's last effort to keep hold of the secrets and control Cole.

"The past is over. You have to let it go," Cole shouted over the roar. "I'm going to live in the future. I am not going to be afraid of the past. This house is no longer yours. It's mine. This house belongs to me and my future legacy. Do you hear me?" he shouted. "I belong here, not you."

The tension in the whipping flames melted away. The flames fell back and the fire sizzled, then went out. A serenity filled the house.

Eerily quiet, Cole looked around the room. This was his room, his mansion. He had accepted it too.

The need to get started on the process of creating that future overwhelmed him. He'd wasted a lifetime already on things that didn't matter. It was time to move forward. He couldn't waste a minute more.

CHAPTER 33

A NGELA PACED HER white living room carpet, back and forth, back and forth. She'd checked her phone dozens of times since she'd left Cole in the mansion hours ago.

"Here, drink this tea." Emma shoved the warm cup into her hands.

Angela folded her fingers around warm ceramic. "I need this to calm my nerves. She took a sip of the steaming chamomile. "Why hasn't he come here yet? He said he'd come."

"Give him time. His world has just been blown apart."

"I know." She took another sip.

"The pieces will fall together in all the right places."

"How do you know that?"

Emma simply gave her a shrug and a knowing smile.

"I hope you're right. I have a bad feeling. He should have at least called me by now. When things go wrong, he runs away. Instead of facing things head on, he avoids problems." She set the mug down and some of the pale liquid sloshed onto the glass tabletop. "I have to try to call him again."

Angela's stomach tightened when the call went directly into voice mail. She ended the call without leaving another message, then flopped on the couch.

"I saw how upset he was that day you were hurt. He has feelings for you. He touched you like porcelain. He'll call."

"Emma, if you'd seen his face when he read those letters. He looked like he had seen the scariest ghost. And in reality, he had. Everything he thought he knew about himself was a lie."

"It was a good thing. He got to see the ghosts of Christmas past. I'm sure that was pretty upsetting, but it had to be done." Emma said. "I'm glad for it. I would want to know something like that. Now he can move on. Both of you can move on."

"But what if he doesn't come back?" Angela's eyes filled with panicked tears. "I think this was too much for him. He doesn't think he's good enough. He doesn't believe in me enough." She covered her face in her hands.

Emma knelt before Angela. "You're wrong. You'll see. He's found love in you. You've given him what no one ever has. If he doesn't realize it that's his problem."

"I'm the one who didn't realize it." She remembered their love making and how she'd ran off to help the ghost.

"I don't like to see you upset." Emma wiped the tears that slipped down Angela's cheek. "Let his thoughts rattle around in his fat arrogant head."

That made Angela smile. "He's not as arrogant as I thought he was. You're right." She rested her head on the pillow and resisted the urge to call him again. She had a sinking feeling he'd run again, from his life, his past and from her.

"Three days. I still haven't heard from him in three days. No call, no texts, not one single word," Angela said. She was at her desk in her office, wearing the sweatshirt he'd given her by the river. She hadn't taken it off in days. It and his car were the only connection she had to him right now.

Emma leaned in the doorway, her face filled with pity. Angela looked at her computer screen to avoid the pathetic gaze.

That was it. He'd run off, away from his life again. She wished it didn't hurt so much. She was taking it personally and her heart felt like someone had reached in and cut it to ribbons. "When the going gets tough, he gets going." Her laugh was bitter. He'd abandoned her and his life.

"Here are those papers you asked for," Emma said. She'd been tiptoeing around Angela like she was shattered glass.

"Thanks."

Emma handed her the papers and left her alone.

Back to her ordinary life, Angela was pretending like she wasn't devastated.

Her next appointment, Mr. Bainsley, would be by in a few moments to talk about his experience with a ghost that appeared when he started to remodel his home. Mrs. Andrews had just left after discussing her séance for a Halloween party. She was very unhappy when Angela declined the invitation.

Yup, back to her daily routine, though somehow things seemed different. Without Cole, she had lost her verve for the business. She wanted to head back to her apartment, climb under the covers and forget about everything.

Tears clouded her eyes again. She'd cried a lot these last few days. She must have been wrong about him, thinking he didn't need to be alone anymore. He had her. But he was rejecting her and choosing a life alone where he'd bound himself into a safe cocoon where he wouldn't let anyone in.

She was going to call one last time, where she would spill everything in that last message. Then she would be done. He would know where she stood. It would be his choice, but at least she knew she had tried.

As she pressed the first button, the phone chirped. Cole's name registered on the screen and her heart skipped. She had to read the name a second time before she could believe it, then quickly, she answered the call.

"Cole, hello, is it you? Where are you?"

"It's me." His voice held a cheerful tone that was opposite to the anxious feelings she'd harbored for days. That annoyed her.

"Where have you been? Why haven't you called?"

His chuckle came through, rich and clear, and

she gritted her teeth.

"So many questions so fast."

"You made me leave that day and I haven't heard from you since."

"I know. I'm sorry for that. I've been trying to get some things finalized. But I'm heading home now."

Home? When had he ever considered Dalewood as home? "Where are you?" she asked.

"I'm in Chicago, but I'm about to jump into a rental car and drive back to Dalewood. I should be back in a few hours."

Her heart thrummed with the thought of seeing him. She gripped her phone tighter in her hand. "You'll be back today?"

"Yes, and I need to see you." His voice had lost all of its joking mannerisms and had lowered to a husky rumble.

She couldn't let go of her pain so quickly. He'd really hurt her by abandoning her so easily.

"Why didn't you call?"

The question hung between them for a moment before he answered.

"I needed to handle a few things on my own. I needed to keep my mind clear and focused." There was silence. "After reading through the papers..." He paused as if he was trying to find the right thing to say. "When I read the love letters, I didn't know what to do. I'd spent most of my life planning ways to get rid of that mansion. Then I had the chance."

"What do you mean?"

"I almost burned the place down. I wanted to

burn it all, the papers, the mansion, the past. But all I could think of was you. I saw you in the smoke and then I knew I was burning my entire world. When I saw you and the future going up in smoke, I knew everything was going to hell, like everything else in my life has gone to hell. When I saw that happening I knew. I knew I needed to change. I knew I needed to end my condominium contracts and keep Penniberg for us."

He paused, but she couldn't say anything through the lump that had formed in her throat. He was saying everything she'd wished he would ever say to her. Everything but the words she needed above it all. He'd told her once that he loved her but she needed to hear them again.

"Will you meet with me?"

"Yes."

"I'm going straight to Penniberg mansion. Will you meet me there?"

"Yes. I'll meet you." She couldn't wait to see him, but she had to understand why he left like that. She needed to talk to him. He'd returned to Dalewood. What had made him change so that he felt like this was home?

CHAPTER 34

A NGELA GOT INTO Cole's silver Camaro that had been sitting at her apartment since she'd seen him last. The scent of leather and car and Cole, manly, clean, surrounded her.

She hadn't sat in his car since he'd left her. The scent of him made her feel close to him, but it made her long to be with him.

She gripped the steering wheel tightly as she pulled out of the garage. What did he want to tell her? Maybe he was going to move on. He had left her for days without one word. But she reminded herself that he'd called Dalewood home. He was thinking of this place where she was as home. He had used the word us.

She drove down the road that led to the mansion. The road was no longer canopied by changing leaves. All the leaves had blown free. The light shone through the clean branches, making the road bright and glowing as she drove up to the mansion.

The sun's rays sent shafts down and the stones glistened and glowed white in the light. The mansion looked bright and warm and happy.

Beautiful.

She felt like she was coming home. A black SUV rental sat in the drive. It was empty, so Cole must be inside already. Her heart skittered and she was filled with nervousness at seeing him. She put the car in park and jumped out. She rushed to the mansion.

Pushing through the unlocked door, she headed to the drawing room. The memory of Cole holding her in his arms and passionately loving her flooded her brain. The cloying scent of burnt wood greeted her when she entered the room. Black soot covered the lion head, and the oriental carpet was burned in spots.

He had his back to the door while he faced the fireplace. His gray T-shirt outlined his strong shoulders, framing the muscles of his back and arms. Afraid, she rushed to him and touched him with tentative fingers, though every being in her body wanted to grab him, wrap her arms around his waist and never let go.

"Cole," she whispered.

He turned, the charred box in his hands. His smile brightened the entire room and part of her concern faded away. She'd never seen him smile like that, completely opened, unhesitating, fullness of his heart right out for anyone to see. Her breath caught in her chest as she rushed into his waiting arms and pressed her face into his chest. She felt his beating heart and her racing heart matched his in a syncopation.

"Don't ever leave me like that again." She pushed at his shoulder. "How could you do that to me? You ran away without a single word."

"Will you accept my apology? I had to figure a few things out. Fix some things."

She looked at him through her brimming tears. "Can we call it even? I left you in this room when I ran to help the ghosts."

He dipped his head and kissed her deeply, giving her all the answer she needed.

When they broke away, breathless, he held up the box. "At first I wanted to run away. You're right about that. I wanted everything to be over. I wanted to burn the past. All of this. I wanted to destroy everything, to leave the past in the past and let everything die with it." He set the box on the table. "But I couldn't. I couldn't let it end. Not here, not this way. I envisioned you here and I knew I needed you in this place. You are the key to my future." He touched her cheek. "I realized I didn't want an ending. I needed a beginning."

"Then why did you leave?"

"I took the documents to Chicago to have them authenticated. They're real. Everything in the box is legal. My father, I mean Hank, had already learned about the past. He was in the process of fixing things. In his own hard way, he was protecting me. He wanted to make things right with me, but his death ended that. That and my focused need to destroy him." Cole opened the lid of the box and held up a crisp white page. "This is a deed to the mansion. I had all the paperwork signed and my name is on everything. My father was in the process of signing the mansion over to the historical society. I also met with a lawyer in

Chicago. Since my father died before all the documentation was finalized, the historical society no longer has a hold on this place. It's mine clean and clear. I've accepted this place as mine." He waved his arm to encompass the room. "All of this." He put the letter back into the charred box.

"But it was always yours."

Cole stared into her golden eyes and hoped he was worthy to enter paradise. He was finally willing to take the chance. "I didn't want it then. But things are different now. I have a father to find, Patrick Allen. We have a future to start." He took her hands in his. "I didn't want this before you. I couldn't see a future before you. I can see one now and I see it with you. We can bring happiness back to this place. What do you think?" His heart was about to thud through his chest.

He couldn't read her expression. Maybe it was too late. Maybe he'd taken too long. He shouldn't have left her that way. But he'd needed to figure it all out and get everything situated. He swallowed. He had to convince her that they were meant to be together. "We can bring this home happiness. I need you here with me. I love you and I hope you can learn to love me." He wanted to grab her and pull her close, but he was too afraid she would refuse him.

She stood very still for a moment, then her face changed like the sun rising from behind a bank of dark clouds. The beautiful rays gave light and joy to all the darkest places in his soul.

"You bring warmth and life to all my places that once seemed lost. Will you start a future with me in this place?" The words pushed from his throat like dry gravel.

"Yes. It's time to let the hurt and anger of the past go and create a new future."

Those weren't the words he wanted to hear. He wanted her to tell him of her undying love and her need to be with him. His heart sank. She wanted to help the ghosts and make the mansion a lighter, happier place. But then she continued.

"I want that future with you too." Angela wrapped her arms around Cole's waist and laughed through her happy tears. "I don't know how it happened, but I love you so much."

He loved this woman with all his heart and he was about to tell her.

Floorboards creaked and they both turned. The ghosts of Brooke and Hank shimmered in the doorway as they stood together, watching. Cole could barely believe what he was seeing. The reality was that he could believe in anything now.

Brooke's face shined at them as if to say she approved. Hank gave one nod of his head.

"His aura has changed," Angela whispered. "It's no longer ominous and dark. The air is light and filled with warmth. Finally, things will be made right. Both Brooke's and Hank's secrets have been revealed and so have your connections to the Dalloway family."

Both ghosts smiled, each full of hope. Brooke grasped Hank's hand and both images faded into a sparkle of white light.

Angela wrapped her arms more tightly around Cole's neck.

"Still don't believe in ghosts?" Her eyes flashed golden sparks.

Pulling her closer, he kissed her quick on the lips. Half laughing and half breathless he spoke, "There are a lot of things I believe in now, Angela. You've possessed my heart and soul. I love you." He cupped her cheeks and kissed her again. This time it was soft and lingering and filled with a lifetime of promises.

ACKNOWLEDGEMENTS

It may take only a few hours to read a book, but writing a book takes much longer than that, months, even years. It takes lots of thinking, planning, researching, writing, rewriting and rewriting and rewriting. Writing a book can be a very solitary act, but there are lots of people involved in helping bring a book to the world.

Windy City and Chicago North RWA chapters helped me learn so much about writing. Thanks to editor Catherine Snodgrass for her help in the middle stages of this book. Thanks to the Aphrodite Writers and the many hours of creative fun and friendship. Thanks to the Goldies who helped me when this book was in its earliest stage of mostly ideas. Thanks to those who critiqued chapters, or even the entire book multiple times. That thanks goes to Katrina Bauer, Dyanne Davis, Sonali Dev, Denise DiLeo, Sarah Kayes, Clara Kensie, Vanessa Knight, Robin Kuss, Nicole Leiren, Cindy Maday, Hanna Martine, and CJ Warrant. I am especially thankful to India Powers and Savannah Reynard, my SISs, for spending endless hours chatting about our books and the plans for publishing them.

My family gave their endless support and without them there would be no book. My dad, Edward who was my biggest cheerleader when I chose to become a writer. My mother, Portia "D" who showed me how to love reading. My sister, Maria who is there no matter what to help with everything. To my brother, Lou who kept me motivated by continuously asking when the book would be finished. To my nieces and nephew, Roxanne, Louis and Katherine, I love you so much. To Conor, my little heart, who came after the book was almost finished, but can't be left out. And to Tim Kelly who knew every part of this book, inside and out, before ever actually reading a word of it.

ABOUT THE AUTHOR

I love books! Reading them and writing them. As an avid romance reader for many years, I always knew I wanted to write a romance novel of my own. As a kid, I created a list of five life goals. One of those goals was to write a romance novel. I'm happy to say I have been able to cross that off my list (along with visiting Venice, Italy). Once I wrote my first novel, a passion for writing burned inside me and one book was not enough. If you like sweet, steamy paranormal romance, you'll love my haunting ghost stories with heart.

Visit my website to learn more about the POSSESSION SERIES.

www.ciciedward.com

CONNECT WITH THE AUTHOR

Website:
www.ciciedward.com

Sign up for my newsletter
for the most current updates.
www.ciciedward.com/contact-me

Facebook
www.facebook.com/cici.edward1

Instagram
@ciciedward

Twitter
@CiciEdward

THE POSSESSION SERIES

by Cici Edward

———⌘———